Charlotte Grimshaw is the author of five critically acclaimed novels, *Provocation*, *Guilt*, *Foreign City*, *The Night Book* and *Soon*, and two short-story collections, *Opportunity* and *Singularity*. She has been awarded the Buddle Findlay Sargeson Fellowship, and is a winner of the BNZ Katherine Mansfield Award. *Opportunity* was shortlisted for the Frank O'Connor International Prize, and won New Zealand's premier Montana Award for Fiction or Poetry. *Singularity* was a finalist in the Frank O'Connor International Prize and the South East Asia and Pacific section of the Commonwealth Writers' Prize. *The Night Book* was one of the three fiction finalists in the New Zealand Post Book Awards. *Soon*, a bestseller in New Zealand, has been published in the UK, Canada and the US. Her monthly column in *Metro* magazine won a Qantas Media Award. She lives in Auckland.

STARLIGHT PENINSULA

—

CHARLOTTE GRIMSHAW

VINTAGE

ST

AR

LIG

HT

PEN

SU

LA

VINTAGE

UK | USA | Canada | Ireland | Australia
India | New Zealand | South Africa | China

Vintage is an imprint of the Penguin Random House group of companies,
whose addresses can be found at global.penguinrandomhouse.com.

Penguin
Random House
New Zealand

First published by Penguin Random House New Zealand, 2015

10 9 8 7 6 5 4 3 2 1

Cover design by Megan van Staden © Penguin Random House New Zealand
Text design by Megan van Staden © Penguin Random House New Zealand
Cover photograph by rvika (background) and alslutsky (foreground) © Shutterstock
Author photograph by Jane Ussher
Typeset in Palatino Light
Printed and bound in Australia by Griffin Press, an Accredited ISO AS/NZS
14001 Environmental Management Systems Printer

A catalogue record for this book is available from the National Library of
New Zealand.

ISBN 978 1 77553 822 6
eISBN 978 1 77553 823 3

The assistance of Creative New Zealand towards the production of this book is
gratefully acknowledged by the publisher.

penguinrandomhouse.co.nz

— *FOR PAUL* —

ONE

It was summer when everything changed. On hot stunned weekend mornings, Eloise Hay woke alone, left the house and walked clear across the Auckland isthmus, through green parks, over volcanic cones, in and out of suburban malls, past waterfront cafés and rows of rickety wooden houses, and gardens backed by corrugated-iron fences, spending whole days roaming into sunstruck corners of the sprawling city, the streets buffeted by warm wind, or silent under hot black cloud, or bathed in white light under an enamel sky. The bumpy asphalt sent up waves of heat retained from weeks of summer, the green shoulders of Rangitoto Island appeared and disappeared on the horizon.

From the edge of the crater on Mt Hobson she saw cloud shadows cross crazily fast and a plane slip over the edge of the earth, and walking down the mountain track she had the sensation her head was not descending at the same rate as her body; it was lifting off, about to fly into the sky. She walked all day, sometimes not reaching home until the low sun was setting the windows along the peninsula on fire.

She said to her psychotherapist, 'You know those mad people who never stop walking? Driving, you see them in one suburb then another.'

Dr Klaudia Dvorak was German. She had blonde hair, blue eyes and was very tall. Her special research interest was the study of phobias, but she also ran a private clinic in Herne Bay, for the mildly mad. She listened to Eloise, who said:

'Weekdays I go to work, but in the weekend I wake up with one fixed idea: Sean is lost and I have to find him. So I walk. Saturdays, Sundays, that's all I do. If I found him I'd probably punch him. But I can't stop myself. It makes me feel as if . . .'

'Yes?'

'As if I'm an animal and this is instinct, and it's beyond my control.'

They were silent, listening: cicadas sawed in the shimmering hot air, a lawnmower started up. An elderly woman crossed the grass in front of the French doors, carrying a pot plant.

'So. Klaudia. Do you think that's all we are? Just animals?'

TWO

Eloise Hay lived on the Starlight Peninsula. She caught the bus home from work in the evening, getting off on the main road and walking through a series of side streets to the land on the edge of the estuary. This land formed a strip between the sections and the shore, and she walked to her house, which was sixth in the row, passing the back gardens of her neighbours.

The suburb, close to the inner city, had been shabby but was now becoming fashionable, and all the houses but one were either brand-new, built on the site of demolished rentals, or were freshly, expensively renovated. The house next to hers on the main-road side was the exception. It was a disreputable rental, not yet sold off by the landlord to a private owner despite the high land value, a big, dingy stucco house, two storeyed, with an unkempt garden and no permanent residents Eloise could make out, just a steady stream of people who came and went day and night. They didn't bother Eloise except when they played loud music in the evening, but that didn't happen very often. A one-eyed cat often lay on the concrete balcony at the front, and sometimes a tattooed girl sunbathed on the lawn.

Eloise walked home, carrying a bag of shopping. Hot wind combed the grass, washing blew on lines, there were diamonds of light on water shirred by the breeze that smacked down and spread like a hand pressed on the surface. Here the estuary narrowed to a creek as it wound inland, and on the other side of it lay the dog park. In the distance you could see the city buildings, to the east and west the row of houses, and out in the estuary where it opened into the sea the tide was rising, water meeting sky in a haze of shifting light.

When she passed her neighbours' sections she kept her eyes forward, not looking at the lawns and decks and open ranch sliders. There were children playing, voices inside the houses, sprinklers throwing spirals of water over flowerbeds.

A child screamed. Eloise saw a small girl lying on the path, her tricycle tipped sideways, one wheel slowly spinning. From her sprawled position, cheek flat on the asphalt, her foot still on one up-ended pedal, the kid looked at her, motionless.

'Are you all right?' Eloise said.

But a woman in a yellow dress, a phone held in the crook of her neck, crossed the yard, swiftly and casually righted the tricycle, pulled the child up by one arm, slapped her not too hard on the bum and set her pedalling along the path again. She said intently into the phone, 'No, he would say that. He *would*.'

Eloise walked away, hearing the slow squeak squeak of the tricycle wheels.

At the next-door house the neighbour was hanging sheets on a clothesline. She had a full sleeve of tattoos on one arm and a series of coloured patterns inked on her neck, red and yellow stars and diamonds. Eloise waited for the usual glare. The girl paused with a peg in her hand and scowled and Eloise felt heat rise in her face. Well, same to you. The anger was unexpected.

She turned away and headed along to her property, which had an old gate that wasn't attached to anything, no fence between her and the neighbours on the other side from the tattooed girl's house. She looked up at the sky and her eyes burned — burned and stung. This weight dragging at her; it was the feeling she started to have at the end of every week. Because tomorrow was Friday.

A noise had stopped. Silence. Then it started again. An oily sound: snick snick. Someone clipping a hedge. A man appeared from behind a tree and stopped with the clippers held loosely in front of him. She had met him, once, out on the street when he'd introduced himself and said his name was Nick or Ned or Neil. Their eyes met, and because of feeling angry and because it was Friday tomorrow and she could barely face the thought of the weekend, she didn't greet him and turn away without paying attention as she normally would. Instead she stared at him, hard, and he stared back.

THREE

'So, picture it. This massive storm. Night time, pitch dark. Great booms of thunder. The flashes lit up the sky in a place where there were no clouds. And what I realised is this. The sky at night is blue. Bright blue. It's just that you normally can't *see* it because it's *dark*.'

The make-up girl gave a fondly sarcastic smile, a little roll of the eyes. She was dabbing pancake on Ed Miles, the Minister of Justice, who was about to be interviewed about Andrew Newgate.

Scott Roysmith went on, 'Great blue patches in the night sky. In the *blackness*.'

'Amazing,' the politician said.

Scott leaned on the door frame for a moment, blinked and said to Eloise, 'Anyway. See you in ten.' He went off along the corridor.

The make-up girl stepped back, gave a critical look, angled in again with her sponge. 'His wonder of the world mood. It's a Friday thing.'

'Isn't he always in that mood?' Ed Miles tipped back his head and glared at the make-up girl who was thin and quite sexy, although her teeth sloped inward like a shark's. The politician looked tired, dark circles under his eyes despite the pancake, also as if he'd like to put his hand on her narrow waist.

'Scott Roysmith. He doesn't smile, he *beams*. And that is why we love him.' She turned his swivel chair around for him, definitely flirting. 'Done.'

Eloise walked behind as Ed Miles was led to the green room, where he sat in front of the tray of snacks, scowling down at his phone, tapping the screen with clumsy fingers. There were beads of sweat on his nose. The green room was perhaps the least soothing place in the building, with its harsh light and dry air, the litter of paper cups and tissues, the slangy girl and boy assistants slouching through, the atmosphere of behind-the-scenes cynicism and cool and anti-glamour.

'Can we get you anything?' the assistant was asking.

The politician ignored her and looked at Eloise. He had a stillness about him that was unsettling.

He said, 'What's your name again?'

'Eloise Hay.'

'That's right.' His eyes were so pale it was hard to tell if they were green or blue.

She didn't say, What's right?

'You work with Roysmith.'

The way he was staring unnerved her.

Eloise got out of there. She and Scott didn't work here; they'd called in to the news side of the building so Scott could have a casual word in passing with Ed Miles. They'd made a documentary about Andrew Newgate, next they were going to film a piece about the internet millionaire, Kurt Hartmann. Ed Miles had refused compensation for Newgate; no doubt he would refuse to comment about Hartmann.

She walked tentatively, taking care not to brush against the walls, hesitating before pushing the metal handle of the heavy swing door. The make-up girl, Naheed, tip-toed past. It was busy. Mariel Hartfield was preparing to read the news, and Naheed and others were starting to go after her. In this part of the complex, known as Q Wing, Mariel Hartfield would arrive and move about the corridors, and rustling respectfully behind her with their iPhones and tablets would follow various functionaries, her assistant, the waspish Selena, and sometimes her co-presenter Jack Anthony, elbowing his way through the crush.

At the exit door an ironic little pantomime took place between Jack Anthony and Ian the cameraman: 'After you.'

'No, after you.'

'Christ, all right then. When are they going to . . . ?'

And Jack Anthony swept through the door saying, 'Cheers, mate. One for the team.'

Jack's eyes now rested on Eloise, who was standing outside the staff cafeteria. He was variously described as 'handsome', 'gorgeous', 'incredibly handsome'. The boy and girl assistants sometimes reached for alternatives: 'awesome', 'hot'. He was tall and telegenic with a fleshy face and thick hair swept back off his forehead. Eloise saw his bland symmetry as a mask (those rubbery jowls) behind which might lurk, she speculated, something odd and possibly unpleasant, a powerful misogyny say, or a hidden liking for cruelty. It was whispered he was religious. She'd overheard him being unfashionably lenient about Fox News, also making approving noises about the American use of drones for extra-judicial killings (shrugging off the odd accidental frying of forty innocent villagers). But you couldn't judge him on those pronouncements, because you could never tell whether he was serious.

He threw the odd quiet tantrum (he became cutting, sarcastic) when people messed things up. Mariel Hartfield, according to her media profile, 'maintained serenity through meditation and yoga', but Eloise had seen her turn on Jack as if she were about to smack him in the mouth. When Jack got sarcastic, Mariel faced him down, the light went out of her eyes and she spoke very quietly. Their working relationship was supposed to be warm and easy-going, and that was how it came across during news broadcasts. But Eloise knew Mariel didn't like Jack, and Jack was wary of Mariel — the way her eyes could turn to ice. Only Eloise had noticed; everyone else just believed the hype and bullshit put out by the network.

Eloise prided herself on being observant.

Mariel Hartfield, who was popular, guarded her privacy jealously, but a version of her life could be found in the pages of gossip magazines. She was featured in the current edition of the *Woman's Weekly*, photographed by the pool at her 'beautiful, architecturally designed haven', where she lived with her partner, 'hunky journalist, Hamish Dark'.

Eloise, along with everyone else, kept up with Mariel's life while waiting in the supermarket queue. (But Eloise wasn't everyone. She was an insider. And she was observant.)

This month, Mariel and Hamish were 'talking weddings' (he pressed her to marry, she valued her independence). This made a change from 'thinking about baby number three' or 'discussing a renovation'. Currently, Hamish was installing a large tropical fish tank in their family home. Other documented activities included having arguments (frowning and gesticulating in public), being targeted by a troubled stalker, and shopping with their children 'bubbly daughter Maxie' and 'sporty, curly-haired William'.

The couple's romance began in Sydney, the magazine had revealed, where Mariel was a reporter at Channel Nine and Hamish was working for *The Sydney Morning Herald*. As soon as he met Mariel, he knew she was The One, and wooed her with daily bunches of red roses. 'The house looked like a florist's shop,' Mariel laughingly told the *Weekly* in its spread, the pages of which were coloured a garish pink.

Hamish Dark, a successful writer and prizewinning journalist 'both in New Zealand and Australia and with wider interests elsewhere', was a doting father to their children. What had first attracted Hamish to Mariel was her awesome beauty, specifically her amazing eyes.

And after that he was just blown away by her incredible mind.

Evading Jack Anthony, who was staring, Eloise walked out the door and crossed the forecourt to the opposite building: Z Wing. She took the stairs to Scott's office, where they were scheduled to discuss upcoming interviews. *Roysmith* was a weekly show of supposedly hard-hitting current affairs, although they were forced by the network to cover a lot of human interest and fluff.

Scott was on the phone. She stood at his office window with its long view down the harbour. A ferry moved out from the wharf, the churning wake spreading behind it in a long white V. On the street a tall man with black hair and a thin, hawkish face walked past a mirror-fronted building and was reflected, through some trick of refraction, upside down. She watched the slanting, bubbled figure, legs scissoring in the air.

'Christ,' Scott said. 'It's outrageous.'

Watching the upside-down man, she signalled, Want a coffee? He nodded.

Eloise went to open a cupboard and hesitated, eyeing the metal handle unhappily.

'I don't believe this. I hear you, Terry. It's actually malicious. All the more reason for us to . . . Yep, yep. Be in touch.'

He hung up, started pacing. 'That was Terry.'

They'd spent a lot of time on Andrew Newgate, the convicted

murderer whose cause had been taken up by businessman Terry Carstone. After years of public campaigning and an appeal to the Privy Council, Newgate had been granted a retrial and acquitted. Now he was looking for compensation.

Scott said, 'You know the new rumour doing the rounds — that Andrew caused his parents' death when he was eleven, mind, *eleven* years old. Ridiculous. Well, now there's another one: that Andrew's being investigated for the murder of a girl who lived about twenty ks away from him when he was a teenager. It's tabloid stuff.'

Eloise looked out and away. The ferry moving towards Rangitoto, the sun blazing through the tinted glass, and Scott's reflection, furred with golden light, standing in the blue space out there, pacing on the air.

'Terry's livid. He's looking at legal action.'

'Again? He's the king of defamation suits.'

'The rumour about the parents, Terry says it's based on a misunderstanding. Andrew was quoted years ago as saying he wasn't in the car when it crashed, and then someone found out he *was* in the car, and that he'd been hospitalised with a head injury. And there was no explanation for the crash, blah, blah, straight road, good weather, broad daylight, sober driver, car just veers off into a ditch, so of course they start saying Andrew was a child psychopath and grabbed the wheel. Started killing young. Terry says Andrew never said he wasn't in the car, that he was misquoted and it's all gone from there. It's malicious. It's all to wreck his compensation claim.'

Scott picked up a long wooden ruler and hooked it behind the cupboard handle, flicking the door open.

'Thanks,' Eloise said. She took out two coffee mugs.

Scott rummaged in the mess on his desk. 'I've lost my glasses. I must have left them at Q. What do you think of Ed Miles at close quarters?'

'He watches. In silence. It's disconcerting.'

'His "quiet menace" act. It's not an act. I wouldn't like to be the PM with Miles breathing down my neck. Anyway, re Newgate. Terry has concerns. He wants boundaries. He's been so burned. So . . . let down.'

Eloise thought about Carstone, Newgate's champion, the 'campaigner for justice'. The 'ball of energy', with his roguish winks, his anecdotes of times when he'd 'singlehandedly' exposed injustice and conducted whole court cases, and stayed up all night writing submissions and negotiating, this (he continually implied) without the help of any lawyer. He was 'battle-hardened', 'a bit of a rebel', 'fearless' — it all gained greater accuracy when surrounded by inverted commas.

'Did he mention money again?'

'Terry? No! Terry's not in it for the money. And what a brain. What a *mind*. The way he powers through the evidence, he's got it all stored in his head. Ask him about any aspect of the case, he'll come right out with it. He's amazing. The energy of the guy . . .'

Eloise picked up the ruler and tried to prise open a drawer with it. She put the coffee cups down and said, 'Actually, let's go out for coffee.'

'Good idea. Let's go out. Let's get out of this death trap. Our side of the building's the worst apparently. Selena came into my room with her hair standing on end. She said there was this huge click. And then a silver flare came off her stapler.'

'Everyone's on edge.'

'Jack said there was a sort of St Elmo's fire in the lift yesterday. People freaked. What are they doing about it, is what I want to know. People can't work, they can't focus. They don't dare touch anything. They're developing learned helplessness, like abused children . . .'

'You all right?' he asked five minutes later.

'Fine,' Eloise said.

They were on the back stairs, having decided against the lifts. In the foyer a group had gathered to discuss the state of the building. For a week now, staff in Z and Q wings had been terrorised by a strange new hazard: static electric shocks. Every door handle and metal object had become a potential source of fright and pain. The working theory, tentatively put about by management, was that it had to do with renovations in the building next door. Some issue with wiring, with the electrics. Technicians moved about the building, gathered in groups, frowning and discussing.

Scott now said, 'Thee and I are planning . . . a bit ambitious but the kids will . . .'

Eloise listened to him talk about his life: his clever photographer wife Theadora (he called her Thee) and the children, his daughters Sarah and Sophie and the third afterthought child, little Iris. He said things like, 'When you have children, it's like being in love all the time. Surrounded by love.'

He doesn't smile, he beams. Eloise smiled faintly. She thought about her own domestic scene: the wind combing the grass over the peninsula, the white sky filling the window of the upstairs bedroom, the melancholy cries of gulls over the dog park. The Saturdays. Even worse, the Sundays.

He said, 'You and Sean got a nice weekend planned?'

Her whole body tingled. 'A few things. Nothing special.'

Later, on her way out, Eloise called in to Q Wing looking for Scott's lost glasses. She inspected herself in the harsh light of the mirrored room. People passed in the corridor; there was a general rush, someone speaking urgently and angrily about a delay. There was a line of dresses and jackets hanging on a rail; she tried a few against herself, too frilly, too shiny, not her style.

Should she change everything about herself?

The connecting door to the next room was slightly open and she heard a cough, voices.

Through the crack in the door, Eloise looked at Mariel and Jack

Anthony facing each other. Mariel leaned forward and rested her forehead on his shoulder. He stood for a moment, then took her by both arms and pushed her back and looked at her. Neither said anything.

Eloise raised her fingers to the door handle. There was a painful snap and she whipped her hand away, stumbling against a chair. They both turned. Jack Anthony walked across and closed the door, and Eloise hurried out of the room.

On the bus she stood up for an elderly woman whose grateful smile turned to a gasp as they lurched around a corner and she fell. Her bag of shopping crashed down, fruit and tins rolled and scattered. A man, half-risen from his seat, held the woman up, preventing her from subsiding into his lap. Passengers began gathering the groceries as the woman, still hopelessly off-balance, pawed feebly at the man, flecks of spit at the corners of her mouth. Someone shouted at the bus driver. Eloise picked up the shopping bag and collected what people had gathered from the floor. She tried to catch the eye of the man who was now lowering the old woman onto the seat across the aisle from him, but he looked away and brushed the sleeve of his jacket, frowning and annoyed. He was tall, with thick black hair and a hawkish face. Uptight, she thought. But — she looked closer — he had a dragonfly tattooed on the back of his hand.

Now the walk along the peninsula in the hot dry wind. In her shopping this fine Friday evening: a bottle of white wine, a ready meal of vegetable curry and a couple of DVDs.

That afternoon she'd seen herself on camera, talking to Scott in the studio. There was a difference: she'd lost weight. It was exactly a month since Sean had left her, and she'd stopped cooking; what was the point? Now, alone, she ate eccentrically and fast, often standing at the kitchen bench: peas and tomato sauce, sardines on toast, pots of ready-made curry. It was strange, she kept thinking, so strange.

In the stone house on the peninsula, she lived through extra-ordinarily long silences: a whole day, two days. Silences that lasted through the Carmelite regime of a long weekend . . .

They'd been married for some years when she got a phone call from a woman telling her Sean was having an affair. The woman said her informant was a secretary at Jaeger's, the firm where Sean worked as a commercial lawyer. Eloise was very calm, listening. The woman's tone was weird and rambling, possibly mad, and Eloise thought her spiel about Sean and a young actress might not be true. But when she confronted him there was a terrible pause. He didn't say anything — and then he confessed. They had a ferocious shouting match — she shouted and he mostly just listened; she threw a coffee cup, smashing it on the wall near his head. She threw another. When she threw the third he packed a bag and left. Now he was holed up at the actress's house across town. It was as abrupt as that.

There were nights of frantic distress when she demanded explanations, sent furious emails, expected him to come home. One evening he did come home and she angrily told him to leave, thinking she should out of pride and some vague idea of tactics but not actually wanting him to. And then a final message from him saying he wasn't coming back.

In all the time they'd lived together, they'd spent very few nights apart. Now she was in shock. She'd got lazy about keeping up contact with friends, and she was very alone. The situation seemed so unreal that she hadn't got around to telling Scott, or any of the people she worked with. It was so strange . . .

She opened the wine and turned on the TV news. Mariel Hartfield was squeezed into a bright white top, very sexy, and her glossy black fringe was just slightly too long, giving her a sleepy look. Eloise knew that Mariel took a beta-blocker before going on air, more reliable than yoga for keeping you calm if anything went wrong. Eloise had read the label on the prescription bottle, and had seen Mariel popping the pill while getting her hair done. At the time, she'd congratulated herself for noticing. Because she was observant . . .

The pill dilated Mariel's pupils, giving her a benign and distant air. She said, 'The Minister has declined to comment on the speculation. Political editor Sarah Lane has more.'

They crossed to Sarah Lane, live in front of a flax bush in the grounds of Parliament.

Eloise refilled her glass. Should she get a dog? She imagined it: greeting her at the door, joyfully wagging its tail. Barking at intruders. A companion on her weekend walks . . .

Sarah Lane said, 'Mariel, while Minister O'Keefe has now confirmed her due date, she has, until today, declined to comment on persistent rumours surrounding the paternity of her child. Prime Minister Jack Dance has also refused to comment, saying only that he has full confidence in Ms O'Keefe and that her personal life is not a matter for him or anyone else to discuss. However, following publication yesterday of an article by Ian Ramsey in *Witness* magazine, the Minister has released a statement expressing concern at what she calls an unprecedented intrusion into her private life, and reiterating that she is not obliged to discuss the question of paternity with anyone unless she chooses to. She also says she is considering laying some kind of complaint against Mr Ramsey in relation to the *Witness* article.

'Mariel, you could say the Minister's statement is notable for what it doesn't say. It obviously doesn't shed any light on the paternity question, and it doesn't make any denials in relation to any of the male government ministers and one prominent businessman named in the article, who've been the subject of rumours in this matter for the past few months. Those individuals may also want to lay complaints against Mr Ramsey, but so far none is prepared to comment. Look, the government will be wanting to tread very carefully here. There'll be a general desire not to let things get out of hand with what ministers are calling everything from a side issue to a distraction to an outrageous intrusion into a member's private life. Adding to pressure on Minister O'Keefe is the roll-out of her new child poverty initiatives next week, which she won't want overshadowed, and, even more delicate, her policy outlining new measures for sole parents on benefits. The Opposition will obviously want to proceed carefully here too, but let's put it this way, Mariel, they won't be ungrateful that the government's having to deal with this distraction at this time. I think the only thing we can safely say at this point is: Watch this space. Mariel?'

There was now a shot of Minister Anita O'Keefe walking towards the cameras, elegant in her tight dress and high heels, her hair pulled back, a fixed smile. The microphones appeared in front of her. The questioning wasn't rough or persistent, she wasn't mobbed, she passed easily, ignoring, smiling. Did she get behind the door of her office and lean against it with her eyes closed? If Sean had been here Eloise would have said to him, 'Look at her, that little smile. Mona Lisa. Like she's hoarding something, like she's in possession of something.'

Yeah. A baby.

Already slightly drunk, Eloise walked into the kitchen and contemplated the curry. She spooned it into a bowl and shoved it in the microwave. While it heated she went out on the deck and looked across the estuary to the dog park. The tide was on the turn, the banks of the creek glistening with purple mud, and she watched a man and dog playing fetch, the arc of the ball and the mad speed of the dog, and behind them the evening sky crossed with delicate ropes of cloud.

Perhaps she should have got pregnant, not consulted Sean, just let it happen. She thought about Anita O'Keefe, whose refusal to comment had caused speculation about her pregnancy. It was being said (excitedly rumoured, fervently hoped) that the father was a serving politician, and married. A cabinet minister perhaps. Minister O'Keefe, who was young, unattached and very attractive, had been the subject of gossip since she'd been given a cabinet post. She'd been popular with senior politicians, who squired her about looking modestly proud and discreet, as if they'd invented her themselves. Maybe she'd worked her way through all of them. Secretly slept with all of them, and now the whole male front bench was terrified of the pregnancy — and of their wives. Or maybe there was no father. She'd got herself a sperm donor. Gone down to the lab and ordered a baby off the plans.

A single brown bubble had surfaced in the curry, like a blister. Eloise squeezed rice out of a plastic bag and ate the hot fragrant mess, her eyes on the TV. Mariel turned to Jack Anthony, there was the usual chatty feed into the topic of weather, and they both turned to the weather presenter — the haggard one Eloise called the Sinister Doormat — who now told Eloise that tomorrow would be a continuation of the Big Dry.

All along the peninsula the drought had turned the grass brown. A network of cracks had opened up on Eloise's lawn. She glanced through the glass ranch slider — out in the gulf the water was like steel — and wondered how much longer it would be her lawn. Sean was going to force the sale of the house. His mother, Lady Cheryl Rodd, had recently visited Eloise. She still felt cold rage at the memory, the tyrannical old bag, barging in and coldly patronising her, like a social worker. 'Are you sleeping, dear? Keeping your strength up, dear?' Her beady eye on the chattels, and implacable in defence of her son. The house, Lady Cheryl confirmed, would have to be sold, since Sean had his heart set on what she called 'his new course'. Eloise would understand this. A tough decision, but someone had to make those.

What did she care, so long as her son was happy?

While Eloise was trying to freeze Lady Cheryl off the property the cleaner backed out of a spare bedroom with his knapsack vacuum cleaner, and Lady Cheryl jerked her thumb at Amigo and whispered stagily, 'What about him? I know you've got that TV job, but you might have to cut down on a few expenses.'

Well, Lady Cheryl was the little actress's problem now.

Sean's family, the Rodds, were so rich he could afford to let her have the house, but Eloise knew some terrifying Tulkinghorn from Sean's law firm would soon arrive, bringing papers from the Rodd dynasty. She also knew she needed to visit a lawyer herself, but so far she'd lacked the will. All she could manage was to cling onto the routine of work.

And then there were the weekends.

It was very unhealthy and unwise and she deplored it and it was a disgrace and all, but she couldn't help getting drunk, sitting in front of the big plate-glass window, watching the sky turn red over the estuary and the last figures — small, black, slanted against the wind — making their way across the dog park in the fading light. She tried to watch one of the DVDs but her attention kept wandering, and there were many trips to the fridge for more wine, and then a long session in front of the computer, searching through Facebook and Twitter for electronic traces of Sean, virtual views of Sean — the online version of her weekend wanderings. She also checked the Facebook pages and Twitter accounts of Minister Anita O'Keefe and other members of the government. Ms O'Keefe had been in the habit of tweeting about the cities she was visiting, and Eloise, who'd been watching her for a long time, had noticed she'd often been in the same city as the prime minister. Since the minister's pregnancy had become public, Twitter had never shown Anita O'Keefe and Jack Dance to be in the same place at the same time.

Running out of material on the politicians, she looked at Mariel Hartfield's Wikipedia page. Mariel was Ngai Tahu, had worked for the *Melbourne Herald*, in Britain for *BBC World*, at Nine in Sydney, as a reporter and sub-editor for *Eyewitness* and *News1*, and was currently co-presenter with Jack Anthony on *Evening News1*.

Later, when Eloise was so tired and tipsy she'd lost the ability to touch type and was reduced to stabbing with two fingers, she wrote Sean an email. In her mind she called it emailing the dead. She was sending words out into the void. *I am in rather a bad way* was her next vague thought, as she rested her forehead for a moment on the desk.

Later she slid off the chair, wandered over to the sofa and lay down. There was a moment when she lucidly, sternly, examined the state of affairs. (And rebuked herself for being drunk.) Sean's departure was the second loss in her life. Marriage to Sean had been a way of remedying (and perhaps not facing up to) a loss that had occurred before. And now Sean was gone . . . *That* was why she was in a bad way. You pick yourself up once, but twice? It was too much. Eloise frowned. Now Sean was gone, she thought, all my chickens. All my chickens . . . they're coming home to . . . root? No.

That was it: since Sean had left her, all Eloise Hay's emotional chickens were coming home to roost.

She slept, she flew into dreams. Scott Roysmith floated in the air upside down, he was a kite, his string held by a lone figure in the dog park — Andrew Newgate. Newgate turned, and his glasses were filled with red light.

When Andrew Newgate smiled his eyes stayed watchful, and his eyes followed you. With Terry Carstone, it was different. Terry's eyes didn't follow you. They were looking at something no one else could see: the mind of Terry Carstone. They were always looking inward. And they said, *Watch me. Watch me. Look at me . . .*

Outside, on the edge of the peninsula, not far from the dog park, shapes were moving in the dark.

FOUR

I'm not fooled by surface appearance. I read between the lines. I am observant.

But Andrew Newgate looked at her and his eyes were unreadable. His glasses mirrored the red sky over the park and then a tiny black shape, the reflection of a dog, crossed them, crossed over the arc of the glass and disappeared into space . . .

This weight on her. It was the weight of the weekend, of loneliness and childlessness, the ticking of the biological clock, of one loss and then another, the second making the first come home to roost. All that weight, but there was something else. As she swam up into consciousness there was matter pressed against her face. Eloise surfaced with a gasp and pushed her way clear of the heavy cushions.

Her head was pounding and her mouth was dry, and she had the beginnings of a searing hangover — hypersensitivity, suicidal ideation, *tristesse* — but now there was something else again. A rhythmic thumping. She stood up, and her heart, already racing, sped with alarm as the thumping turned into battering and there was a crash, followed by shouts and then, terrifyingly, actual screams. Her hands flew to her ears.

She was standing with fists clenched and pressed against the sides of her head when she saw, beyond the ranch slider, a torch beam crossing the bottom of the garden. The beam played on her lawn, then disappeared as it reached the spill of light from the deck. She'd fallen asleep with the living room lamps on. Beyond the deck, all was black.

Eloise crossed the room and turned off the lights. There was another scream followed by a man's shout. The torch beam crossed the lawn again, falling briefly on the creek, the water glittering. Eloise dug among the sofa cushions for her phone. She found it, looked up, and saw the shape of a man against the glass.

She heard him knock. He waved. As she was grappling with her phone he found the handle, slid open the unlocked glass door and stepped into the room. Eloise backed away, putting furniture between them.

There was another loud bang outside, a dog barking. She said, 'What is it? Oh, what is it?'

He felt around on the wall and turned on the lights.

'It's okay. Sorry,' he said, and then, 'I hope you're not going to hit me with that.'

She was holding a heavy book at shoulder height.

He walked to the window and looked out. 'I knocked on your front door but you didn't answer, and then I came around on the deck and saw you. I thought I'd better explain.'

'What's going on? The *noise*.'

'Come and see. It's the police. They're doing some kind of raid over there. They actually broke the door down, I saw them, and then the girl, the one with the tattoos, was in the upstairs window screaming her head off, going nuts. I ran into the police about half an hour ago, they were sneaking around outside my place. I thought they were prowlers so I went out, and they grabbed me and told me to keep quiet. Then they went in. Dogs and all. I've been watching from the edge of your property.'

He beckoned her forward and she looked out at the big stucco rental next door. There were figures moving in the windows upstairs and the garden was lit up with spotlights, a man in a white boiler suit bending to look at something in the grass.

'I feel . . . slightly sick.'

'Oh look, sit down. You got a fright.'

He steered her over to a chair and she sank down.

'I could make us a cup of tea?'

She nodded, watched him moving around in the kitchen, opening drawers, finding things, filling the kettle and switching it on. She rode out another wave of nausea and said, 'I'm sorry but I can't remember your name?'

'It's Nick Oppenheimer. I remember yours. Eloise. I had no idea this was such an exciting neighbourhood.'

'Is it just you at 27?'

'Yeah. I've just moved in. Love the peninsula, the dog park.'

'Do you have a dog?'

'No.'

'I thought of getting one.' She added stupidly, 'I'm trying out living by myself at the moment.'

'Dogs are good company,' Nick said.

The shouting had stopped; there was the sound of voices, the slam of car doors and the crunch of boots on gravel. A dog let out a series of deep barks.

They listened. Eloise said to fill the silence, 'Dogs. Um, there's a man who parks his Jeep outside the supermarket up the road, and twice when I've passed it I've heard the most eerie sound. Howling. I looked in, into the Jeep, and what he's got in there is a wolf. It's huge, twice the size of an Alsatian. I went home and Googled pictures of wolves — and it's a wolf. It doesn't bark, it howls.'

He was studying her face.

'It must be illegal,' she said.

'To own a wolf, I'm sure.'

'It really *is* a wolf. It can't be anything else.'

'Yes, I believe you.'

'It's a mystery. How did he bring it into the country? How does he keep it without people complaining?'

'I'll look out for it.'

'God . . .'

'Are you all right?'

'Nerves a bit shot, that's all. The woman screaming.'

'It was unnerving. And me creeping about on your lawn. Sorry.'

He waited, then said, 'This is an interesting house. So much glass. It must have incredible views.'

'We had an architect. I don't know how long I've got here. I'll be moving out soon.'

She pressed her fingers to her temples. 'Can you actually *see* my head throbbing?'

He laughed.

Eloise said, 'I've always thought of myself as observant. I thought I was the one who noticed what was going on, while everyone else was in a fog.'

'Oh. Right . . . ?'

'And it was a complete delusion. I didn't notice anything going on over there. Drug dealing or whatever.'

'I doubt anyone knew.'

She went on, 'I didn't notice my husband was about to leave me. Never saw it coming. Yesterday at work I saw something happen between two people I thought hated each other. And I had it completely wrong. Instead of hating each other they're probably having an affair. I don't know why I'm telling you this.'

Nick handed her a cup of tea. He was tall, thin and athletic, with even features, almost handsome although skin slightly rough. Blue eyes.

'Oh thanks. You've put sugar in it. What I need to do,' she said, 'is get some fresh air. I think I'll just walk around to the dog park.' Her voice quavered. She sounded mad and proud and unwell.

'By yourself? In the dark?'

'It's fine. I do it all the time,' she lied.

'How about I come with you, Eloise,' he said.

The lawn next door was harshly lit, with a group of police conferring on the porch. The scene, figures in white boiler suits moving in white light, stirred a memory in Eloise, a feeling of dread that passed and was replaced by a kind of doomed brightness, as if all was lost and any feeling futile. They followed the path along the edge of the creek, where Starlight Peninsula broadened and joined the land, and a bridge led across to the dog park. There was a dull orange glow in the sky over the city, the warm air smelled of dried grass, and tiny sounds came from the estuary, little clickings and rustlings, small creatures maybe, crabs or water rats, scuttling through the mangroves.

'Looks like a spaceship's landed.'

Two figures in white shower caps moved silently across the grass. The darkness curved over the bubble of light.

'I saw them arresting the girl, the one who was screaming. She made such a fuss they actually picked her up and carried her.'

Eloise saw it: the struggling girl, a dynamic, furious thing amid the black-and-white strangeness of the spotlit garden. She remembered her dream, the shadow of a dog crossing her vision.

Looking back at her own house she saw that the lighted interior was visible from the park. During the day the glass was opaque, but at night she would be seen clearly as she moved around the sitting room.

'I'll have to start closing the curtains.'

'But there's no one in the dog park at night.'

She said, 'This area used to be much rougher. It was a bit of a slum apparently. Up the top was the worst pub in Auckland — the Starlight Hotel. There was a murder there. The peninsula only started getting respectable after they demolished the Starlight.'

They walked to the edge, where the land ended in the estuary and the water lay still and calm, giving off stray flashes of light. Something rose and disturbed the surface, a splash, bubbles. A car alarm started up far away.

He said, 'Do you really come out here often? At night?'

'Oh sure. Why not?'

They headed back across the park, walking slowly.

Nick said, 'So, tell me about your job. It must be interesting working for Roysmith.'

'Did I tell you my job? When?'

'At the gate when we first met.'

'Oh? We've just done a piece on Andrew Newgate. About Ed Miles turning down his compensation claim.'

'Do you think Newgate's innocent?'

'Roysmith thinks he is.'

'So you don't think so?'

'Yes, I do.'

'Most people think he's guilty as sin. That he's only got off because of Carstone's campaign.'

'Not most. Fifty per cent.'

'Anyway. What are you working on now?'

'Well, just between us, we might do the internet mogul, Kurt Hartmann.'

'Isn't he about to be shipped off to the US?'

'He's fighting extradition.'

Nick said, 'It all seems rather complicated.'

Eloise stopped and pointed. 'Did you see that flash? A fish jumping. Quite a big one.'

They looked out at the estuary, brimming at high tide. A line zig-zagged across the water, then the surface went calm, a dull silver, like mercury.

She said, 'Kurt Hartmann owned websites where people could store data. He says he was — effectively — operating a big electronic warehouse and it wasn't his business if people were storing material in it that breached copyright. He didn't know what was in there and he didn't care. But the Hollywood studios and the US Government say he knew he was storing copyrighted material, that he's a pirate and that he's ripped off the movie and music industries five hundred million US dollars.'

'Right.'

'And then it was discovered — actually it was leaked by someone — that he'd been spied on here illegally, also at the behest of the US. Illegally because he's a New Zealand citizen and the GCSB can only spy on foreign nationals. Although Ed Miles is working to change that rule. Scott wants to find out who leaked it that Hartmann was spied on illegally. The word is there's a faction in the PM's own party who are leaking against him. An Ed Miles faction, probably backed by the old guard, by people loyal to Sir David Hallwright.'

'Hallwright's in the South of France. I read an article about his house,' Nick said.

'That's right. Lounging around the Med. In St Tropez or whatever. On his millions.'

'Are you going to the Hartmann mansion?'

'I hope so. It's meant to be unbelievable. Anyway, what do you do, Nick?'

'I used to be a teacher. Then I started working for NGOs. Aid work. Save the Children.'

'That sounds very worthy.'

'I grew up in Cape Town. My father's South African, he's a newspaper editor, and my mother was a Kiwi. They split up and she came back here. I'd been working in Africa, various countries, and my ex-partner and I decided to try Auckland. My ex is a New Zealander. I like Auckland, less crime. You don't have to live in a fortress.'

'Carjackings,' Eloise said vaguely.

'Places over there, you need to own a gun. Although, I'm a black belt in karate.'

'Really.'

'It's a discipline. It's a *way*.'

Eloise looked sideways.

'I inherited the house from my mother when she died, some other property, too, so now I'm a landlord. At this point I'm not sure whether to sell up and go back to Cape Town, or stay here.'

They crossed the bridge and followed the path back to the sections. A man in white overalls was kneeling on the lawn in front of the stucco house, photographing something.

She watched Nick leap neatly over a low fence. A 'way'. He was good-looking. Was he slightly weird?

He said, 'I do volunteer work, for search and rescue. I used to do it in Cape Town, so I signed up here. We look for demented old people, kids gone missing, trampers lost in the bush. Also corpses. Last week they rang me — did you hear about the woman's body found in a drain in West Auckland?'

'Yes.'

'Actually they only found half of her in the drain. It had washed in there from a stream. I got the call, they wanted us to come out and help find the other half.'

She stopped walking. 'Did you find it?'

'No. We were looking for bones. Clothes. Got nothing.'

'Had she been sawn up?'

'Maybe.'

'Why do you do it?'

'Look for people? I enjoy it. I love tramping, going up in the helicopter, scouring coastlines. Slogging through the bush. And to give back, obviously.'

They walked on. Eloise hesitated at her gate.

He said, 'I've got some brandy at my place.'

She followed him round the side of his house and in through the back door. They entered a hall smelling of floor polish and then a spacious room with glass doors opening onto a deck, a view of the estuary and the city beyond. There was a sofa, one armchair, a glass coffee table, a flat-screen TV and a couple of prints on the walls.

'All my books are in boxes still. I need shelves.'

Eloise sat on the sofa and looked at the city buildings against the night sky. He handed her a glass and she drank, the alcohol hit her, waves travelling down her body.

'Want to know something funny?' she said. 'On the subject of looking for people.'

He sat down beside her.

'Ever since my husband left, there's something I can't stop doing. I go looking for him. It's some primitive impulse, like a panic — he's gone so I have to find him. I walk for hours. I'm not sure where he's living; I haven't found out and he won't tell me. I just walk and walk, looking in places where he might be.'

'What would you do if you found him?'

'I don't know. Yell at him. Punch him. It's not rational. None of it's rational.' She tipped back the glass, drank. Strange, it was nearly empty. 'I'm not looking for him in order to punch him,' she added.

'I understand.'

'What do you understand?'

'The impulse. To go looking.'

She stared. 'Really?'

'Sure. I split up with someone not long ago.'

'You've got me drunk again.'

'You're fine.'

Eloise felt a slackening, she wasn't able to shut up. 'My marriage was a cure. A barrier. A remedy.'

'For what?'

She whispered, 'Grief.'

'I see. For a previous relationship?'

'He *died*.'

'Oh. Sorry. Did he have an illness?'

She looked sadly at her glass. He filled it.

'I shouldn't drink this.'

'Yolo.'

She snorted. 'Did you just say "yolo"?'

'Go on, tell me about it.'

'My partner, before Sean, he was found dead outside his flat with his neck broken. The police found he'd been taking pills for insomnia, and they thought he might have sleepwalked. There was a flimsy wire fence; he fell against it and it gave way. He went over the retaining wall.'

Silence. The sudden deep barking of a dog along the peninsula.

'It was strange.'

'Why?'

'He never sleepwalked. He might have taken the odd pill, but they told me he took a huge dose. The police told me he had a bruise on his thigh. They never found out how he got it.'

'So what do you think happened?'

'I don't know. Arthur was a journalist. We both worked in TV, that's how I met him, just after I'd done my communications degree at AUT. He was older than me.'

'Was he an investigative journalist?'

'He did all sorts of things, TV One current affairs, wrote for *Metro* and *North & South*. Worked on screenplays. We were living between his flat and mine. I was about to leave mine permanently and move into his. That morning I'd been in Sydney, I went straight to his flat from the airport.'

She paused, sipped her drink. It was the crime scene at the house next door that had brought it back. Summer. A hot morning on the side of Mt Eden. Towing her suitcase up the hill to Arthur's, she'd passed a man wearing a white boiler suit and a shower cap, his shoes encased in bags. When she stopped outside Arthur's gate a group of people with notebooks looked towards her. They'd been clustered at the top of the retaining wall, looking down.

Opening the flat she went in, called out, walked around. The rooms were full of sunlight. The doorbell rang.

On Arthur's front steps a blonde woman, a detective, asked for her name and spoke strange words. 'A man has been found dead. We haven't identified him. We've had a suggestion from a resident he might live here.'

They took her to him. He'd fallen against the rickety wire fence and gone over when it gave way. He was lying on the hot asphalt terrace below the retaining wall. She saw his thin ankles, one dusty shoe come off. She wasn't allowed to touch him, but she saw that his eyes were closed, his mouth was pursed as if in shock or surprise, and a part of his skull was broken and sticking up out of his matted, bloody hair in a triangular shard.

After that, the morning had turned unreal, toy-coloured. There were seams of evil pulsing behind the sky. Eloise stood on Arthur's back deck looking at the grassy mountainside, the walking track winding to the summit. There were police up there, searching through the waving grass, pacing along the path, inspecting the wire fence and the stile. She turned to the detective and said, 'Why are they up there? You must think it wasn't an accident.'

'We don't know anything at this stage.'

She remembered arguing, 'But they're looking for clues. Why go searching up the mountain if it was an accident? Do you think someone hurt Arthur then ran up there?'

'We don't know.'

The blonde woman detective and her partner drove Eloise away from Arthur's flat and into Central Police Station. She was distracted by the woman detective's odd-coloured eyes: one blue, one brown.

'After he died everything was terrifying. I was afraid all the time. I went back to living in a flat my father owned. I got burgled. Or someone broke in, anyway. They didn't take anything.'

'That's bad luck.'

'It *was* bad luck. I knew that's all it was, but it made me even more scared. I met Sean and he seemed so solid. That's what attracted me, he was all wholesomeness and muscles and honesty, like a big strong bodyguard. Honesty, so I thought. I didn't know at first that he was rich, that he had family money. That's how we got the house so quickly. Which we now have to sell. We got married quite quickly. I blotted Arthur out. We were close, happy. And now my marriage, all that I built up between me and ruin — it's gone.'

'So you have to confront the past. It hasn't gone away.'

'It might kill me.'

Nick topped up her glass. 'It won't kill you.'

'You think?'

'No, it's good to look back. Helps sort out the present and future.

Stop walking the earth and confront the situation. I'll tell you something, when my ex and I broke up, I was depressed, couldn't sleep. I was angry. She told me to see someone about it, and I ignored her. Maybe I shouldn't have.'

He splashed a large helping into his own glass, leaned back and put his shoes up on the glass coffee table. 'You know, the dog that howls, the one you think is a wolf.'

'Yes?'

'See, it may just be a husky.'

FIVE

Something had wormed its way into her chest and was pinning her down, making her writhe like a speared fish. It was early morning, and it was foggy. She was in her bedroom, the glass door to the upstairs deck was open, the white curtain not stirring. Silence, no wind. The dog park was shrouded in mist, the city buildings a grey blur on the horizon. It came back to her, how much she'd drunk, how much of herself she'd given away. To someone she didn't know.

Oh God, she'd made a fool of herself with the wine and the fright of the police raid next door, and then the brandy tipping her over the edge. The vile taste of it now rose in her throat and lit up her chest with a miserable sick heat. The memory swam up: walking back to her gate with Nick, raising her voice. 'They asked you to look for the *other half* of someone? The police wouldn't invite search and rescue volunteers into a crime scene.'

'They do, we've been trained. We follow their lead, don't touch, just look. If we find something we call them over.'

And her repeating, 'It can't be true.'

Remember what Sean used to say, *When you're drunk, Eloise, you're like a dog with a bone.*

Nick standing straight, looking down at her. 'You calling me a liar?'

'A crime scene. I don't know . . .'

Later she'd said, 'Anyway, you think a husky. Not a wolf?'

He said, 'If you're going for a walk tomorrow, why don't we look for your wolf together?'

Going for a walk. That *so* didn't cover what she'd been doing. Had she said no to his offer to come along?

One thing she was sure about: no more drinking. Not for at least two days.

She walked out onto the deck and stared at the white world. There were banners of mist hanging around the trees and in the east the obscured sun was a silver disk, surrounded by a ring of light. It was going to be hot. Silence and stillness along the peninsula. The fog muffled sounds. Two shapes, a man and a dog, crossed the bridge to the park, disappearing into swirls of air. She watched the vapour rearrange itself behind them.

It was impossible to see if the tide was in, and the dog park was hidden, but she was close enough to the stucco house to catch sight of a person in one of the upstairs rooms. The figure moved past a window, appeared at another, and disappeared. Eloise waited, but there was no further sign of life.

Down in the kitchen she turned on the TV and watched a clip of Minister Anita O'Keefe being interviewed on the introduction of her families package, involving tax credits, a baby bonus, and legislation governing liable parent arrangements. The minister fielded questions smoothly. Brushing off a final enquiry, on a certain magazine's insinuations about the paternity of her unborn child, she managed to seem both steely and poised. She would not comment, of course.

Of course. Eloise stooped, and rested her cheek on the cold bench top. Outside the air whirled and collapsed in on itself, the sky fallen onto the lawn. A seagull landed, edging along the deck rail on its red feet, and Eloise opened the glass door and threw it a crust. Screams as more gulls bombed down onto the deck, scrapping over the bread.

Prime Minister Jack Dance appeared in the studio endorsing O'Keefe's package, before moving on to his core message: Opposition leader Bradley Kirk was so unpopular he'd lost control of his caucus, so busy dealing with internal wrangling and 'chaos among his members', he was unable to lead his own party.

'It's bedlam on the Opposition side, I'm afraid,' said Dance, whose public nickname was Satan.

The news crossed live to Wellington and a shot of the Beehive. There was a barber's chair set up on the sunny forecourt outside Parliament, and Richie Carter, the youngest member of the Opposition shadow cabinet, stood beside it, two girls in matching T-shirts holding his arms. Carter's smile was forced. A jokey spiel from reporter Chad Going: Carter had been volunteered by his leader, Bradley Kirk, to have his head shaved as a fundraiser for Cancer Research. Kirk himself would do the shaving, and now appeared wielding a hedge trimmer. A laborious joke. Eloise sipped her tea as Kirk roguishly posed for the cameras. Then he took up a hairdresser's razor and started shaving off the young man's hair.

Oh how hilarious. Carter began to look smaller as his hair came off, his pale scalp showing, his reddened ears sticking out.

The camera panned back and there was a shot of the crowd, among them Anita O'Keefe and a junior woman MP, who was filming the proceedings on an iPhone, and laughing.

Eloise went on thinking about it in the shower. It was for a cause. You shaved your head to raise money, in solidarity with those who lost their hair through chemotherapy. But who gets shaved against their will? Prisoners, collaborators, traitors. The subjugated.

Opposition leader Bradley Kirk was famously a nice guy, his niceness one of the reasons why his leadership was being questioned. You wouldn't pick him as a bully.

The older man humiliates the younger, while a beautiful woman watches. Sean would dismiss it as a lame stunt, 'desperate stuff from Labour', because Sean votes National, because his family funds the National Party. Scott Roysmith will call it a selfless act of charity. What would Arthur have called it?

Atavistic, was the word she was looking for. Arthur would have said, What's Carter done to piss Bradley Kirk off? And maybe, Who's screwing who here? Arthur noticed details, things she missed. He would have seen something ancient and primitive and savage in it, something sexual.

The sun was rising, hot behind the fog. She walked around the outside of the stucco house. It was closed up, windows locked and the doors sealed with tape. So how could she have seen someone upstairs?

She set off, worried about running into Nick, walked towards Ponsonby, headed in the direction of Newmarket, then the waterfront. There was a thin covering of cloud over the sun but it soon burned off and the sea glittered, chemical blue. It was beautiful, but it was the wrong place. She turned inland, and kept walking.

To Maungawhau, Mt Eden, the highest cone, its green terraces rising steeply above the city. She turned onto a path that led between wooden fences and through suburban gardens, onto the hillside and up to the summit, where the coaches parked, and the tourists milled around, photographing the rock-strewn volcanic crater and the slopes where Maori once built their pa and fought off marauding tribes, the view of suburbs stretching all the way south to the airport and north to the city. Haze of sun over the Sky Tower, shining dust.

She crossed the summit to the west, climbed a stile and walked down the hillside track. She had only been back twice since the morning Arthur died, both times to take away clothes she'd left there. The detective with the odd-coloured eyes had been with her. When the policewoman briefly left the room to talk on her cell phone Eloise, suddenly angry at being watched, and at being told she could take nothing of Arthur's, pulled a file of his papers from under the desk and concealed it in the sports bag containing the clothes she'd collected. She'd taken it home and hidden it.

Now the track led through the long grass under a stand of trees and came out above the concrete deck where she and Arthur used to sit on summer mornings, listening to the sounds of the city below.

From here she had a view of the roof and the deck, the back door and the kitchen window. A wisteria vine grew up a trellis, and there was an orange beach towel hanging on a wooden chair. She left the path, treading carefully on the uneven ground, avoiding holes and stones hidden by the long grass. She recalled summer mornings waking with Arthur to the sounds of cicadas and birds, the scent of hot grass and pine through the open window. Arthur's jokes and crazes, his obsessions. He would get up in the night and make notes. He said, 'I'll change my name to Abelard,' and explained when she didn't get it.

She stood on the hillside remembering, the patch of sun on the deck, light catching a metal water bowl left there for the cat, stillness, and she saw a man cross the deck and behind him Arthur getting up from the wooden chair, talking to the man who was just inside the kitchen now, Arthur pulling a leaf from the wisteria vine as he talked, rolling it between his fingers. Arthur's eyes, his face, his thin body and long legs. Turning to follow the man, he kicked the metal bowl of water, she caught the flash and shimmer of light. The door closing.

Eloise sat down in the long grass and watched the cloud shadows crossing the suburb. The cicadas sang so loud they had no meaning, no essence, only sound. The green mountain, once a plate of fire spilling lava, site of ancient wars, the clouds above it filtering sunlight, sending down the beams that Maori call the ropes of Maui. She lay in the grass and dreamed.

Killing time.

She was halfway along Karangahape Road when she remembered sitting in a room at the police station with the woman detective. Her name was Marie Da Silva. She had blonde hair, long at the back and sticking up like gold wire on top of her head. She had a male partner who seldom talked, only watched — she remembered his steady stare. Detective Da Silva showed her a note written by Arthur. In his scrawling handwriting in black felt pen, there were names divided by a forward slash.

'This mean anything to you?' Da Silva asked. 'Do you know these names?'

Eloise, who had been silent, began to talk. Words spilled out of her. Arthur always had a lot of projects on the go. He wrote copious notes. He was working on a play. He was part of a team of writers on a TV comedy show. He was finishing a screenplay about a National Party prime minister. He wanted to plan his first novel. Arthur was a barrel of energy, he was curious about everything. He wanted to experience as much as possible, to come up against things, institutions, people. He was especially interested in politics. He wanted to write about right-wing politicians, and he wondered how he could get into their world, which he didn't belong to.

The names he'd written down could relate to any of those projects.

She'd felt as if she were defending Arthur against a terrible accusation.

'They're not the names of politicians,' the detective said, giving the list a push across the table. 'Are they.'

There was some kind of question behind her question.

Eloise said, 'You know who they are.'

'Are you asking me if I do?'

'It sounds as if you do,' Eloise said. The detective's eyes were disconcerting.

The detective tapped a finger on the paper. Her hands were small and neat. 'I might know who one of them is. But you don't?'

'No.'

What Eloise remembered was feeling embarrassed afterwards that she'd said a 'barrel of energy'. She'd meant a 'ball', got mixed up with 'barrel of laughs' and stumbled on, not correcting herself.

All that time gone by and still, today, she winced. As if anyone would have even noticed, barrel or ball.

Those hours in the police station, she'd felt she was defending Arthur against the suggestion that his death was his fault. But she'd turned away from detail, shielded herself from questions. She'd pushed the piece of paper back across the table, saying numbly, 'I don't know the names. I've got no idea.'

After they'd finished investigating and told her Arthur had been affected by sleeping pills and had probably fallen off the wall by accident, she hadn't argued or asked questions, she'd accepted the verdict and carried on.

Already learning to live without him.

Evening on the peninsula. The walkers stood in groups while the dogs sniffed and chased. The tide was full, the estuary brimming, tips of the mangroves sticking out of the slow green water.

She put the laptop on her knees and Googled Detective Marie Da Silva. A few entries, mostly newspaper reports of criminal cases where she was quoted giving evidence or making statements to media, a couple of pictures: there was the strong angular face, blonde hair, unmatched eyes, one blue, one brown. She didn't look much older. No sign of her on Facebook or Twitter.

Absent-mindedly, Eloise wandered over to the kitchen and shoved a plastic pot of curry in the microwave. Waiting for the ping, she realised she'd already poured a glass of wine and drunk half of it, contrary to her earlier resolution, which meant she'd have to postpone not drinking until tomorrow, otherwise it wouldn't be proper abstinence.

Resignedly drinking, she watched Mariel Hartfield, who was reading a news item about a plane crash. Beautiful Mariel with her rich, resonant voice, her face framed by thick, glossy black hair, the fringe slightly too long. Smooth brown skin, perfect full Maori mouth, those sleepy eyes.

Strange — might as well have another glass of wine — strange how newsreaders become celebrities. You go to AUT, get your journalism degree, work your way up through radio and TV, then they decide you can read the news and suddenly you're a celeb and a national icon, and it's all about what you're wearing and what silly, ersatz names you call your kids and not much about the actual job: broadcasting the news. The latest *Woman's Day* had 'bubbly A-lister' Mariel and her 'hunky husband' musing on the subject of 'heritage'. 'I'm a Mozzie,' Mariel said, a Maori Aussie, brought up in Queensland, had to be persuaded to come here by her husband, 'but now I'm in love with all things Kiwi, of course'.

Eloise watched the bulletin: crime, politics, crime, human interest, international, crime, crime. Tired, she drifted a little. She saw Arthur standing in front of the TV, ruffling his curly hair, making it stand on end. He said, 'Listen.'

She sat up, tipping the plate sideways off her knees. Mariel was still talking. Her voice.

Listen.

But Satan Dance appeared, making a statement in Parliament. Eloise turned off the television. It was dusk; the sky was high, pale, a single star just becoming visible. She sat in the dark looking across to the dog park, where she could see figures moving against the sky. The laptop was beside her on the sofa. She picked it up and a photograph of Marie Da Silva appeared on a wall of Google images.

Her eyes travelled up and fixed on the patch above the sofa where one of the cups she'd hurled at Sean had made a hole in the wall. The plasterer who'd fixed it had said with a wink, 'Wild parties, eh?'

When the phone rang Eloise had her head in the hall cupboard and her arse in the air and was rooting around in a mound of shoes, suitcases, sports bags and tennis racquets. She backed out and ran to the phone.

'It's me.' It was her sister, Carina.

Eloise removed a cobweb from her face, leaned on the wall, blew hair off her forehead.

'I was in the hall cupboard.'

'Any news?'

'He's not coming back.'

'God. Arsehole. Listen, can I bring the Sparkler over tomorrow? And Silvio? I've got to finish something and I don't know what to do with them.'

'Sure. We can go to the dog park.'

'Oh that's great thanks, maybe around three? And then after we could get takeaways.'

'Yeah, that'd be good.'

'Did you say you were in the cupboard?'

Eloise sighed. She heard barking, a bang, a scream, childish laughter, her sister's voice, 'Christ. Will you *shut up*. Okay. Bye.'

She went back to the cupboard and started making a pile. Old shoes, a golf club, a pot-plant holder, a folding chair. Wedding presents:

a vase, a framed lithograph of a Pacific scene, bowls, an impossibly complicated food processor still in its box, cushions, a bedspread. She dragged the stuff towards the back door then changed her mind and hauled it through the living room, across the deck and onto the lawn. An old vacuum cleaner, a suitcase, a spring-loaded exercise contraption. A tartan beret, surely belonging to Lady Cheryl, who went in for hats. She held it between finger and thumb.

Would any of it go up?

Seagulls screamed on the deck rail, and across the estuary in the dusk the dogs ran crazily to and fro.

SIX

Eloise was lying on the deck wearing dark glasses and attempting to read.

> *But his heart was in a constant, turbulent riot. The most*
> *grotesque and fantastic conceits haunted him in his bed at night.*
> *A universe of ineffable gaudiness spun itself out in his brain*
> *while the clock ticked on the wash-stand and the moon soaked*
> *with wet light his tangled clothes upon the floor . . .*

She thought: spin, wash, soak.

There was the sound of a car, then a dog barking. Carina and the Sparkler came through the side gate, arguing.

'It's true. I know it's true.'

'Oh shut up,' Carina said good-naturedly.

Eloise rose on one elbow, pushed the shades to the top of her head and squinted into the glare.

'Hi. God. Dizzy,' she said, blinking. Something warm and wet touched her leg: the nose of the dog, Silvio.

'Ugh. Hello, Silvio.' She touched his fur or wool, whatever it was, and he turned and stuck his arse in her face and wagged his tail, and generally showed himself keen to be friends.

She got to her feet.

Carina's phone rang, she answered, pacing. Eloise looked at her sister with glazed tolerance. She shook her head gently, trying to get rid of the dazzling silver hole floating in front of her eyes, a visual distortion that probably had something to do with last night — with the postponement of stopping drinking.

Stabbing her phone with her index finger, Carina said, 'I've got six things to do at once, and Giles is in Georgia again, and Mum's getting her hair done.'

The Sparkler kneeled and held the dog's muzzle in her hands. She whispered in his ear and the dog cocked his head and turned up one side of his mouth, and actually smiled.

Eloise looked at her sister, who in turn stared fiercely down at her phone. Carina was tall, thin, dark-haired, with deep brown eyes and a sharp face. Carina seemed to Eloise always to be *on a slant*: leaning forward, hurrying, frowning, the furrow deepening between her eyebrows. She wrote features and a weekly column for the *Record*, which was the North Island's biggest paper. She complained (everyone complained) that the *Record* was turning into a tabloid, the real news squeezed into a diminishing space between crime and celebrity gossip.

'Right, I'd better go,' Carina said.

'Wait.' Eloise drew her away from the child and dog and said, 'Do you remember years ago I gave you a bag of stuff belonging to Arthur, that I'd taken from his flat?'

'Yes, sure.'

'Have you still got it?'

'It's in our basement. I hid it, like you told me to.'

'I wasn't supposed to take anything of his. I'll come and get it soon, okay?'

'Sure. Why?'

'I'd like to have a look. I can't even remember what's in it.'

And then Eloise and the Sparkler stood at the side of the road, waving Carina off. The car droned up the peninsula and Eloise followed her niece down the path past the stucco house.

The Sparkler was a small, wiry, brown-haired girl, dressed in jeans and a T-shirt, a bag printed with *Soon and Starfish* cartoons slung over her shoulder.

'You've got earrings,' Eloise said.

The girl nodded. 'Mum got a tattoo and I got my ears pierced.'

'Is the tattoo nice?'

'It's like, a bird. Is this the house?'

'Yes, they burst in, in the middle of the night, see where there's a big dent in the door, they had a battering ram and sneaked up and smashed the door open. Then they sent in dogs. You should have heard it. It was chaos.'

The Sparkler climbed the steps to the concrete porch. She had a broad forehead, intelligent, deep-set brown eyes, gold studs in her ears. Her face was bony, with strong cheekbones and a Roman nose. When she smiled, sharp dimples appeared in her cheeks. Her real name was Rachel Margery.

'You heard of tear gas?' Eloise said.

'No.'

'The police shoot it at people, it makes their eyes sting so the police can arrest them. My neighbour, Nick, told me you can fire tear gas into a house and then send in police dogs because dogs aren't affected by the gas. The humans are blinded and gagging but the dogs don't feel it at all.'

The Sparkler, on tip-toe, peered through the rippled glass panes beside the door. 'Where are the people?'

'In jail, I suppose.'

'I'm hungry.'

'Didn't you have any lunch?'

'No.'

'You like curry?'

'No!'

They untied Silvio and walked to the shops. Eloise talked about the man who owned the dog that looked like a wolf.

The Sparkler said, 'By the way, Silvio's full name is Silvio Le Bron Hay.' Silvio heard his name and turned his head.

He fixed his strange, knowing, golden eyes on them.

They bought bread, cheese and ham, then went to the pet goods and hardware aisle where the Sparkler selected a bag of rusks shaped like bones, and Eloise lingered before putting a bottle of methylated spirits into the basket.

Silvio was waiting patiently out the front, chained to a pole. They fed him a treat and headed for the dog park. Eloise undid his chain and he shot over to another dog, his tail quivering.

The Sparkler said, 'See how he bends his front legs and sticks his bum in the air. That's a play bow. It means let's have a chase. Watch this.' She took the treats out of a zipper pocket of her bag, called the dog, made him sit, and rewarded him with a treat.

They sat on a bench. It was hot and bright, a shine coming off the flax. Eloise broke off bits of cheddar and folded them with the ham to make lumpy sandwiches.

'So, what about school.'

'I'm the best at maths. And reading.'

'Good teacher?'

'The usual.'

'Nice bag. You like the *Soon and Starfish* books?'

'I like them on TV, too. Mum got it at LA airport. She brought me a *Soon and Starfish* T-shirt too.'

'Do you like Soon or Starfish?'

'Both. And the Green Lady and the Bachelor. Who do you like?'

'Maybe the Bachelor, and the Cassowaries. I like the way they're drawn. They look cool. Like Tintin.'

'Mum says, um, they're iwonic.'

'Oh. Okay.'

Silvio got hot and waded into the mangroves looking for water but the tide was out and he came scrambling up the bank, his belly smeared with black mud. He was now pie-coloured, tongue hanging out, panting and reeking, the Sparkler scolding him in her high, shrill voice. They clipped on his chain and pulled him back along the creek edge, over the bridge.

They put the garden hose on the dog. With his hair slicked down he looked much smaller, his legs and tail rakishly thin. Eloise laughed at his long nose, drooping silken ears and martyred expression.

'He looks like Jesus. Like Silvio of Nazareth.'

The dog sank down, put his chin on his paws, heaved a theatrical sigh and appeared to go straight to sleep.

'That's him taken care of,' said the Sparkler responsibly.

Eloise considered her niece. 'Actually, let's put him in the garage, out of the way. There's something you can help me with.'

It took them a long time to build a pile on the grass in front of the deck. When they'd balanced the last items, an old golf bag and a wicker picnic basket on the top, Eloise turned on the hose, and wet the ground around the pile.

She hunted in the house, came out on the deck. 'I can't find any matches.'

The Sparkler rummaged in her bag and brought out a Bic lighter.

'What's that for? You taken up smoking?'

The girl shrugged.

'Okay. Sean burnt some garden rubbish here once. You're not supposed to but it should be fine. Stand back. And hang on to the hose.'

Eloise crouched down and set fire to a cardboard roll of posters. The flame bloomed up and burned halfway along the roll before fizzling out. She tried again. The cardboard resisted the flame. The whole pile shifted to one side.

The Sparkler danced around, hugging herself. 'Let's use the stuff you bought. The meffs.'

Eloise looked doubtfully at the pile. The Sparkler scurried inside and came out with the plastic bottle.

'Gorn, do it.'

'Give me that.'

Eloise took the bottle, made the girl stand back, hesitated, then poured liquid down the sides of the pile.

'That's not enough.'

'All right.'

She splashed out more, lit a piece of paper and tossed it on. There was a whoomph, and the whole pile went up.

The Sparkler screamed.

'Fire, fire.'

Sparks flew up, there were pops and cracks and flames shot high, blown by the afternoon breeze. A suitcase lid peeled back like a mouth, curling, melting. The Sparkler capered and shouted, picking up handfuls of dry grass and throwing them on the pyre.

'Keep back,' Eloise said.

They watched. The fire roared, grew intense at its centre.

Eloise had hold of the hose with one hand and was reaching for the Sparkler to pull her back when the whole pile started to topple sideways.

'Look out,' they both shouted, and the burning tower fell, flaming in all directions, sending embers whirling into the air and depositing a thick wad of burning material into the stand of toe toe along the boundary. The toe toe, parched after months of drought, went up like a bomb. They felt the rush, the fire sucking in air as the white plumes crackled and curled up, exploding into sparks that blew into the long grass beyond the fence. Embers began drifting onto brown lawns, clinging to dry bushes, settling in the long grass in front of the stucco house.

The Sparkler stood on the edge of the deck, her face fixed in an expression of savage delight. Embers floated in the air above her head.

They jumped at Nick's voice. 'What are you *doing*? You'll set the whole peninsula on fire. Give me the hose.' And then, 'It's gone too far. Ring 111.'

Eloise gave him the hose, went inside and rang the fire brigade.

'Someone's garden fire's out of control,' she said politely.

She could see Nick on the lawn, shouting directions, training the hose on the stand of toe toe, a couple of other neighbours stamping out embers in the grass.

It was surprising how quickly the firemen showed up, their massive hose so powerful that much of what remained of the toe toe blew apart in a watery explosion of ash and earth and sticks. They had it under control fast, although they stayed for a while to make sure Eloise hadn't set any roofs on fire, and that the dry grass wasn't going to reignite.

Not much remained of the pile, apart from a burned patch of lawn and some unidentifiable rubble. The toe toe, once a large stand of beautiful feathery white plumes, was a charred mound, and most of the bushes along the fence were blackened. A long dark smear stretched out from the toe toe like a shadow, a black finger pointing towards the dog park.

Beyond the lawn Nick was listening to two people, who gestured towards Eloise and spoke animatedly.

The senior fire officer had pale blue eyes and cheeks ravaged by fine wrinkles. Eloise watched him coming towards her in his creaking silver coat. He began to talk about public nuisance, damage to council property. Her actions had endangered the entire peninsula. Open burning was an offence under the Resource Management Act. Was she not aware of the drought, of current fire restrictions?

Nick came across the grass, looping the garden hose around his hand and elbow.

The fireman said to Eloise, 'Your daughter could've been injured.'

'Yes I'm sorry, it was stupid. Actually, she's my niece, I'm just looking after her for a few hours.'

The fireman said something about completing paperwork. A fine.

She was seeing them off at the front door when Carina turned up.

'Oh my God, what's going on?'

'Everything's fine, we had a little fire.'

'Quite a big fire actually,' the fireman said.

Eloise faced her sister. 'I'll explain, the Sparkler's fine, she's on the lawn.'

Carina went inside.

The firemen left and Eloise went to find Carina, who was inspecting the lawn with her hands on her hips.

'Sean did it once. There was never any danger.'

'But there's a drought. Have you gone crazy?'

'I didn't think. I'm going to have to pay a fine. And the neighbours will hate me.'

Carina looked at her narrowly.

'Please don't be angry. Shall we have a drink? There's some wine in the fridge, I'll be back in a minute.'

Nick's back door was open. She knocked, called out and he came along the hall shirtless, drying his hands. She looked at his thin, muscular chest and thought: karate.

He said, pained, 'The toe toe was beautiful.'

'And all your bushes. Sorry.'

'They'll grow back.'

'I got the idea after we talked. I decided, okay, clean slate.'

He leaned on the door frame. 'So you thought torch everything.'

'I really am sorry about your toe toe. Would you like to come and have some takeaways? My sister and I are going to order pizza. If she's not too angry with me. She'll think I'm not a fit babysitter now.'

'Let me just get a shirt. Come in.'

She stood in the hall, looking into the bare rooms. He seemed to be camping in a virtually empty house.

'What were you burning?' he called out.

'Stuff from my marriage. Junk.'

'From the recent relationship or the one before that?' He came out, buttoning up a shirt.

She looked at him, surprised. 'The recent one.'

'Oh?'

'It was all just junk,' she said.

Eloise introduced Nick to Carina and the Sparkler, who fingered her gold earrings, bobbed her head shyly and said, 'Demelza's here.'

Demelza Hay appeared on the deck, an elegantly dressed old woman with dyed blonde hair, painted eyebrows and an angular face. She was trailed by a dachshund of significant girth and pomp: Gerald.

'Hello, all. Come on, Gerald. Carina! If you could just . . . ?'

Carina rose and went outside to park their mother's car, which she'd abandoned, in her usual way, in the middle of the street.

Demelza greeted her other daughter and granddaughter, shook Nick's hand and sat down at the table, fixing her sharp eyes on Eloise.

'Any news?'

'Sean? He's not coming back. I'm going to have to sell the house, leave the peninsula.'

Demelza looked at Nick. '*Men*,' she said. Her gaze rested on the blackened grass, the mounds of burnt vegetation. She sniffed. 'But, chuck, your bushes are all black. And what a pong. What's happened?'

'We had a bonfire,' the Sparkler said.

Carina and the Sparkler argued about the pizzas, Eloise got on the phone and ordered, and they sat on the deck drinking wine and eating crisps.

Demelza said to Nick, 'Eloise's husband has taken up with an actress. She's very attractive, I understand. My husband, Terrence, now, Eloise's father. He was a right terror with the women.' Her expression turned distant; she seemed to suppress a brave, bitter laugh. 'Any road, he wasn't going to give up his fancy women. I lived with it. I became a *realist*.'

Carina snorted. 'No you didn't. You were furious when he had affairs.'

The Sparkler, all studied innocence, was watching Demelza and secretly feeding the dogs crisps under the table.

Demelza said, haughty, 'I accepted it.'

'Right. Sure. As well as wanting to kill him. And fair enough, too.'

'No, *Carina*.' Demelza drummed her fingers on the table. 'I believe in telling the truth, see.'

There was a silence.

Eloise tipped up her wine glass and said in a faint voice, 'It doesn't make much difference whether I accept it or not, since Sean's gone.'

'Men are hopeless,' Demelza said, holding out her glass. 'Carina, if you could just . . .'

Carina didn't move. Nick poured more wine all round.

'Thank you, that's champion,' Demelza said. 'Do you wish me to pass the crisps, Nick, or have you had sufficient? Terrence and I came from Manchester, Nick, when we were in our twenties. We've been very happy, once we got used to the heat and the problems, the insects and the diarrhoea, which we all suffer from here, goodness knows.'

Carina said, 'God! She's been here fifty years and she still makes it sound like she's living in the tropics.'

A phone went off. 'My editor,' Carina said and wandered off over the lawn. Demelza and the Sparkler made stick figures and words on the table out of crisp crumbs. Demelza said, 'How are you getting on at school?'

'I like it.'

'Your mummy hated school. She was always in terrible trouble. The teachers were right nasty to her. Are yours horrible?'

'Mrs Reid is a Nazi.'

Demelza laughed, clapped her hands. 'A Nazi.'

'If my socks are the wrong colour, Mrs Reid says I'll have to be sent home.'

Demelza narrowed her eyes. 'Does she *say* that? See, she shouldn't say that to you, I reckon. That's petty. That's wrong-uh.'

The Sparkler struck a pose. 'I accept it.' Her expression was deadpan. 'I'm a realist.'

'Well, what a character you are,' Demelza said, sweeping away the crumbs and gathering them in her fist. 'Just like your mummy.'

She turned to Nick. 'Carina was a wild girl. Hated school. She was always falling foul of the law when she was a teenager. Getting arrested and the like.'

'By the police?' the Sparkler said, big-eyed.

'Ooh yes. You know, Nick, we'd get the call, come down to the police station. There she'd be, just out of the *cells*. What with that and the troubles at school, she could be terribly difficult, you know.'

Eloise said, 'Carina mightn't want people to hear that stuff.'

'What stuff?' Carina said, sliding into her seat.

'How you used to get in trouble at school,' the Sparkler said.

'And be arrested,' the little girl added.

Carina fixed her mother with a steady look.

The old woman laughed, her bright eyes on Eloise, 'Ooh, I can never keep my mouth shut. You know what Terry says about me, I can't tell a lie. Not one falsehood, me. I just can't.'

Carina leaned forward. 'Who's asking you to lie?'

Demelza's tone hardened. 'Well, I can't see what the harm is, *Carina*.'

Eloise watched her mother's fingers drumming on the table.

They were interrupted by the delivery man bringing boxes loaded with pizza; they lost focus, the conversation shifted, they talked about the GCSB scandal, about the local security services caught spying illegally on the internet millionaire Kurt Hartmann.

Carina mentioned the mayor, Edward Mack, who'd been caught having an affair with an employee.

'Edward Mack then,' Demelza said, looking at Nick. 'With that high-pressure job, I imagine the poor chap *had* to have an affair, just to help him get through the day.'

Carina glanced quickly at Eloise, then leaned back in her seat and closed her eyes, her whole body expressing irritation. Eloise stared out at the estuary, where the silver water was running fast with the incoming tide.

Silence. Nick coughed. 'Eloise tells me Roysmith's interviewed Andrew Newgate.'

'Andrew Newgate! He's right creepy, that one.'

Eloise said quietly, 'He was acquitted. He was found not guilty.'

Demelza snorted. 'The jury found him not guilty, but they were blinded by that smoke-and-mirror merchant, that Carstone. With his sports cars and his girlfriends and his lawsuits. Him, a campaigner for justice? Don't make me laugh. It's symbiotic, that's what it is. You scratch my back and I'll get you off a murder.'

'That is an incredibly simplistic interpretation,' Eloise said.

Nick's tone was polite, cautious. 'So, Eloise, you and Roysmith are totally convinced?'

'Roysmith's always thought Newgate was innocent. There were too many holes in the evidence.'

Demelza's laugh made Eloise furious. She stared at her hands. Demelza said, 'I've read Carstone's books. All three of them. They're badly written, unconvincing and without intellectual merit. Narcissistic, that's what they are. He's even put big glossy photos of himself in them. He's *fabricated* the holes in the evidence. They don't exist. Smoke and mirrors.'

'Really,' Eloise said.

'And your Roysmith, with his emoting and his silly hair, he helped get Newgate acquitted. All through the second trial, the reporting was right biased.'

'The jury isn't allowed to look at news reports.'

'Oh, I'm *sure* they don't,' Demelza said.

Carina said, 'I've read Carstone's books.'

'Well, you'll know what I'm talking about then,' Demelza said. 'Load of rubbish.'

Eloise banged down her glass. 'We've all read the books. Okay, Carstone's not a great writer, but that's not the point.'

Carina traced a line on the table with her index finger. 'So, Eloise, are you going to go into the case, or is it going to be magazine-style, "the wronged man speaks about his new life"?'

'The point about most television,' Demelza said loudly to Nick, 'is that it's just not intellectually good enough.'

Eloise turned to her. 'So Roysmith's thick.'

Demelza sipped her wine and said in a hoarse, amused voice, 'Not *completely* thick. But . . . a lightweight.'

Nick said, 'I heard Newgate's supposed to have killed his parents when he was eleven.'

'That's just a malicious rumour. It's just pure . . . tabloid.' Eloise turned her glare on Nick, who flinched. His phone rang in his pocket and he jumped up to answer it, walking away across the grass.

Carina said, 'Want another slice, Mum?'

'Has it got garlic on it? I won't have that foreign muck.'

Demelza was inspecting the Sparkler's bag. 'Fancy Roza Hallwright selling her *Soon and Starfish* books to Hollywood. She must have made a right fortune.'

'She was rich to start with.'

'Who?' the Sparkler said, reaching for the bag.

Carina told her, 'Roza Hallwright is the wife of Sir David Hallwright, who used to be our prime minister. She wrote the *Soon and Starfish* books. Which were then turned into the cartoon, the movies and TV series.'

She added, 'I got the bag in LA. '

'I'm not sure the books have much literary merit.' Demelza gestured at the house. 'I suppose *Soon* built this house. Since Sean works for Jaeger's and they act for the Hallwrights. Since they made the *Soon* movie, the whole country's gone mad. Terrence and I flew to Wellington recently; I couldn't believe it. There was a gigantic statue of the dwarf — Soon — hanging from the departure lounge ceiling, looked like a right death trap if you were sat under it in an earthquake. And signs saying *Welcome to Soonworld*. And out on the tarmac there's a 777 with Soon characters painted all over it. And when you get *on* the plane you have to sit through a *Soon and Starfish* safety video.'

'There's *Soon and Starfish* Lego now.'

'Merchandising. Soon tourism. The Soon Village at Rotorua.'

'The National Party will never be short of funding.'

Carina said, 'Although the party's divided, since Hallwright's faction's backing Ed Miles. Miles is breathing down Dance's neck.'

'Who's Ed Miles?' The Sparkler, leaning on Carina's chair, was interrupting for the sake of it — her way of signalling she was getting tired.

'Ed Miles is our Minister of Justice.'

'Who has hopes of overthrowing our current prime minister, Mr Dance, according to the gossip. With the help of David Hallwright.'

'With the help of Sooncorp.'

'Roysmith says Miles is leaking against Satan Dance, that it could have been Miles who leaked that Dance knew Kurt Hartmann was being spied on illegally.'

'Miles is *so* after Dance's job.'

'Dance managed to deny he knew anything.'

'But the leaker went to the Opposition, and they've said there's going to be proof.'

'Of what?'

'That Dance knew Hartmann was being spied on illegally. Proof Dance acted illegally.'

'The internecine stuff is really heating up.'

'Funny that the Hallwrights are "Hollywood money" now.'

'Was Hartmann's website ripping off the *Soon and Starfish* movies?'

'No doubt!'

'Do you think Satan Dance's the father?'

'Of Baby O'Keefe? Not him, surely.'

'The way he used to look at O'Keefe, like he was licking his chops.'

'He looks at everyone like that.'

'Most men look at her like that.'

'Except not any more. Not the front bench.'

'They look away, guiltily.'

'Nervously.'

'Heard any clues, Carina? Any rumours at the paper?'

'No one's found out anything as far as I know.'

'I thought maybe David Hallwright.'

Nick came across the grass, putting away his phone. 'David Hallwright what?'

'We're wondering who's the father.'

'Oh, Baby O'Keefe? What about Ed Miles.'

'He's only interested in power.'

'O'Keefe wouldn't go for him. He's too chilling.'

'When it's born we'll know. There'll be a resemblance.'

'Babies usually look like their fathers.'

'A tiny Satan.'

'A tiny Ed.'

'Oh these *men*,' Demelza said, picking up Gerald.

Nick clapped his hands. 'Anyway. Do these dogs know how to play fetch?'

'Course.' The Sparkler's piping voice, all competence and scorn.

'Got a ball?'

The Sparkler produced a tennis ball from her bag and they coaxed Silvio and Gerald down to the grass strip by the path. Eloise watched, imagining Nick in a white karate outfit. He had a strong throwing arm, was well co-ordinated. The sausage dog couldn't keep up, and resorted to jumping on the spot and barking insanely. She noticed Nick glancing across at her.

Later, Demelza rose to her feet and lightly kicked Silvio, who was trying to get at a pizza crust under the table. 'Look at your silly dog, Carina. What a ridiculous name you've given him. Funny, he looks gay to me.'

She leaned down to Silvio. 'Are you gay? Are you *gay*, little pussy cat?'

There was a silence.

'Well, I must love you and leave you. Carina, here's the keys. If you could just . . .'

She shook the jingling bunch at Carina, who stared at her for a further beat of seconds before rising from her seat, taking the keys and leaving the table.

When Carina had manoeuvred the car out of its park and positioned it on the road outside Eloise's house, ready to be driven, Demelza kissed the Sparkler and Nick, neatly side-stepped Eloise, turned her back on Carina, and worked her way into the driver's seat. Gerald bobbed in the back seat, his long nose sliming the window. They waited respectfully while Demelza put on a different pair of glasses and pressed the button to lower the back window, allowing Gerald to poke his nose and one long ear out.

She revved the motor and engaged the gears. The engine whined and a scorched rubber smell rose. They heard a last hoarse bark from Gerald, a toot, and she was gone.

Eloise, Nick and Carina cleaned up while the Sparkler and Silvio slept sprawled together on the sofa.

Nick put his hand on Eloise's arm. 'Want a brandy at my place?'

'I've got to stop drinking so much.'

'Do you good.'

'I've got to get up early, so . . .'

She imagined going to his house, drinking brandy, waking in his bed. Did she want that?

But he was already saying, 'Good night, ladies . . .'

After he'd left, Carina stood on the deck smoking a cigarette. She blew out a long stream of smoke. 'Strange guy.'

'What do you mean?'

'I don't know. Intense. Hard to place. He likes you, he stares at you. Did you see him playing with the dogs, checking to see if you were watching? He fancies himself — bit of an athlete. He's got a good torso. Works out.'

'Anything else?'

'Did you say he lives alone? Is he a "loner"? Gay? What's he doing at your place?'

'He's my neighbour. He's separated. Single. He hasn't been back in the country long.'

'What does he do?'

'He owns the house over there, and he's inherited some other property. He worked for an NGO in Africa. He does karate. There was something about trying to decide what to do next, doing up houses in the meantime.'

'Well, he's interested in you.' Carina looked up at the windows of the stucco house. 'Do you mind being here by yourself?'

'It's intense. I like it.'

'Is there anyone living in that house?'

'No, that's the one that was raided.'

Carina ground her cigarette butt on the deck rail. 'I thought so. But I saw someone upstairs.'

Eloise looked uneasily at the blank windows. It was a still night with a clear sky. Out by the dog park the trees were humped black shapes; beyond them the city lights sent up a white glow. The air smelled of smoke. Below the gardens the slow tide was creeping through the mangroves, over mud and roots and crab holes. She heard the harsh, chilling cry of a possum in the flax.

'I had a dream about Andrew Newgate. The killer, as Mum would call him.'

She heard restraint in Carina's reply. 'It must have been interesting, meeting Newgate.'

'He was very pleasant.'

'Oh, well, good.'

'So what are you saying, you agree with Mum he's guilty?'

'Well, I hardly ever agree with Mum, but . . .'

'He seemed ordinary. Boring even.' Eloise frowned.

Carina flicked her dead cigarette off the deck. 'Well, trust your instincts. You've always been observant.'

Eloise looked at her in silence.

Carina put on her coat. 'It's late. I'd better get home.'

Eloise looked over at the stucco house. The night air seemed close, something electric in it. Sudden memory: a wooden staircase, warm rain outside, a view through a window of the garden, green underwater light. The door of the flat standing open, a footprint on the doormat, something spilled and trampled back over the threshold . . .

She helped carry the little girl to the car. The dog climbed into the front passenger seat, where he sat staring solemnly ahead.

Carina said, 'You want me to lend you Silvio? He's an excellent guard dog.'

'No thanks. He's sweet but he stinks.'

Eloise went from room to room, locking doors and windows, which made her uneasy. She drew down the sitting room blinds, but once she'd shut out the view she felt as if she were trapped in a large, silent white box. She listened to her own breathing, the loud clink of her glass on the coffee table. How could she keep watch if the blinds were lowered? She pulled them up and faced the black windows.

Out there, beyond the glass, the night had a glossy sheen.

At the computer, finishing off the wine and roaming through cyberspace, she searched aimlessly, not knowing what it was she wanted.

What is the question? What is the thing I look for and can't find?

She tipped back her glass, but the wine wasn't doing its job. She peered at the bottle. What was this toy drink? Some lite or diet brand brought over by Carina? Sober, alert to every sound, she drank, and felt no warmth.

Only something tipping her sideways, out into the night.

———

The possum sent out its eerie cry as it crashed around in the undergrowth, making the flax spears clatter. Smoky air mixed with the stench off the estuarine flats, and the stream banks were alive with clicks and splashes, the plop of a rat hitting the water, the running of the tide in the channel.

She hesitated at the edge of the dark. The keys were in her pocket. She'd pulled the back door closed, but not deadlocked it, and in her hurry she'd come out with no jacket, her shirt half-unbuttoned. She crossed the path, entered Nick's garden and saw him standing in his lighted front room.

Eloise buttoned her shirt by feel in the dark. Combed her hair with her fingers. It was like being in the wings, about to step onto a lit stage to deliver lines that seemed unreal, unconvincing, and painfully important. Changed my mind. Brandy after all. Why not.

Nick was leaning on the glass ranch slider, his arms folded. He changed position, looked up at the ceiling, lifted his elbow and rolled his arm around in its socket. He gestured with his hand, looking into the room. It looked, oddly, as if he were speaking to someone.

Eloise stepped back into the shadows. Beyond the flax the moon had risen, and the estuary glittered. A cricket cheeped in the long grass.

Was she, after all, despite the fake wine, very drunk indeed? When she closed her eyes, the light off the water superimposed itself on her lids. Tiny sparks exploded and scattered outwards and she registered the suggestion or rumour of one of her migraine attacks.

The night and the dark were entering her mind. When she blinked, emerald sparks flew out of her eyes and up into the black sky, mingling with the stars. The warning of migraine made her feel as if she were some tiny creature, hunched down under a vast, threatening sky. She wanted to be touched, held.

But there was a man in the room with Nick.

He was wearing black. He was tall, with a hawkish face and thick black hair. She saw his long wrists and bony fingers, the jacket sleeve riding up as he leaned against the glass. The back of his hand. She stared, light flowed around him as if his fingers were on fire. He was talking. Nick listened to the man, shook his head and made a quelling gesture, palm down. His manner was different, he was at ease; he looked handsome, alien and tough.

The visitor was so unexpected, she couldn't think what to do next. Her eyes throbbed, a stab of pain. She saw a waterfall of light at the edge of her vision and a trickle of nausea made her mouth dry. In the grass the cricket relentlessly sang. She blundered back across the lawn and up the path. She would go to bed, sleep it off.

But her back door was standing open.

Ahead of her was the boxed air of the hallway, with its bright, forensic stillness; behind her the peninsula was alive. The wind rustled the flax spears, clouds crossed the moon, striping the grass and casting patches of blackness that could be shadows or the holes opening in her vision. Moonlight on the mangroves, on the tidal basin, a big patch of sky near the moon that was clear and full of stars. She faced the hallway again and the stars had lodged in her eyes, their silver glare obscuring something dark that moved beyond the brightness.

Had someone crossed the doorway at the end of the hall?

Her phone was lying on the small table inside. She listened, then ran into the hall, grabbing for the phone and sending it flying off the table. She scrabbled for it on the floor and seemed only to be chasing it with the clumsy tips of her fingers. There was a sound somewhere in the house, and she went still, crouched on the floor. Her fingers closed around the phone. She straightened up and walked to the door, pulling it closed it behind her. Then she was away up the path, not looking behind.

From the pub at the top of the peninsula, she rang her sister.

———

She lay in Carina's spare room in a bed that smelled of dog, with a flannel over her eyes. Scattered on the table beside her was a collection of pills mined from Carina's bathroom cupboard. At intervals she would moan, and reach blindly up, and shakily crack the seal on another foil tray. Pain made tiny, evil seams of light that pulsed in her brain. Pain was a network of lines in the darkness, as fine and bright as a spider's web.

SEVEN

Dr Klaudia Dvorak's office was the back room of an elegant old Herne Bay shop, its French doors open to the garden. A grey-haired woman gardener tended the flowerbeds on the lawn outside.

Eloise listened.

'I have always had a special interest in violence,' Klaudia was saying.

The Nazis, Eloise thought.

'This started because of the war, the role of previous generations of my family in . . .'

Genocide, thought Eloise dreamily, watching the old woman cross the lawn, knocking earth out of a plant pot with a trowel. The tapping of the trowel against the clay pot, the drone of a car in the distance.

'I was thinking more of my mother,' Eloise said.

Klaudia smiled. 'Ah. Your mother, yes. She worked in your father's business, you said, now retired?'

Eloise leaned forward. 'That's right. My father is an architect. My mother was his assistant. She didn't go to university actually, but she reads a lot. By war, I meant domestic warfare. All the aggression under the surface. Isn't life hard enough without it? It's all so . . .'

'So . . . ?'

'It's all so *unnecessary*.'

'We humans are not famous for being rational,' Klaudia said.

'The things she comes out with, bearing in mind my husband's just had an affair and left me: "The poor mayor, his life's so stressful he needed to have an affair just to get through the day." It implies men are justified in having affairs, which implies Sean's affair was justified. Maybe I wasn't giving Sean enough. It fits with her new line that she accepted our father's affairs, because she was a "realist", when the truth is she was furious about his affairs. She attacks and plays the submissive wife in one breath.'

'Very subtle.'

'What we're all supposed to know about her is that she's not subtle, she's an open book. An honest Mancunian. She's unable to tell a lie. She's so simple and innocent, she just comes out with things, inadvertently. It's always, Ooh, what did I do? Did I say something wrong? I'm an open book, me.'

'Hmm. It's called plausible deniability.'

'She's so "honest" she "can't stop herself" telling my niece about my sister's wild youth, even though my sister's asked her not to. My sister's paranoid her daughter will get into trouble, because she knows how damaging it was to her. And our mother, she wants to *regale* the kid with that stuff. She used to encourage Carina to rebel at school, too. It was always, Did the teachers really say that to you? That's bad. They're right fascists. And then she'd tell everyone how badly behaved Carina was. Carina still gets our mother's old friends coming up to her, saying, Is your daughter as difficult a girl as you were?'

Eloise pressed on, feeling how absurd it was to be talking like this about her mother — *at her age*.

'The Sean situation. My mother seemed sympathetic at first, but she started to introduce a line about how I had to accept that men have affairs. She told me about men she knew who'd gone off with younger women and never come back. She talked about ageing, wear and tear, how time ruins us. She said my husband's new girlfriend must "give off a strong charge", whatever that means. I started to think it was a trip for her, that I was in the down position.'

Klaudia nodded, making notes.

'I'm here because it's all got too much. I told you about Arthur. He died. Then I married Sean, then he left, and just after that happened I had to confront the fact that my mother wasn't supportive. The marriage was my safe haven and when it was gone I had no base, no defence.'

Eloise paused. Klaudia would now say, *Come now, this is paranoia, hysteria. Your mother cares for you deeply.*

'Sometimes I think she really dislikes me.'

She waited to be corrected.

'Sure,' Klaudia said briskly. 'From what I'm hearing, we're talking at least ambivalence.'

Eloise blinked. 'Ambivalence?'

'It's family dynamics. Jealousy. Competitiveness. Perhaps she is narcissistic. Were you your father's favourite child? Or perhaps your sister was?'

'*Ambivalence?*'

'Let's call a spade a spade.'

'So, I should go away feeling even worse than I felt when I came in? I thought this was supposed to make me feel better. Now you want to tell me I'm not imagining it, she really *does* dislike me?'

'Possibly. But at the end of the day, it's her shit not yours.' Klaudia's tone softened. 'Somewhere deep down, she probably knows she messed up. So. I want you to learn to have empathy for the child you once were.'

'Christ.'

'I am German, so I am blunt. Excuse me. You tell me about walking all day. I think you have been walking away for a very long time.'

'I met a man who told me I should confront things. We were a bit drunk at the time, or I was. I'm drinking rather a lot, by the way.'

Klaudia laid down her pen. 'Okay, sure. We'll come to that. But perhaps the walking is a metaphor for escape. You have reinvented yourself in order to escape bad things that have happened in the past. There was the mother who was clearly ambivalent. The partner who so sadly died. You reinvented yourself to escape these blows, and now, with this fresh situation, you feel the old terrors are jumping out at you all at once.'

'Well, it's been bleak . . .'

'You need to look back and find some empathy for that unloved child . . .'

Eloise pinched the bridge of her nose with two fingers. 'I'm starting to feel like I need a drink.'

'Ah yes. Drink. How many units a day, please, and what time do you start? In the morning?'

'Never until the sun's over the yardarm.'

Out there in the bright garden the old woman was using a hose, the water spooling out in beads of silver. A sudden gust flipped the leaves of the flax, making the spears shine. Eloise was surrounded by light and silence.

'It's a beautiful garden.'

'Yes.'

'Perhaps my mother doesn't mean any harm. Perhaps she's just a simple, honest person who blunders, tactlessly says the wrong thing.'

'You say she's interested in literature. She understands fiction — character, motivation, subtleties. If she understands these things, how can she be so simple?'

'Maybe she's like one of those mathemeticians who's a genius at maths but simple and childlike in life.'

'People can be childlike, sure. Childhood usually involves narcissism, lack of empathy and a sense of entitlement. And then the child grows out of it.'

Another silence.

'Or not,' Klaudia added.

Eloise shifted unhappily. 'You said reinventing. When I married Sean I felt I'd become a different person and left the bad old self behind.'

'It was not a bad old self, it was the same self. You don't have to repress things, hide things. You can be more accepting of yourself. You can ask questions. Why did things happen the way they did? Sure, look back. Ask yourself, what do I know of those bad times? Be open. Are there things you don't understand? Find out.'

Eloise started to speak, thought better of it.

'Go on?'

She hesitated. But she could say anything in here, it was confidential. Why not? 'Well, okay, I burned a whole lot of stuff on the weekend. It turned into a bit of a disaster. Long story. I may be prosecuted. Anyway, I was clearing out, and it made me think about the past. I remembered there are things belonging to Arthur that I took from his flat and never looked at. Stuff nobody knew I had.'

Klaudia tilted her head.

'What kind of things, please?'

'Notes, papers, photos. I don't know whether I'd have burned them if . . .'

'You didn't burn them?' Klaudia said softly.

'No.'

'You shouldn't burn them. That would be a bad thing.'

'Okay.'

'What did you do with them?'

'I . . . Well, I haven't burned them.'

Klaudia smoothed her writing pad, gently smiled.

'Now. You say things have got a bit too much. You're drinking too much, you're doing the continuous walking. Are you sleeping?'

'Yes. Although I wake up often.'

'You wake early, can't sleep again? I would like to recommend some medication.'

'I don't like the idea of sleeping pills.'

'There's no need for concern. I'll get you a prescription from our psychiatrist. This will be good for you. Give me one moment.'

She got up and went out, holding up her hand to forestall any argument.

Eloise listened. Footsteps on the street outside, low voices. There was a wisteria vine growing up the veranda pillar outside. She walked to the open door and picked a leaf from the vine, rolling it in her fingers. The gardener backed across the lawn pulling the hose. She tugged it over to the garden shed, disappeared into the dark doorway.

The footsteps came back along the hall. Klaudia said, 'Here's your prescription, something to help you sleep. Start tonight, you will feel much refreshed. After four days, you can build up to two pills. It's fine to drink one glass of alcohol with them, no more. I think you need to come and see me regularly. There's a lot we need to get to the bottom of.'

They went out together, along the hall with its antique mirror, past the closed doors, the other offices.

Eloise paused at the door. 'Do you get tired of listening to people? Do you start to hate some of them?'

'Tired? Never! I love to go on a journey with my patients. To explore lives, motivations, it is the source of great interest. You know, my tutor in Germany once said to me, Don't think of studying psychology until you've read the Russian novels!'

'Well. Thanks. See you next time.'

Klaudia said, 'I meant to say, those items you remembered you had, belonging to Arthur. They're part of your past. Keep them. But there's no hurry. Don't look at them until you're ready. Be kind to yourself. Take your time.'

The heat struck up off the asphalt and the car had turned into an oven. Eloise gripped the steering wheel — it was hot. She looked back at the old shop, its rooms full of secrets. These 'items belonging to Arthur' — actually, what were they? That day at Arthur's flat, she'd arrived with the woman detective who followed her closely, making sure she took only clothes and some kitchen items that belonged to her. She remembered the air was still, musty, dead, Arthur's presence sucked out of it, as if the place where they had lived happily had been inundated, and she had dived down and was peering from room to room in the blurry, silent space. She viewed light switches silvered with fingerprint powder, Arthur's desk with a yellow arrow taped to items on it, a pair of surgical gloves on the kitchen bench, a man standing on the back deck talking on a cell phone; he was the woman detective's taciturn partner, whose eyes followed Eloise as she passed the open door. In the silence she opened a drawer, took out clothes and put them in her gym bag. Why this anger?

When someone dies an unexplained death, the world enters every private space. Everything sacred is trampled on, everything you loved is covered in footprints, and the explanation you make of a life, all its subtle and delicate detail, is turned crass, ugly and inadequate. Sudden resentment at the presence of the woman detective turned, when the woman's phone beeped and she stepped onto the back deck with her partner, into a determination to find something of Arthur's and keep it for herself. Her eyes fell on the cardboard file in a shelf under the desk, where Arthur kept his current projects. She put it in her bag just before the detectives came back into the room.

Arthur could be secretive. He guarded his writing; no one was allowed to read a piece of work until it was finished. He was a perfectionist. After he died, the police had questions. They asked, Did Arthur have enemies? Had he annoyed anyone? Once the woman detective asked Eloise, Had she ever wondered about any of Arthur's male contacts? Was he bisexual or gay? Like many of the questions the detective asked, it gave Eloise the impression she had something specific in mind.

She asked them, Are you thinking of someone in particular? They hadn't told her anything. Arthur was one hundred per cent heterosexual. So what had they meant?

The male detective had offered to carry the bag down the steps to the car. She zipped it up and handed it over with a show of carelessness, feeling trapped and furtive and cunning. She remembered passing the back door, Da Silva on her cell phone, twirling one golden strand of her wiry hair between her fingers, one corner of her mouth turned up in a sarky grin, and Eloise heard her pronounce a word, as though repeating the punchline of a joke: 'Gynaecologist!'

Their eyes met and the detective lowered her voice and turned away. It was one of many fragmented memories, of random words, and questions and phrases overheard, odd details that she had stored in her mind but neither processed nor pursued. Arthur, with his usual daring and originality and boldness, had gone too far this time; he'd been caught in a forbidden and terrible place, and this pair of cops, with their tough faces and sharp eyes, knew that Eloise had crossed over, too; she was implicated, always would be, in Arthur's transgression. It was a strange discovery: that calamity brought with it this burden of fear and shame.

Shame had made her fail Arthur. She should have paid attention to details, tried to find out what had happened. Shame had made her defiant. She took Arthur's file back to her flat and hid it in the ceiling, frightened that the police would come looking for it. Later she'd given it to Carina. She imagined herself denying to those two dour, good-looking cops, Da Silva and — what was his name? O'Kelly? — that she had any idea how it had come into her possession. In all the years since, she had never looked at what the file contained.

EIGHT

'How was your weekend? You and Sean get up to much?'

Eloise looked, she hoped, blandly non-committal. 'Oh, you know. Nothing special.'

Scott was wearing a bright blue three-piece suit, with turquoise lining. His hair, thick and glistening with gel, sat on top of his head like a brown turban. The bridge of his teeth was too narrow for his mouth; now he smiled, showing pale pink gums.

'You like this suit? I hope I don't look like a banker. God, I love suits. Ronald at RJB has this new range, just absolute masterpieces.'

'What a nice waistcoat.'

Eloise had just received two messages on her cell phone: one from Carina wanting to know if she would be staying again, and the other from a real estate agent. Sean had passed on her number. The agent wanted to discuss the sale of the house. Prospects were excellent. Values on the Starlight Peninsula had rocketed; the area was hot right now. Would look forward to her call.

She deleted the message.

Scott stroked his blue sleeve. 'Ronald talked me into the suit. Thee freaked out at the price. Then she calmed down and said, Oh well, as Shakespeare said, "The apparel oft proclaims the man." Isn't that great?'

She looked at him: his wonder-of-the-world grin, his big hair, the *blink* he did, the blink that set off the smile that showed how much he relished life, how genuine he was, how enthusiastic and passionate. Sometimes she had a sense of a small busy person inside him, pulling the levers for smile, blink, beam, bray.

'Reports are coming in that Jack Anthony got a shock off the urinal. Apocryphal at this stage.'

'Ouch,' Eloise said.

'Also Selena says over at Q the coat hangers in hair and make-up are making clicking and sizzling noises, and there's an electric smell. Why haven't we all gone out on strike?'

'I know. Someone's going to get killed.'

'I wonder if it's like, carcinogenic,' Ian the cameraman said.

'What if you're pregnant? Karen's pregnant. So is Hine at reception. You don't want to be getting shocks when you're . . .'

They waited for the car outside reception. Under a cloudless sky the light was impressively clear, the shadow of a plane tree making a perfect shape on the asphalt, the reflections of leaves sliding over the car windscreen as it drove up. They loaded their gear and got in, Scott on the phone to Kurt Hartmann's man, Chad Loafer, who was getting a lot of talking done.

'Chad,' Scott said, rolling his eyes at Eloise, 'mate, I understand.'

An hour later they entered the gates of the Hartmann estate and approached the mansion, with its grey-pink castle battlements and dinky turrets, its flagpole and helicopter pad, and garaging for thirty cars.

A security guard bustled out of the topiary and waved them towards the front door, where they were met by a small black-clad man with a shaven head.

'Chad Loafer, head of Mr Hartmann's security,' he told them.

A great door creaked open, all oaken and Narnian and faux-gnarled, and Loafer led them into a large reception lit by lamps in the shape of flaming torches. He withdrew, silently. The room was filled with large squashy white sofas flanked by pedestals on which sat dishes of colourful sweets. Eloise imagined Hartmann arriving in a witch's hat, on a sleigh, driven by a dwarf.

'Jesus,' Scott whispered, looking around the room. One whole wall was a mirror. They eyed themselves, wary.

'I wonder if he's watching us.'

'Yeah, cameras. No wait, the mirror's two-way. He's behind it. In, like, a control room with a big chair.'

They could see into another room beyond the reception, in which armchairs faced large computer screens. The internet mogul and his business partners were enthusiastic gamers; in fact Hartmann had first discovered he was being spied on by the security services when his computer games started running slow by one seventh of a second. He picked this up straight away, had the problem investigated, and found his entire system was being routed through an external system run by the spy agency, the GCSB.

Next to the chairs and screens were more stands holding dishes filled with sweets. It was a child's fantasy: the sweets, the screens, the fake swords crossed above the doors, the suits of armour standing at attention by the dungeon-style doors. One entire wall of the gaming room was covered by a photo of Hartmann's face.

A door opened and Hartmann entered, followed by his head of

security. Loafer was dwarfed by his charge, who was obese and six foot six.

'Good morning,' Hartmann said, lightly wringing his hands. He had a massive face, a shaven head, a smile full of wicked little teeth and an air of amused, cartoonish criminality. Loafer did a rapid check of the room, touched his ear and spoke into his sleeve. Scott blinked and beamed. Eloise's mouth involuntarily twitched. It was impossible not to feel a certain hilarious amazement, here in the fairytale castle, standing before the elven king of criminal kitsch. Loafer smiled; for a moment they were all grinning.

Through the window there was a view of a glowing green lawn, and topiary in the shape of battlements.

'Roger that,' Loafer growled into his sleeve.

'Welcome,' Hartmann said. There were introductions all round. After shaking hands, Hartmann drew a bottle of hand santiser from his pocket and briskly lathered.

He said, 'First we are going to do something I love. Chad, would you please?

They followed him out to a courtyard where two cars were parked, their gleam and burnish enhanced by the extraordinary clarity of the day. A man wearing a fluoro vest was polishing a pink Cadillac sporting the number plate COCK. Parked beside it was a black Humvee, whose number plate read: KILL.

'My babies,' Hartmann said. 'In fact these are the only two not yet taken by the court. I had a fleet of sixteen classic cars, as you probably know, all taken after the police raided my house. It was here,' he pointed at a gap between the manicured hedges, 'that the squad came through. They landed their choppers out on the green, and burst through. All armed to the teeth. They took my staff at gunpoint. Nearly shot brave Chad on the lawn. I had made my way to the panic room; they smashed their way in. They put boots on my neck.' He gestured for them to follow and went on formally, 'All this at the behest of the United States

Government, who had spied on me, who requested the New Zealand Government to spy on me illegally. All because I run a file-sharing website that Hollywood says rips the studios off.'

'Absolutely,' Scott said.

'The People decided what material they stored on my site. I played no part in their choices. I was merely the host. The People are going to retake the internet. Do you know that?'

'For sure,' Scott said. 'Where would it suit you to sit down so we can set things up and discuss all this properly . . .'

'First we do the nice thing.'

'Oh yes?'

Hartmann clapped his hands. 'Chad, if you please.'

Loafer now whirred up behind them on a golf cart. He dismounted respectfully, and indicated that Eloise and Scott should get on.

'All aboard,' Hartmann said, hefting himself behind the wheel. 'We are going to feed the chickens.'

They trundled slowly across the estate, driven by Hartmann.

Scott leaned close to Eloise and whispered, 'Feed the chickens. Think it's some sort of code?'

They got off beside a wooden shed with a silver iron roof, and Hartmann produced a paper bag, into which he plunged his hand. He took Scott's hand, gently turning it. Holding his own great fist above Scott's upturned palm, he allowed a stream of small pellets to trickle into it.

Hartmann opened a wooden gate, and they followed him into the yard, wading through straw. Scents of wood chip and pine mingled with the big man's smell: spearmint, peppermint, cherry.

'Chook chook,' he said softly, and folded Eloise's hand in his own. She felt the heat of his huge soft palm, looked into his small eyes and saw, or thought she saw, behind the ageing effect of the bulk and the camp and the Bond-villain persona, someone intelligent, gauche, amoral, young.

'This,' Hartmann said, 'is my Zen.'

On the toy grass, in the implausible brightness, they fed the crowding chickens. Nearby towered Hartmann's giant statue of a grazing giraffe, its black shadow crossing the gentle hills. Eloise found herself looking at the internet mogul's trousers, which were black cotton and necessarily stretchy, due to his height and bulk. They were poignant, unfashionable, slightly too short, revealing black socks and soft orthopaedic shoes; they pointed to the sartorial trials of the oversized. Movie villain, hacker, fugitive from US justice and struggling fat guy: condemned to wear uncool pants.

Eloise had done the research: since the raid on his property, Hartmann had been out on bail, fighting extradition by the US Government. His file-sharing website, on which his customers had stored copyrighted material, had allegedly deprived artists and studios of five hundred million dollars' worth of intellectual property.

Depending on who you asked, Hartmann was hero, maverick, hacker, pirate, internet freedom-fighter, crook. He was undeniably a philistine. He played computer games all night and slept half the day. Books, according to Hartmann, were today's equivalent of cave drawings. Books were *over*. His interests included gaming, girls, cars, lollies, bling, bad art, his Narnian castle, Twitter and, more lately, bringing down the government of Jack Dance, which had collaborated with the Americans first to spy on him illegally, then to arrest him.

It had been leaked, although denied and not proven, that Jack Dance, as minister in charge of security services, had known personally about the illegal spying, and this had caused Dance political difficulties. The Dance Government was keen to grant Hartmann's extradition and speed him out of the country with a swift boot to the arse. As far as Dance was concerned, Hartmann had caused him so much grief he could rot in an American supermax jail for the next fifty years.

'Chook chook,' Hartmann called, throwing the last of the feed in the air. Out near the stone battlements, Loafer patrolled in his own golf cart. Hartmann looked over at him fondly.

'Chad was Special Forces. He can kill with his bare hands.'

Scott brushed his suit sleeve. 'Do you feel threatened?'

'The US wants to extradite me, but it's a hassle. It takes time. Wouldn't it be easier for them to kill me?'

'But, here? Surely not?'

'One day I might be found dead. They will say, Heart attack. They will announce, Stroke. Who would know? A big guy like me. I got it coming,' he said ambiguously. 'Climb on board. I will show you around my house.'

He led them on a tour: the ballroom with giant black chandelier, a dining room decorated with suits of armour and mounted deers' heads, more luxurious gaming parlours, a succession of brothelly bedrooms decorated with gilt and fur. In one grand, pink-lit bathroom, bathers could swim towards a giant photograph of Hartmann's face.

After inspecting a huge kitchen, in which women in Orwellian smocks were working in silence, they arrived in a room that looked like the bridge of the Starship Enterprise. There was a half-circle of screens, as if Hartmann was in the habit of making conference calls to high places: White House, Kremlin, International Space Station. Eloise wandered about the room, hands behind her back. She kept glancing at Hartmann, studying his face, his bland, inscrutable smile. The house was unbelievable. To what extent was Hartmann's life, for him, a vast, camp joke?

Hartmann gestured to a large black-and-gold throne.

'What a perfect spot, my friends. Let's do the interview here!'

They came away with a decent amount of material to edit and a bag of promotional odds and ends: a miniature giraffe sculpture, a pink toy Cadillac and DVDs of Hartmann performing hip hop and rap songs with a troupe of girls in hot pants.

In the mansion's forecourt Hartmann rested his big hand on the car door.

'Don't forget, my friends, now you've interviewed me, the security services will be watching you. Every communication will be monitored. Just because they got caught spying on me illegally doesn't mean they stopped. They changed the rules to suit themselves, and they went right on spying. And you should look into leaks. Who leaked that Jack Dance knew I was being spied on illegally? Dance denies he knew, and he's got away with it — but he will want to know who dropped him in it. Was it his opponents, or one of his own team?'

He turned away from Scott and said, 'It was nice to meet you, Ms Eloise Hay. You have enjoyed feeding my chickens?'

'Yes. Thanks. They were lovely.'

'You know Eloise, when I was young, I was the best hacker in Europe. I was caught a few times, jailed even. I made some mistakes! And then, you know, my country's government gave me money, they paid me, to break into security systems, to test their vulnerability.'

She nodded, mesmerised by his giant head and tiny little teeth.

'And so, Eloise, I can hack into systems that exist now. But did you know data can be mined from the past as well as the present? Emails, calls, texts, you name it. Information is power. It can be used to expose, but it can also be used to bargain. As *currency*. In that case, when information is used as cold hard currency, it is nothing personal, Eloise. It's just business.'

It's chust business.

'Goodbye, Eloise. Goodbye, my friends.'

He raised his hand and the car moved slowly down the gravel drive, towards the mock portcullis.

As they crossed the dinky bridge over the moat, Scott looked at the bobbing ducks and said, 'You know what else? Now we've interviewed him *he'll* be monitoring everything we do, too.'

'Really?'

'In fact, he's probably been doing it since we contacted him. He's the master hacker, remember. He'll be into our emails, texts, everything. So no fat jokes. Show respect. We don't want to piss him off.'

There was a short silence, Eloise mentally reviewing her communications thus far. No sharing about Hartmann's poignant pants, then.

'Is there any actual evidence for who leaked against Dance?'

'Not yet. But I bet it was Ed Miles — backed by the Hallwright faction. Hallwright wants Dance out and Miles in. Dance's denied he knew about illegal spying, but having to deny it made him look bad, right. So the fight's on.'

'The Opposition are saying there's going to be proof that Dance knew, that he acted illegally. Someone's armed Bradley Kirk with some dirt.'

'So Dance will be looking for ways to shaft Miles in return. Any dirt on Miles.'

'Presumably,' Scott said. 'And there's something else, too. Last night my friend Mrs Twitcher told me to stand by for information about Baby O'Keefe.'

'The father? Is someone going to leak that as well?'

'There's not much else to the story other than who's the daddy. We can only hope he's not a civilian.'

'Cos we want the fall-out.'

'Yeah, the hoped-for fall-out.'

Eloise said slowly, 'With everyone talking about it, the fact that she hasn't named the father suggests . . .'

'That it's someone who doesn't want to admit it. Or maybe she just quite rightly thinks it's no one's bloody business.'

'Maybe it's a sperm donor.'

'She's a workaholic. The whole thing about her is that she's sexy as hell but she's married to the job. Lives and breathes policy. Mad for select committees and late-night debates. She only hangs out with politicians. If it's not a sperm donor, it'll be one of them.'

Scott stared out the window. After a long pause he clenched his fists and said, 'Children need a father.'

'Oh. Right . . .'

'I, I love my children so much, it's crazy. You'll find out, Eloise. If, *when,* you and Sean decide to have kids, it's the most wonderful, the most marvellous thing you can do. You find yourself immersed, just *surrounded* by love. Just the other day Thee and I . . .'

Eloise half-listened. She was remembering the person hidden behind Kurt Hartmann's eyes. How many of us are living so deep below the surface, no one knows who we are?

Out on the northwestern, the gridlocked traffic queued and slowed. By the time they got back, Mariel Hartfield was up on the big screen at reception, sleepily gorgeous in a tight black jacket, and halfway through reading the evening news.

Anita O'Keefe wasn't telling. Satan Dance wasn't commenting. Ed Miles, the Minister of Justice, was available and was commenting: 'I will not review my decision to deny Andrew Newgate compensation for the ten years he spent in prison.'

And later in the bulletin, Ed Miles appeared again: 'The Opposition,' he said, 'should put up or shut up. As far as I can see, there is no truth to the allegation that Prime Minster Dance acted outside his powers by allowing illegal spying on citizens. I do not, and never have had, leadership ambitions. I am one hundred per cent behind our current leader, Jack Dance.'

And now came the weather. The Sinister Doormat was predicting weather that would surprise us. It would surprise us by not changing. By going on day after day, giving us worryingly more of the same.

NINE

Along the peninsula, the air was hot and still. The iron roofs blazed with reflected evening sun, and the boardwalk was busy, a steady procession of dogs and owners making their way across the bridge to the dog park. Eloise was walking on the edge of the estuary. She shaded her eyes and squinted at the gulf, where the water lay silver and flat. Heading home for the first time in two days, she was thinking: Make a plan. It would be good to make a plan. But there was so much, so very much, that needed fixing.

Drink less. Find a hobby. Join a club. Meet a nice man. She passed one of the neighbours who'd tried to stamp out the fire on her lawn. The look he now gave her was scandalised, reproachful. Look at that glare. Go on, get your staring done. *Whatevs.*

She frowned. See, I love living by myself. Living alone: what a thrill.

The freedom. You can do what you. No need to answer to. When the impulse takes you, you can . . .

The migraine had gone but its effect had lingered — rawness, dizziness, a feeling of teetering at the edge of a cliff. At one point during the night at Carina's a shaft of darkness had split her vision, as if a door had opened, and she'd seen the shape of a man, blacker than the darkness, at the end of the bed. She lay watching the black figure, her whole body poisoned with adrenaline, until he passed across the room and was gone. She dreamed that behind the fabric of the night there was a deeper blackness, only glimpsed when the night had frayed. When she woke in Carina's spare room she was wired, exhausted, with a yearning for touch so strong she would even have hugged smelly Silvio, if he'd snuffled his way onto the bed.

She had woken with a memory, of a story in a book Arthur had given her a long time ago. But who was the author?

Now, just off the bus, she was carrying a DVD of Kurt Hartmann's hip hop tracks, a vegetable curry hot pot, a box of Panadol Extra, a memory stick of interview notes, and a bottle of chardonnay. She passed two boys hauling up a bait-catcher on the edge of the creek, the plastic cylinder filled with writhing sprats. She thought: Yoga. Meditation. The whole mindfulness thing. Or Nick's hobby: search and rescue. Finding lost kids, bewildered oldies. Camaraderie. The satisfaction of it. Their relief and gratitude.

Book clubs. Karate?

Now she came up against the singed bushes, the new line of black at the boundary of her property. Nick, at least, had taken the fire calmly. She summoned up his face: strong jaw, clear blue eyes, slightly rough skin. A tall, lean figure, thin even. Ruggedness mixed with a gentle manner: that was an appealing combination.

She looked up at the blank windows of the stucco house. A layer of the world was hidden from her. She'd thought her marriage was solid, that Andrew Newgate was an innocent man, that Mariel Hartfield and Jack Anthony hated each other. That there was no sense in wondering about the death of Arthur Weeks. Was it her own fault that she was lost? Had she been wilfully blind?

The evening light shone on the blackened bushes and the sooty base of the toe toe; the air was full of shining dust. Beyond the line of gardens the estuary stretched away to the horizon, crossed by ripples as the tide turned. Eloise walked on under the high light sky, hearing the cries of seagulls, the shouts of children on the playing field along the peninsula road, melancholy sounds, distant in the summer evening. The air still smelled of fire.

Nick came down the side of his house, dragging a load of cut ponga fern fronds. He was in jeans, sunburnt, his eyes bloodshot from the dust and sun, his hair messy. The light was turning golden behind him, dust and fern fibres floating in the air, and he stood scratching his head and looking at her with a slightly dopey smile.

'Where you been? You been away?'

'No. Oh yes, I stayed a night at . . . a friend's.'

She went on, awkward, 'I nearly knocked on your door the other night, after you'd gone home. But you had someone with you.'

He dumped his load on the ground. 'Oh?'

'A tall guy, black hair. I came across the lawn and saw you, and thought I'd better leave you to it.'

'You should have come over. Did you interview the mogul?'

'We did. The house is incredible. We fed his chickens.'

'Chickens?'

A pause. Stupid grin on her face. She tried to frown.

He said, 'Why don't you come over tonight and tell me all about it?'

'I've got work to do.'

'Come over when you've finished.'

'Well, thanks.' She turned to go. 'The man in your house . . .'

'Which evening was it? A man did come over. He was a cop, asking about the stucco house. I said I'd never noticed anything untoward.'

'Did he have a tattoo on his hand?'

'A tattoo? I didn't notice. Why?'

'I thought I'd seen him somewhere, I can't remember where.'

Nick shrugged.

She shouldered her bag.

'Might see you later then?' he called after her.

The door was deadlocked. She used both keys and entered the cool, dim hallway, closing the door behind her, and passed into the sitting room, where the evening light was casting a rhombus of tangerine light on the wall. She set out her shopping on the bench, turned on the television, then changed her mind and switched it off again.

She listened: the ticking of an art deco clock Sean's mother had given them. The fridge motor. A car driving up the peninsula road. She turned the television on again. The Sinister Doormat, her face rendered more sepulchral by a tight ponytail, was standing in front of the weather map, predicting the usual: no rain.

Listening, she walked through the hallway to the internal garage door, checking rooms, behind doors, even, with a flustered shake of her head, how stupid, opening cupboards and looking behind beds.

Outside, the low sun picked out bare branches along the fence. From the estuary there was a flash off a boat, glass catching the last rays. The Doormat was now addressing a chart decorated with rows of little yellow suns. Eloise drifted to the windows and watched the children out on the path. One boy had his bait-catcher slung over his shoulder, the other carried a stalk of toe toe, like a spear against the blue sky.

She poured herself a glass of wine and walked around the rest of the ground floor, noticing a trail of Silvio's and the Sparkler's black footprints in the hall, the Sparkler's handprints on a glass door, on a coffee table. The Sparkler's drawings on scraps of paper in the sitting room. Evidence of a crime: Silvio had, in an idle moment, gnawed a wooden edge of the steps.

At the bottom of the stairs, she stood with a hand on her stomach, thinking of Hine at work, who, in the café that evening, had taken Eloise's hand and pressed it to the hard mound of her stomach, the skin suddenly, astonishingly, moving under Eloise's fingers, making her jump and pull her hand away.

'So freaky!' they all said, wanting to feel again. The baby was pushing its foot against Hine's stomach. You could feel the hard bulge moving under the skin. Imagine it. The presence inside you.

'Alien,' someone said.

Stop thinking about babies.

Speaking of babies, she had kept up her surveillance of Anita O'Keefe. Her latest theory was holding: that the father of Baby O'Keefe was Prime Minister Dance, married father of adult children and secret lover of the beautiful young Minister for Social Development, whose travels around the country, revealed on Twitter and Facebook, used to, before the pregnancy, mirror his own. That was the theory anyway. But stop thinking about babies.

Eloise was on the stairs. She looked out the window at a patch of dry grass and a pepper tree, its long shadow crossing the garden. Ahead on the landing, the door to her bedroom was open. She entered the room and saw that the window to the balcony was closed, that all was tidy and unstained, the Sparkler and Silvio not having passed this way. She heard whispering behind her.

In the bathroom a tap was running a thin stream of cold water. She turned it off, returned to the bedroom and sat down to take off her shoes. A cushion had fallen on the floor. She picked it up and noticed that the door of the cabinet next to her bed was open. The book she'd been reading was not on the top of the pile. She searched, found the book at the back of the cabinet, behind the stack.

How had it moved?

Everything was uncertain, as mysterious as a migraine dream. In the next room she found the book she'd been trying to recall: Arthur's copy of a collection of Chekhov stories. She sat down on a deckchair on the upstairs balcony to read:

> *A thousand years ago a monk, dressed in black, wandered about the desert, somewhere in Syria or Arabia . . . Some miles from where he was, some fishermen saw another black monk, who was moving slowly over the surface of a lake. This second monk was a mirage. Now forget all the laws of optics, which the legend seems not to recognise, and listen to the rest. That mirage cast another mirage, then from that one a third, so that the image of the black monk began to be transmitted endlessly from one layer of the atmosphere to another. So that he was seen at one time in Africa, at another in Spain, then in Italy, then in the Far North . . .*

The sun was going down behind the stucco house, the windows blazing with reflected light.

I can't stay here.

But her phone was ringing.

'Hang on a second,' she said half an hour later, and tilted the wine bottle. The level seemed oddly low. She filled her glass. 'Go on.'

'I said to him, You say Pilger lacks balance. I say . . . I say Pilger has a point of view. He *cares*. He cares and he has a point of view and he *gives* it to you. He *socks* you right between the eyes. And I said, So *what is* this thing you call balance? Do we *always* need to provide the other point of view? Tell me this. What if there *isn't* another point of view? What if there's just *the truth*? Know what I mean?'

Eloise, who had been looking at the ceiling, allowed her chair to fall gently back onto its four legs.

'E? You still there?'

She sipped, swallowed and said, 'You get sick of the endless "on the one hand, on the other hand". Sometimes there's just the truth.'

'Exactly. *Exactly*. I knew you'd . . . But we need balance to assess the truth. We need a balanced attitude. As I said to Thee . . .'

She drank, tilted back her chair, listened. Scott roamed away from his central point, came back to it, veered off again. She liked the sound of his voice. She loved the fact that he was talking. In fact, at that moment she loved *him*, tireless Scott: his enthusiasm, his goodness.

Keep talking.

'Now, Pilger on the Aborigines. It's searing stuff. I'm not saying there's *never* another point of view. Obviously some things are subtle and you've got to cover the whole picture. But to dismiss it out of hand just because you want "two sides of the story". I said, Mate. There's a place for belief. There's a place for *anger*.'

Balance, she thought. Balance. Her mind wandered and she was back in Dr Klaudia Dvorak's office at the rear of the old Herne Bay shop, the French doors open to the garden. Eloise was talking, elaborating, and something had caught her eye out there in the garden, a movement.

This was true: while she was sitting with Klaudia, a large, pale brown rat had emerged from under a mound of leaves, and begun sniffing around the edge of the patio. Eloise didn't stop talking, she droned seamlessly on, all the while watching the big, sleek rat picking its way through the undergrowth. Its nose so busy, its progress so cautious . . . While talking, she'd considered mentioning the rat, decided it wasn't relevant, and carried on without missing a beat.

I edited out the rat. And if she was editing, was there balance? How could she know she was telling Klaudia the truth? Wasn't it all selective, and didn't any conclusion Klaudia drew from their discussions depend entirely on Eloise's subjective take? She wondered if *balance* was a question she could raise with Klaudia herself.

'Know what I mean?' Scott said.

'Totally,' she said into the phone.

It really was surprising, the way the wine seemed to be emptying itself out of the bottle. There was soft twilight outside the window, the black horizon seamed with orange and gold, a wavering stain of light on the water. People hurrying home with the last of the sunset.

Listening, the phone held in the crook of her neck, Eloise reached up to the very top kitchen shelf and edged a gin bottle into her fingers. She nearly over-balanced as Scott went on, 'Have you watched Hartmann's hip hop tracks? He does the whole gangsta DJ thing. Stupid backwards cap and bling, all that. The songs are absolute shit but the girls in hot pants are amazing.'

Eloise primly slid the wine bottle back into the fridge. Best not to finish it off. You don't want to overdo things. She upended a slug of gin into her glass, and searched in the fridge for tonic.

She poured, sipped and said in a thick voice, 'He's being a Man of the People. He talks about the People reclaiming the internet. He doesn't mention how much money he makes out of the revolution.'

'Mmm,' Scott yawned.

He was fading. Eloise said quickly, 'He's got his political ambitions.'

'Right.' Scott livened up. 'Totally opportunistic ones. He wants to prevent his extradition, right. Like I said to Thee . . .'

Eloise tilted back in her chair, fixed her eyes on the ceiling.

It was late when he finally hung up. She was by the lamp, in a little bubble of light. Beyond its glow the darkness seemed to throb, as if in time with her heartbeat. She pitched herself forward and up, into the warm shadows. As she went around the room turning on the lights, her heart, which was already racing with the alcohol, sped up so fast it ached. In the estuary the water reflected the lights of a fishing boat, making its way out to sea.

Her chest hurt. She felt odd. But when had she last eaten anything? She and Scott had dipped into a bowl of chewy lollies at Kurt Hartmann's; that was it. No wonder she felt light-headed. She found her shopping, selected the packaged curry meal and slid it into the microwave, watching it revolve on its glass plate. She turned, and her eyes fell on the book she'd been reading when Scott rang, the Chekhov story called 'The Black Monk'.

She picked it up.

Then he passed out of the atmosphere of the earth, and now he is wandering all over the universe, still never coming into conditions in which he might disappear. Possibly he may now be seen in Mars, or in some star of the Southern Cross. But my dear, the crux of the legend is that exactly a thousand years from the day when the monk walked in the desert the mirage will return to the atmosphere of the earth again and will appear to men. And apparently the thousand years is almost up . . .

According to the legend we can expect the black monk any day now.

The microwave pinged.

There. A bit of food, a calming drink. No problem. With her plate of hot curry and her drink, she settled carefully into a chair. It was like . . . It was like being on a plane, with the pilot's voice on the intercom: Slight technical problem, folks. Nothing we can't handle, but we're going to have to change our course . . .

And so she sipped, and gingerly ate her packaged meal, and plaintively sought more drinks, and didn't look at the night out there, at the teetering height of the sky, the pitching blackness of the air.

Eloise woke, but nothing was clear. The previous hours presented themselves as a series of images.

She had virtually no memory of leaving the chair and going to bed, only a fragment to do with climbing the stairs. At 3 a.m. she had sat up and looked at the clock, and in the darkness she had seen something move. Then she was locked in the bathroom, sitting hunched on the edge of the bath. She saw the mirrored door of the bathroom cupboard opening, her image sliding quickly away, then swinging back. Her face shuddering, then still. Her eyes big and dark, spooked. But then she had left the bathroom and was lurching across the dark living room, pushing down a curtain that was billowing up in the night breeze. She was fighting down the curtain and closing and locking the ranch slider, which had been standing open.

This yearning for touch, for someone to anchor her. She was lost, the night was all splinters and shards. And then the information came to her, as if the darkness had shifted just for a moment, revealing what lay behind. The door had been deadlocked when she'd arrived home. But when she'd last left the house and fled to Carina's, she had not deadlocked the door.

TEN

Carina and the Sparkler were sitting on stools at the kitchen bench, their work spread out in front of them. Giles, a structural engineer (a builder of bridges), was away, in the Sudan or Somalia or Niger, Eloise hadn't quite paid attention to which. The Sparkler was leaning over her maths book and Carina was typing on a laptop with extraordinary speed, occasionally looking over and saying things like, 'Christ, what does that even mean? Turn the fraction upside down maybe?'

'You *suck* at maths.'

'Ask Eloise.'

'I suck even more.' Eloise, who was lying on the sofa, spoke from under a cold flannel. Silvio had settled himself across her feet and she was tentatively enjoying the weight and heat of him, although not the smell. His eyes were uncanny: yellow flecked with brown, weirdly intelligent. He was a strong presence. Earlier she'd stroked his head and he'd pulled away as if irritated, and she'd felt hurt. When he draped himself over her feet half an hour later her spirits lifted. Really Silvio, old boy? So I'm not that bad?

'You all suck. Total *suckedness*.'

'Just get on with it. Put something down. God, homework's a drag.'

Silence. Eloise lay low, occasionally turning the flannel on her brow. The doorbell chimed. Silvio leapt off her feet and hurled himself into the hall with an explosion of barks. The noise was unbelievable.

Eloise sat up, taking note. He was good, Silvio: he was mild and friendly but big enough, with a deep enough bark, to sound like a proper guard dog.

The door opened. They heard, 'Ooh, you're a big softie. Lick me to death will you? Ooh, hello, all.'

Demelza entered, with a jingle of keys. 'Carina. If you could just . . .'

Carina rose without a word, and went out to retrieve the car from where it had been left in the middle of the road.

Demelza's eyes fell on Eloise. 'What are *you* doing here?'

Eloise sat up. 'Just visiting.'

'Pardon? What are you *muttering* about? And what've you got that thing on your head for? Ooh, hello, Sparkles, darling, I've brought you a present. Look, it's for your room.' She presented her granddaughter with a plant pot, from which a small cactus reared up, furred with prickles.

The girl took it with care. 'Thanks. It looks like an evil gherkin,' she said.

'That's all right,' Demelza said. She sniffed. Her gaze moved to Eloise again. 'Look at you, your hair all on end. What's the matter with you?'

'Nothing.'

'You been living it up?'

'No. Want a cup of tea?'

'I don't mind.' Demelza lowered herself into a chair and sat pushing her hair off her temples in quick movements. She was wearing a short skirt and a tight jacket. She crossed her shapely legs, now mottled with age, and flexed her feet in their high-heeled pumps.

'Your father's under the doctor. He's not himself. I've had the locum pop in, she's been wonderful with me. So attentive and kind.'

'What's wrong with him?'

'I understand it's the lungs.'

'What about them?'

'I don't know. They're not right, is all.'

'Was there anything specific mentioned?'

'Hark at you. Goodness me. It's his *lungs*, chuck. Mind you, I've not been right myself, with the hot weather. It comes to us all, doesn't it, the stomach troubles.'

Eloise presented her mother with a cup of tea.

'What's this then? A mug? It's terrible isn't it, the way I am: so fussy. Only wanting the best china, me. Now, Sparkles, how are you dear? Enjoying school? Doing your homework are you? Ooh, your mother never did her homework. Mind, she practically never went to school. Played truant the whole time. I don't know how she managed to get any qualifications at all, to be honest.'

Carina came in with the car keys.

'Thank you, dear. Did you leave a window open for Gerald? He does get so hot. Carina, if you could just . . . Goodness, Eloise dear, what's that you're wearing? What a lovely jacket. Look at that. The colours. You do always manage to look so elegant.' She looked pointedly at Carina, who stood holding out the keys, in her jeans, her faded hoodie.

'Look at your sister's lovely jacket, Carina. I suppose she does have to maintain standards, working in the television environment. That

Roysmith, mind, he's all hairdo, that one. If you ask me. Right clothes-horse. All style and no substance.'

Eloise closed her eyes. Carina dropped the keys on the coffee table.

'Anyway, I just thought I'd pop around, since your father and I never see you. You're always so busy, I don't know. Your brother comes and sees us all the time. He's been wonderful with us. Let's see, he's reconcreted the driveway, done the lawns, painted Terrence's study, and that's just this week. Let me tell you about a fascinating book I've been reading. You're welcome to borrow it if you wish.'

'Want some pasta? There's a lot left over.'

'Full of garlic, is it? Why don't you make a nice shepherd's pie?'

'It's only got a few capers in it.'

'I don't eat capers!'

'Do you want a muffin then?'

'I don't eat *muffins!*'

Eloise opened a high cupboard in Carina's basement and reached for the old sports bag. Down here in the homely, cobwebby space, with the bikes and the humming clothes dryer and the smell of hot laundry, it seemed possible to take a look at the past.

She unzipped the bag. And look: the fashions of yesteryear. That jacket, those shirts. She'd never worn them again. Could you believe you needed to wear that colour? Or that cut? She drew out a pair of dated shoes, an ornate belt. Unlike Carina, who didn't much care, Eloise had a strong fashion sense. The once-valued items now looked clumsy, absurd even.

Underneath the clothes was Arthur's cardboard folder.

Most of the file was the typewritten script of Arthur's play, a political satire that had been put on at a small theatre. It was funny and original and got some excellent reviews. He'd been discussing a run in a bigger theatre and had been improving and editing parts. The script was covered in notes. She flicked through it. There was also a screenplay for a satirical TV show he'd been working on with a group of writers.

Just Arthur's current work, then. Time to go and have a glass of wine.

Under the screenplay was a thin pile of handwritten notes. Here was Arthur's small, cramped scrawl that she'd always found hard to read. It sloped backwards, perhaps because he was ambidextrous. He wrote with his right hand but batted left at cricket, kicked a ball with his left foot. She bent to decipher the handwriting.

Notes for The Night Book Screenplay.

Back then, he'd been working on a film script about a National Party politician. He was interested in the prime minister, David Hallwright. He wanted to write about society: rich, poor, high, low, good, corrupt.

He said, 'I want to write about money. To do a *Père Goriot*. I want to create my own Rastignac. A man who comes up against society, is horrified by its cruelty and then says: *I am ready for that world. I will not lose. I will not go back.* But I don't know any rich people,' he'd added. 'I need to find some money. I want to get into Hallwright's world.'

Was *The Night Book* the name of the screenplay Sean had mentioned when she first met him?

She lifted the handwritten pages and found an envelope; inside was a stack of photos of Eloise and Arthur. A trip they'd taken to the South Island: Eloise on a rock, waving, Arthur on the Cook Strait ferry, the stormy sea behind him, the two of them in front of a motel on the West Coast.

She sifted through the pictures. A day of rain, and they'd walked beside a river banked with grey stones and come upon a melancholy, sinister scene: a pile of severed deers' feet, left by hunters. The rain falling into the slow river, the grey stones, the hunters' gruesome leavings. She remembered a tree fallen across the riverbank, its roots thrust up into the air. Rusted farm machinery in a paddock. The wooden motel in the distance under a giant bank of black cloud, its windows glowing through the watery dusk like a Jack o' Lantern.

Here was Eloise sitting on a bleached log, on a rocky beach. One of Arthur throwing stones. She turned up a photo of him sitting on a rock against a bank of intensely green bush. He was wearing his old oilskin. His hair was slicked down with rain, his potent gaze fixed on her. That look he could give you, his startling eyes.

Arthur.

In the first shock of his death, random phrases came. Arthur's died, but he'll be all right. Something has hit Arthur so hard that he's died. The thing was, you couldn't understand it. These odd phrases came to you out of the confusion, and you tried them out in your head.

She drew out a Polaroid. It was a faded picture of a girl sitting on a bench, looking away from the camera. There was a background of sand, lupins and marram grass. The girl looked to be early teens, Maori, thin and pretty with glossy black hair and intense, pale eyes. She turned the photo over and found a name written in Biro on the back: *Mereana*.

Eloise listened. The dryer had stopped rumbling. She could hear Demelza talking upstairs, and Silvio's claws clicking as he crossed the wooden floor.

Mereana. There was a memory, but she couldn't retrieve it. Now she heard her mother preparing to leave, asking where she was, an inaudible reply from Carina, and the Sparkler's high voice. The front door opening — Carina would be out in the street, positioning Demelza's car.

The front door banged again and her sister started making bedtime commands: teeth, pyjamas, book.

While Carina and the Sparkler were arguing in the bathroom, Eloise took the file to the spare room. After she'd got into bed, Silvio poked his nose around the door, and with surprising grace leapt up, turned a number of times and settled himself hotly, with an emphatic sigh, against her body.

———

The handwritten pages were dated just a few weeks before Arthur died:

Lin Jung Ha 021 233 9436. Housekeeper, boss of the help. Runs Hallwrights' city house, now staying at Hallwrights' summer residence, Rotokauri.

Also at Rotokauri, David Hallwright's closest circle:

His wife Roza.

His children.

His oldest friend and fellow campaigner, Police Minister Ed Miles.

His best friend, and the adoptive father of Roza's daughter Elke, Dr Simon Lampton.

Simon Lampton's wife, Karen.

The Lamptons' son, and Elke.

Hallwright's Deputy PM and Finance Minister, Colin Cahane.

Also on site, domestic staff, political and security staff, and children's nanny Tuleimoka Faleuka.

That summer: Arthur was preoccupied, full of enthusiasm one moment, silent the next. He always had too many ideas; she'd thought he should concentrate on just a few. He was usually working on three or four projects at once.

Re Hallwrights and Lamptons: the Lamptons adopted Elke Lampton when she was eight. Former adoptive parent had died. They didn't know at first she was the daughter of Roza Hallwright. RH had given birth when she was a teenager, and had the baby adopted. (Parents strict Catholic. After the adoption RH became alcoholic and drug user — is now sober — ref Roza's old friend Tamara Goldwater 027 436 6602). The Lamptons discovered the

connection with Roza after becoming National Party donors and
meeting the Hallwrights. The two families are now close friends.

Eloise paused. These people were real and so were the connections between them. Everyone knew about Roza Hallwright and the daughter she shared with the Lamptons. Back then, there were magazine pieces about it, also about Rotokauri, the luxury compound north of the city, where the Hallwrights went during the summer break. But Roza Hallwright a recovered alcoholic? A drug user? That wasn't common knowledge. Had Arthur uncovered a secret, or had he invented it?

There was a soft knock. Carina stuck her head around the door and said, 'There you are, Silvio. Want me to drag him off?'

'No. He stinks, but I'm touched he finds me acceptable.'

'You can stay here as long as you like, by the way.'

'Thanks. Sorry.'

'No, honestly, the more the merrier.'

'Well, thanks.'

Eloise thought, for the thousandth time, how much better she would be if she was like Carina. How much saner, cleverer, kinder.

'Just kick Sil off if he gets too hot,' Carina said.

Eloise wanted to say, *I love you and I'd be dead without you.* But not wanting to be uncool said, 'I will.'

She went back to reading Arthur's notes.

The names: there was something about the names.

ELEVEN

'I've been wondering about balance,' Eloise said.

Klaudia positioned herself in her seat, holding a coffee mug in both hands.

Eloise considered, then decided against mentioning the rat she'd seen during the last session. 'Balance. How do we know I'm not sitting here editing out the truth? How do we know, either of us, that what I'm saying isn't a load of subjective invention? Delusion?'

Klaudia had a smile that turned her mouth up at the corners like the Joker. She had an especially fairytale quality today, her eyes large, bright and intensely blue. Eloise thought of lost children, wicked stepmothers. Dark forests. Snow.

'Balance. Big question.'

Would it be rude to mention the rat? Would the rat seem to represent something Klaudia hadn't been privy to, and therefore a kind of assertion on Eloise's part, a piece of one-upmanship: You weren't anticipating *that*, were you? You didn't see *that* coming. Eloise considered this while saying, 'Also, I have the slight concern that since I've been seeing you I've got more mad, not less.'

'Ah.'

'Well, perhaps not more mad. But my life seems to have got more chaotic.'

The rat was in league with Klaudia. The rat was part of her repertoire. It emerged and showed itself to the patient, and then Klaudia measured the reaction. After the session, the therapist and her colleague, the rat, conferred. Eloise thought this while saying, 'Talking about my mother, for example. It seems, potentially, a recipe for disaster. The only way I get on with my mother is by not thinking about her too hard.'

It was quite difficult to say all this. And Klaudia, it had to be said, was being disconcertingly tight-lipped today. Eloise, whose headache was so bad she felt like screaming, selected a tissue from the box on the desk and wiped her brow. *Honestly, Klaudia, let me know what you think. Jump in whenever you feel like it.*

She went on, 'Now I've talked to you, I notice everything my mother says. I don't skate over things. I've become too aware. It's going to lead to fights, is all I'm saying.'

'You mention balance.'

'Oh yes. Two issues.' (Was it terribly hot in here?) 'Balance, and the fact that raking up family problems might lead to fights. Perhaps,' Eloise tried a smile, winced and thought better of it, 'perhaps there's a lot to be said for the good old-fashioned stiff upper lip. Everyone bent into their dysfunctional shapes and the ship moving along just fine. Whereas if you start unpicking the family dynamic, you undo the winning formula that keeps the ship, er, afloat . . .'

'I notice you looking at the garden. Is it too cold with the French doors open?'

'Too cold? No. I . . . sometimes there's an old woman out there.'

'Yes, she is the gardener.'

There was a pause. Eloise said, 'I just wonder about the wisdom of opening this can of worms.'

Klaudia smiled. 'The can of worms — horrible expression — the can of worms was already partly open, don't you think?'

Eloise shifted in her seat, embarrassed to have used a horrible expression.

She said, 'Perhaps one should just force the lid back on.'

'Better to let those worms out!'

'Oh God,' Eloise said. How would Klaudia interpret it if she crossed the floor and threw up all over the patio?

Klaudia's voice softened. 'It can be painful, I know. And sometimes, through therapy, you will find you are raising things with your family that may in the past have been kept usefully taboo. If you kick a holy cow, you can ruffle a few feathers!'

A short silence. Eloise frowned.

Trying to sound normal and even upbeat, she said, 'I'm wondering if I should get a puppy.'

'Ah. They are a lot of work. You have a full-time job?'

'That's the problem. Maybe I couldn't look after it properly. But I'm so . . .' She stared at the desk with mad intensity. 'I'm living alone, and I'm having trouble sleeping at night.'

'You have been using the sleeping pills?'

'I want a guard dog.' It came out like a demand.

'I see. But of course if you got a puppy, it wouldn't guard for about a year.'

Eloise stared, baffled by this piece of wisdom. It hadn't occurred to her — puppies don't start work straight away. Should she take up

Carina's offer of Silvio? Noisome Silvio . . . But what would *he* do all day while she was at work, apart from shit on the floor and gnaw the stairs. She would have to borrow the Sparkler to see to him, and she went to school most days, presumably. Think of the mess. Trashing the place would certainly annoy Sean and Lady Cheryl.

Klaudia had swivelled a photo on her desk. Eloise looked at the picture: a large brown dog with a noble head and soulful eyes.

'I am a dog-owner myself, so I know a bit about them. The alternative for you would be some human company, wouldn't it?'

A hot sigh rose in Eloise's chest. 'Well, I thought maybe a hobby, involving a club. There's a book club on the peninsula with some nice women. Or yoga or zumba, or whatever. And there's a man. A neighbour, who's friendly.'

'We have to keep building those bridges.'

'Yes. Bridges.' Like Giles, she thought. The bridge builder.

'Tell me about this man.'

'Nick? He owns properties. He's sort of good-looking, athletic. A nice manner, not rough. There was a fire, near my property, he helped put it out.'

'A fire?' Klaudia raised her eyebrows. 'The one you started?'

'Yes.'

Out there in the garden, the wind flipped the silvery fern leaves and shivered the colourful heads of the flowers. She saw a line of rats performing a song-and-dance routine on the bricks. Little top hats and sticks and tails.

'I'm glad to hear he's a nice man. Puts out fires.' Klaudia smiled.

But had they actually answered the question about balance? Eloise gathered her strength and said, 'What I mentioned before. Balance. How do we know everything I tell you isn't so subjective that it's giving you a false picture? What if I tell you my mother makes comments that seem designed to attack, but in fact she's not doing that, and I'm just deluded and paranoid?'

'You don't seem so paranoid to me. But think of this as a conversation. An exploration. I'm not the judge. I'm the mirror. In a way, you are having a conversation with yourself. When you talk about the past, you have a strong reaction. It can be helpful to focus on the Now. Things that happened in the past are gone, but their effect still reaches you, like light travelling from a dead star.'

'The past is a dead star,' Eloise repeated.

'Yes. Its light still crossing the universe.'

Klaudia sat up straight. Glancing at the clock, she tapped her notepad with her pen. 'We talked before about the past, how your current situation has brought it flooding back to you. Certain things for you have been unresolved. The mementos you mentioned, belonging to Arthur. You felt they were significant. Have you explored your feelings about those?'

A conversation with the self. A memory: the image of her face swinging back in front of her in the bathroom mirror. Her eyes wide and black . . .

Eloise wondered if she were perhaps slightly frightened of Klaudia. They were talking so intimately, but Eloise didn't know who she was. She kept talking to Nick, and she didn't know who *he* was either. Perhaps this was what happened when you went mad: eventually everyone was a stranger. You went on talking and in the end you were surrounded by faces you didn't know.

She heard herself: evasive. Avoiding the question. 'That's a beautiful dog, Klaudia. What a glossy brown coat. Is it some kind of rare breed . . . ?'

She drove away from Klaudia's office, windows wound up and the air-conditioning roaring. Instead of heading straight back, she parked at the Herne Bay shops and went to a café.

Over a calming trim flat white, she mentally replayed the conversation with Klaudia. The past was a dead star, its light still reaching her.

Was therapy making her saner? This was unclear.

Deep breaths. Right. All serene. She rang Sean's cell phone.

A woman answered, 'Sean Rodd's office.' It was that awful little bitch, his secretary, Voodoo.

'It's Eloise. Let me speak to Sean.'

Voodoo tried to fob her off and then made her wait. Eloise remained composed.

Sean came on the line. She said, 'Right. It's me. Please thank your secretary for making me wait. I suppose she's just had to get up off the floor. Off the . . . off the desk. Whatever.'

'What? Who?'

'Your secretary. With the tiny neck and the big round eyes. Voodoo.'

'Oh,' Sean said.

'Anyway. I have a question, okay?'

'Okay, sure. Shoot.'

'Shoot. Shoot. You would say that, wouldn't you.'

'Eloise, I have to go to a meeting.'

'Right. A meeting. You know what, *fuck* your meeting.'

Silence.

'Okay, Sean. I just want to say one thing.'

'Yes?'

'*Fuck* you *and* your meeting.'

'Right. Is that it?'

'No. Actually. What I want to know is have you been in the house?'

'In the house? No.'

'In our house. In our ex-marital home. Have you been sneaking in?'

'No. I wouldn't dare after last time.'

'Very funny. You haven't, not once? It's important. Do you promise you haven't been back when I was out?'

'I swear, Eloise. I haven't been back since you threw the whole kitchen at me.'

For a moment, Eloise couldn't decide how she felt about this. 'I think someone's been in the house.'

'What, broken in?'

'Just, got in. Things were moved around. I left the door unlocked and stayed at Carina's and when I got home it was deadlocked.'

'The cleaner. Amigo.'

'No, it wasn't his day.'

'Was the alarm on?'

'No. I never bother. I'll start using it.'

'Well, you should. Are you all right?'

'Of course I'm all right. What's it to you? What do you care?'

'All right. Jesus.'

'Where are you and Barbie holed up? In some student flat?'

'Actually, Danni has her own house.' His tone was aggrieved, and faintly proud.

Eloise's whole body filled with nausea and pain. And yet it was easier if he was hateable. She sighed, sounding like Silvio at his most weary and long-suffering, and said, 'I suppose you'll be wanting me out soon. Of the house. The sale.'

'Eloise, don't cry.'

'I'm not crying.'

'Yes, we have to sell soon. We'll make a lot. Values have really gone up. Starlight Peninsula was a dump when we bought there, compared to now. Now it's hot. I don't mind talking, but I've got to go. The Hallwrights have flown in from the South of France. They'll be here in a minute. The whole team's working around the clock, we're doing a due diligence. Eloise? I promise, I haven't been near the house.'

The waitress said, 'Can I clear that for you? Are you okay?'

'Fine, thanks.' Eloise pressed the heel of her hand to her cheek, nodding: yes she would like another flat white. And if you could throw in a slug of rum. Or horse tranquiliser. Or cyanide.

Sean was still on the line so she said numbly, 'What are you doing for the Hallwrights? Taking over Sony?'

'I can't tell you. It's a big deal, that's all.'

'Perhaps you could rename Auckland, now Wellington's called Soonworld. What's Auckland going to be: The Idiot's Village?'

'Actually the village idiot characters were edited out by Hollywood. As offensive to the differently able. Eloise, I . . .'

'What?'

'Sometimes I wish . . .'

'What?'

'I miss . . .'

She waited.

'The thing is, Danni . . .'

'Good *bye*.' She slammed down the phone, only it was an iPhone, and there was a distressing crack as it hit the table. Around the café, heads turned.

Stare all you like. Whatever.

Sean. Sitting in his high-rise office at Jaeger's. Jaeger's: Auckland's oldest and richest law firm, advisors to the Hallwrights, and the Hallwright group of companies. She'd stood there in that office many times. Waiting for him on a cold clear day with a roaring wind, everything harsh and full of white noise and Sean coming in as she stood looking at the harbour and the bridge and the yachts and saying, Let's get married.

His specialty was intellectual property and entertainment law, which was why he was running round after the Hallwrights. Jaeger's was a big commercial firm with a lucrative sideline; they acted for TV stars, film directors, for the country's only famous pop star. She'd met Sean after Arthur had died, when he'd come to ask whether she had any copies of a screenplay Arthur had apparently written for a film-director client of his. Later, he came to the set of *Roysmith*. He was accompanying a Jaeger's client, a rich Chinese businessman who was being interviewed and wanted to be seen sweeping around town with a team of suits. On first meeting them the businessman had whipped out photos of himself with Prime Minister Jack Dance: connected, see. Sean asked her out to lunch in front of Scott, who'd immediately (warmly, richly, melodramatically) urged her to accept.

Now, outside, the sun made a burning cross on a shop front opposite, filling the window with glare. There was a tall, dark-haired man walking past, in front of the glass. She stood up and looked after him, but he'd disappeared.

Eloise sat down and opened her diary.

One: Silvio just for a few nights? Discuss with Carina.

Two: Nick? Cook him dinner? Invite to pub?

Three: A hobby.

Four: A flatmate?

Five: Who is Mereana?

TWELVE

'Get the email on strike action?'

'Oh yeah.'

'Jack Anthony's not happy about getting zapped in the toilet. Personally I'm going to use the pub across the road.'

'I haven't had a shock for a while.'

'Like a rat in a maze, you've learned what to avoid.'

'Everyone looks so tentative, so unrelaxed. Scared to touch.'

'All ginger.'

'Tip-toeing around.'

'Maybe it's a management tactic.'

'Or a big science experiment.'

Selena walked past, talking on her cell phone. 'And then I did this amazing course. I was blown away by it. It's about finding your inner awesomeness.'

Scott rolled his eyes.

They were watching film of Kurt Hartmann. The tycoon on his throne, with his smile, his wicked little teeth. Another one with a fairytale quality.

'Put simply,' Hartmann said, 'I am a citizen of this country. The security forces of the GCSB, who do not have jurisdiction over citizens, spied on me illegally. Prime Minister Dance is in charge of the security services. How can he say he didn't know?'

Scott paused the clip. 'Bradley Kirk keeps saying he's got proof that Dance knew about the spying, but he's not coming up with anything.'

He pushed play. Hartmann, who was strikingly articulate when he got going, began talking about the US Government's application to extradite him, which he'd been fighting since the police raid on his house.

In the room beyond, there was a cry of pain.

Scott nudged her and said, 'Selena holds the record for the number of times shocked. It proves to me—'

'How does the Prime Minister justify any of this?' Hartmann said. *Chustify any off ziss.*

'—It proves once and for all how thick she is.'

'Hey, Selena's not thick. She's got inner awesomeness.'

Hartmann went on, 'I am a businessman. I owned a large, popular file-sharing website. That is all. To this day, I don't know what was stored in it. I have done nothing wrong.'

'See, I always knew Selena was the dumbest rat in the maze,' Scott whispered.

They edited in a clip of Jack Dance at his weekly press briefing, dismissing Hartmann's claims that he knew about illegal spying. His tone was contemptuous. 'Mr Hartmann is simply trying to avoid extradition.

I had no idea he was being spied on. That was an operational matter.'

'Satan's looking a bit haggard.'

Dance had recently developed a new crease down the side of his face, and dark loops under his eyes.

'All the gossip's about Ed Miles making his move. Backed by the Hallwright faction. I wouldn't underestimate Satan, though. He'll be looking to push back.'

'How's he going to do that?'

Jack Dance was a right-wing hardliner. His handicap was the perception that he was aloof. Miles, who was now Justice Minister under Dance, was centrist, populist, and had recently been working on his friendly 'down-to-earth' persona. Dance's smoothness made people wary, but there was something about Miles that made you uneasy too: those noticing, calculating eyes. Neither had the charm of the ridiculously popular Sir David Hallwright, whose sunny goofiness, during his reign, had concealed layers of cunning and guile.

When Hallwright was in power, Scott used to reckon the real political brain was his wife, Roza Hallwright, who, while her husband was in office, spent her time writing children's books. 'Hallwright's lady,' Scott once mused to Eloise. 'What a brain. What a *mind*.'

Opinions were divided on this. Eloise wasn't sure what she thought. Carina, who disapproved of the Hallwrights, called them a *folie à deux*, which didn't seem quite right to Eloise.

And Demelza said, 'There's only one political brain in that pair, and it's him.'

Eloise now thought of Sean, holed up at Jaeger's with Sir and Lady Hallwright and their due diligence. There was a slight confusion in her mind about Roza Hallwright. The TV series and movies, *Soon and Starfish* and *Soon and the Friends*, which had been described as post-post-modern, contained jokes for adults as well as children, and featured Mrs Hallwright and her son Johnnie as characters; they were the creators of *Soon and the Friends*, who continually argued over plot in a slapstick mother-and-son power struggle. When Mrs Hallwright was mentioned, Eloise saw her cartoon — Mrs H as rendered by some witty Hollywood geek: bendy, curvaceous, faintly menacing. Her son Johnnie's cartoon image was reminiscent of one of the Sparkler's early favourites, SpongeBob SquarePants. 'Johnnie' was a brick-like figure with freckles, tiny legs, big sandals and billowing shorts.

Eloise didn't have an opinion about which Hallwright was the brains, but she did sometimes wonder what the *Soon* hype said about the country. Wellington airport, these days, was so tricked out in *Soon* merchandising it looked like a theme park. It wouldn't have been a surprise to hear that New Zealand schoolchildren believed they were born in Soonworld. That they were citizens of the Land of Soon . . .

She went on watching Kurt Hartmann, who had revealed, at this point in the tape, that he had political ambitions. He wished to help anyone who wanted to get rid of Jack Dance. This had much to do with the fact that Dance wanted to get rid of *him,* by sending him to an American jail.

'I have considered starting my own political movement,' he said. *Moofmint.* His tiny, avid eyes gleamed behind his tinted glasses. With his brutal jowls, wide mouth and pointy teeth, he'd been described as 'Bond villain', but Eloise thought he looked like the Ort Cloud in the *Soon* stories, a giant, gaseous character who sometimes landed, shimmering and pulsating, in Soon Valley. Hartmann was a creature massive yet somehow dainty, his pinky finger fussily crooked as he sipped his mineral water, reached anxiously for his hand sanitiser. He looked scandalised by the low level of debate (who were these agonising simpletons, these Luddites, who didn't understand his brave new megaworld?), yet at the same time he played the teenager: scoffer of lollies, game addict, gangsta.

Now, in the dark room, Scott made one of his noises: a cross between grunt and sigh. It signified deep thought. He was known for being a deep thinker, a real journalist, who hadn't succumbed to the network's pressure on content. At *Roysmith* they did real stories, not fluff. Scott made his noise again. Eloise looked at her watch.

Scott leaned over and whispered, 'What do you think of this suit? Too much?'

Eloise said automatically, 'It's gorgeous. Lovely lining. When it sort of falls open. That mint green and pink combo — is it paisley?'

'It's a lightweight weave Ronald sourced from Italy.'

'Right.' She was gearing up to make an excuse.

'I hope I don't look like a stockbroker.'

'Oh God, no.'

'I don't want to look shallow. Like Mike Hawkens, say.'

'Everyone knows you're deep. Into the arts and, um, literature. A reader. A thinker.'

'Thanks, Eloise. You and Sean must come over some time. As James K Baxter once said—'

'I've got this appointment. I'd better go now or I'll miss it.'

He flourished his hand. 'Go. *Fly.*'

There was a loud click and a shriek from the hall outside.

'Ouch,' Scott said, pitilessly.

She left the building and hurried through town. She was walking on the right-hand side of the road, and there was a bus stop twenty metres ahead. A car passed the bus stop, slowed and braked next to her, and a girl opened the car door and called back towards the stop, 'Want a ride?'

Eloise thought: The girl in the bus stop is crying.

The bus stop was a walled shelter and she couldn't see who was inside it until she reached it. Sure enough, it was a girl, and her face was contorted, and smeared with tears.

Eloise walked on. She didn't believe in ESP, or star signs, or fortune tellers or God. So how did a thing like that happen? How did information fly in, out of the blue? Perhaps something in the manner of the girl who'd called from the car had suggested it: that she was calling out to another girl, and that the girl was crying. Perhaps it showed that Eloise wasn't going nuts. That she could still read the world accurately, at least some of the time.

The police station loomed ahead of her, like a giant block upended on the hill. It was a brutal and unlovely building, all flat concrete surfaces, grimly functional. You reached the front office by way of a pebble-dash walkway. From across the road, the rectangular windows looked as small as arrow slits. What a dump.

Eloise had visited this dump before, having been driven there on the day Arthur died. She had spent hours in a CIB office high above the city, watching a neon sign on the horizon, while the murder squad milled and bustled outside the door. At that time, Arthur was the subject of serious CIB interest: the white boards, the diagrams, the hurrying detectives. And then his death had been downgraded, relegated, the squad moving on to new mysteries. He was no longer a homicide; he wasn't suspicious or even unexplained. He was just an accident.

Yesterday's fish-and-chip paper, she thought. Old news. Life goes on. Best not to dwell. Her phone rang. Absent-mindedly, Eloise answered.

'Ooh hello. It's your mother. I know you're at work, but I just wanted you to know your father's having tests with the specialist.'

'What specialist?'

'The one he's been recommended. I understand he's wonderful.'

'What's he a specialist of?'

'Of? Goodness me, I don't know. The internal organs, I imagine.'

'Any hint which organ? Organs?'

'Listen to you. Which organ. Which organs. The organs he's having the twinges in.'

'Mum, I'm actually in the middle of the road.'

'The middle of the road? What are you up to?'

'I've got an appointment.'

'Are you under the doctor, too?'

'I'll have to ring you back.'

Eloise reached the top of the pebble-dash ramp. A piece of paper taped to the smeared glass of the front door read: *Doors broken. Buzz and WAIT.*

She buzzed. Waited. After a few minutes a heavily tattooed couple with a toddler came up the ramp and buzzed, and resignedly waited. They were joined by a youth with a shaven head, who buzzed and waited and then, with a look of amazed affront, as if this really was the last straw, began kicking the door and shouting. A policeman appeared and opened up.

Eloise avoided the altercation between the youth and four officers, and went to the desk. Directed to a waiting area, she sat. A buzzer sounded, a door opened, and Detective Marie Da Silva appeared.

She hadn't changed. Wiry white-blonde hair sticking up on top of her head, short at the top and long at the back: an eighties hair style. A straight, freckly nose on an angular face. Strong features, defined cheekbones. Eloise thought: leonine. That pale hair and the feline face, and the unusual eyes. You noticed her eyes immediately. One was blue and one was brown, and they made you feel just slightly disorientated. You started focusing on one or the other, because both at the same time seemed wrong.

'Hi,' Da Silva said with a sharp glance, and put out her hand. She looked extremely alert, also impatient, as if she had little spare time. She was wearing khaki pants, boots and a short jacket.

They rode up four floors in silence, in the scarred lift. Eloise followed her along a corridor and into an office. Da Silva pointed to a seat, and Eloise sat, while the detective shifted books and files on the desk, and drew out a cardboard file.

'So. Eloise Hay. How are you?'

'Fine.'

'What can I do for you?'

'I wanted to talk to you about Arthur. Arthur Weeks.'

'I remember.'

'You interviewed me. He was my . . .'

Da Silva opened the file. 'Arthur Weeks. Died after falling from a retaining wall on the side of Mt Eden. He was your partner, you and he had been living together, half in his flat, half in yours. Detective O'Kelly and I interviewed you, let's see, here and here.' She sifted through pieces of paper, reading.

'They said he was drugged with pills when he fell.'

Da Silva lifted a page. 'Fractured skull. Spinal injury. Tests showed levels of . . .'

What was she doing? Eloise stood up. 'Actually, I think I should go.'

Da Silva paused, her gaze steady.

'I don't know what I was thinking, really. Just a whim.'

'A whim.' Da Silva looked amused, then her smile dropped and she said, 'Perhaps you'd better sit down and explain yourself.'

Silence.

'Since you're here,' Da Silva added.

Eloise looked at the door, hesitated.

'Otherwise I'll just go on wondering why you came,' Da Silva said.

Another silence.

'Oh, all right.' She sat down.

Finally Eloise said, 'It's just that I never asked anything. I didn't ask questions.'

Da Silva folded her arms and leaned back, considering her. 'That was our job.'

'But I don't believe it, that he fell off the wall because of pills. Arthur wasn't like that, he was never stoned.'

'He was a barrel of energy,' Da Silva said softly.

Eloise stared. 'You remember.'

Da Silva smiled.

'I can't believe you remember I said that. I meant ball. Ball of energy. I got it wrong. I got everything wrong.'

Da Silva's eyes were fixed on her. 'What do you mean?'

'I was so . . . I was so ashamed.'

'Ashamed?'

'It's hard to explain.'

'Is there something you want to tell me?'

'What? No.'

'Something about Arthur?'

'No. I mean ashamed because I felt that Arthur and I were both in such trouble.'

'Both in trouble? But Arthur was dead.'

'I know. But I couldn't grasp it. I felt as if Arthur and I were both in terrible trouble. I was out of my mind.'

Da Silva waited, then said, 'Why have you come here today? What's happened?'

'There's something I want to know.'

Another silence, then the detective said, 'Okay, sure. Just let me do one thing.'

She got up and went out of the office. Obviously she thought Eloise was crazy.

'Remember this guy?'

Eloise looked up. It was the taciturn partner, O'Kelly. He sat down in a chair next to Da Silva's desk, clicking his ballpoint pen.

Da Silva said, 'So, now we're all here. What did you want to know?'

Eloise leaned forward. 'You showed me something Arthur had written, some names. You asked me if I knew who they were and I said no.'

'Okay.'

'What were the names?'

'Why?'

'Because I didn't want to know then, but now I do. I've realised I let Arthur down. I should have asked questions.'

'All this time later you've decided this? Why?'

Silence. The clicking of the ballpoint pen.

'Well?'

'Why? I don't know. My husband left me.'

The two cops glanced at each other. 'And so . . . ?'

'I'm alone. I feel like I'm being visited by Arthur. And he's saying to me, Why were you so useless? Why didn't you ask a few questions, instead of sitting around being embarrassed because you said *barrel of energy*.'

It sounded angrier than she'd intended. A long pause. Da Silva glanced at her partner again. His eyes were on Eloise.

Finally Da Silva said, 'You didn't need to be embarrassed. You were fine. You were very together.'

'Was I?'

'Yes, sure.'

Eloise sighed. 'You see those stories on TV about people whose loved ones have been killed and they swear they won't stop until they find out what really happened. Until there's justice. You know those stories?'

'I suppose.'

'Well, I just accepted it. I didn't lift a finger.'

'There wasn't anything else you could do. It was pretty straight-forward.'

'Do you really think that?'

'Sure.'

'Will you tell me the names?'

'I'm not sure which names you mean.'

'They were divided by a forward slash.'

Da Silva regarded her steadily. 'Just give us a minute,' she said, signalling to O'Kelly. They went out of the room.

Should she leave? Would they let her? What must they think? They'd be arresting her next, for suspicious behaviour. It seemed a long time before they came back in and sat down. The ballpoint pen clicked.

Da Silva said, 'Arthur's death was filed as accidental.'

'I know.'

'I'm saying, Eloise, the questions were answered.'

Da Silva drew out a booklet from the cardboard file. It contained photographs. She flicked through the pages, not showing Eloise, until she came to one, which she turned over. The photo was of a piece of paper, on which was written in Arthur's handwriting:

Simon Lampton/Mereana Kostas

Eloise put her finger on the photo. 'That's it. You showed me those names, and I didn't know who they were.'

'Do you know now?'

Eloise looked away, suddenly unsure. 'Mereana' was the name written on the back of the photo of the girl in Arthur's file. And Simon Lampton was on Arthur's list of the friends of David Hallwright; he was the one who'd adopted the daughter of Hallwright's wife.

Why had Arthur connected the names?

She looked at Arthur's handwriting. 'Who is Mereana Kostas?'

'Well, it's an unusual name. There was a Mereana Kostas in Auckland and she's a missing person,' Da Silva said. 'She disappeared years ago. No trace.'

'Why did Arthur connect her name to Simon Lampton? And who is Simon Lampton?'

The male detective leaned over and put a hand on Da Silva's sleeve. She nodded, picked up the file. 'Eloise, just give us another second.' They got up and went out into the hall again.

Alone in the room, Eloise wished for a giant gin and tonic, a mountain of Valium. Perhaps if she just tip-toed out now, they could draw a veil, forget all about . . .

Da Silva marched back in and sat down, slapping the file on the desk. 'Right. Sorry. We don't know why Arthur put the names together. We interviewed Lampton. He was staying, would you believe, at the Prime Minister's summer compound at the time. Apparently Arthur contacted him twice by phone because he was a friend of David Hallwright, and Arthur wanted to write about Hallwright. Lampton fobbed him off, and that was it. Didn't Arthur tell you this?'

'He was cagey about projects, or so busy he didn't get around to telling me. He used to do too much, too many things at once. I always thought if he could just slow down and concentrate on a few . . .'

'He didn't tell you who Mereana Kostas was? Didn't mention her?'

'No.'

Should she tell them about the photo of the girl in Arthur's file? But look at silent O'Kelly's expression: not so deadpan now. A flicker of interest there, in his hard grey eyes. Eloise fell silent herself. A missing woman and a friend of David Hallwright. Arthur had made notes about these people, had even contacted Lampton and not told her, a fact she put aside for later, as possibly hurtful. But the notes in Carina's basement included current politicians too, powerful ones: Justice Minister Ed Miles, the Finance Minister Colin Cahane.

It was back, the sense that Arthur had got himself in trouble, had somehow gone too far. She'd dismissed it as irrational . . .

Concentrate. Focus.

'Is Simon Lampton still in politics?'

Da Silva made a wry face. 'He was never in politics, he was just in the PM's circle. Best friend of the Hallwrights, big party donor. He's a doctor. Obstetrician and gynaecologist.'

Eloise frowned, some vague memory stirring. The sun was suddenly shining directly into the office, casting a harsh glare on the drab furniture and lighting up Da Silva's wild blonde hair. O'Kelly's face looked feral, too avid. Something new had entered the room.

She stood up.

They didn't move, only looked at her.

'You'll be busy. I'll let you get on.'

'No rush,' Da Silva said. 'Is there anything else you'd like to talk about?'

'I've got an appointment.'

'Oh, really?'

Their interest frightened her. She'd expected to be fobbed off. It was a mistake. She shouldn't have come.

'Like I said, just a whim . . .'

Stop talking. Just stop.

Riding down in the lift with Da Silva she asked, 'What happened when you interviewed Simon Lampton?'

'Not much. He said Arthur was just another journalist wanting gossip on the Hallwrights.'

'What's he like?'

'Lampton? Nothing special.'

'You made a sort of face when you said his name.'

'Did I?'

'As if you had an opinion of him.'

Da Silva shrugged. At the door, she gave Eloise her card. She took it and said, 'But all the questions were answered.'

'They were.'

'I see that now.' Eloise bowed her head.

Da Silva looked amused, as if she detected something false in Eloise's tone.

'Barrel of energy,' she said, and walked away.

THIRTEEN

'I couldn't even see who was in the bus stop and it came to me: The girl in the bus stop is crying.'

'Spooky,' the Sparkler said.

'The information just arrived of the blue. And so I walk past and there she is, sobbing away.'

'ESP.'

'Actually, life's usually the complete opposite. Mostly you have facts in front of you, staring you in the face, and you can't work them out.'

Gulls cried outside. There was the sound of steady crunching. The Sparkler and Silvio were eating popcorn while watching a *Soon and Starfish* cartoon, the girl lying along the top of the sofa, the dog lounging on the cushions. Eloise was in the kitchen, fixing herself a drink.

She looked over at her niece's comically skinny legs, made slimmer by a pair of over-large sneakers. And the girl looked up and met her eye, with a steady gaze. Rachel Margery Hay Hillman: she was a powerful child. Eloise had a photo album of her niece in her head; she was vital, she was like electricity. The Sparkler running, or dancing around in the rain, or out on the dry peninsula, watching the toe toe go up in flames . . .

'I promised Carina I'd cook something healthy. So I got sushi.'

'Cool.'

The details of the evening had been worked out. It being a school night, the Sparkler would be picked up by Carina later in the evening, but Silvio had arrived with luggage, because he was going to sleep over. Eloise had unpacked his bed, also his blanket, bone, leash, chew toys, and sack of biscuits. There was a list of instructions on his routine: hydration, feeding, walks, shits.

'No fires,' Carina said, and Eloise had promised.

'So, after the news, we'll take him over to the park and then have our sushi and then you can watch your film, okay?'

Eloise squeezed in beside Silvio on the sofa. She was unsure how it was going to go with him. What did he do most of the time? Just lie around? Did he need to be talked to, entertained? He was a disturbing presence, too intelligent to be ignored.

Soon and Starfish ended. They switched to the news: Mariel Hartfield and Jack Anthony wore matching colours, her jacket, his tie. They shared an upbeat moment over a quirky item, then their expressions went solemn; he introduced a piece on an African famine and warned: Some scenes may disturb.

Now politics, Jack Dance, answering questions in the House. Yes, he was the minister in charge of security services. No, he had not known the GCSB was spying illegally on Kurt Hartmann. If the Opposition had proof, they should produce it. Put up or shut up. To a question from Opposition leader Bradley Kirk on unemployment, Satan Dance responded with a taunt: he wasn't surprised Mr Kirk was worried about unemployment, as his own job security was shaky.

Then a live cross to political editor Sarah Lane, and reports that Justice Minister Ed Miles was doing the numbers, in the hope of unseating Jack Dance.

'The polls, Mariel, are ringing alarm bells for the National Party. If the party's and Dance's personal ratings don't improve, we may start to see a serious push for change. Former prime minister Sir David Hallwright arrived in Auckland this week, and there has been speculation on several blogs that Sir David will meet with Ed Miles and his supporters.'

Ed Miles, caught on camera emerging from a lift, said, 'I have no leadership ambitions at this stage. I'm not even thinking about the question at this point. As I stand here now, I unequivocally support my leader, Jack Dance.'

Mariel Hartfield thanked Sarah Lane and the bulletin moved on: crime, celebrity gossip, international news, crime, unusual weather events around the globe, the drought, traffic, crime. And then the Doormat, with her spiel and her rows of little suns.

Eloise herded niece and dog out into the hot evening air. *The girl in the bus stop is crying.* Information had come unbidden, out of thin air — but it was useless information. Layers of the world were hidden from her. She kept going around it: Arthur had been interested in a missing woman, in Simon Lampton, who was a friend of David Hallwright, and in Colin Cahane and Ed Miles, who, back then, were Hallwright's Deputy Prime Minister and Minister of Police. What was Arthur's angle?

As they walked, the Sparkler outlined Silvio's routines. They discussed where they should put his bed, Eloise eventually settling for the bottom of the stairs. From there he could sound a warning and she could hole up in her room upstairs with the phone.

'I might get my own dog, see. So I thought I'd try out Silvio.'

'Mum said you could move in with us if you wanted.'

'Did she say that? Really?' Eloise looked away, more touched than she wanted to admit.

They were standing on the edge of the dog park. 'It'd be great to live with you. But I love the house and the peninsula. I'm going to have to move, but I don't want to.'

They ate sushi. Eloise drank chardonnay and proved herself useless with homework, with maths and science. A studious silence: the Sparkler bent over her spelling book, mouthing the words *Because Through Harmony Bright*, while Eloise tried to concentrate on her book.

The Sparkler finished her homework and moved on to her treat: a movie about teenage vampires.

Eloise sipped and frowned down at the page. She was nearly through *The Great Gatsby*.

> *He must have looked up at an unfamiliar sky through frightening leaves and shivered as he found what a grotesque thing a rose is and how raw the sunlight was upon the scarcely created grass. A new world, material without being real, where poor ghosts, breathing dreams like air, drifted fortuitously about . . . like that ashen, fantastic figure gliding toward him through the amorphous trees.*

What a grotesque thing a rose is. It was true. Not just the thorns but the soft, fleshy folds, as grotesque as ponga stems covered with hairs, their fronds curled like ears. And what were trees but growths erupting out of the land? But look at the peninsula, how beautiful it was.

Her hands flew to her ears as Silvio erupted in a shocking explosion of barks, and half a glass of chardonnay shot across the carpet.

On her knees mopping with a napkin, she said, 'God! If he does that in the night I'll have a heart attack.'

'There's someone at the front door,' her niece said, without taking her eyes off the screen.

Eloise went silently to the hall and looked through the peephole. Relief: it was Nick, wearing a plaid shirt and jeans, holding a shopping bag. How rugged, how nice he looked. But he raised his hand — and waved. She drew back from the peephole, disconcerted.

She opened the door. 'How did you know I was looking?'

'Hi. I don't know. I heard you, I suppose. How are you?' He came in. There was a smell of cut grass, of the lemon-scented verbena bush that grew along the edge of the property.

He held out the shopping bag. 'Apples.'

She took the apples, thanked him. 'I'm looking after my niece. You want a drink?'

Turning, they bumped against each other. Eloise's scalp prickled.

Out on the deck, so as not to interrupt the movie, she poured him wine, eyeing his brown hands. So suntanned and capable.

She took a recklessly large sip of wine. 'I did something unusual today.'

'What was that then?'

'I visited the police.'

He didn't say anything.

She waited and then said into the silence, 'It was probably a bad idea.'

Still he didn't say anything.

'It was partly because of what you said, about it being good to confront the past. I realised that when my . . . when Arthur died, I didn't ask any questions. I just accepted what I was told. So I wanted to go back and ask about it.'

He leaned back in his chair. 'But it was a bad idea, you said? I suppose they fobbed you off.'

'No, that's what made me nervous. They didn't. They seemed to want me to hang around. I wished I hadn't gone there.'

'They thought you were going to confess. It was me, officer. I pushed him.'

Eloise didn't say anything.

'Sorry, that was a stupid thing to say.' He reached over and touched her arm.

'No, it's fine. They probably did think something like that. I should've let sleeping dogs lie.'

'I wouldn't worry. They'll be super busy, overworked. They won't want to bother with a closed file.'

'I suppose.'

Nick looked away over the estuary, as though thinking about something else. Birds flew over, high and late. In the distance a gull was screaming.

The way he'd brushed past her in the hall. Now he seemed distracted, only half-listening. She said, 'There was some mention of politicians.'

Silence. Nick suppressed a yawn and rubbed his face.

'Past and current ones,' she added.

Now he looked at the backs of his hands and said lazily, 'What kind of mention?'

'Arthur was interested in David Hallwright's close circle when Hallwright was PM. Apparently he contacted one of them not long before he died.'

'Contacted who?'

Eloise hesitated. 'One of them.'

'How do you know?'

'It's in the file.'

'Arthur never told you?'

'No.'

'Is there anything else in the file?'

'I don't know. They didn't show me.'

'So you're not much further on. Unless you've got some other information.'

Eloise looked away.

Nick said, 'Did Arthur leave any clues?'

'Well, there is something . . .'

His eyes were on her, but now they heard Silvio making a racket and the Sparkler's voice, and Carina appeared in the doorway.

Nick stood up. 'I'd better get going. Things to do.'

Eloise made herself look neutral.

He nodded to Carina and left by way of the deck, crossing the lawn past the charred toe toe stump.

Carina watched him go. 'Did I interrupt?'

'No, he's got things to do.'

'He's sort of . . .'

'What?'

'I don't know.' Carina frowned. 'Nimble, shadowy.'

'Why shadowy?'

'I don't know. Because he's so nimble.'

'Right. Thanks for that, genius. How useful. Want a drink?'

'No, school night. Well, actually, the movie's still going.' She sat down, and Eloise got her a glass.

'I did something today. I went to the police.'

'What police? Why?'

'CIB homicide. I wanted to ask about Arthur.'

'But, you know what happened.'

Eloise stared at the estuary. How much had she just told Nick? Too much? She turned to her sister. 'I've been worrying about it all afternoon.'

'Worrying about what?'

'Okay. Arthur died and I accepted what they said. But it doesn't seem enough of an explanation, that he was stoned on sleeping pills, walked out of the flat and fell down a retaining wall.'

'It was a freak accident, sure.'

'When he died, Arthur was interested in the Hallwrights. He wanted to write about a National Party prime minister. He'd researched Hallwright's inner circle, and before he died he contacted Hallwright's best friend, Simon Lampton, who was the doctor who adopted Roza Hallwright's baby. He rang him twice.'

'Did you know he'd done that?'

'No. The police told me today. Listen, in Arthur's file, the one I took from the flat, there's a photo of a girl with the name "Mereana" written on the back. I don't know who she is. And in the police file there's a picture of a note in Arthur's handwriting that says Simon Lampton forward slash Mereana Kostas. When I asked who Mereana Kostas is, the police said she's a missing person. She disappeared from Auckland years ago. So Arthur's put together the name of Hallwright's friend Lampton, and a missing woman. And he had a photo of the missing person — or at least of a girl called Mereana. Which isn't a common name. He's rung up Lampton twice and been given the brush-off. Then he died.'

'He didn't tell you anything?'

'He was hyperactive, remember, always thinking up some new scheme. I couldn't keep up. I wanted him to slow down and focus. I nagged a bit — I think he deliberately stopped telling me what he was up to.'

Carina reached into her bag, brought out a single bent cigarette and lit it.

'Rations,' she said. 'You're thinking about all this now because Sean's left and you're out here by yourself.'

'Maybe.'

'Come and stay with us for a while. We'd love to have you. Honestly.'

Eloise refilled her glass. 'I keep dreaming about Andrew Newgate.'

'Come and stay. Tonight. I mean it.'

Focus. Concentrate. 'Carina, think about it. Arthur's death was unexplained. It had to be investigated. Right? So the police must have looked into it: Lampton, the missing woman, Arthur's death, and asked themselves whether any of it was connected.'

'I suppose.'

'So that means, at the very least, there was a police inquiry that involved Hallwright's circle, of which parts are unexplained. The missing woman is still missing. And we don't know why Arthur put her name with Simon Lampton.'

'Well . . .'

Eloise said, 'The detective told me Lampton was staying at the Hallwrights' summer residence when Arthur contacted him. It was the holidays when Arthur died, remember. Arthur's notes say that there were other people at the residence, too, at the same time.' She tipped up her glass. 'Want to know who?'

'Who?'

'Ed Miles. He was police minister back then.'

'How did Arthur know that?'

'He would have stalked them, like any journalist. He's got a phone number for a housekeeper with a Chinese name. Maybe she was his source. The finance minister was there too — Colin Cahane. Some of it would have been common knowledge. Hallwright was our first "celebrity PM", remember. There were all those magazine stories about what he was doing.'

Carina said, 'So at some point Ed Miles, Hallwright, old Cock Cahane and this Lampton are all at Rotokauri and Arthur phones Lampton twice, we don't know why.'

'What if he was asking about the missing woman?'

'Did Hallwright and co know Arthur rang Lampton?'

'No idea.'

Carina ground the cigarette out on the rail. She bit her fingernail. 'Miles and Hallwright.'

'So if there was something to find out . . .'

'I wonder why the police *told* you about Arthur ringing Lampton. They're usually so cagey.'

'It's a closed file, all explained. They don't care. Maybe they assumed I knew.'

'Or, they did it on purpose because they don't mind stirring things up again.' Carina stood up. 'I think you should come and stay with us. You're making yourself anxious. Ghost stories.'

Eloise looked out over the estuary. 'I've tried to understand what Arthur was doing. He wanted to write a screenplay, something fictional, but the people he was making notes about are real. I suppose he was going to research them — he talked about getting into their world — and then fictionalise them. Base fiction on them.'

'He did sort of mix up truth and fiction, if you think of that play he wrote. The comic satirical one. Wasn't there a real politician in it?'

Eloise sat up. 'There's something else. It says in his notes that Roza Hallwright is a recovered alcoholic and drug user.'

'How did he know that?'

'Maybe the housekeeper told him.'

'I suppose it could be true . . .'

All the wine seemed to be gone. Eloise looked at her empty glass and said, 'Layers of the world have been hidden from me.'

'What? You're getting drunk again. Let's go inside. I'll make you a cup of tea.'

Eloise looked up at her. 'Can we do one thing? Can we hide Arthur's file somewhere else?'

'It's fine at my house.'

'But you're my sister. It's an obvious place to look.'

'Who's looking? Come on. I'll make you a coffee.'

'Carina, wait. I think someone's been getting into this house.'

'Have you been burgled?'

'No. Someone's been getting in, looking around.'

'Then you have to ring the cops. And you're definitely coming to our place.'

'I've got Silvio.'

'But that's temporary. You can't have him. Much as I'd love it, the Sparkler won't allow it.'

'Can't you just hide Arthur's file somewhere no one will look? Please. You're right, I have made myself anxious. I shouldn't have gone to the police.'

'Why not?'

'What if someone hears I've been asking?'

'Why would it matter?'

'I'd come over and move it myself, but someone might see me doing it.'

'Someone might *see* you? Come on. You *definitely* need to sober up.'

'We're making a programme on Kurt Hartmann. Scott says we might be under surveillance.'

'Oh, rubbish.'

She allowed herself to be hustled inside by Carina, who now turned off the television, quelled the Sparkler's protests, put on the kettle and inspected Eloise's kitchen.

She turned, hands on hips. 'There's no food!'

'I bought bread and cheese,' Eloise said vaguely. Although, when was that? Last week?

'Right. I'll make you a sandwich.'

'Just another thimble of wine would be fine,' Eloise said. She rested her hand on Silvio's hot head.

Carina moved swiftly around the kitchen. 'Here, eat this. And no more wine.'

Eloise looked at the sandwich without enthusiasm.

Carina said, 'Do you insist on staying here tonight?'

'Yes.'

'Then eat the sandwich and don't drink any more, or I'm not leaving Silvio with you. I'm not having you minding him if you're off your face.'

'Okay. Sorry.'

Eloise started eating, and found it good. Silvio leapt up and settled himself on her legs. Carina brought her a cup of tea.

She sighed. 'This is nice. How about you two stay the night? Or move in. Bring Giles, bring Silvio.'

The Sparkler had her face pressed to the ranch slider. 'I saw Nick down there,' she said.

They looked out at the dark, listening.

Carina glanced at Eloise, who said quietly, after a pause, 'Please. Move the thing?'

'All *right*,' Carina said. She looked down at Eloise, thinking. 'When we go, you won't go out will you? Lock up and go to bed.'

'I will,' Eloise lied.

She stood at the back door, airing Silvio. The darkness had not made it any cooler. Above the door the lamp was crawling with insects. Silvio drank from his water bowl and snuffled his way out to the edge of the light. She would station him in his bed before locking him in and crossing the lawn to Nick's.

Silvio went still, sniffing in the direction of the dog park. He hurled himself forward, his barks lifting him off his front feet.

After the barking, silence. The spears of the flax bushes clacked and sighed in the hot wind.

'What are you barking at? What are you raving on about? Good boy.'

She pulled him inside, and led him to his tartan bean bag at the bottom of the stairs. To her relief he turned a few times and settled down without complaint.

Eloise contemplated the dog, curled peacefully in his bed. She looked out at the dark beyond the glass. Carina's words: *You're tired. Don't drink any more. Just go to bed.*

Which version of the night was preferable? It made her dizzy and hot and thirsty all at once, trying to decide.

FOURTEEN

'Planes,' Klaudia said. 'I've been hearing too much about planes. This one crashing, that one plunging to the earth.' She grimaced.

'Oh?' Eloise waited.

'A colleague has been researching pilots who deliberately crash. I said to him, Don't forget, it's not just suicide, it's mass murder.'

Eloise thought about it. She said politely, 'I suppose some are political, where they shout God is Great and point the thing at the ground, and others are just, as it were, going postal. A way of getting back at their employer. Since it ruins business for the airline.'

'It's certainly a form of workplace violence,' Klaudia said.

Silence.

Klaudia shook her head. 'They're trained to look after their passengers, and then they turn around and kill them. It's like these men who decide to kill themselves in front of their partners. Then they get the idea, why should I be the only one to suffer, and they kill the partner, too.'

Eloise looked at her, nervous. Was she angry? There was another silence. Klaudia looked as if she were waiting for comment.

To fill the silence Eloise said, 'The pilots. They're stressed but they can't complain about it, in case they get fired. Um, maybe they're sick of all those patients they're saddled with. Having to look after their safety while no one's looking after *them*.'

'Patients, Eloise?'

'Sorry, I meant passengers!'

Klaudia smiled.

'Anyway, Eloise. How have you been?'

'Oh, I don't know.'

Klaudia's gaze seemed to harden. 'You don't know?'

Eloise quailed slightly. 'Sorry. Sometimes I wish I'd got pregnant.'

'Even though your husband has now gone?'

'Especially now. He could have left me with something.'

'You have the house.'

'But I have to move out. Soon. Once he's got himself organised, I'll be served with papers.'

'Is he delaying sorting out your affairs?'

'No.'

'Are you?'

'I'm just going from day to day.'

'Do you wish for reconciliation with him?'

'I don't think that's likely.'

'But you have been thinking about children,' Klaudia said coolly.

'Anita O'Keefe doesn't think she needs a man.'

'Ah, the cabinet minister?'

'She's just gone ahead and done it.'

'Indeed.'

'I think the PM's the father.'

'Really. How does that make you feel?'

'Not sure. Should we applaud his virility? Sympathise with his plight? Did he think she'd go through with the pregnancy? Does his wife suspect? How are they going to play it when the baby's born? Will it look like a tiny Satan? Should they just come clean and make an announcement?'

'What makes you think it is Mr Dance's child?'

'Facebook and Twitter. For a long time he and O'Keefe were following each other round the country. And the way he used to look at her, and now doesn't.'

'Not very strong evidence.'

'Well, everyone's playing the same guessing game.'

Silence. The image of Prime Minister Dance and O'Keefe together. She with her glossy hair and white teeth, he with his sports jackets, his chinos, his smooth, ageing skin.

'But back to you . . .'

Eloise frowned. 'I was in the supermarket car park yesterday and I saw it again. The wolf. It's huge and shaggy and it sits in the back of the SUV and howls.'

'You have mentioned this wolf before. Interesting. But to return to earlier issues. We should focus . . .'

'Sorry, Klaudia. I'm having trouble focusing.'

Eloise's eyes were on the summer garden, shafts of light angling through the leaves. Klaudia's French doors stood open and the gardener was moving along the fenceline, using a spray on the plants. The fine mist whirled in the air, creating a rainbow.

'You mentioned you went to your neighbour's house at night?'

'He'd left a bit abruptly, earlier in the evening. I wanted . . . I went onto his deck but his house was dark. I knocked and there was no answer. I was going to leave . . .'

Eloise paused to decide how honest she was going to be.

'I discovered . . . It became obvious that . . . Well, I somehow found that the glass door was unlocked. I opened it and called. I heard a sound in the kitchen and there was a light back there, so I called out again, and went into the room . . .'

'Go on.'

'I was standing in the dark. A voice said my name. Eloise.'

Klaudia tapped her pen on the pad.

'A voice?'

'It wasn't Nick.'

'Oh?'

'I ran back to the house and locked myself in. I sat downstairs with the dog for a long time. I had a few drinks then I went to bed.'

'It wasn't your neighbour. Whose voice was it?'

'A man's. I couldn't see. It was dark. All I know is it wasn't Nick.'

'Was it someone else who lives in the house?'

'Nick lives alone. I met him the next morning on the way to the bus stop. He was walking back from the shops. I didn't want to admit I'd gone inside his house. I said I'd knocked on the door but it was all dark and there was no answer. He said . . .'

Klaudia was writing on her pad, nodding.

'He said he'd gone to bed early, that he was asleep in bed, upstairs.'

'So . . . whose voice?'

'I don't know.'

Klaudia paused. Her smile was gentle. 'Perhaps a friend of his, staying.'

'Who knew my name.'

'Nick may have pointed you out, from a distance.'

'I suppose.'

Klaudia allowed another pause to play out. 'Or, do you think this voice was in your head?'

'No.'

'You had been drinking.'

Eloise's mouth was dry. 'Drinking doesn't make you hear voices.'

Klaudia shuffled some pages, checked. 'You've had migraines recently. With visual distortions.'

'I never heard of a migraine making you hear things.'

Klaudia folded her arms. 'It's rare, but it's possible.'

'Really?'

'Sure.'

'But I didn't have a migraine that night.' Eloise stared at the photo of the soulful brown dog on Klaudia's desk. 'Or did I? I was so tired.'

'Tired and a bit drunk, perhaps?'

'But no migraine.'

In the garden the cicadas made their bright wall of sound. The sound shook the air, it was silver, a waterfall — and what lay behind the falling curtain of noise? A migraine made brightness and then the shimmer parted and you saw the blackness that lay beyond.

Eloise said, 'It was Arthur's voice.'

'Your partner who died? You heard him speak to you?'

Klaudia turned her head on one side, her smile distant, as if she were trying to hear something curious and quaint, from a long way off.

'No. Only joking.'

'How did this voice make you feel?' Klaudia said.

Arthur's back deck, the view across the mountainside, the dry paddock sloping up to the crater of the volcanic cone. A summer morning, iron light, bees in the grass, sun shining on a silver water bowl left for the cat. Arthur, crossing the deck, kicks the bowl and the surface shimmers and the light breaks and splinters. Standing at the door is a figure, and Arthur follows, into the cool, dark interior of the flat, and into nothingness; Arthur will be seen again but nothing of Arthur will remain, only the vulnerable head slicked with blood, the broken triangle of skull, the hand with fingers lightly curled, the thin ankle and loose, boyish sock.

'Klaudia, do you believe in ESP?'

'Psychic stuff? No.'

'If I told you I was walking towards a walled bus shelter — no view of who was inside it — and before I got to it the information came to me: The girl in the bus stop is crying. When I reached it, there *was* a girl in there, and she was crying. What would you say? ESP?'

Klaudia's gaze was steady, bright, sharp. After a moment she said, 'I would guess you had seen or heard something prior to reaching the bus shelter that gave you a clue.'

'So it's not ESP. It's that you've read the signs.'

'Sure. Picked something up. Maybe subconsciously.'

Towing the suitcase up the hot street. Something is wrong. There are people with bulky notebooks tucked under their arms; a little way off a man, wearing a white boiler suit and a shower cap, stands at the edge of the retaining wall, talking to someone below. A woman with odd eyes stands at Arthur's door and speaks strange words: 'A man has been found dead.'

They walk down a concrete staircase, past a lemon tree and a back door. He looks thin and young lying there, surrounded by the living. Look at the trouble he's got himself into, the heat he's brought down. Tough cops, the intent forensic team, the busy photographer. *Look what you've gone and done.* Should she admit it's really him? This is a question she considers for a moment in the stalled silence, as if it's possible that Arthur could get away with this, could quietly rise from the concrete and stealthily slip away, leaving the puzzle of his body behind. Can I help him escape? If we play this right . . .

Arthur's flat that morning. A rectangle of sunlight on the kitchen bench, light seething on the curved flank of the kettle, a fly braining itself against the glass, dying for the unreachable blue beyond. The policewoman, who is full of authority despite her girl combat boots and her unruly teenage hair, orders Eloise to sit down, but Eloise goes to the back door and walks out onto the concrete deck. There are men and women on the hillside, searching in the grass. Colours have turned candyish and surreal; seams have opened in the sky which is not blue any more but 'blue', just as Arthur is not himself any more but has suffered a violent change. He is not somebody. He is 'the body'. *Where are you? Come back.* She remembers: a circular line of purple shading the delicate skin below his eye. She remembers: a gash in his cheek, in the shape of a Y.

Look what you've gone and done. She let on, down there at the bottom of the retaining wall. She cracked, grassed, admitted it straight away. It's him. Yes, that's Arthur Weeks.

If the very air turned toy-coloured and surreal . . .

If the morning coloured everything it touched . . .

'Why do you mention ESP?' Klaudia said.

Eloise watched the spray falling onto the shining grass. 'Layers of the world have been hidden from me.'

'Can you explain?'

The bees, the hot paddock, the mountainside. Arthur crossed the deck and entered the cool dark hall.

If that morning coloured everything it touched, if it splashed an indelible stain . . . Was there someone else it touched?

Eloise was on a flight from Sydney when it happened. So how could the information come to her?

There was someone in the flat with Arthur on the morning he died.

FIFTEEN

'Have you noticed a man, tall with black hair and a tattoo on the back of his hand?'

Scott said into the mirror, 'Tattoo of what?'

'A dragonfly.'

'No. Why?'

'I saw him this morning.'

Scott smoothed gel into his hair, wiped his hands, turned. 'Nice dress. What do you think of this suit? It's Ronald's new range. Russet, earth tones, looking ahead to autumn.'

'Hint of dead leaf. Very nice.'

'The cloth — Ronald had to go to the ends of the earth. It's a one-off. Limited edition. It's light as air. You feel like you're naked.'

'Mm. Great.'

'See the lining?' He opened the jacket.

'Silken. Quite a riot of colours.'

Scott checked his watch. 'Let's go.'

They walked through the busy corridors of Q Wing to reception, where Thee was waiting, frowning down at her cell phone. Scott swooped, embraced, and held her at arm's length, blinking.

'Look at *you*. My wife. Goodness me.' He drew her close to the reception desk. 'Just look,' he said, running his hand, palm up, along the contours of his wife.

Thee rolled her eyes.

'Wow,' Hine said. 'Want your cab now?'

'Hi, Hine,' said Thee. 'Hi, Eloise.'

'Perfection,' Scott said. His phone beeped. 'A feast for . . . Roysmith. Hi, Chad.'

Eloise and Thee went ahead.

'Iris was up all night, puking,' Thee said. She rummaged in her bag.

'Oh?'

'She's got some bug. Now I'm feeling a bit delicate, too. But I had to come, I'm taking photos.' She had her big camera slung over her shoulder.

Scott bounced down the steps. 'That was Loafer.' He winked. 'With *demands*. Mr Hartmann wants previews, discussions, editorial control. Sure. Like hell. Where's the cab? Here it is. Off we go. I didn't say to him, our emails have been quite slow lately. Is that because your boss has hacked his way in there? Getting a preview at his leisure?'

They rode through town.

'Put the window down,' Thee said, her hand over her mouth. They waited. She sighed. 'No, it's passed.'

'My poor darling.'

Eloise looked out at the crawling traffic. 'My email and internet at home is really slow now.'

'Assume everything's being read. Emails, Facebook, texts.'

'Right. No fat jokes.'

'From now on it's either encryption or by hand. Face to face. And your iPhone's a bloody bug, don't forget. It's a listening device. If you want privacy, put it in the fridge.'

'Window!'

They waited.

'Poor love.'

Thee slumped back in her seat. Her face had a faintly yellow sheen. 'God,' she said in a weak voice.

'Here we are, quite a crowd already. By the way, E, I got a tip-off: management's assembling a panel of experts to review the shocks. And the great thing is Selena quit today. She's going to sue . . .'

They threaded through the crowd outside the theatre, Scott and Thee pausing at the entrance for a photographer. They were early. Scott made his way, was laughingly stopped, nabbed, buttonholed: he was from TV, everyone wanted to be close.

Eloise and Thee peeled off, and found seats in the bar.

'How's Sean?' Thee pressed her glass to her forehead. The ice cubes gave off tiny cracks.

'He's . . . working.'

'I haven't seen him for a while.'

Eloise looked away. It was such a burden. It wasn't easy to lie to Thee: Thee with her sharp cheekbones, her wide mouth and clever eyes. Her permanent expression of irony and exasperated humour. Apart from Carina and Scott, Thee was Eloise's favourite person. Like Carina, Thee had opinions, got into arguments, fearlessly said her piece. Afterwards she shrugged her shoulders, despaired, laughed, wound her dark hair into a bun and secured it with a chopstick, pushed up her sleeves, waded into whatever mess her children had created. She didn't have Eloise's problem, which was increasingly (it seemed) the inability to see people clearly. Carina and Thee: they saw things straight away.

Thee was forthright and frank; Scott was cautious and circumspect — he was, despite his admiration for Pilger, studiously balanced. (Because he was on TV.) He was devoted to his wife, and admired her, and whatever she said went. 'Ask Thee,' he'd say. 'No, Thee's the brains.'

'I used to think I was observant,' Eloise said.

'I'm sure you are.'

'Well, I didn't notice anything was wrong. And now . . . Sean and I, we've separated. I'm going to have to sell the house, leave the peninsula.'

'Oh, God, sorry.'

'Thanks. It's not so bad. I'm enjoying the freedom really. The Me time.'

Thee fanned herself with a programme. 'He's mad. She's a complete drip.'

'Who?'

'Danni Whatsername. Wannabe actress, long chin. She's into self-help seminars.'

'How d'you know about her?'

'Not sure. Just a guess.'

'A guess. Right. I suppose everyone knows.'

'Well, not *everyone*.'

Eloise wished for a second large glass of chardonnay, followed by a tankard of gin and tonic. Topped up with a mountain of Valium.

'Unbelievable,' she said.

'I'm really sorry.'

'What else do you know?'

'Nothing. Just that she was on some kids' TV programme once, and looks like a Barbie doll.'

'A complete drip, you said?'

'Sort of New Ageish. Humourlessly into self-help.'

'Syrupy and cloying,' Eloise suggested.

'Looks like a mite or poppet in a painting on a motel wall. Big eyes, long eyelashes, babydoll fringe.'

They sat back, thinking about this.

'Quite a problem then, isn't she,' Eloise said eventually.

Thee sat up. 'Ah, forget Sean. He'll be regretting it already. We need to find you someone new.'

'There you are,' Scott said, emerging from the crush. 'How are you, my love?'

'Moderately better thanks. We're just talking about Sean.'

'Oh. Sorry!'

Eloise threw up her hands. 'God, so you know, too, do you? You could have *said*.'

'Everyone— Anyway, let me just get a beer. Another wine, E?'

He headed for the bar. The crowd parted around him, approving and soft-eyed.

Eloise said dully, 'It must be weird being stared at all the time.'

'He used to find it strange. We both did, seeing him on billboards, his face driving by on buses.'

'He's frighteningly popular.'

'Anyway, Eloise, are you living by yourself? Is it okay?'

'It's fine. Great. Loving the freedom. You don't have to cook. The . . . uh . . . spontaneity. No planning. Long rambling walks. Nature and that.'

'Oh, good,' Thee said.

'I'm trying out seeing a shrink, too.'

Scott emerged — was reluctantly released by the crowd. Thee pointed at him. 'His sister's a clinical psychologist.'

Eloise reached for (snatched) her glass of wine and said intently to Scott, 'You were talking about Pilger and balance the other night. So I started thinking about balance with the shrink. When your sister's treating a patient, how does she know she's getting a balanced report? What if it's false, and she ends up basing her assumptions on lies?'

'She works to sort out the distortions,' Scott said.

'I went to a shrink once,' Thee said. 'I felt I was telling him a series of stories. He wanted to talk about my childhood, and I wouldn't do that.'

'I suppose she reads between the lines,' Scott went on. 'She gets the patient to call a spade a spade.'

Eloise said, 'At the beginning my main problem was I felt like a bore at a party. After a whole hour talking about myself, I went away feeling incredibly sorry for the shrink.'

'But has it helped?'

'I don't know. I was thinking about this when we were talking about Pilger. The therapist's office has glass doors onto a garden, right. One day I was talking and I looked out and saw a rat. First it balanced on a stick, then it started walking around on the bricks outside. I didn't even pause. I carried on talking, but at the same time I was deciding what to do about the rat, whether I should I mention it. I decided no, it wasn't relevant.'

Scott let out a big laugh. People glanced over with tender, indulgent smiles.

'I edited out the rat,' Eloise said. 'So if I was editing, could I say there was balance?'

'You don't have to discuss everything,' Thee said. 'You can leave out the odd rat.'

'I wanted to mention the rat in the next session. But I wondered whether it would be rude. To say, actually, the whole time I was talking to you, I was looking at a rat.'

'And not telling you about it,' Scott said.

'Secretly looking at a rat,' Thee said.

'Would it seem somehow hostile?' Eloise said. 'Maybe she'd think, How sly to spring this rat on me now!'

Thee rattled the ice in her glass, 'She'd think you were making up the rat.'

'But to what end?'

'To raise your concerns about balance.'

'What's balanced about Pilger,' Scott said, 'is that he calls a spade a spade.'

'He confronts the elephant in the room.'

'He would have mentioned the rat.'

'Or would he have edited out the rat as irrelevant? Because he's only concerned with truth.'

'The rat was true. It was real.'

'But it wasn't relevant to the truth you were discussing.'

'Pilger would certainly have *smelled* a rat.'

Eloise said, 'Anyway, this shrink. I can't work out how I feel about her. It's possible I find her incredibly frightening. The other day she started talking about pilots who deliberately crash their planes. She sort of clenched her fists and said, They're entrusted with people's safety. And they turn round and kill them. So I said, Maybe they feel burdened by all those patients they've been saddled with. All that pressure to perform, and no one caring about *them*.'

'Patients?' Thee said.

'Exactly. I said patients when I meant passengers!'

'Maybe I should go to a shrink,' Scott said. 'The pressures of fame . . .'

'Darling, you love fame. You're made for fame.'

Eloise said, 'Have you read *The Information* by Martin Amis? The hero writes a novel; agents, publishers, editors enthusiastically set to work reading it, but as soon as they get to about page nine they can't go on. One has a stroke, another has a catastrophic migraine, another has a breakdown. The novel is simply . . . unreadable.'

'Relevance?' Scott said.

'I fear I am that novel.'

Scott laughed and the crowd turned and stole a look, and warmly smiled. A group of women edged nearer to them, beaming secretively, as though contemplating a pile of gold.

'You should run for office,' Eloise said.

Thee said, 'Mr Popular. It reminds me of another novel actually — *The Swimming Pool Library*, where the gay guys are crowded in the showers at the gym, and when one gets a hard-on it creates a wave of hard-ons in response.'

'What on earth do you mean?' Scott said, taking her hand with a fond glare, a little mime of reproach. He eyed the women, who eyed him back.

'You laugh, they laugh.'

'You're a snake charmer.'

But Scott's expression altered. He lowered his voice, 'Here's a real snake charmer for you, ladies.'

And the crowd followed his gaze . . .

There was a pause, and then a rapid shifting and regrouping, women craned and stood on tip-toe, there was some subtle shoving, an excited laugh among the group standing near.

'She's really tall. Is she taller than him?'

'He looks the same. Only a bit more grey.'

'Look at her dress.'

'Could she be six feet tall?'

'They don't pay tax. They keep their money offshore.'

'She's had a boob job. A facelift. A derma-peel. She's had *work*.'

'You know it when you see it.'

Eloise stood; she, too, craned to see. The Hallwrights were heading for the entrance to the stalls, the crowd parting ahead of them. He walked with a slight limp, she had a hand on his arm. They looked the same only more so: they used to look like money, now they looked like more money. Both tall, expensively dressed, she in a tight-fitting dress, he in a costly suit, they moved with stately slowness through the crowd. The ex-PM and the kids' book writer . . . Which one was meant to be the brains?

'Which one's the brains?'

'Her.'

'Him.'

'Her.'

'They're good-looking.'

'That suit,' Scott said, 'is definitely one of Ronald's.'

'I hope it's not the same. One of you would have to go home.'

'My wife mocks me,' Scott said.

'Christ, someone has to. Let's go in.'

The bells had started to ring.

'We'll try and catch them after,' Scott said. 'Come on.' He drew their arms through his and blinked, and said, 'Look how lucky I am, with the two most beautiful women in the room.'

'Oh shut up, Scott.'

'The two cleverest—'

'Look, is that the madwoman who stalked Jack Anthony?'

'No! Is she wearing an electronic ankle bracelet?'

'She's got pants on. Let's get closer.'

'The cleverest and most beautiful—'

'Um, *The Marriage of Figaro*. There's Figaro and Susanna and the Countess — but what happens in it again?'

'Here, read the programme.'

Arm in arm, they followed the Hallwrights in a procession towards the auditorium. A crush developed at the door and they slowed, waited, Eloise's mind wandering in a haze of wine and pleasure: Scott's random jokes, Thee's laugh, Scott's arm holding her, the heat of bodies. *See, Arthur, we're dogs. We're pack animals. Wanting to be held close like this, hard up against the people we love.*

In the stalls there was shuffling along and making way and squinting at programmes, and a dicey moment when Thee leaned forward with a hand over her mouth, her eyes squeezed shut, and

Scott laid his big hand on her forehead and whispered, We can go home if you can't manage, and then the curtain went up and the day of madness, *la folle journée*, began in the household of Count Almaviva.

'I feel better actually,' Thee said, as they made their way out at the interval. 'It's good. Sitting in the dark with my eyes closed. Beautiful music. No bickering kids.'

Eloise was in two minds: the music was beautiful, Susanna's voice was sensational, but there was something about the Countess. . . She checked the programme. The singer, a visiting star, hailed originally from Lancashire. The voice, the face . . .

'The man next to me — his nose keeps whistling.'

'I've preordered drinks and snacks,' Scott said, ushering them forward. 'All taken care of.'

'Scott, can we swap after? So you have a turn with the nose-whistler.'

'Of course, love.'

'Do you think the Countess is singing in a Northern English accent?' Eloise said.

Thee frowned. 'Is that even possible?'

Eloise said vaguely, 'A sort of *eh oop* delivery. And the way she laughs dismissively, and combs her hair in quick movements with the ends of her fingers.'

Remember, Arthur? Next she'll be singing, I don't eat foreign muck. Oh no, chuck. Does it contain garlic?

'Anyway, who do you think's the father?'

'Minister O'Keefe? I reckon sperm donor. Cos she's a workaholic.'

'She's secretly gay. So, a gay friend.'

'Who needs to be *secretly* gay? No one's secretly gay these days.'

'Wasn't she a Mormon?'

'Can Mormons be gay?'

'She's not gay!'

'She's pretty hot.'

'Every time Bradley Kirk gets near her he looks misty.'

'So do they all.'

'Not any more. Now they look shifty.'

'Here comes trouble,' Scott boomed.

A change in atmosphere (one of the Sinister Doormat's high-pressure systems, approaching from the west) made the crowd turn, faces shining like a row of little suns. And the two television stars came together and collided, with soft kisses. Beyond, everywhere you looked, a constellation of shining eyes.

'Mariel, darling.'

'Hi, guys! Thee, you look amazing.'

They were used to this: talking as though no one was looking. And they were being doubly scrutinised, now that there were two television people on display. Mariel Hartfield was all smooth brown flesh and striking eyes: she was media glamour, fashion, money. She wore a parody of a tuxedo, with a tight, revealing white shirt. She was almost too thin yet sexily curvy, and her heels were wickedly high.

Eloise found herself next to Mariel's husband, Hamish Dark.

'Hi,' she said.

He was tall, lean and sarcastic, rumoured to be depressive. He was a journalist, but he didn't disguise his allegiance to the National Party; in fact he had a sideline as the MC at National Party functions. Eloise had seen him jogging in the Domain, fully clad in lycra, his teeth bared as if he were in an agony beyond the physical.

'Hello, *Eloise*.' His tone was knowing: he was too cool for all this.

Arthur would have had a *take* on Hamish and Mariel: he resents her fame, but also likes it. He's cleverer than she is, but she's more successful, because he's thin-skinned and she's not. Her lack of subtlety is her armour, his complexity predisposes him to the Black Dog.

Or something like that.

Hamish said, 'Amazing how everyone loves opera all of a sudden. Even ZB DJs. Even weather girls, celebrity chefs.'

'Well it's for child cancer, right.'

'Exactly. They turn up because it's a charity event. Not because they love Mozart.'

Eloise felt vaguely that this was kind of a redundant thing to say. Hamish Dark: keeping it real. Behind the pretension, with Hamish Dark. The master of the scathing quip, the guy who 'sees through things'. And here comes another brilliant statement of the obvious. She had a sudden yearning to say something earnest, impassioned (and therefore uncool). Sure, life is absurd. All is bullshit. Quite a few of us can see that. But what do you love, Hamish? Is there anything that you love? That's what'll save you from the Dog.

But what did she know? Hamish had a partner and kids; all she had was an empty stone house. Not exactly qualified to give advice, then. Who do I love — whom? Carina, the Sparkler, Scott and Thee. It's not a very long list. Well, you have to start somewhere . . .

The Sinister Doormat walked by in witchy red shoes, and winked.

And the bells rang, and they trooped back in.

After the hysterics and the high jinks, after the drama in the garden, after the celestial singing . . . Tinsel floated down onto the stage in jubilant celebration. The audience erupted in applause and eventually rose in a ragged wave to its feet; there were hoarse and ironic cries of bravo from the high-spirited invited guests, some of whom had whispered and checked their cell phones throughout.

Then they were filing along the seats and out into the foyer, most of the crowd surging away into the night, but others washing up against the bar, where a lively group was jostling for drinks: reward for having sat through that boring shit for so long, in a good cause.

'It's a good cause.'

'Mate, all for a good cause.'

'Starship. Kids' cancer. You've obviously got to do it.'

'You've got to give back.'

Eloise sipped the wine Scott had brought her and looked across at Thee, who'd got her second wind, and was talking intensely to Hamish Dark. Thee had agreed to take photos of the event. She took out her camera and moved around the room, lining up shots.

Beside her a group of women were discussing the performance.

'The costumes were amazing.'

'I know. And what an amazing turn-out.'

'Look, it's an amazing effort all round.'

'I'm amazed by it, to be honest.'

And here came Scott Roysmith, walking among his people. Beaming, frowning — the beam, then the frown. Shades, layers — he was known as a deep thinker. And then he was standing in front of her and saying, 'Eloise Hay, meet Sir David Hallwright.'

'Oh. God. The PM,' she said.

'Ex,' Hallwright said, smiling down, offering his hand. How tall he was. He had deep eyes, an angular face, a pink and gold complexion, blonde-grey hair.

'And Roza Hallwright.'

'Of *Soon* fame,' Eloise said — and blushed and laughed at her own brilliant statement of the obvious. The Hallwrights' smiles were warm as they paused, on the brink of turning and moving on. They smiled beautifully, they were all surface, opaque, beautifully unreadable.

Which one was the brains?

Him, Eloise thought. Those noticing, calculating eyes, the air of intelligence and control.

And then the Hallwrights were passing by, shaking hands, murmuring greetings. They reached Mariel Hartfield and stopped to talk, turning occasionally to the crowd, as if almost inviting them in.

The crowd frankly staring. David Hallwright put his hand on Mariel's arm. Roza Hallwright looked away, and her eye fell on Eloise, whose cheeks went hot again.

Maybe we're pack animals, and maybe a crowd is one animal, its nervous system linked by all the five senses . . .

Roza Hallwright and her glamour, its pixelated shimmer. Money and fame. What would Arthur have made of the Hallwrights, if he'd ever got to meet them? He wanted to know what lay beneath, beyond.

The Hallwrights moved on again. Now Mariel Hartfield walked away from the bar. She took out a cell phone, went to the plate-glass window and began to talk. She made her fingers into a claw and inspected her nails. She stood briefly on one leg, and adjusted her high-heeled shoe.

A man came and found a space to lean against the window near her. He was facing ahead, also talking into a phone. They were so absorbed in conversation they didn't notice each other. Look at that, Scott would say. What a paradox. The way technology connects us and yet keeps us apart. The phone traps us in our own little bubble, the crowd becomes a group of individuals, loses its sense of itself.

The man and woman, so close and yet so far apart. Behind them the black window, and the city spread out beyond, all the yellow windows stacked along the curve of the motorway and the cars flowing through the glossy dark, like a river of jewels.

SIXTEEN

It was evening. In the upstairs bedroom, the rays shining through the thin blind turned the room sepia. The blind stirred in the breeze; gulls cried on the roof; from along the peninsula, a distant radio sent out a tinny, reverberating pulse. Silvio lifted his head and listened, then rested his nose on his paws again.

Eloise had finished *The Great Gatsby*, and had now gone back to the book Arthur had given her: *The Chekhov Omnibus*. All the books she owned had been bought by Arthur, or belonged to him.

Arthur used to come over all scandalised: You haven't read any Dickens? What, *none*? No Balzac?

You and your Balzac. Damn your Balzac.

But there was this: even though she'd failed him (by not asking questions) she'd finally taken his advice. Not when he was alive — when he was alive she ignored his carping and stuck to TV box sets and movies — but after he was dead Eloise, for no apparent reason, went over to her parents' house, looked through their extensive library, and borrowed *Wuthering Heights*. She'd been making her way through the classics ever since.

Arthur said it was a mystery. How had the daughter of a bookworm managed to avoid the canon? Was it rebellion? It was something to ask Klaudia. She told Arthur (who laughed strangely) that the closest she'd got to a Brontë was a novel whose cover portrayed a muscular jock (dark, heavy-browed, lowering) leaning against a locker, while a blonde schoolgirl gazed up at him. It was called *Wuthering High.* 'Pretty Cathy's the star of her cheerleading team, and set to be prom queen! But a chance meeting at the ballpark with troubled track star Chip Heathcliff . . .'

'Listen,' she said to Silvio.

Andrei Kovrin, a master of arts, had exhausted himself, and had strained his nerves. He did not seek treatment, but casually, over a bottle of wine, he spoke to a friend who was a doctor; the latter advised him to spend the spring and summer in the country.

Silvio licked his paw with a slow, clopping sound.

So it was a mystery, her late arrival at books. But her mother's disdain for schoolteachers — 'Oooh, Sparkles, you shouldn't put up with that' — it wasn't new. Perhaps it was Demelza who'd steered her away from the classics, and from doing well at school. She heard Demelza's voice:

That teacher sounds a right Nazi.
A right Gauleiter.
Ooh, they would say that, wouldn't they?
Load of fascists.

Conformists.
The way they try to turn you into a drone.
Another brick in the wall.

Demelza was the owner of the copy of *Wuthering Heights*. She was well read. But she had left school at sixteen, had no university degree.

'Question, Silvio. Does the autodidact despise formal education?'

Silvio turned his head, lolled his tongue sideways and smiled. *Only when he fears a loss of power.*

Eloise turned the pages. A long, peaceful silence. How comforting to feel the hot weight of Silvio across her legs. The sunlight crossed the bed through a crack in the blind, and a spicy smell came off his woolly flank. She was starting to feel unhappy at the thought of giving him back.

> *'But you are a mirage,' said Kovrin. 'Why are you here and sitting still? That does not fit in with the legend.'*
>
> *'That does not matter,' the monk answered in a low voice, not immediately turning his face towards him. 'The legend, the mirage and I are all products of your excited imagination. I am a phantom.'*
>
> *'Then you don't exist?' said Kovrin.*
>
> *'You can think as you like,' said the monk, with a faint smile. 'I exist in your imagination, and your imagination is part of nature, so I exist in nature.'*

Eloise marked her place and closed the book.

'Right. Shits,' she said.

On the wooden bridge, she looked dreamily down at the slow, brown water. Crabs edged between holes in the creek bank. The mangroves stood in the shallow, blood-hot, impure water, their reflections wavering. The estuarine mud sent up its briny stink.

'Last chance,' she said.

And as they crossed the dry lawn, 'Are you sure? Nothing?'

Silvio paused and turned. His eyes were deep, steady.

'I hope you're not going to do anything while I'm out.'

The dog trotted delicately over to the blackened toe toe stumps. He sniffed the sooty dust, sneezed, but declined to squat or lift his leg.

'Okay. On your head be it . . .'

She went through the house, checking and locking, and positioned Silvio's bed and water bowl at the bottom of the stairs. The burglar alarm would have to stay off; the dog would trigger it unless she locked him in the garage, and she didn't have the heart. She wanted Silvio to like her. (She wanted him to adore her!) So far he seemed to tolerate, rather than openly welcome, her charm offensive. His tail wags were more polite than effusive. She would look up from her book and find him regarding her levelly, with his shrewd golden eyes. *Come on, Silv. Give me a bit of love. Tell me I'm not so bad . . .* She plied him with dog biscuits and choice bits of sandwich; he would take the morsel delicately from her fingers, and look away while he ate it. *Come on, Silv, a penny for them . . .*

'Right. Anyone comes to the door, make a massive racket. Ditto anyone walks past the deck. Got it? Loud as you can.'

He looked up at her.

'I really like having you here, Silv. There you go. All fluffed up nice for you.'

But he ignored his bed and headed for the sofa, which was already marked with paw prints, and giving off an earthy smell that Amigo the cleaner hadn't managed to shift. He fixed his eyes on the television.

'You got a clock in your head, Silvio? How do you always know what the time is?'

Eloise put on make-up, listening to Mariel Hartfield: 'Kurt Hartmann has appeared in the High Court on matters relating to his extradition. He's vowed to expose what he calls the Prime Minister's "lies" about spying in this country. Andrew Newgate has revealed he will go to court to seek a judicial review of Justice Minister Ed Miles's decision to deny him compensation for wrongful imprisonment. Anita O'Keefe has confirmed that despite earlier reports she has not made a formal complaint against *Witness* magazine over an article detailing her personal circumstances. And more bad news in the polls for Jack Dance.'

'I'll be back,' Eloise told Silvio. 'Be good.'

She drove the Honda, which she rarely used. Sean had taken his sleek black Audi when he left: the Audi was one thing she kept an eye out for, on her weekend walks.

Golden light along the peninsula; a red sky blazing off windows as if the houses were burning inside. Cars slid by, lightly buffeting the Honda as it beetled along. Face it, in a city ruled by giant SUVs and 4WDs, the tiny vehicle was a death trap. Reaching the top of the peninsula the apologetic car trundled into the traffic, a toy-town whine in the engine. It would be good, Eloise thought now, whirring and battling along in the slow lane, to sit behind the wheel of a big car like Carina's. Driving the masterful Holden, the model all plainclothes cops used, Carina looked like a detective, and other cars got out of her way.

At this hour the motorway was a river of metal sweeping her into its path; it was also a zoo and a jungle and a war zone. The rip and zip, the whine and snarl, the swerving, cutting off and messing up. Everyone was in a tearing hurry, and murderous with it. Damn you. No, damn *you*. An old bomb crossed the lane in front of her, tiny pieces of debris flying off the rim of the temporary wheel on which the chassis wobbled, too loosely balanced. Soon after, police cars with sirens sped through, causing dangerous swerves in the current. And near the city, like the contents of a clogged pipe, the whole stream slowed, banked, and came to a noisome halt. Eloise sat hunched over the wheel, furiously texting.

Untangling itself, the motorway sped up again and spat her out below the slopes of Mt Hobson. The tiny car shot out of the exit lane like a rocket. Eloise flew over a sleeping policeman, and checked the speedo. Whoa. Really? Who knew the Honda could go that fast? She changed down, barely braking, and took the tight bend with style. There was a tortured shriek from the tyres.

Here, below the mountain, the streets were orderly and quiet. The Hay house stood on the highest ridge of the affluent eastern suburbs. Down a long drive off the main road, you passed through the gate to a terraced lawn with a view over the valley, and across the suburb to the sea. Rangitoto Island shouldered up against the horizon, and beyond it stretched the gulf, with its haze of distant islands. The driveway led past a willow tree on an island of grass to the house, a spacious classic villa with a return veranda covered in bougainvillea flowers.

Eloise swept down the drive, parked up against the stone wall and cranked the brake. The car ticked and creaked, giving off a smell of burning rubber. She slammed the door. One day the tinny little bomb would disintegrate while she was driving.

'Oooh, helloo, chuck.'

She kicked the Honda's tyre and went to greet her mother.

Eloise sat on the sofa drinking gin and tonic, and blandly smiling. She seemed to have developed a new preoccupation: with breaking things. Fresh from punishing the Honda, she was now looking at the dining table, which was laden with the settings for a family dinner: china, glassware, a tall vase of flowers. To pick all that lot up and hurl it off the veranda . . . Only yesterday she'd sat in the staff café with Scott and pictured herself throwing cups and cutlery against the plate glass.

Her mother's sister Luna settled herself on the sofa.

'How *are* you Eloise?' Aunt Luna asked, with a hopeful smile.

The desire to break things: it was something to discuss with Klaudia.

'*Great*, thanks.'

'Oh *good*.'

Silence. Luna gently blinked.

She was spending a lot of time thinking about Klaudia. At the end of the last session, Klaudia had suppressed a yawn, and Eloise had thought with dismay, she's bored. I'm boring her. She's going to fire me.

Did she care if Klaudia fired her? Evidently she did, because she'd spent an afternoon thinking out how to describe her maddest attributes, in order to rekindle Klaudia's interest. You could imagine it becoming like the *Thousand and One Nights*: introducing a new set of symptoms each week so the shrink didn't decide you were cured, and give you the chop.

It was all there when you looked on Google: it was called transference. Reactions to the shrink coloured by your past experiences of significant others. Which included something worryingly called *erotic transference*, where you developed a powerful sexual fixation on the shrink, even if he or she wasn't *remotely* what normally lit your candle. What Eloise was worried about was countertransference — of the negative kind: putting Klaudia off. *I fear I am that novel.* It was a bit like trying to win over Silvio. Come on, Klaudia. Wag that tail. Tell me I'm not so bad . . .

Carina was beckoning from the hall.

She interrupted her aunt and excused herself. Luna gave her a smile of great sweetness.

The two sisters strolled out on to the veranda, holding their glasses.

Because she could tell Carina anything, Eloise said, 'I was just thinking about the shrink.'

'Really? Are you in love? You're meant to fall in love with the shrink.'

'She's a woman. I'm a failure at being gay. I've never been able to manage it.'

'Me neither.'

'People have tried. Remember that butch Traci at school? She propositioned me. I couldn't see my way to it.'

'God, that school was like a woman's prison. Anyway, I know you went on about it, but I've been so busy — I can't think where to put the thing, you know, Arthur's file.'

'Surely there's somewhere.'

'How about here? I've got it with me.'

'No. Not here.'

'Well, I don't *have* anywhere else. No safety deposit box, nowhere at work. I mean, I could bury it if you like.'

'Give it to me. I'll think of something. I suppose I could open a bank deposit box.'

'Isn't this all a bit unnecessary?'

Silence. Eloise put down her glass. 'Okay. Forget it. It's unnecessary.'

'Don't fly off the handle. No need to go berserk.'

Eloise drew in a long breath. 'Just humour me for a minute. Just bear with me: If there was something funny going on with Hallwright and Miles at Rotokauri, and Arthur rang Lampton about it . . .'

'That's a big if.'

'*If* Arthur did go looking for a missing woman called Mereana, and then died shortly afterwards, just say there was something funny about that . . .'

'It was investigated.'

'Yes, but if there was more to it, I want to find out. I know Arthur thinks I let him down. I never asked any questions.'

'You know Arthur thinks?'

'I mean Arthur *would* think, if he was alive.'

'You should definitely keep going to the shrink.'

'What if the missing woman was murdered?'

Carina shook her head. 'Just keep going to the shrink. And stop thinking about murders. You've spent too much time with Andrew Newgate.'

They both looked into the sitting room, where their mother, with her sausage dog Gerald in her arms, was holding forth, while her sister gazed up at her, her small bulb of a head faintly wobbling.

'The shrink says the past is a dead star, its light still reaching me. She says it helps to live in the Now,' Eloise said.

'How's that going?'

'I'd quite like some more wine *now*.'

They went in search. In the kitchen Eloise said, 'Maybe I could give Arthur's file to Klaudia. She has security, locked cabinets.'

'Who's Klaudia?'

'The shrink. The one I'm supposed to be in love with. Klaudia of the Thousand and One sessions.'

'She'll say no. There'll be a rule.'

'Give it back to me anyway, and I'll think about it.' She filled their glasses.

Demelza summoned them to the table. Eloise sat next to her father, who nodded and waved a hand. He'd been in bed with laryngitis, and was reduced to whispering. Demelza drummed her fingers on the table. There was an expectant silence.

'The doctor,' Demelza said, 'has had a look at Terrence's vocal chords. There could be a polyp there, I understand. Go on, Luna, help yourself. Don't stint. Of course, in many instances, it turns out there's cancer. That's a dreadful thing to contemplate. But still, life must go on, as long as it can. Have another slice, Carina. Goodness you're looking well, dear. Quite ruddy. Have you lost some weight? No? I thought not. What a wonderful shirt, Eloise. That's a lovely shade. You always do look so elegant. Not all of us can get it quite right, can we. I sometimes wonder if there's a colour-blind gene in the family, on Terrence's side. Carina's just like her father, can't tell her oranges from her reds. Her greens from her blues. Eloise just has that extra visual sense. I'm sure that's why she's gravitated to the television environment. Now, Luna, did you know Nancy Deans has cancer? Of the throat. Terrible. Started out as a bit of a dry cough. They say she's got just weeks.'

Eloise felt a hand on her arm. 'Sorry Dad? You want the water? The salt? Oh, the wine!'

'Me too,' Carina said.

'More,' Terrence mouthed, making tipping motions.

Demelza went on, 'I've had a bit of spare time. So I've read just about the whole of Dickens. I've got it on my Kindle. It's wonderful. Exhilarating, really. Sparkles darling, have some chicken. I was fortunate to be able to cook it this morning, before the day got too hot. Go on, dear. Now Luna, I meant to tell you, I wrote to the judge.'

Luna drew down her brows, solemnly leaned forward. 'Ah, the *case.*'

'Exactly. The case.'

'What case?' Carina said.

'A dreadful, dreadful case.'

'Dreadful,' Luna echoed.

'Whoops.'

'Christ.' Carina clicked her tongue with exasperation and gently repositioned her daughter's chair, handing back the fork she'd dropped.

Demelza spread her hand over her chest and said in a thick voice, 'I've had sleepless nights, thinking about it. You must have read about it in the papers.'

Luna nodded, with a soulful expression.

Carina shrugged. Terrence made a small snorting sound.

'What, Dad?' Eloise said.

He shook his head and raised his eyebrows. He had his eyes on Carina, who laughed.

Demelza drummed her fingers. 'The Parkinson case, *Carina*.'

Luna said, 'The poor woman, Terrence, Sheryl Parkinson.' She turned to Eloise and Carina. 'She was left caring for her autistic grandchild. Her daughter, the mother, had run off. The child was impossible to deal with. Woke every night. Would sing at the top of her voice at 3 a.m. The grandmother, at the end of her tether, she . . . It's tragic.'

'She killed the child,' Demelza said in a deepened voice. 'And there's been such an outpouring of self-righteousness, I can hardly stand it. They convicted her of manslaughter and she's been given a huge jail sentence. Just huge. My heart goes out to her. People's cruelty. The inhumanity. I've been so moved that I wrote to the judge to protest.'

'Courageous of you,' Luna said. 'Bravo.'

'You can only do what you can do.' Demelza squared her shoulders. 'I believe in telling the truth, see. The truth. That woman was pushed to the limits of her endurance. Oh, I know people will think I'm unconventional. That I'm not thinking of "the victim". But no one's thought of that woman, and what she went through. *I know.*'

Luna drew in a deep breath, through her nose. 'The suffering,' she said vaguely.

'Human beings,' Demelza said, with a shudder. 'Man's inhumanity to man. The way they've thrown a woman to the wolves, who . . .'

'How did she kill the child, just out of interest?' Carina asked.

'Oh don't,' Luna said, putting a hand to her neck. 'It's too . . .'

'She drove her to a bridge and strangled her.'

'And how old was the child?'

Demelza met her daughter's gaze. 'She was fourteen. But you know this.'

'Yes, I know this.' Carina didn't look away. 'Must have taken quite a bit of doing, strangling a teenager.'

Silence.

Luna gazed at Carina with watery eyes. 'Demelza's always been like this. She's able to care about *all* human beings, even those society's thrown on the . . . on the . . .'

'Scrap heap,' Carina said.

Demelza shook herself, as though from a reverie. 'Anyway! Would you like some ice cream, Sparkles, darling?'

She looked sideways. 'Of course *you* could have ended up coming a cropper, Carina. You weren't afraid of authority, see. You had a wonderful spirit. Such independence. That's why you were expelled from school. And ended up in custody all those times. The police saying to you, Get in the car! Oooh, it was a time, Sparkles, when your mother was a teenager. Terrence and I would get the call, and your mother would have done some new rebellious thing. And then she'd be appearing in the District Court, or some big copper would be at the door.'

'You were lucky you had such an enlightened mother,' Luna said richly. 'Imagine if you'd had parents who were *repressive*. It's marvellous, really. You've been lucky, Carina, and you, Eloise.'

'You can only do what you can do.'

The willow cast its drooping shadow over the drive. Beyond the branches the moon was pinned like a stud in the dark, swelling sky. All day the clouds had piled up in the west and yet there was no storm, and now the promise of rain was broken and the moon was out, shining down on the parched city.

Demelza's lawn, fed by sprinklers in breach of hosepipe bans, glowed a rich, unnatural green under the garden lights.

Carina took a plastic bag from the car boot.

'Now you're not going to drive. You're going inside and ringing for a cab.'

'Yes. Promise.'

Carina handed over the bag. 'Here's Arthur's stuff.' She paused. 'Listen. Something's just occurred to me. If there was something funny going on at Rotokauri and Arthur found out, which is obviously very unlikely, but if there was . . .'

'If the missing woman was murdered . . .'

'If there was anything funny, and David Hallwright and Ed Miles were involved, then I suppose you should ask . . .'

'You should ask what happened. I *am* asking. I want to know.'

'Not just what happened, but who would benefit from finding out.'

'Arthur would benefit.'

Carina opened her mouth, hesitated. 'Um, Arthur's dead.'

'Arthur's ghost would benefit.'

'Christ. Okay. Arthur's ghost would benefit. But who else? *Cui bono?* Theoretically. If your *fanciful* idea of something funny was remotely possible.'

Eloise, who had been drinking with some dedication, put her hand over her right eye, looked up at the moon and said, 'Dunno.'

'The Prime Minister would benefit,' Carina said. '*Jack Dance* would benefit.'

Eloise started up the Honda. Arthur's file lay on the seat beside her. She'd considered hiding it at her parents' house, but thought better of it. You couldn't hide anything in a house occupied by Demelza.

You couldn't ask her to hide anything *for* you either, Demelza being such an open book. If you asked her to keep a secret, she'd try her very best, but it would just pop out. *Eloise's husband has left her for another woman. A very attractive actress, I understand. Carina's been feeling much better since she had her piles seen to. Oooh, did I say the wrong thing?*

She was always remorseful; it was just that she couldn't tell a lie. The more important it was that she not mention a secret, the more likely it was that Demelza would come out with it. Carina had complained about this, and Demelza had explained (while Eloise listened).

'Now Carina, I can't help it! I'm the victim of the power of suggestion! It's the fear of doing something, chuck, *once you've thought of it*. Take this example, Carina: when you were a young girl, there were a phase when I was right depressed. Terrence was off with one of his fancy women, Eloise was a dear little baby, and you were a challenging child. Every time you came near me, chuck, I couldn't look at knives. Why knives? It was fear of the power of suggestion!'

Cold-blooded old times. Eloise pointed the Honda towards the street. She had to be over the drink-drive limit. Carina would have taken the car keys off her, but she'd sensibly buckled up the Sparkler, and soberly driven away. Eloise had waved them off, before ambling inside in search of a nightcap or two for the road.

Suitably refreshed and fortified, she'd taken her leave from her mother. As they stood on the veranda looking over the suburb spread out below them Demelza said, of her sister, 'Poor Luna. She's entirely unreflective. She insists everyone sees things her way. It's a serious neuroticism, I'm afraid. She's quite mad.'

Stepping back to avoid any possible drunken attempt at a farewell kiss or embrace, Demelza added, 'Hurry home, dear. I won't come out to the car. Sure you wouldn't like another nip of brandy for the road? There's plenty more. No? Well, it's late. Drive carefully. Don't spare the horses. The motorway's quickest. Godspeed!'

The engine whined as Eloise flew up the dark driveway. At the top, she reached out and freed part of the hedge from the windscreen. And then she started driving very fast.

Dutch courage. Why am I here? Dutch courage. Like on the plane: the turbulence, the funny noises, and then you have the pre-dinner gin, a couple of wines and it's okay, let it bump and roll, let it swoop and shudder — you're laughing.

See, I'm laughing — and so are you. Because it's funny me turning up at ten-thirty on a hot night on the peninsula, saying just passing, and haven't seen you for days and hi neighbour, and guess what I've got a dog now but it's only a lend, and I love him. Already I love old Silv, the heat and weight of him, the smell, his golden eyes, because we all want to be touched, we're all dogs, we're pack animals, we want to lie against each other, to be held close to the people we love. We're all animals, Nick.

That was just on the doorstep. And none of it was said.

He stood in the lighted doorway, wearing a jacket and jeans, scratching his chin, his eyes tired. 'I've been out. Just got in.'

'You smell of smoke.'

'Couple of friends were smoking cigars.'

'I love the smell of cigars.'

'Come in.'

'Is it too late?'

'No, no, come in, Eloise. I'm glad you came over.'

'I just wanted to tell you I've got a dog.'

'I've looked for your wolf by the way. Haven't seen it.'

'I saw it again. It was howling.'

He smiled with his mouth closed. He looked weary, tolerant, his hair messy; he sat, leaned down and unlaced his boots, rested his hands on the arms of the chair and slumped, feet squarely placed. Eloise took in the jeans, the unlaced boots, the stubble on his chin; he looked pleasingly rough but there was something elegant about him, too: the skin on his cheeks just slightly blurred and softened, the expressive hands. Think of him out on the peninsula, coming along the path in the hard light, the way he pauses, goes still, looks sharply at you and then dips his head, relaxes and comes forward, all his movements suddenly fluid.

She said, 'I saw someone in the stucco house. But it's all sealed up.'

'It must have been a ghost.'

'Do you believe in ESP, Nick?'

'No. Yes.'

He poured a drink. 'You know, I went to Chernobyl once. The men who work in the Exclusion Zone call themselves Stalkers, after a Russian movie called *Stalker*. You heard of it?'

'No. What were you doing in Chernobyl?'

'Working for an aid agency. In the Russian movie, there's a guy called the Stalker. The Stalker takes two clients into the Zone. In the Zone is The Room, where anyone who goes inside will be granted wishes. But here's the thing, The Room grants *subconscious* wishes, so it's dangerous; you don't get what you think you're going to.'

'The Zone . . .'

'I don't believe in ESP. Just the subconscious. Have a drink, Eloise.'

'Dutch courage. It's why I'm here.'

'Come here,' he said. 'Eloise. Come here.'

She woke up in bed with the dog. The clock told her it was almost time to get up and go to work. She lay on her back, and the night replayed itself, a series of scenes.

He said, Come here. He kissed her. She wanted him, but then she pulled away.

I have to get back to Silvio, she said. I came straight here. He needs an airing.

So he'd walked her home, over the blackened toe toe stumps and across the lawns, and together they'd aired the dog. Silvio ambling about in the spill of light from the back door, lifting his leg against the blackened bushes. The night full of sounds, the clack of the flax spears, the cheeping of crickets, the sigh of the tide running in the creek.

He kissed her again. He smelled of smoke. She wanted him to stay, but then she came out with some awkward cliché, what was it? Raincheck? How awful!

She woke once after he'd gone, and experienced a feeling of regret so intense she sat straight up. When it was light she came down to the kitchen and found he'd left her a note, signed with an x.

On the way to the bus she went out to the Honda, opened the boot and slid her hand under the carpet matting. Arthur's file was still there.

She went to work. Kurt Hartmann was appearing in court again on another matter, his frozen assets: they were due at ten to film.

Leader of the Opposition Bradley Kirk was facing questions: had he met with Kurt Hartmann to discuss the internet tycoon's spying allegations against the Prime Minister? Was Hartmann working with the Opposition to bring down the government of Jack Dance?

Selena was clearing out her office and talking litigation. She and the Sinister Doormat had fallen out: each accused the other of defamation and theft of stationery.

Management put out a statement: they were processing a number of complaints from staff about the alleged 'shock' issue. Enquiries were progressing well, and experts were being consulted. Details to follow.

In the course of a long phone call to Eloise, Demelza mentioned that Andrew Newgate had appeared in a women's magazine, talking about his quest for a girlfriend. Women would have to convince him, Newgate said, that they were 'not just interested in his fame'.

'I can't believe it, chuck. Lord Muck. *They* have to convince *him*. Nothing about *him* having to convince *them* he won't *murder them in their beds.*'

In the same women's magazine, it was foretold that Mariel Hartfield and Hamish Dark (both in their forties), would be trying for another baby, if that was what they were doing when they were seen near a building that possibly housed an IVF clinic. (A rival magazine had recently photographed Mariel walking near a children's clothing store and announced: *Mariel: Twin baby joy.*)

On TV, Mariel wore sky blue and announced: Jack Dance's polling woes deepen. She went on: Opposition attacks continue, amid allegations Mr Dance ordered or at least knew about illegal spying against Kurt Hartmann. Justice Minister Ed Miles has refused to comment on the US bid to extradite Kurt Hartmann, other than to say that the extradition procedure is 'on track'.

Jack Anthony, in a summer-blue suit, explained: The true economic toll of this summer's drought.

The Sinister Doormat stood at the door of Q Wing's hair and make-up suite and hissed, 'Stuff you, bitch.'

Not just a pencil-thin blonde with huge breasts but a qualified meteorologist, the Sinister Doormat's job was to 'add value' to the weather. The weather formed a significantly large segment of the evening news. The Doormat and the weather had had a lot in common these last few months. They both went on and on being beautiful and golden, and not changing, and never getting old.

SEVENTEEN

Eloise sat sweltering in the Honda. The air-conditioning wasn't working, and the car was parked in full sun at the top of a quiet suburban street. She started the engine and drove slowly, checking mail boxes. Number 18 Pukeora Place, the Epsom address she'd found in an electoral roll at the local post office, was a sizeable white villa with a landscaped garden, a beautiful stained-glass front door in blues, greens and reds, and an orange tiled roof. There was a fig tree on the front lawn, which was fronted by a dry stone wall.

The slope of a small volcanic cone, Mt Matariki, rose steeply beyond the line of houses. She got out, went to the gate and leaned over to check the mail in the letter box. She took hold of an envelope and pulled it out. It was addressed to Mrs Karen Lampton.

Now she stood, glazed, her eyes fixed vacantly on the blue wooden bench on the front porch. It would be easy to open the gate, walk up past the twin ornamental trees in pots, ring the bell beside the stained-glass door. But what then? The thought of trying to explain made Eloise feel exhausted. She went back to the car and drove away.

At home on the peninsula, Silvio lying across her legs, a glass of wine at her elbow. Trying to frame it: a sad story. Long time ago now. There are things I never asked. So sorry to bother. There's just this thing I've wondered about. If you wouldn't mind. Your name.

Your name and the name of a missing woman. Mereana. The detective, Marie Da Silva. You remember, with the odd-coloured eyes? She must have. Did she? You see, the man I loved. The man I wanted to marry. The love of my life. He wanted to write a screenplay about a National Party prime minister. He had brown curly hair, deep-set eyes, he was tall and thin. Did you ever? His name was Arthur Weeks.

Arthur.

Scott rang. They talked about Kurt Hartmann, who was trying to seek discovery from the Crown to support his bid to resist extradition. Scott passed the phone to Thee, who made Eloise laugh.

She rang Nick, but he wasn't picking up. She rang Carina, who read extracts from the Sparkler's school report: *Rachel Margery has achieved the highest marks in her class in Maths.* (Maths!) *Also the highest mark in reading and spelling. A very capable student who must learn not to chat so much to . . .*

But Carina had to go. Eloise picked up her book. 'Come here,' she said to Silvio.

'If only you knew how pleasant it is to listen to you!' said Kovrin, rubbing his hands with satisfaction.

'I'm very glad.'

'But I know that when you go away I shall be worried about the question of your reality. You are a phantom, an hallucination. So I am mentally ill, not normal?'

'What if you are? Why trouble yourself?'

'Want to come for a ride, Silv?'

On the west side of Pukeora Place, she unclipped Silvio's leash and allowed him to run up the pedestrian walkway that led through the gardens and onto the volcanic cone. She panted up after him, and they emerged on the terraced slopes, heading for the top. On the rim of the crater she looked down and saw that the water that usually pooled in the dip had dried up. Silvio was already down there sniffing around in the yellow grass. She walked a circuit around the crater, while Silvio ran up and down the inside of it.

From here, she could see the orange tiled roof of number 18. She headed down the slope, calling the dog, and reached the dry stone wall at the end of the back lawn. Beyond the lawn was a swimming pool, and glass doors opening onto a deck. She was about to turn back, when Silvio ran ahead, found an open gate and appeared on the lawn. He lowered his head, sniffed, raised his head and looked at her. The white dog against the green lawn, legs squarely planted, like a Matisse cut-out, and beyond him the wavering plastic blue of the pool. She walked towards him.

Like walking into something new, a world of perfect forms — white dog, green grass, the hushed air of a dream. What was the thing she looked for and couldn't find? To cross the line, to find what lay beyond the colour and shimmer, the bright, block-like form of the world . . .

Eloise found she had entered the gate and was crossing the lawn, calling and shaking the leash. The glass door opened. A man came down the steps and dumped a plastic bag in an outside bin. Eloise walked around the side of the swimming pool, calling Silvio. The man turned and stood looking at her, at ease, unhurried.

He was tall and slim, with broad shoulders and greying curly hair. He was wearing suit trousers, a white shirt, black shoes. He reached for the tea towel draped over his shoulder, and dried his fingers. His hands were square, blunt, unusually large.

Eloise hesitated. Using Google, she'd found his picture on his practice website. In person, he looked different. Those big hands. Had she seen him somewhere before?

'Nice dog.'

'Sorry. This is Silvio. We were on the mountain. He has no respect for private property.'

The man smiled, a lazy, benign expression. Not bothered. He was almost turning away.

'I'm sorry, are you . . . Dr Lampton?'

He turned to face her.

'Dr Simon Lampton?'

Silvio sat down. He looked from one human face to the other. The swimming pool filter made a rhythmic, slopping sound and an intricate pattern of sunlight played on the white weatherboards behind Simon Lampton's head. His face was suntanned, weathered, his eyes were sharply fixed on her. He shifted position, carefully pulled the tea towel off his shoulder and gathered it in his big hands.

'Have we met?'

'No.'

He made a slight gesture, a twitch of the shoulders, dismissive, impatient.

Eloise put her hand flat on Silvio's head. She swallowed. 'I'm sorry. I can't . . .'

Now he looked at her with closer attention. She could see him shifting gear: this was no longer a meaningless encounter. It was some sort of *situation.* When he spoke his voice had a clipped, professional edge.

'Is everything all right?'

'Sorry.' She bent down, put her hands on her knees.

'Do you need help?'

Eloise thought about it. 'Yes.'

'What's wrong?'

'I feel dizzy. Can't breathe.'

'Here, sit down.'

He guided her to a wooden seat. His tone had softened. 'Do you have medication? An inhaler?'

'I'm all right now.'

'Allergies?'

He sat beside her and put two fingers on her wrist. She looked at the crisp white material of his shirt, his chunky silver cuff-links. He smelled of clean clothes, aftershave. They sat, listening. He let go her wrist, looked her in the eyes and said, 'Still breathless?'

His expression was serious, respectful.

'Sorry. No.' Eloise squeezed her eyes shut. 'There's nothing wrong. At least not physically — it's more psychological.'

He stood up. 'Ah.'

'Have you got time to talk?'

'Actually, not at the moment. I'm pretty busy. My wife's in the kitchen, we're about to have some people over.'

Silence. He waited, then said, 'Do you live around here? I haven't seen you.'

'No.'

After a while he looked at his watch. 'If you're okay, maybe you could take this nice dog, Silvio, did you call him, and finish his run. Do you think? The gate's open down there.'

'I'm not mad.'

'No. I'm sure. But I'd better be getting on with things, so . . .'

There was a woman's voice inside the house, the sound of a door closing.

'I wanted to talk about the man I used to live with.'

Now he had a little exasperated laugh in his voice as he said, 'I'm really not the person for that.' He stood over her and she looked up at him, his arms crossed, his face set with wary calculation. He looked competent, tough, his expression closed, calmly set against her, deciding how most safely and efficiently to deal with her. He was checking her out, trained eyes measuring available data, at the same time edging away. He was used to dealing with 'situations', appropriately, within ethical and professional guidelines, all that. He was also coolly searching his memory, since she'd mentioned his name — *query:* some odd acquaintance of his wife? Patient? Stalker? Eloise could see him considering all this, so it was with a weird sense of comedy that she said, 'Can I come in?'

He raised his hands, palms outward, fingers up. 'We're busy at the moment. My wife and I, like I said, we've got people coming. Would you like me to call someone for you?'

'Okay. I'm fine now. Made a mistake.' She picked up Silvio's lead.

'Breathing okay?'

'Yes, fine thanks. I'm sorry.'

She walked away over the lawn, turning once to look back. He was watching her and raised a hand. Making sure she got off his property.

'Come on, Silvio.' She herded the dog into the car, agitated, in a hurry to get away. The drive ahead seemed too far, it would take ages, too long before she could sit down, think, get her head straight . . .

She sat at the lights, cursing the slow traffic. A giant, bloated snake of motorway lay between her and the peninsula, every inch of it crammed.

You're running away.

Getting your head straight: what did that mean? Relax, sit yourself down. Open a bottle. There you go: an interlude of clarity and calm before the gradual increase in speed, the enjoyable lurches into sentimentality, melodrama, delusions (of coolness, charisma, rich bravado), the end dash towards the vortex. What was not to like?

She sped on; here came the three-lane roundabout and motorway junction at Highway Ra, one of the most famously testing intersections in the city. At rush hour it was a maelstrom, requiring maximum aggression, a take-no-prisoners poise. She accelerated, forcing her way into the right-turn lane *comme d'habitude*, but then something happened. She changed her mind.

There was resistance. There was an emphatic blast of horns. There were forearms twirled out of windows, shouts. But the Honda shot through the gap between two trucks, cut off a taxi and dodged a bus. Forcing a Holden to brake hard, she made it to the other side. Silvio tried to stay upright, his claws scrabbling on the seat. Eloise turned left.

She drove to the road at the base of Mt Eden.

The tiny Honda seemed to hesitate and cough, as if to gird itself, before bouncing over the cattle stop and entering the park road. Then it rallied, and whirred bravely up to the top of the volcanic cone.

They sat in the grass above Arthur's flat. Below the slopes, the suburbs lay in grids, and lights were beginning to come on in the wooden houses. Arthur's deck was in shade and the sunset was like an advancing army, banners of red cloud above the dark line, all motionless, as if painted on the taut canvas of the sky — all as still as the single, tiny star above the horizon, and the pale moon.

Eloise talked, Silvio listened. All those stars. Some of them are dead, but they are so far away that their light is still reaching us. The night sky glitters, Silvio, but it doesn't move. Except for the fleeting passage of shooting stars and the steady, beetling progress of satellites, the firmament appears frozen. When you go outside the city, to a place beyond light pollution, the millions of stars are arrayed with such cold, dense fixity that they make life on earth seem impossible. Flowers, colour, skin, fur, softness, swiftness, movement, your beautiful woolly coat, Silvio. How? By what strange fluke? Extraordinary that such things exist or survive when you look up at the mineral blackness, the diamond-studded infinity.

She talked, Silvio listened, until Arthur's deck was lost in shadows, and the sunset deepened, and began to pour itself like lava down the curved back of the world.

EIGHTEEN

Eloise received a text from Klaudia. Hers was the last appointment of the day, and the office had just had its driveway concreted. Klaudia sought to warn her that she would have to climb around the wet cement by holding onto the white pole at the gate.

Having easily achieved the manoeuvre with the white pole she went inside and met Klaudia in the hallway. The therapist was hitching up her trouser leg and peering at her shoe.

Klaudia straightened. 'I went out on an errand, when I came back I stood in the concrete. The men were angry with me, but they'd put no warning sign, no plank over. I walked in it and they had to redo the concrete. That's why I texted you.'

'Do you want me to come in now?'

'Yes, yes.' She limped in and sat behind the desk, shaking her head, frowning. The workmen had been annoyed with her; she was embarrassed, flustered. She said, 'It was my fault but it was their fault, too. There was no sign.'

'Are you . . . wearing concrete shoes?'

'No. It's fine. How are you, Eloise?'

'I'm still having trouble sleeping . . .'

Eloise was in mid-sentence when she saw it: the widening of the nostrils, the gradual tensing of the jaw and neck as Klaudia, with the utmost delicacy, suppressed a yawn.

It *was* hot in here. The sun was shining directly in, dust motes turning in the light. Klaudia thrust her shoulder forward, bent her elbows, clenched her fists, covertly stretching.

Eloise said hurriedly, 'Can I put something to you? A hypothetical question.'

'Of course. Just a moment.' Klaudia got up and limped across the room. Eloise tried to get a look at her shoes. She'd started talking in a rush, Klaudia nodding, while under the desk perhaps the cement was hardening around her foot. Would she have to lever her shoe off with a chisel?

Klaudia stood by the door, a hand up to her neck, moving her shoulders. 'Right. Where were we?' She sat down again, fluttered her eyes, and put a hand politely up to her mouth.

Eloise took a tissue from the box on the desk. Obviously she needed to take things up a notch. 'Do you think confiding is important? The mere fact that you've told at least one other person?'

Klaudia paused, considered. 'Put it this way, Eloise. Why do we suffer when we are prevented from telling our true story? It has to be existentially important.'

'Klaudia, if you perceived that your mother would be indifferent to your death, wouldn't that be one of the most frightening things you could contemplate?'

Klaudia held her pen above the page.

'That would be the abyss, wouldn't it.'

'Go on?'

Eloise looked at the terrace outside. There was no sign of the rat. 'Not your stepmother or adoptive mother or wicked aunt. Your *mother*. Wouldn't care if you died.'

'I am listening.'

'And it's not because . . .' Eloise paused, trying to reign herself in, and gave up, 'it's not because she's a junkie or an alcoholic, or poverty stricken, or a battered wife. And it's not because you're autistic or schizophrenic or because you're violent towards her. There's no reason like that. You're her child and she wouldn't care if you disappeared for good.'

Klaudia was looking out at the bricks now, too. Summoning the rat perhaps. Wanting the rat to show up for moral support. For light relief.

'Her wish would be unnatural, wouldn't it? *Against nature*,' Eloise said, sweating.

'Sure,' Klaudia said. 'A mother is supposed to love her child.'

'And wouldn't it also be an invitation to suicide? For the child?'

'Why so?'

'Philosophically. If you came from your mother and she hates you, then you hate yourself.'

Klaudia placed the tips of her fingers on the desk and frowned down. She swallowed. 'In your theoretical scenario, Eloise, the mother doesn't necessarily hate the child; she hates an aspect of herself. She is not seeing the child, she is seeing a projection of herself, that blinds her to the real person. She cannot see outside herself.'

'Or, she just hates the child.'

'But if to love your children is natural, perhaps there is something to make this mother unnatural — a pathology that prevents normal emotion.'

'If the mother's a freak then the child's a freak,' Eloise said.

'No one is a freak here. There is neuroticism.'

'It's the abyss.'

Klaudia gently smiled.'It's an old abyss. One that can be left behind. It's possible to be on a different mountain now.'

'With only a can of worms to eat,' Eloise said.

Klaudia looked down, curled one hand and glanced at her fingernails.

Looking at your nails was a sign of boredom, wasn't it? Eloise had a sense of sorrowful comedy. What a funny life Klaudia must have. Dealing with an endless parade of bores and creeps and nutcases, and, meanwhile, what was going on in *her* life? What pains and tics and doubts, what waves of ennui. Not to mention the concrete now hardening on her shoes.

What did it mean when you started to feel sorry for your shrink? You start out all beady-eyed and vigilant, suspecting she's the Harold Shipman of her profession (or your mother) and within no time you're bleary-eyed with sympathy and ready to tip-toe away, so sorry for the agony you're putting her through.

Klaudia stared out at the bricks and said,'You mention philosophical questions. In fact, it's Shakespearean.'

Eloise paused. Shakespearean: that was quite good, wasn't it? Better than being told your issues were trivial. It was nearly as good as biblical.

'Can I ask you another hypothetical question, Klaudia? If I wrote you letters, what would you do with them?'

'I would read them and put them in your file.'

'And they'd be confidential.'

'Of course.'

'What if I gave you a document written by someone else? Would you put that in the file and keep it confidential?'

Klaudia turned her head on one side, with the expression she had, of listening to something very faint, a long way off.'I am not sure what you are suggesting?'

'What if I gave you something that relates to my state of mind — showed it to you to demonstrate how I'm feeling. Would you keep it locked in my file?'

'Yes, I would.'

'And keep it confidential?'

'Of course.'

Eloise experienced a gap, a beat of time, in which she thought nothing. They were both looking out at the mossy bricks, and beyond, the wind flipping the leaves, making them shine. The sky was hard, clean, bright.

'My neighbour and I, Nick. We might have started something.'

'Oh, a relationship?'

'I went over to his house.'

'But weren't you afraid, after hearing the voice in his house?'

'I got drunk. Dutch courage.'

'Is that wise? It is better to make important choices when you are sober. Especially choices about your safety.'

'I don't feel safe being alone.'

'But still. Have you heard the voice again?'

A sudden needle of pain in her head made Eloise hesitate before saying, 'Do you believe in ghosts, Klaudia?'

'No. But perhaps the dead are present to us.'

'I let Arthur down.'

'What do you mean?'

'Klaudia, if I gave you a whole file, would you keep it for me?'

'Of course, Eloise. If you think it would help. Where is this file?'

'I've hidden it. I'd have to bring it to you.'

Klaudia's smile, so wolfishly pretty, lit up her face. 'Of course. No problem.' She gave her thigh a little slap, and a cloud of dust rose, sparkling, into the air.

'We have made great progress, Eloise,' she said.

'Some, Silvio, have called my problems Shakespearean.'

They were down in the laundry. Eloise measured out a cup of dry, smelly biscuits.

'Here you go. Here's your dinner that you hate.'

Silvio sniffed, unenthusiastic.

'I can see why you're not keen. You want a bone. A steak. A chop. But Carina says these give you the full range of nutrients.'

Silvio looked at her with his golden eyes.

'I know. You're saying you're not a hen. You're not a mouse. You don't want *pellets* for dinner. Only thing is Silv, I haven't got anything else.'

The dog lowered his long nose into the silver bowl and stirred its contents.

Eloise watched. She was thinking about Klaudia — again. Always brooding about Klaudia. Would erotic transference come next? Turning up at Klaudia's house, asking for a date. Or her hand in marriage. It was true, Klaudia did have very nice blonde hair. And a pleasingly sly, characterful face . . .

She directed a wry smile at Silvio. Dogs, Carina had told her, can read faces. They can distinguish a frown from a grin.

The dog crunched up his pretend meat, dry as dust. The fur on his legs was black. That morning, while he was sniffing near the blackened toe toe, a cloud of ash had formed itself into a cone beside him, and whirled away along the peninsula.

Godspeed.

It's Shakespearean, Silvio. You come from your mother. If your mother doesn't love you, it sends a powerful message. Nature is whispering, You don't belong. You are, in the Shakespearean sense, 'unkind'— inhuman, unnatural. It feels like a malign invitation. It feels like a glimpse into the Godless universe, into the void.

NINETEEN

Passing the supermarket, Eloise kept an eye out for the wolf. With her phone, she was going to film it howling, for Nick.

On foot, without Silvio, she walked east across the city. She was without Silvio because the Sparkler had protested, and requested his return. She was looking, as usual, for Sean's Audi — for any evidence of Sean. But she was heading in the direction of Mt Matariki.

Around noon, she reached Hillary Road. It was all very staid and buttoned up, here in the plush eastern suburbs. None of the raw atmosphere of the peninsula, with its scorched grasses, high skies, and views of the silvery estuary. Here were lawns, pools, tennis courts tended by the silent help: Comrade, Buddy, Angel. In the streets, the children with their hairstyles and their iPhones and their au pairs: Inneke,

Svetlana, Anke. The drone of lawnmowers, the roar of leaf blowers. The svelte blondes, in their tanklike SUVs. Sporty, burnished lycra-clad couples, bedizened widows with stiffened stacks of dyed hair. This was Jack Dance's constituency: true blue. This was where the affluent lived and rejoiced in the gap — the gap between rich and poor. Because what would be the point of being rich, if everyone else was rich too? Look how far away the poor were! The further away they got, the more enjoyable everything was. And the clearer it was that you'd arrived. Obv.

Eloise knew all this: she grew up here. She knew the hilarity, the tolerant mirth that ideas like 'wealth distribution' and 'fairness' were met with around these parts. Left-wing candidates were laughed off doorsteps at election time: they just didn't get it. David Hallwright had got it, when he was prime minister. Jack Dance got it. Eloise got it, and didn't entirely approve, although she hadn't argued with or minded Sean's firm right-wing allegiances. (His parents, Sir Jarrod and Lady Cheryl, along with the Ellison family, practically funded the National Party.) Carina was sternly Labour: she could never have married Sean Rodd. Carina had principles. She had, for her paper, interviewed members of the Labour Party in this electorate. There were nine of them, and two were dying.

Now, Eloise climbed the side of Mt Matariki. She looked down into the crater and thought of Silvio. His nose, his tangled white fur, his strange, deep eyes. The wind blew in the dry grass; cloud shadows swiftly crossed the suburbs. *Look Silvio, how the wind flips the leaves. Notice, there is something about the air today, as if soon there will be a change — to the iron light, the great wide skies of autumn. And Klaudia, you here, too! (What a fetching shirt you're wearing, such a pretty blue, to match your eyes.) Sit down here on this bench in the sun, Klaudia. I'm all ears. Let me hear your best lines: Treat yourself well. Go easy on yourself. Don't judge yourself so harshly. No, you are not boring, Eloise.*

That was the best thing Klaudia had said: *No, you are not boring,*

Eloise. But she'd said it a while ago, possibly before she'd found herself growing terribly, terminally bored . . .

She hadn't been on the mountain for more than an hour when Simon Lampton emerged from his front gate, wearing shorts and a T-shirt. He set off, jogging slowly up Pukeora Place.

Eloise headed down to his gate and waited.

Forty minutes later, she heard him pounding along the pavement. He came around the curve of the street, his face sweaty, a dark stain on the front of his shirt. He stopped in front of her and roamed around, his hands on his hips, steadying his breath. He looked at her, wiped his face with his forearm and said, 'Jesus.'

'I saw you. At the opera,' Eloise said. 'You were leaning against the window in the foyer, talking on the phone.'

'Right.'

'*The Marriage of Figaro.*'

He went on looking at her. He took the hem of his T-shirt and wiped his face. She could smell his sweat. Politely, and as if speaking to the village idiot, he said, 'Lost your dog?'

'I had to give him back.'

He nodded, about to pass her.

Eloise followed and he turned, with a flash of cold firmness.

'What's this about? You mentioned my name. When you came on my property.'

My property. Meaningful words, around here. Like taxpayers' money and welfarism and slap on the wrist with a wet . . .

Focus. Concentrate.

He took hold of the gate, about to close it. He moved around, jogging on the spot, fidgeting, impatient.

'I wanted to talk to you. But it's hard to explain.'

He dropped his head, waited. Flexed his shoulders.

She got it out in the end. Her voice quavered, and sounded quaint and formal, 'My enquiry concerns . . . It's about Arthur Weeks.'

She coughed, to get her voice under control. But look at him. He'd stopped moving. His whole body had gone completely still.

Silence.

'Arthur Weeks,' she said. 'Arthur is actually dead. He was my partner — we were going to get married. The reason I've come is . . . it's a bit difficult to explain . . .'

No response.

'I know it must seem a bit weird.'

Silence.

Finally he said, 'Okay, come inside.'

'Really? Are you sure?'

He nodded, held the gate open, gestured for her to go ahead up the path. His big hand was twisted in his T-shirt.

Directing her around the side of the house, he led her through a gate to the back, where he unlocked the glass doors. They entered the big, sunny room, and he pointed to a seat at a wooden table.

'Back in a minute,' he said.

She waited, looking around. It was a very big villa. There were shelves crammed with books and ornaments and photos. Pictures of Simon Lampton with his family. A blonde woman. A glamorous girl, presumably Elke Lampton, a plain young woman with Lampton's features, a young man holding a tennis racquet, a dark, curly-haired boy with freckles on his nose and striking, pale eyes. There was an expensive kitchen, a view through to a wide hall with a polished wooden floor and a staircase that he'd presumably just run up — she could hear him moving on the floor above — large windows with a view over the lawn to the mountain. She watched a figure climbing the slope and then she saw eyes, a face in the glass — he was standing behind her.

He had a towel around his neck, and a clean T-shirt.

'I'm going to make a coffee. Would you like one?'

He moved smoothly into the kitchen; she followed and watched him. His movements were controlled. Those big hands: so very steady. Surgeon's hands. The life seemed to have gone out of him. His tone was flat, unanimated, 'How d'you have it? Milk? Sugar?' A little twitch at the corner of his mouth made Eloise think of Demelza: he was probably suppressing his irritation. She felt bad.

'Sorry about the intrusion,' she said.

'I *do* have things to do. I'm catching up on work.'

'You go and get your PE and then you can focus,' Eloise said warmly. 'I can't concentrate at all unless I've been for a walk.'

The look he now gave her was complex: incredulous (he really couldn't believe he was having to put up with this) and potent. His face was oddly white, and set.

Potent: full of potential. But potential for what?

'My name's Eloise Hay.'

'And you know my name.'

He handed her a coffee. They sat down, faced each other. Eloise coughed.

'My partner, boyfriend, Arthur Weeks, died some time ago, and I was told the reason why he died, and I accepted it. But now I feel like I let him down. I didn't ask any questions.'

Silence.

'And this relates to me how?'

Eloise paused. She focused on his face. His expression faltered, his brow creased, then his eyes went hard again.

'Arthur rang you,' Eloise said.

Their eyes were locked.

'Arthur *rang* you. He was a journalist. Do you remember?'

She put down the cup, leaned forward. 'You were at Rotokauri with the prime minister, David Hallwright, and Arthur called you. He wanted to ask about the Hallwrights and you fobbed him off. After that he died.'

'Right. I remember.'

'I would have *thought* you'd remember, since the police asked you about it.'

'Of course.'

'So why do you ask, relates to me how?'

'I'd forgotten. Sorry.'

Eloise sat back, sighed.'I know, it was a long time ago.'

'It was.'

'Do you remember anything? Any clues?'

'He had a fall, didn't he? From memory. I have no idea. It was nothing to do with me. And so long ago. They only came to me briefly because they'd checked his phone records, and my number came up.'

'The Hallwrights had a housekeeper, a Chinese woman. I think Arthur might have talked to her, maybe got information.'

'Really. I don't know.' His expression was closed, set against her.

'Are you still friends with the Hallwrights?'

'Sure.'

'Have you seen them? They're back in the country.'

He just looked at her: no comment. None of your business. He put a hand up to his head and calmly smoothed his hair. He swallowed.

Eloise went on, 'I got an idea. There was a piece of paper with your name and a woman's name on it, that the police found in the flat. Did you know about that?'

'No.'

'They didn't ask you about it?'

He shrugged.'Not that I remember.'

'I wondered if Arthur was talking to you about the woman, when he rang you.'

'No.'

'Because your name and hers are together on the bit of paper. Separated by a forward slash.'

He mimed puzzlement, mouth turned down, slowly shaking his head.

'A forward slash. As in, Simon Lampton forward slash Mereana Kostas.'

Silence.

'And the woman, Mereana Kostas — she's a missing person.'

A bird flashed past the window and swooped towards the green slope of the mountain. Beyond the glass were the rings within rings of yellow light, dancing in the blue pool.

He was speaking.

'I have helped people all my life. Every week I look after women. I help them deliver their babies. When they need surgery, I fix them. I fix them.'

'I understand.'

'And you come here. You come here.'

'I'm sorry.'

'You come into my house and question me. These people, these names, I don't know who they are.'

Something rising. Eloise put up her hands. 'I'm sorry.'

He blinked, hard. His jaw working.

'I'm just trying to find out. I want to know what happened. I loved Arthur. He was the love of my life.'

Arthur.

Remember that morning, on the side of Mt Eden. Try to describe it. All the world dissolving, falling down . . .

She couldn't stop talking. Sitting there, holding the coffee cup in both hands, explaining herself while the man, the stranger, ranged near, came close, veered away again, his movements smooth, like liquid, he waited out near the edge of her explanation — watched and waited, in a zone of his own.

TWENTY

Eloise said, 'The way the rings of light move in the pool — they're not just "dancing". They move like fat people with big round arses, bumping and grinding.'

Rhythmically. The bump, the grind, the rings of light. The interval between the words could be expressed as a forward slash.

Double rings, circles but not round, they are wavering, elliptical, like smoke rings, yet their motion, conforming to the movement of the water, is regular and muscular.

It was hypnotic: the twanging, elastic samba on the pool's blue walls. On the white paint of the weatherboard house.

Simon Lampton was standing at the edge of the pool, one thumb hooked inside the waistband of his shorts. Eloise was sitting on a deckchair six feet away from him, holding a glass. They were surrounded by the patterns of light.

This was after she'd sat at his table, explaining herself. After she'd talked, and he'd listened, until she'd suddenly stopped talking, her throat closing over, and he'd stood over her, inspected her warily and said, 'What can I get for you? Would you like me to call someone? A friend? Your mother?'

Call Demelza. How taken aback he was when she laughed.

Eloise had looked up, swallowed, and said, 'Can we go outside? Get some air?' And then, 'I'd like a *stiff drink.*'

The bump/the grind/the rings of light.

Now he came near and squinted down at her, shading his eyes.

'Can I have another one?'

'You've had quite a lot.'

'Can I call you Simon?'

'Of course.'

'We've been brought together by a forward slash,' Eloise said.

He sat down heavily on the seat beside her. 'Christ.'

'I'm sorry.'

'Eloise. Eloise Hay, did you say? Let me make sure I've got it straight. Because you've told me quite a tale, and you've been a bit incoherent.'

'Sorry,' she said again.

'Your boyfriend's, partner's, name was Arthur Weeks. You and he spent half your time at his flat, half at yours.'

'I was partly living in a flat my parents owned. But I was about to move in with Arthur.'

'You arrived at Arthur's flat after getting off a plane from Sydney, and the police were there.'

'I walked up the hill, and they were on the road outside the flat. A woman had come out her back door and found Arthur dead in her yard. She hadn't heard anything, apparently. The police said he'd been taking sleeping pills, and that he'd walked out of the flat and fallen off the retaining wall. I didn't question. But there was a bruise on his leg and they didn't know how it had got there.'

Simon nodded. 'Right. So they looked at his phone records and found my number. And they found a note among his stuff with my name and the name of a woman.'

'And the only woman of that name they could find is missing.'

'But you don't know who the woman is, why Arthur wrote down her name?'

'No. I don't know why you and she are connected with a forward slash.'

'Neither do I,' Simon said. He shaded his eyes against the sun. 'Although, Arthur was a journalist, right, so maybe we were just the two people he'd decided to call that day. He called me because he was interested in the Hallwrights.'

'He didn't mention Mereana?'

'No. I hung up on him pretty quick. We were used to journalists taking an interest. Given that we shared our daughter with David Hallwright and his wife.'

'Arthur was a lovely person.'

Simon looked at her, expressionless.

'He was so talented. I used to tell him, just focus on one thing at a time, but he had so many ideas. There was the screenplay, and he'd written two plays, and he wanted to write a novel. And he worked for television, he did some writing on comedy shows — he was hilariously funny, did I mention that?'

'He sounds too good to be true.'

'I know, but he was.'

'But after he died, you got married?'

Eloise sat up. 'What do you mean "but"? Do you think I should have pined forever, never got with anyone else?'

He made a quelling motion with his hand. 'No. Sorry. I didn't mean it like that. It's just, this is all very confusing — you turn up out of the blue, you spring all this detail on me.'

'Yes, I married Sean. The thing is, getting married was so conventional, it made me feel safe. I really loved Sean. Now he's left me. And suddenly I realised I've been living in a kind of denial, a fog. I never asked any questions.'

'How did you know to look for me?'

'The police showed me the piece of paper with your name on it, when they were questioning me. Actually I remember overhearing the woman detective mentioning a gynaecologist at some stage.'

'The woman detective?'

'Her name's Marie Da Silva. She's got odd eyes, one blue, one brown. You'd remember her.'

He shrugged. 'I don't think so.'

'She remembers *you*.'

'Why do you say that?'

'When she mentioned you she made a kind of face. As if she had an opinion of you.'

'You've got a good memory, Eloise.'

'Well, it wasn't long ago I saw her.'

'Not long . . . ?'

'I went back to Central Police Station. Recently. I told them I regretted not asking any questions. I asked about the names.'

Simon got up so abruptly, she blinked. He went inside and came back with a glass and a bottle.

Eloise looked up from her phone. 'Just going to text my sister.'

He smiled, without warmth. 'Ah. That's an iPhone, is it? Where would we be without our smart phones.'

She shrugged. 'Yeah?'

'Can your sister wait? We're talking.'

'Okay, sure. I was going to ask her when I could borrow her dog again. You remember Silvio?' She put the phone away.

He refilled her glass and poured one for himself.

Eloise said rapidly, 'Thanks. It's good to talk. This is a beautiful house by the way.'

He was looking at her closely, tipping back his drink. He reached across, picked up a phone that was lying on the next chair, checked its screen. There was a kind of grace about him, as if the air around him was heavy, liquid and he was moving against it.

'I bet your hands never shake,' she said.

The rings of light played on the white wall above their heads.

Eloise followed a line of thought. It wavered, faded. She tried to organise her mind. 'When Arthur rang you, you were at David Hallwright's country place. Rotokauri.' '

'I remember.'

'I met the Hallwrights at the opera. Scott Roysmith introduced me.'

He looked sharply sideways, as if distracted from some intense calculation. 'Roysmith from TV? You know him?'

'I work for him. That's how I met Arthur, we both did degrees in communications, then worked in TV, although he was older than me. I had an internship at TVNZ back then; he'd already been there for years. He started doing freelance work, the comedy shows . . .'

'Have you talked to people about your . . . enquiries? Talked to Roysmith?'

'No. Not at all. I haven't even told my shrink about it.'

'You have a shrink?'

'Well, a therapist. I'm trying it out. I've been a bit unhinged since Sean left.'

'What about your sister?'

Eloise hesitated, lied. 'No.'

'Maybe the best thing is not to tell anyone at this stage.'

'Do you think?'

He settled himself closer to her. 'It occurs to me that this interest-ing story, this little mystery — even though I don't actually think it's a mystery really, just an awful, tragic accident — it might have things about it that make it a bit sensitive.'

Eloise said thickly, 'Yes. I agree. You were at Rotokauri with the Hallwrights when Arthur rang you. The Mereana woman is presumably still missing. And *Ed Miles* was at Rotokauri too. The Minister of Justice. Although he was police minister back then.'

'How do you know that?'

'Arthur made some notes. I took them from his flat after he died. I was only supposed to take my clothes . . .'

Simon swallowed. His face was flushed. 'Notes.'

'Just a few notes — and also I've got a photo of Mereana.'

His eyes were fixed on her. 'Really.'

'Well, it's a faded photo, like a Polaroid maybe, with the name Mereana written on the back. It's old. She's a girl. Maybe about twelve, thirteen?'

Eloise stared into her glass, which was empty already. 'It's funny, Simon, I wasn't going to tell you all this. I was just going to ask you a few things, non-committally. Without really explaining. But you've been very nice.'

Automatically, he refilled her glass.

'And I've been short of company. I borrowed my sister's dog . . .'

He was looking down at his phone. 'My wife's coming home in a minute.'

'Oh. Sorry. I'd better go.' She got up, and the world tipped sideways. She caught hold of the top of the deckchair. 'Whoops.'

His voice at her elbow. 'You're drunk.'

'Nonsense. I'll be fine.'

'You can't drive.'

'I walked here actually.'

'Oh, okay.'

Eloise thought for a moment. The surface of the pool was so dazzling, so dizzy-making. 'I'm going to call a taxi. What number Pukeora are you?'

Simon rubbed his face hard, an agitated movement.

'No, look. Don't bother calling a cab. I'll drive you home. Where do you live? You could show me these notes of yours.' He caught hold of her arm. 'If there's any mystery, Eloise, perhaps you and I could solve it together.'

He said, 'You *walked* from Starlight Peninsula to my place? All the way? It must have taken hours.'

'It's not that far. People never get out of their cars; they don't realise how easy it is to walk. When I was a kid, if I was bored, I used to walk from Remuera out to Avondale.'

'Quite a weird kid, were you?'

'Well, slightly weird, maybe. My sister's a more normal version of me. Carina. She's a journalist.'

The BMW shot smoothly up the motorway on-ramp, merged, accelerated. The wheels of the heavy, expensive car made a clicking sound, like a train. Simon Lampton was still and alert, gripping the wheel.

'What kind of journalist?'

'Carina Hay Hillman. She writes for the *Record*.'

'Oh yes. I've seen the name.'

Eloise gave directions. Simon drummed his fingers on the wheel, looked at his watch.

She said, 'When I took Arthur's notes from the flat, I wasn't supposed to. So I hope you won't mention them to anyone.'

'I won't.'

'Not that they're particularly significant, necessarily.'

He glanced at her. 'You don't think they would have been useful to the police?'

'There's nothing there they didn't know already.'

'Okay,' he said.

Eloise rested her hand against the cold window. 'Do you believe in ESP?'

'No.'

'Would you say it's just the subconscious, reading signs?'

'Yes. Or coincidence. Or nothing. There's no science.'

They drove through an area of industrial sprawl: car yards with lines of fluttering flags, a warehouse standing in a field, the sun sending a flash off its iron roof.

Eloise said, 'When the policewoman and I were in Arthur's flat, I was so shocked I couldn't think straight. They'd told me he was dead. Everything was incredibly intense. All the layers, everything I expected had been taken away, and I was raw.'

'Everything you expected?'

'Arthur and I had a life we'd built up. Routines, habits — expected life. It made a barrier. And that morning it was as if the barrier had been smashed, and suddenly there was nothing between me and . . . information. I built up another life with Sean, and now that's been smashed too. Nothing between me and the world.'

'You've been unlucky.'

'When Arthur died, I was frantic to find someone else. To get away from the information. But now I've started to think about it, to face it. I've been back to Arthur's flat. It's on the side of Mt Eden.'

'Right. I suppose that's why there was a high retaining wall,' Simon said. His tone was level, smooth. His fingers gripped and twisted on the wheel, making the leather squeak.

'In Arthur's flat that morning — the morning he died. All my defences were stripped away. The scene hit me, when I was completely raw. I've been back. I remember that moment now, and I'm convinced.'

'Convinced of what?'

'That there was someone in the flat with Arthur on the morning he died.'

Silence. He glanced sideways, his smile crooked, unconvincing. Finally he said, 'The plot thickens.'

Eloise winced at his tone. He was humouring her. And she was boring him. It was too weird. Telling all this to a complete stranger, whose home she'd invaded, who was now having to drive her across town to get rid of her, in order to spare his wife the unpleasant intrusion. Simon Lampton was simply someone Arthur — reckless, hyperactive Arthur — had rung in his solipsistic quest for interesting material. She had a sudden terrible vision of herself as an ageing, drunken bore, forever having to be *dealt with* by normal people.

'Never mind. It doesn't matter.'

'Go on. It's all very intriguing.'

But he sounded so politely insincere. What a disaster she'd become. Even Carina was starting to look a bit fed up, what with the night-time phone calls and dramatic appearances, not to mention the fire. Although she'd been very forgiving when Eloise had absent-mindedly returned Silvio in a blackened state, covered in toe toe and soot from nose to tail.

Finally she said, 'I don't know exactly *why* I think someone else was in the flat. That's why I went back, to try to recall. Maybe it was a smell, or an indentation in a chair, or things out of place. It was something the police wouldn't have noticed, but I picked it up because I spent most of my time there.'

'But wouldn't there have been visitors often? And even if there *was* a visitor, it wouldn't necessarily mean he or she had anything to do with Arthur's death.'

'The police checked. None of our friends had been by that morning. So if anyone was there, it was a stranger.'

'Did you tell the police you felt someone had been there?'

'No.'

'Why not?'

'Because it's only a feeling, and I'm not sure I even had it back then. I've only uncovered it now.'

'Pretty tenuous,' he said, looking ahead.

'Exactly. You can't tell people, the police, you have a *feeling*. That you've developed a feeling you didn't even know you *had* back then.'

'It wouldn't have much evidentiary value, no. Also, you said he died the morning he was found, that's a fact, right? The neighbour came out and found him. So even if you were noticing some missing item or whatever, it could date from any time when you were in Sydney. Not necessarily on the morning he . . . passed away.'

'You drive very fast, don't you.'

'Sorry. I wasn't thinking.' He slowed down, then almost immediately speeded up again.

Eloise gripped the top of her seatbelt.

After a moment she said, 'Missing item.'

'Do I turn left here?'

'First left and then right, onto the peninsula road.'

Silence. The big car hissed over the chip seal.

Eloise bit her nail. 'You said *missing item*.'

'Did I? No. I'm not sure.'

'I didn't think of that. I thought I must have seen some clue, or sensed it. I didn't think maybe something was *missing*.'

It was a high tide, the estuary a brimming stretch of silver beyond the tip of the land. Inland, the water looked viscous, almost bursting, like the skin of a blister. The creek was full almost up to the bridge, and only the tops of the mangroves were visible in the still water. Skeins of high cloud stretched over the dog park, a line of grappling ropes thrown towards the horizon, their angle making the whole vista seem as if it was on a slant.

Simon parked and she led him down to the creek, showing him the wooden bridge and the path along the peninsula.

He stood shading his eyes, looking over at the dog park. He was very tall. Broad shoulders, curly hair, big hands. Something so self-contained about him, so controlled. She had a moment of — what could you call it — incredulity? That she was standing here with this unknown person. It was entirely improbable he should be here at all. Sudden memory: when she was a student she used to think, I like that person. Somehow, I am going to find my way into his house. It was usually a man — she was better at making friends with men. She had managed to enter Lampton's house, now he was about to enter hers.

Did she like Simon Lampton? The way he'd led her to the wooden seat in his garden, sat her down and placed two fingers on her wrist. Looking into her eyes, his expression intent, respectful, serious. The freshness of his shirt. The clean, masculine smell of him. His big hand resting lightly on her arm.

Don't get carried away. It's called a good bedside manner. They all do it; they learn it at medical school. They touch you somewhere nice and safe, a brief comforting squeeze on your arm or foot, before leaving you to get on with your dying.

All that. But yes, she did like him. He had a way of looking sideways, as if, beneath his smooth politeness, there was something more real. His patients were women; he must be used to covering his male nature under a veneer of gentleness, concern. Not scaring the ladies — he was good at that. But sometimes his smile dropped and he gave you a shrewd, assessing look, as if, during a crisis, he would swap the pleasantries for toughness, efficiency, pragmatism.

Funny, he is most charming at the exact moment he stops smiling.

He followed her along the creek path; now they surveyed the blackened bushes on the fenceline, and the base of the toe toe, rising crookedly out of the grass like a dead tooth.

'What happened here?'

'We had a little scrub fire.'

'This weather. Everything's tinder dry.'

'And then some moron drops a cigarette . . .' Eloise pointed across the lawn. 'This is my house.'

'Very nice. Someone's home, I see.'

'No. I live alone.'

'Someone's upstairs. At the window.'

She squinted up, shading her eyes. 'There shouldn't be anyone in there.'

He shrugged. 'Your ex. Your sister.'

'No. No one. And it's not Amigo's day.'

'Well, let's go and see.'

The door was deadlocked. She opened it and called, 'Sean?' The hallway was silent and hot, crossed with sunlight from the high window. Dust motes whirled in the air. The alarm was switched off. Hadn't she set it, since there was no Silvio to trigger it?

She called out again.

There was no sound except the seagulls crying above the house and the ticking of the noisy clock in the kitchen. And a faint, metallic clang, as if someone had bumped against the garage door at the front. Could Sean have gone out through the door that connected the garage to the house?

But there were voices behind her.

Nick and Simon Lampton were facing each other on the path, Nick slowly raising his sunglasses, pushing them to the top of his head. He was wearing jeans and a red T-shirt.

Simon turned to Eloise, his face inscrutable.

'Oh Nick, hi! Nick, Simon Lampton.'

The two men shook hands. Nick looked hard at Simon, who declined to meet his eyes, only looked at Eloise with an odd, smiling expression.

'Simon says he saw someone in the house. At the window. Did you see anyone?' she asked.

Nick shook his head.

Simon smiled with mouth not eyes. He was impatient, keen to move on. 'The sun was right on it. Impossible to see really. Probably a curtain blowing.'

Nick said, 'A trick of the light.' His tone was faintly derisive.

Silence.

Nick tried to engage, to catch Simon's eye, but Simon turned away, jingling his car keys.

Eloise said to Simon, 'Are you in a rush?'

'I was just going to ask if you wanted me to cut your grass,' Nick said.

'Oh, thanks, that's really nice of you, but I've still got Goodfellow. Goodfellow Nkemba — he does a lot of lawns around here.'

'Okay. See you later, Eloise.' He flipped his sunglasses down over his eyes and went off along the path, with a backward glance.

Simon passed his keys from one hand to the other. 'Who was that?'

'Nick, he lives across the way.'

'All right, is he? Seems a bit, I don't know . . .'

'A bit what?'

'What was he doing on your property?'

She laughed. 'We're a bit more relaxed about boundaries here. Not like over your side. With your gated communities. Your security details.'

'I hope you trust him.'

Eloise thought about Nick's backward stare. He was much younger than Simon Lampton. Next to Nick, Simon appeared smooth, affluent; everything about him, from his clothes to his expressions, was infinitely more complex. She looked at his expensive shoes, his air of competence. He was a doctor. Well respected. A pillar. It was right to trust him.

'So, Eloise . . . ?'

She refocused, understood the tone: he meant she was using up his time. Time is money.

'Do you want to see Arthur's file?'

He nodded casually. 'Sure. Why not?'

'Come inside. Nick's okay, he's just a neighbour. He's incredibly useful around the place. One of those practical guys. Always has his toolkit on him. Do you want a drink? Just sit there if you like, sorry about the paw prints, that's Silvio, he's always covered in mud. From the estuary. He likes to get down and wallow in it. I'm thinking of getting a puppy, but I'm at work all day. I have to move out, my husband and I will have to split the assets, you know, go fifty-fifty. Because he's left me, and he's not coming back. His family's rich, he's an heirloom. He's got this actress. This bimbo, *narcissist*. Everyone says she's an idiot; she's into spiritual self-improvement, all kinds of humourless New Age bullshit. He's making us sell the house but I love the peninsula; I love the dog park but it's a bit challenging at night sometimes. That's why I borrow Silvio. For the company.'

She left him and went out to the Honda, sliding the file out from the cavity under the spare wheel. Should she take it to Klaudia next session?

Klaudia. An image of the therapist appeared, along with a lingering sense of *tristesse*. Transference again. Not erotic exactly (not so much about Klaudia's soft, fair hair and wry, crafty smile), more just a yearning for her large, square, blonde presence. Note to self: think up something very 'worrying' for next session. Something to get old Klaudia frowning intently and reaching for the textbooks . . .

Eloise now entered a daydream she'd begun to have lately: filling the house with people. Klaudia, on an extended house call. Carina and the Sparkler. Silvio. Nick. Scott and Thee. Maybe Simon Lampton, too. The more the merrier. Having them move in and stay. After an earthquake, say. Catastrophic floods. All in it together. Camaraderie. Never a moment to yourself.

Simon hadn't moved. He was staring out through the ranch slider, over the brown grassland to the dog park. His expression was far away, distracted.

'Air,' he said, vaguely.

She sat down next to him with the file on her knees. 'You want the window open?'

'You said your ex is an heirloom. You mean an *heir*.'

'That's what I said. He's an heirloom to the Rodd family fortune.'

'An *heir*. To the Rodds. The *Rodd* family, no less. How did you meet him?'

'He's an intellectual property lawyer. He came to ask me if I had a copy of a screenplay Arthur had written for one of his clients. Then one day he came to the studio with a Chinese businessman who'd been buying up farms. The guy presented us with photos of himself and the prime minister. Sean was part of the entourage. He's a lawyer at Jaeger's.'

'Jaeger's act for the Hallwrights.'

'Yeah. The *Soon* franchise. Soonworld. All that.'

'All that,' Simon repeated. A look of intense calculation in his eyes.

'Here,' Eloise said. She turned over the photo of Arthur sitting on a rock, the green West Coast bush behind him. The intensity of his expression. His pale, young face and startling eyes.

Simon made a sound in his throat. He swallowed.

Eloise frowned. 'He always wore that shirt. It was his favourite.'

His thin legs crossed, one pale ankle visible, a boyish sock. His face was pale, his lips blue. Faint purple shadows under his eyes. Rain had slicked his hair down across his scalp, and his arms were folded tightly across his chest.

'He's cold,' Simon whispered.

'Yes. It was freezing. The rain was bucketing down. But it was beautiful, in a, you know, melancholy, *atmospheric* way. We were somewhere near Greymouth. We walked along a river that was banked by big grey stones. And we came to a kind of mystery, a pile of deers' feet, heaped on the bank. Left there by hunters. It was eerie.'

'He's so young.' Simon reached out as if to take the picture, drew back. 'I have a son looks about that age.'

Eloise traced the edges of the photo with her finger. 'I'd like to have a son.'

'Maybe you will, one day.'

'I need a man first. At least briefly. Or I could do an Anita O'Keefe. I'm conducting a poll, by the way. Asking everyone. Who do you think's the father?'

Simon looked straight at her, searching her face.

'Of Baby O'Keefe?' she prompted.

'No idea,' he said.

Eloise thought for a moment. 'Most people make a guess. One out of the front bench. Jack Dance. Colin Cahane. Ed Miles.'

He shrugged.

'Funny. For some reason, you've made me imagine you know the answer.'

'I told you, I've got no idea.'

'Maybe you do know, since you're friends with the Hallwrights.'

'Why would they know?'

'As political insiders. Members of the inner circle. Is Ed Miles a friend of yours?'

He made a slight face. 'No.'

'Oh, you don't like him?'

'I didn't say that.'

'I've met him up at Q, when he's been in for interviews. He's unnerving. His eyes bore into you.'

'That's true. He's very observant.'

'What was it like being on holiday with him?'

'Fine. Very pleasant.'

'Pleasant! You know, I met him in passing, at Q, and it was strange, he knew my name.'

'Why is that strange?'

'I hadn't been dealing with him directly. We hadn't been introduced. Why should he know my name?'

'Maybe he makes it his business "to know everything". Part of his scary aura.'

'So you admit he's scary.'

'Well, sure. He's about as cuddly as a lizard. But he's trying to soften his image.'

'Because he wants to take over from Jack Dance.'

'So they say. Dance is low in the polls, and Miles wants the job.'

'And Miles is maybe fuelling the illegal spying allegations against Dance? Secretly helping the Opposition fan the flames.'

'Possibly, but I don't follow politics closely.'

'And your friend Hallwright's helping Miles. Hallwright, back from Monte Carlo or wherever. He's supposedly been meeting with Miles. Plotting.'

'I wouldn't know.'

There was a silence. They were looking hard at each other. Eloise put her hand on his arm. 'Simon. If there was something funny about Arthur's death . . .'

He drew back. 'It sounds like a tragic accident.'

'But if there was something odd about it . . . Arthur rang you at

Rotokauri while Hallwright and Miles were there. The fact that he called you was investigated . . .'

'It was nothing to do with Miles or David . . . with Hallwright. The only *tenuous* link is between me and Arthur, because the records showed he rang me twice. He was looking for gossip. Simple as that. The police made a quick inquiry, found nothing. End of story.'

'It's just, I was thinking, Jack Dance would like to find something on Ed Miles and Hallwright.'

Simon folded his arms across his chest. 'I understand you've got caught up in this idea of looking back. Now that your marriage has ended, and you're on your own, brooding perhaps. And you've got these ideas about "something funny" and "digging dirt" and "mysteries". But from what I've seen, politics doesn't work like that. Not in our boring little country. Jack Dance will be trying to save himself in the usual way. Shoring up support. Rallying his base. Whatever they do. No black ops. No cloak and dagger.'

'*Brooding?* How very patronising.'

'Sorry. I just mean politics isn't like that here. You don't get secrets and mysteries. From what I've witnessed — in the time I spent at Rotokauri, for example — it's all incredibly humdrum and tedious. Admin. Bureaucracy. Committees.'

Eloise sifted among the photos. 'Here's the one I wanted to show you.'

It was an old photo, the colour mostly bleached out of it. The pretty Maori girl on a park bench among lupin bushes, swinging her thin bare legs, gaps in her teeth, hair flying up on one side as if caught by a gust of wind, dark hair, pale eyes.

Simon reached for the photo. He didn't say anything.

'Any ideas?'

'No. Who is she?'

'Look, on the back it says: Mereana. It's not a common name, it's got to be Mereana Kostas, whose name's next to yours in Arthur's note.'

'Me and her and a forward slash. Well, whatever he had in mind, it doesn't mean anything to me. I've never seen this little girl.'

'It's an ancient photo. She won't be a little girl any more.'

'I suppose I could ask Karen, my wife. You could lend me the photo, and I could show her.'

Eloise leaned closer. 'What's that next to the bench? I didn't notice it before. It's a golf club.'

Simon's mouth turned up on one side, an odd, pained smile. 'Yes, well, look just below her feet.'

'Are they golf balls?'

He said, 'Someone's been hitting balls into the dunes.'

'Do you think she's at a beach?'

'Those bushes are lupins. They only grow at the beach I think.'

'Do you think Detective Da Silva should see this? The thing is, I didn't want to admit I had the file after all this time. I shouldn't have taken it. I should have given it back ages ago. I hid it; I didn't even look at it until recently.'

Simon shook his head. 'No need to mention it. It wouldn't tell the police anything new.'

'But it would confirm there really *is* a Mereana somewhere, and what she might look like now.'

'They'll mark the photo as evidence and you'll never get it back. They'll take the file and you'll have nothing of Arthur's to keep. You still won't have any answers.'

'I suppose.'

'That's my opinion. What else is in there?'

'Notes for his screenplay, and on who was staying at Rotokauri that summer.'

'The police already know that, too.' He was looking at the picture of Mereana again. 'How about I take this. Ask Karen.'

'Would your wife know anything?'

'Maybe she'd remember this girl.'

Eloise hesitated. 'I'd like to keep the file together.'

'I could take the whole thing.'

'Your wife could come here. Have a glass of wine, take a look.'

He thought about this, rubbing his hand hard over his face.

'On second thoughts, maybe we should keep it between ourselves. My wife's a lovely person but she's not very discreet.'

'Is it a secret?'

'You said yourself, you stole the file from the scene, from under the noses of the examining forensic team. You withheld evidence.'

'So I should hand it in?'

'No. You shouldn't. Technically you should, but in human terms, it's your memento of Arthur, and you should keep it. Not have it taken off you by some pen-pushing cop who wants to stick it in a file and let it gather dust. It's not going to tell them anything new.'

'That's what I thought. I'm glad I showed it to you. I thought of mentioning it to my therapist. Asking her what to do.'

'No need. Stash it. I imagine a house belonging to a member of the Rodd family would have a safe?'

'No. What would we put in it?'

'Well, put it wherever you put your valuables. Your heirlooms.'

Eloise shrugged.

Simon got up and walked to the window. He looked across the deck to the creek and the dog park.

'Does your neighbour come around often?'

'Quite often. He's new. I like him. We met each other when another neighbour's house was raided by the police. There was a whole lot of noise and screaming and he came over. I'd got such a fright I was glad to see him.'

'It must be lonely here at night.'

Eloise waved a hand. 'I love it. The peace. The tides. The . . . seagulls.'

He smiled, although he looked pained. 'You sounded like my daughter when you said that.'

'The one you share with the Hallwrights.'

'No, the other one. Claire. She's my biological daughter. The other, Roza Hallwright's daughter, is adopted of course.'

He looked around the room. 'Life's so strange. You're here all alone in this stone house . . .'

Eloise waited. He seemed to have lost his composure.

'You arrive out of the blue at my house, you're describing this dead boyfriend of yours, you're talking and drinking my wine, you've got me driving you across town and you're talking intensely and showing me pictures until you've almost got me convinced it all *does* have something to do with me. And yet I have *no idea* who you are, or who *he* is, or who the girl in the picture is, or why I'm here.'

His expression was strained.

She faltered, 'But there is a connection.'

'There is no connection.' He came towards her. 'There is no connection between us.'

Eloise stepped back.

'Did you tell anyone you were going to contact me?'

'No,' Eloise said.

'No one?'

'Absolutely no one. It was an impulse.'

He put his hand on her shoulder, intensity in his eyes. His face was damp; she could smell sweat. Sudden memory: a dream, red light, sunset over the park, a dog crossing the horizon.

She said, 'Only Nick knows you're here.'

Silence.

He stepped away.

'I'm sorry, Eloise.'

She stared. 'What's wrong?'

'Nothing.' He sat down on the sofa and briefly put his head in his hands.

She sat down next to him. 'Why are you sorry?'

He looked up. 'Because you're alone.'

She thought about this. The statement was mildly pleasing; it made him seem kind. She said, 'Oh well.'

Finally he said, 'Listen, there's something I need to explain.'

'Okay.'

He paused, thinking. She waited.

'It would be helpful if you didn't tell anyone about our meeting.'

'Why?'

He put up his hands. 'Just wait. Let me explain. I have a family connection with the Hallwrights, right? My adopted daughter is Roza Hallwright's biological daughter. As a family, as a group, we've had to negotiate that. Over the years we've got very close, gone on holiday together. We've become friends. During some of that time, before David Hallwright retired, my wife and I had to take into account the fact that he was the prime minister. So we had to behave accordingly. Which is why I hung up on Arthur when he rang me. We did everything we could not to make David's life more difficult than it already was. Now, he's not PM any more, but his friends and colleagues are still in government, and the rules still apply. Arthur's death was nothing to do with me, but he did ring me when I was at Rotokauri, and that fact was investigated by the police. It's the most tenuous connection, but one thing I do know is that in politics even tenuous connections have potential for inconvenience.'

'Potential for inconvenience?'

'It's the kind of thing that can be picked up by the media. You can imagine something like, Police Investigated Death of PM's Stalker.'

'Arthur wasn't a stalker!'

'Yes, but this is a set of facts the media would enjoy playing with.

You know that Arthur was a good person. I believe you. He was perfectly pleasant on the phone, as far as I can recall. But he "took an interest in the prime minister", and then he was found dead. You can see how the media, and David's opponents, too, could have spun it back then. Imagine the internet conspiracy theories. Man stalks PM, is then found dead. It would have been totally unfair on the Hallwrights, but that's how it could have been characterised. And let's not forget it would have been unfair on Arthur, too — his name, the memory of him. I'm not sure anything's changed.'

'Hallwright's not in politics any more.'

'He's not in government but he's still very much involved.'

'With trying to get rid of Jack Dance. For Ed Miles.'

'Who was at Rotokauri at the time. You can surely see why I feel that you and I should be discreet. I'm the only actual link to them because I'm the one Arthur called.'

'Is backing Ed Miles Hallwright's way of gaining power again? Without having to be elected himself?'

Simon shrugged. 'Who knows? I really don't follow politics. David Hallwright is my friend. And so is Roza. All I'm saying is that, for them, this is the kind of non-story that could be turned into a story.'

'Arthur's death is a non-story.'

'I'm sorry, don't look bitter. I know it's not a non-story to you, to everyone who . . . loved him, but what I'm saying is it's a non-story as far as the Rotokauri group are concerned. It could have blown into something, and they would have had to spend a lot of energy calming it down. Fortunately, it didn't.'

'Fortunately . . .'

'It was my fault. He rang *me.* It was my fault. Not theirs.'

There was a silence. Eloise looked at him.

She said, 'Why do you say it was your fault?'

He shook his head.

'Why do you say it was your fault, when it was Arthur's idea to ring you? You didn't call him.'

'Okay, not my fault. But he rang me, so I had to deal with it. I had to try not to let the fact that he was dead five minutes later damage them. I mean, Christ, that's all we're talking about. A couple of calls. It's ridiculous. I don't even know why the police came to me. I remember thinking at the time maybe they were just indulging their curiosity. You get a vague link to the PM's circle, so you go poking around just so you can get some more interesting work stories. Talk to more glamorous people than you usually interrogate.'

'Do you really think that?'

'Well, what was *Arthur* doing? All he wanted was to spy on the beautiful people.'

'To spy? He wasn't a gossip columnist. He was an artist. He wanted to find things out. To research. Arthur was interested in the truth.'

'In the course of which he came on like a gossip columnist.'

'That's not true.'

'How do you know? Were you there when he called me?'

'No. I didn't know he'd done it.'

'The Hallwrights were all over the gossip magazines. Especially that summer. There were journalists jumping out of the bushes. David and Roza had the extra exciting detail about them that they were — are — so wealthy. But, no, your Arthur was engaged in something "higher".'

'Yes, he was. He'd written a screenplay. He was going to write a novel. He wasn't interested in gossip magazines. He wasn't doing it for money.'

'But it was all about *him*. He didn't care who he hurt. People were just his material. Fodder.'

'That's not true. People were his subjects, but he loved his subjects. He was a kind person.' She stared. 'Anyway, why are you talking about him like this? You said you just hung up on him.'

Silence.

'Did you meet him?'

'No.'

'Why are you angry?'

Simon made a quelling motion again. 'I'm not angry. I can just see the potential for inconvenience, all over again.'

She looked at his big hand. Rock steady.

'Inconvenience,' she repeated.

He said in a heavy tone, 'Look, I know you loved Arthur, and I know this is painful. I'm just asking if you and I can keep this between ourselves. We have to be aware that our actions can hurt other people. People are *not* just subjects. They're *not* just material for screenplays or novels. People have private lives. They have interests. Loved ones. Secrets.'

He put a hand on her arm. 'People have a right to privacy.'

A long pause. Finally Eloise said, 'Which Arthur sometimes didn't appreciate. That's what you're saying.'

'Yes.'

She looked down at her hands, twisting in her lap. 'He was a kind person. A good person.'

'But in his enthusiasm . . .'

'Sure, maybe he barged in at times when he could have been more sensitive. Maybe he used people's details when he shouldn't have.'

He looked at her keenly. 'Oh? Did he use you as a subject?'

'Only a few times. In his plays. Not as often as he used my mother. He had a running character, this battle-axe . . . Anyway, it doesn't matter.'

His hand was still on her arm. He lowered his voice. 'How did that make you feel?'

'When he used things I'd said or done? Flattered sometimes, other times annoyed.'

'And your mother?'

'I'm not sure she ever knew. She didn't have much time for his stuff. She thought he was a lightweight, that he spent too much time doing TV. When he used her as a character he changed her accent. Made her Scottish or whatever. Very subtle.' Eloise sighed. 'In one skit, he described her to a tee, but he made the character a man. A father not a mother. It's just what creative people do, I suppose.'

'But it can leave people feeling invaded. Or hurt.'

She pulled away. 'All he did was ring you.'

Simon said softly, 'Yes, but he wanted to know about Roza. And her daughter. Our daughter.'

'He said that? You didn't tell me he wanted to find out about your daughter.'

'Didn't I?'

'No.'

He said again, 'People have a right to privacy.'

Eloise stared at him. 'God. I'm sorry.'

He said, 'It's all right. You haven't done anything wrong.'

'Well, I did come barging in to your house.'

'You had a reason. I completely understand.'

'I suppose you think I'm just like Arthur.'

'No, I don't. I don't, Eloise. I think you're lovely.'

'Really?'

'Yes, sure. I think you're actually a sensitive person. I think you understand. I can trust you, can't I? You understand this sort of tightrope I've had to walk, having the Hallwrights in my life. I've struggled with it at times. I'm just like anyone else, there are lots of things I would have liked to talk about, but I've had to keep them private. Because people depend on me. Four kids. The Hallwrights, my wife, you name it.'

'Yes.'

He touched her arm again. 'We could keep this conversation to ourselves, and maybe I could think some more about it, and see if I can come up with anything else.'

She tried to compose herself. Finally she said, 'Okay. Come back soon then. Come and visit. I'll be here.'

He stood up. 'I will.' His face sagged; he looked exhausted suddenly.

'I'm sorry I barged into your house,' she said.

'Please don't apologise. It's fine. I'm glad we've talked.'

She walked to the front door with him.

'Take care,' he said.

'Bye. Thanks for the ride.'

He walked away, turned. 'Eloise, I'm not entirely sure, but the person I thought I saw at the window upstairs?'

She waited.

'Was wearing something red.'

TWENTY-ONE

Eloise lay on the bed, with Silvio across her legs. She had persuaded Carina to drop him off for a short visit, while the Sparkler was at a school camp. He was chewing a strip of dried raw hide.

'Listen, Silvio,' she said.

One day the monk appeared at dinner time and sat in the dining room window. Kovrin was delighted, and very adroitly began a conversation with Yegor and Tania of what might be of interest to the monk; the black-robed visitor listened and nodded his head graciously, and Yegor and Tania listened, too, and smiled gaily without suspecting that Kovrin was talking not to them but to his hallucination.

Silvio yawned. What beautifully white teeth he had. Note to self: ask the dentist about whitening. If she had a smile as pearly as Silvio's, would that help her get dates? Scott and Thee, passing the phone between them, had rung her with two possibles; she had rejected one (you've got to be kidding) and had cautiously requested more information on the other.

And what about Nick?

She put down the Chekhov story, and drowsily addressed Klaudia. Simon Lampton? Yes, I found him. I made quite a hash of things. Intending to introduce myself in a polite and non-committal fashion, I went to pieces, told him more than I'd intended, drank a whole lot of his wine. Even got him to drive me home.

I entered his house. I got him to enter my house. But he didn't know anything. He said, There is no connection between us. He confirmed that Ed Miles was staying at Rotokauri the summer Arthur made contact, and that David Hallwright was there. He confirmed the police had briefly spoken to him. He had no memory of the detective, Marie Da Silva. Together we established that Mereana, whoever she is, appears in her photo to have been playing golf on a beach, as there is a golf club leaning against the park bench, and golf balls at her feet.

Very useful.

I am still alone, Klaudia. I am asking, but I have no answers.

And is it possible that Simon Lampton saw someone at the upstairs window of my house?

'He must have been mistaken,' Eloise said.

Klaudia lightly touched the page in front of her with her fingertips. She frowned.

Eloise went on, 'I guess he saw the blind moving, or the sun shining off the window. I rang Sean to check. I threatened to kill him as usual. He swore it definitely wasn't him. I believe him.'

Out there on the bricks, the leaves stirred, rearranged themselves. And there was the rat! Out it came — look at that — abruptly it was right up on its hind legs, front paws curled, sniffing the air. Watching it, Eloise said, 'But could it have been Nick?'

Klaudia swallowed and said, 'You said you had locked the house. It seems unlikely your neighbour would enter uninvited.'

'He came around the side of the house. He was wearing a red shirt.'

'Eloise, I wonder, have you considered doing something about your living arrangements? Perhaps moving to a different place.'

'Actually I'm going to be forced to move out.'

'By your ex-husband?'

'Yes, and I don't want to go. I love the peninsula.'

'Perhaps you could arrange for someone to stay with you until you leave. Other than the dog you've spoken of.'

'Remember I told you about the girl in the bus stop. *The girl in the bus stop is crying.*'

'Yes. We talked about the subconscious.'

'I was right. She was a girl, she was crying.'

'Yes.'

The rat was sniffing this way and that on the bricks. Move and pause, move and pause. Eloise thought of the rings of light in Simon Lampton's pool. She said, 'I loved Sean. Marriage to him made a protective barrier, and when it was gone, the barrier was smashed, and information rushed in. I've remembered the day of Arthur's death, how the information rushed in then, too. I was raw.'

'I think I understand.'

Eloise paused, listening to the drugged buzz of the cicadas. There was no sign of the old woman gardener. The light in the garden seemed liquid. How peaceful it would be to lie down in the grass out there, in the stripes of shade beneath the wisteria. She said, 'A house is a metaphor for the mind.'

Klaudia steepled her fingers. 'Sure. In a sense, what we are doing with our work here is treating your mind like a house. Together we are opening doors to old rooms, where things have lain hidden.'

'When I was younger, if I met someone I liked I would say to myself, I'm going to enter his house.'

Klaudia's smile was one of tolerant assent. She hadn't yet yawned or looked at her watch, although the air was so hot and close, and they had both slowed to a dreamy pace. Eloise looked at Klaudia's plump wrists, at her manly watch and bronze bracelet. Around her neck today she was wearing an entire small paua shell.

Done up to the nines, Eloise thought. Where was Klaudia going after this? She must be exhausted after five solid hours of nutters and bores. Personally, Eloise would make straight for the pub.

'The man. I went looking for answers. I entered the man's house. He entered mine. But he said, There is no connection between us.'

'And he said he saw someone else in your house,' Klaudia added.

'What does it all mean?'

Klaudia minutely shrugged. The rat had vanished.

Eloise went on, 'There was someone in Arthur's flat on the morning he died. I know it. Just like I knew that the girl in the bus stop was crying.'

'Okay.' Klaudia picked up her pen.

'When I went back to Arthur's flat and sat on the mountainside, I remembered.'

Klaudia's tone was probing, also gently disbelieving. 'And yet how could you know, Eloise, if you were not there?'

'I could tell, when I walked into the flat. The closest I've got is to think maybe there was an item missing. And there was something else.'

'Yes?'

'I don't know. Maybe it was a trace. Or a scent.'

Klaudia smiled, and pointed her pen at the photo on her desk.

'A scent. As if you are my dog, Linus.'

'Yes, as if I'm a dog.'

'I'm sorry, that was just a joke.'

'Maybe we're all dogs, Klaudia. We're all animals.'

Silence.

Finally Klaudia said, 'Well, sure. We do share a lot of DNA. With the . . . animal kingdom.'

'If I was a *dog* and telling you this, if I was *Linus*, it would be completely plausible, wouldn't it. Dogs know when someone's been in a room. They follow scents for miles.'

'Although, Eloise, dogs have millions more receptors for scent in their noses than we humans do. They have very big, powerful snouts.'

'Hmmm.'

Silence. They were smiling at each other. Grinning even. Because the conversation had lurched into the absurd. How absurd, too, to be *paying* Klaudia for this. If only they could just be friends. Go up the road for a coffee.

Would you like to come to my house, Klaudia? My real house. As opposed to wandering around in my mind.

But this would not be possible: Klaudia had explained the 'therapeutic paradox'. She was allowed to enter Eloise's mind, but Eloise was not allowed to enter hers, in other words to know anything about Klaudia. This was to protect Klaudia (from the nutters and bores) and to preserve the therapeutic process, which could not be clouded by the patient's knowledge of the shrink's personal circumstances.

Imagine the chaos if shrinks started befriending people whose minds they regularly messed with.

'Sorry, where were we?'

'Dogs and their noses.'

'Klaudia, information has been hidden from me. A whole layer of the world. I let Arthur down by not asking questions.'

'I see.'

'But if I do keep asking, I don't know what I'm going to find.'

She looked for the rat, but there was only a shiver in the pile of leaves.

Is this what madness is? Everyone is hidden. People are strange. One day you will walk out of your house and discover that everyone is a stranger.

Who is your neighbour? Who is your smiling blonde shrink, behind her therapeutic veil? Who is your mother? The jolly Northern matriarch with a heart of gold? Or the cold, rivalrous witch, who whispers death in your ear, *Godspeed*?

Eloise said, 'They can't be serious.'

Scott leaned back in his seat, linked his fingers behind his head. 'That's what I've heard. Group hysteria.'

'It's just not possible.'

'There was no static.'

'No!'

'They're going to say there were one or two real incidents of static shocks, and then everyone bought into it, and imagined they were getting them. The more nervous people were, the more they thought they were getting shocked.'

'Are you sure that's the line?'

'That's the rumour from my source. There is no scientific basis to say that staff have been subjected to shocks. Engineers, electricians and experts employed by the company will say the phenomenon didn't actually occur, except in people's minds.'

'I can't believe it.'

'There are no burns, E. No scars. There's no evidence.'

'But if everyone testified that they kept getting shocks.'

'Show me the evidence. Did we take a photo of Selena with her hair standing on end? With flames coming out the end of her stapler? Sadly, no.'

'Testimony is evidence. Witness accounts.'

'But where's the damage? The injury was momentary. It left no trace, except in the memory. And we have limited memory for pain. People are already wavering. The weak ones will be called on to say they were mistaken, especially if they're offered inducements. Or subjected to threats. This morning I passed through reception and heard Hine refer to Selena as "hysterical".'

'Scott. You think this is funny.'

They were watching a clip of Kurt Hartmann feeding his chickens. The great fist turned, thumb up, the stream of dusty seeds falling through the shining air. Beyond, a water trough reflected the sky, and the grass was unnaturally green. On the skyline, Chad Loafer idled in the golf cart.

Scott pressed a button and said, 'So much depends upon.'

'How's Thee by the way?'

'She's fine. She's going to contribute some of her photos to an exhibition. A red wheelbarrow glazed with rain water.'

'Good.'

'Beside the white chickens. Oh and another thing, E. Management would like us to do a story on group hysteria. As a psychological phenomenon. You can get onto the research next week.'

'No! That's hilarious, that is.'

Scott blinked, grinned. 'Why don't you come over to our place for dinner. Or the three of us can go out on a date. Me and my two favourite women.'

'Thanks. That'd be good.'

'Thee and I will find you a new man yet.'

'Well, that would be useful. You and Thee are pretty much my favourite people. So any ideas would be welcome.'

'Okay. Shall we do some work now?'

Eloise checked her watch. It was nearly one o'clock, when she had arranged to leave the building for a meeting.

They both frowned at the screen.

The café down the road from Central Police was mostly empty, and the woman behind the counter was arguing with her barista, a sullen youth who kept his head down, operating his coffee machine with moody disdain. The woman took Eloise's coffee order, raised one side of her lip, edged along the counter and resumed her low tirade. 'This is not your final. It's your final final . . .'

Detective Da Silva arrived. She moved with a jinking noise, as of concealed equipment or weaponry. Her hair stuck out like steel wool, the unruly golden strands catching the light. She was wearing khaki pants, a short jacket and girl combat boots.

She ordered a flat white and crossed the room.

'Eloise Hay. How are you?'

Eloise laid the policewoman's card on the table in front of her. 'I'm a barrel of energy.'

'Or a ball of laughs. What did you want to talk about?'

Eloise looked up at her, trying to decide how to begin.

'Well? I assume you have something in mind.'

'I found Simon Lampton.'

Da Silva remembered to sit down. 'Did you, now. How was he?'

'He was very nice.'

'Did he mind you turning up, raising ancient history?'

'He didn't know anything. He didn't remember you.'

Da Silva gave her a quick glance. 'Really.'

'I wanted to know if he could tell me anything about Arthur. He said he'd hung up on Arthur, that they'd barely talked. I asked him about Mereana. He didn't know anything about her either.'

The policewoman received her coffee and sprinkled sugar on top of the foam. For a moment, Eloise could only focus on her odd-coloured eyes, one blue, one brown.

'We're frantic up there,' Da Silva said. She waved her hand in the direction of Central. 'I haven't got time for dead files.'

Eloise said, 'Simon Lampton explained some things to me. How Arthur rang him and how he hung up, thinking Arthur just wanted gossip. How he, Simon, didn't want to create difficulties for the people at Rotokauri. He made me understand how tricky his life was then, sharing a daughter with the Hallwrights when there was such intense interest in them. I understand all that. And that things are still sensitive now. I can see Arthur shouldn't have rung him. Arthur's contacting Simon had nothing to do with the fact that he died, but it did create a potential for inconvenience.'

'Inconvenience. So you and Simon got on pretty well.'

'I liked him. He was nice about me turning up at his house.'

'You went to his *house*? How did that go?'

'It was fine. We talked, he explained things. He said, back then, he wondered why the police contacted him at all about the phone calls. He thought maybe you were curious about the Hallwrights. Which would make you not much different from Arthur.'

Da Silva laughed. 'He said that.'

'He made me feel sorry Arthur had caused him trouble.'

Da Silva played with a sugar sachet, tearing the edges. She had small, nimble fingers. 'I bet he was very calm.'

'He was.'

Da Silva tapped her fingers on the table. 'He has a thing he does. He calms, he quells.'

'I suppose.'

'I remember,' Da Silva said. 'He doesn't waver. He's a flat-line. You ask him something and he blocks. He winds you up then he soothes you down. And every now and then there's a little hint of steel. Like he's your dad.'

Eloise frowned. She said primly, 'It sounds as if you've thought about him quite a lot. Did you develop a crush on him?'

Infinite scorn in Da Silva's eyes. 'A crush. I'm a professional, Eloise. Not a schoolgirl.'

'He must have to stay calm in his job.'

'Sure. I imagine he's a good doctor. Very competent. Also, he's not above deploying the odd name-drop. Tactically. As in, I reminded him I was a detective; he reminded me he was on holiday with my boss.'

Eloise said, 'He seems a sincere person. He said he could tell I was more sensitive than Arthur was.'

'Right.' Da Silva's expression was tolerant, just slightly derisive.

'His whole concern, he said, was for his family. The Hallwrights, his wife, four kids.'

'Three kids.'

'He was kind. He made me see it's not always a good idea to go barging in.'

'Fair enough,' Da Silva said, amused. 'Although, that's what I do every day, Eloise. Barge in places where people don't want me. Barging in on him was a laugh, I can tell you.'

'He said as much. That you were doing it for the hell of it.'

Da Silva rolled her eyes. 'The nerve.'

'I understood . . . it's hard to explain.'

'Go on.'

Eloise frowned. 'Arthur was a lovely, kind person. But he used material from people's lives. Sometimes he might have been a bit insensitive or, I don't know, ruthless about it. He *did* barge in. He used everything.'

'I imagine that's what writers do.'

'But now I can see it from Simon's point of view. He didn't want

Arthur just picking up bits of his life and using them. Or the Hallwrights' lives. He told me Arthur asked about Roza Hallwright and the adopted daughter. Which seems pretty . . . Anyway, the point of this is that Simon hung up on Arthur, and that was the end of it. He doesn't know who Mereana Kostas is, so I guess the forward slash note was just Arthur reminding himself about two unconnected people.'

'Yes, we established that.'

'He doesn't want me to go around talking about it. But since you know about it already, it seems okay to talk to you.'

Da Silva's tone was faintly incredulous. 'Oh, good. Glad to hear it. It's funny, I'm usually the one who decides when it's okay to talk about an investigation. Into a death.'

Eloise paused to gather her thoughts. Da Silva was making her nervous.

She went on, 'I wanted to tell you something else. I think there was someone in Arthur's flat on the morning he died.'

'How do you know that?'

'I can sense it.'

'You can sense it? What does that mean?'

'I sensed it back then but I didn't know I had. And now I've *realised* that I sensed it back then.'

Silence. Detective Da Silva's nose was sprinkled with tiny freckles. Her expression altered as she listened; her small face had now sharpened into a mocking smile.

'Are you a psychic?'

'I'm serious.'

'I'm serious, too. I'm also overworked and short-staffed.'

'I've remembered sensing that someone had been in the flat. Either something was missing, or there was a smell. A scent. I've been back to the flat recently. I sat on the hill behind the flat. By the mountain track.'

'A scent.' Da Silva sat back, smoothed the top of her coffee with a teaspoon. She looked thoughtful. 'I remember that morning. It was a beautiful day. Summer. The hillside was all parched. Dry grass — that's the smell I remember.'

'You said there'd been an accident. But then I saw the police on the mountainside, looking through the grass. I realised they were looking for clues.'

Da Silva said, 'Is there anything else you remember or know about Arthur's death? Anything you haven't told me?'

'No.'

'So, that's it? You've remembered sensing something, but you don't know what.'

'Yes.'

'You remember sensing someone other than Arthur had been in the flat. But surely the forensic team had been in the flat.'

'No, it was locked, I was the first in. He'd only just been found. You came to the door and told me.'

Da Silva looked at her reflection in the back of a teaspoon. She thought for a while.

'Maybe you *have* remembered something. But it's not enough for me to do anything about it. You know what I'm saying?'

'Yes.'

Da Silva frowned, deepening the crease between her brows. 'Sometimes you have to move on. Let it go.'

Eloise sighed. 'I let Arthur down.'

'You said that, but it's a fantasy. He's dead, right. So you should look after yourself. Get some counselling.'

'I've been seeing this shrink.'

'Good. There you go. Stick with that.'

Da Silva drank the last of her coffee. 'Listen, Eloise, I told you I'm overworked. That was a major understatement. Me and my friend Detective O'Kelly, remember him? We've got years of files. Normally I wouldn't have made the time to meet you. But I'll tell you a couple of things, okay?'

'Okay.'

'The first is, Simon Lampton remembers me. There is no way he doesn't. It doesn't mean anything that he denies it. He's presumably got better things to do than talk about the past with you. But he remembers me.'

'Are you sure?'

'No question. Also, he says we were investigating him for the thrill of it. That is outrageous. Police do not investigate people for the "thrill" of it.'

'Okay. Sure. Although cops are human.'

'He really got you eating out of his hand, didn't he.'

'Pardon?' Eloise said.

'The prime minister and the police minister, Ed Miles — my boss no less — were at Rotokauri with Lampton when Arthur called him. We couldn't go barging into Rotokauri like it was some dump in South Auckland. Storm on in there and get the bros up against the wall and see who said something stupid.'

'And Ed Miles is now justice minister. I know that.'

Silence.

Eloise said slowly, 'Were you told not to pursue it?'

Da Silva looked at her watch. 'Put it this way. I didn't know it back then, but I *sensed* we were being told we'd asked enough questions. And now I *remember* that sense. But I have no evidence to show that sense ever *existed*.'

Eloise felt pressure behind her eyes, warning of a possible headache. 'What does it all mean?'

'It means we should leave it alone. Leave Lampton alone.'

'But he's nice. I have a good feeling about him, as if he and I could be friends.'

Da Silva's smile was ironic. 'Really. I'll tell you one more thing, even though I shouldn't. Someone inquired off the record about Arthur's death.'

'How do you know? When?'

'It might have come from somewhere up the chain.'

'Up the chain?'

'Of command. From up high.'

'How do you know?'

'I was told. I haven't seen any evidence myself. It might have been an inquiry relating to Arthur's post-mortem.'

'Who would have done that?'

'I don't know. There's no proper record. Someone has covered their tracks.'

'What about Mereana Kostas?'

'The missing Mereana Kostas had one significant conviction, for a drug offence. She was jailed. She had an ex, a guy she'd had a child with, who told me she might have left the country and gone to the UK or Canada or Australia. But he was probably lying.'

'She left with a child?'

'No. The child had died years before. I didn't believe the ex. I said to him there's no record of her leaving, and no way she could have got hold of a false passport. And he said . . .'

Da Silva paused, as if considering whether to go on.

'He said what?'

'That Kostas, the name her criminal conviction was recorded under, wasn't the surname on her birth certificate. That she had a passport in her birth name before her conviction, and she renewed it, and left.'

'Did you find out more?'

'No. Because the death was an accident.'

'Who was Mereana?'

'No one. Maori mother, Australian Greek father. Five foot nine.

Black hair, green eyes. Scar on index finger. She got the drug conviction here, was in prison, got out, didn't get into any more trouble, probably worked under-the-table jobs in Auckland, vanished. No contact with family. No one reported her missing. This was years ago. She had nothing to do with Lampton or his Rotokauri friends. Completely different worlds.'

Eloise said, 'Arthur and I used to argue. I said he was taking on too many things at once. I thought there was a risk he'd turn into a jack of all trades master of none. So he stopped telling me what he was up to. As if he thought I would nag. He never mentioned any Mereana to me.'

'I'd say she's irrelevant to Lampton.'

Eloise looked at her watch. 'I've got to go and buy a birthday present. For a kid. What do eight-year-olds like?'

'I dunno. Lego.'

'She's a girl. A friend's daughter.'

'Girls like Lego. I did.'

'Have you got kids?'

Da Silva checked her phone, sent a text. 'No. No time.'

Eloise thought for a moment. 'Do you believe Andrew Newgate is innocent?'

'No.'

'Who do you think's the father of Anita O'Keefe's baby?'

Da Silva smiled. 'Good question.'

'Do you believe in ESP?'

'No.'

'Is it easy to disappear?'

'It was easier years ago. It's not now, unless you have help, resources. I'll tell you what I think — Mereana's dead. Most missing people are. Either she died here, or she somehow got to another country and died. She was probably a drug user, moved in nasty circles. Anyway, she's irrelevant.'

Eloise sighed. 'At least I've asked some questions.'

'Yeah. Hope you feel better.'

'I don't know.'

'I've got to get back to work. I've got a gang stabbing to investigate. Just for the "thrill" of it. You go and buy your Lego. Oh, and the father of Baby O'Keefe? It's the leader of the Opposition. Bradley Kirk.'

'No! A cross-party baby. A bipartisan baby. He's married. What d'you base it on?'

'Months ago, me and O'Kelly watched Kirk and O'Keefe together at the Hero Parade. On Ponsonby Road. He was in his sneakers, you know, trying to look like a youth. We were in the car.'

'Really.'

'There was chemistry. You heard it here first.'

'I think it's Jack Dance.'

'No. No chemistry. Wait until it's born. When it's a year old, you'll know. One-year-olds look like their father. It's a biological thing. In the animal kingdom. So the father doesn't kill the kid.'

Eloise winced, put a hand up to her forehead.

Da Silva paused. 'Are you all right?'

'Headache. I get migraines.'

'Oh. Are you driving?'

'No, walking back to work. I'll be fine.'

They parted on the corner, Da Silva walking away towards Central Police. Eloise saw a jagged silver flare just above the policewoman's head, as if her blonde hair had burst into flames. Around her body were small, vivid black holes edged with light, the air fraying like a moth-eaten curtain.

The light effects stayed mild enough for her to reach the toy shop, where she wandered through the bright shelves. There was *Soon and Starfish* merchandising everywhere, from Lego sets to lunch boxes to T-shirts. Blindly, she chose a large and expensive box of Lego.

'Do you do gifting?'

'Pardon?'

'Do you do stuff wrapping up?'

'I'm sorry?'

'God. Sorry.' It affected her like this sometimes. 'Do you do gift wrapping?'

She burst out of the shop carrying a box wrapped in festive blue paper decorated with a bow: some giant droid or Bionicle for little Iris Roysmith. It would probably take her weeks to assemble.

They had the air-conditioning turned up high in the stationery shop. Eloise lingered. The birthday cards were either sugary or frankly obscene; there were few for children. She picked the least awful, came out of the shelves. A tall man with black hair and a hawkish face turned away and headed for the door.

She went after him. 'You're following me.'

His face was tanned, his eyes small and very dark. His black hair was exceptionally thick and slicked back at the sides. Silver holes opened up and bloomed in the air around him. She rode out a wave of nausea.

His expression was open, confused. He shrugged. He had no idea what she was talking about.

She said loudly, 'You were on the bus. A woman fell over on you, dropped her shopping.'

An assistant came out from behind the counter.

'You were in Nick's house, on the peninsula. I saw you.'

'Excuse me. Wrong person.'

'You've got a tattoo. It's you. I've seen you. Show me your hand. Your *hand*.'

But his hands were in his pockets.

A voice behind her said, 'Is there a problem?'

'Wait,' Eloise said.

But he had edged away from them and was gone.

She followed him outside without paying for the birthday card. No sign of him in the street. The assistant confronted her on the pavement, and she had to trudge back in to hand over the money.

Outside in the heat, the nausea rose. Around the back of the store, in the car park, she stood on tip-toe but the fountain came up higher and was unstoppable, a great gout of hot poison rose and rose . . .

She wiped her mouth, looking around the sun-struck car park. No one to see. No witnesses except the CCTV: the grainy figure slinking away from the shameful splat on the asphalt. Crossing screens, vanishing into the space between one line of sight and another. She was there, she was not. She was recorded, she was not. She could see, but she was also blind; the silver edges around the black holes were so intensely bright. Her vision breaking up, she managed two things: to text Scott (the word 'migraine' was enough — he would understand, he would be incredibly nice about it) and to get in a cab.

The taxi drove her to the peninsula. Standing outside the house was Nick. Upstairs, from the window, Silvio silently watched the dog park.

She lay on the bed with a cold flannel on her forehead and whispered, 'Thank you for walking him.'

Silvio now jauntily entered the room, waggling his whole body.

'What have you done to him? He's not brown any more.'

'I washed him,' Nick said. He put a glass of water on the bedside table.

'That's amazing. He's a whole different colour.'

'He stank,' Nick said. 'I've worn him out, fed him, and he's done two shits.'

'God. It's so good of you.'

'Do you want something to eat?'

'No. Could you . . . It sounds stupid. Could you just stay here for a while?'

He took off his boots and lay down next to her.

She said, mumbling, glazed with painkillers, 'When you're sick, sometimes you just want someone near.'

'I know what you mean. I haven't got anyone at the moment, either.'

'When you're sick I'll do the same for you.'

'Okay. Deal.'

'Nick? A man's been following me. A tall, kind of lanky guy, with black hair. I thought he was in your house one night. I was coming across the lawn and I saw him through the glass.'

'No. I don't know anyone who would follow you.'

'He has a tattoo on his hand. Of a dragonfly.'

'I don't know him, Eloise. You're mistaken. Maybe I shouldn't say this, but living on your own's not good for you. You're spooked. Seeing things.'

'Rubbish. I love being by myself. The Me time. The freedom. I wish I'd done it sooner.'

'Hmm. There's one thing . . .'

'What?'

He said, 'I've been meaning to tell you, there was a man on your property a couple of days ago, walking around your lawn. He went on the deck, looked through the glass.'

'Really?'

'I came over and asked if I could help, and he gave me his card. He was a real estate agent. He said the house was going on the market. He mentioned Sean Rodd.'

'Oh no. Stop. Talk about something else. Chernobyl. Tell me about the Stalkers.'

He lay back, his head on her pillow. Silvio leapt up and draped himself across their feet. Outside, above the estuary, the gulls swooped and called, and the tide was running fast in the creek.

'The men who worked on the nuclear reactor at Chernobyl called themselves the Stalkers. Outside the zone, in a rundown hotel, we drank vodka and ate borscht. That borscht was memorable, I can tell you. The cream in it would kill you faster than the radiation.

'The Stalkers had no fear. They worked with minimal protection, with skimpy equipment. The land around the plant was returning to the wild. It was a beautiful, eerie, poisonous place. Ten of us entered the zone on a bus. It was only when we were deep inside, driving through a forest that we . . .'

Silvio blinked his golden eyes, listening.

Over at the park the dogs raced to and fro, chasing each other across the parched ground.

Nick lifted the flannel from Eloise's forehead, turned it and replaced it, smoothing it down. He pushed the tangled hair away from her face.

He said quietly, 'Are you awake, Eloise?'

TWENTY-TWO

On the way to the Hartmann mansion there was a small, brief shower, the first in weeks. The traffic slowed, and a rainbow arced down between two dense black clouds. Rain drummed on the roof of the car.

Normally, this being a Saturday, Eloise would have embarked on one of her walks, leaving early, arriving home when the sun was going down over the peninsula. Now she drove with resolve and a faint sense of disbelief: was she really doing this?

At the ornamental gate, a camera turned towards her and a crackling voice enquired: name and purpose of visit?

She gave her name. 'I have an appointment,' she shouted.

There was a pause before the gates swung open. After the shower, the grass along the driveway glistened and the asphalt steamed. She had entered a *Soon and Starfish* cartoon: the toy colours, the mansion with its fantasy towers and giant oaken door.

In the courtyard she parked beneath a white flagpole from which an unidentifiable black and white flag hung limp. The first person to appear was the security man, Chad Loafer. Unshaven, bleary-eyed, and even smaller than she'd remembered, he ushered her into a room with black furniture, in which lollies were arranged in bowls. Instructed to help herself, Eloise distractedly ate a couple of pineapple lumps, some jaffas, two blackberry jetplanes. Loafer hovered, muttering into his phone.

After ten minutes, the giant door creaked open and Hartmann appeared, dressed in the same outfit as his tiny bodyguard: black pants, a black top, black combat boots. Only Hartmann's pants were stretchy and his jersey was the size of a duvet. Around his neck he wore a black scarf.

'I am an early riser today,' he announced. Loafer fussed around him, arranging his big chair. 'Normally I get up at 2 p.m.'

She looked at him. He should have been consulting a talking animal, a magic dwarf. He should have been sipping from a jewelled goblet containing a foaming potion. Instead, he clapped his hands, and Loafer brought him a small tray on which were arranged two pills and a glass of water.

'Pain relief,' Hartmann explained. 'For tennis elbow.'

Eloise waited and then said,

'Thanks for seeing me. We just have a few extra questions.'

Hartmann smiled, showing his small pointy teeth. 'Of course. No problem.'

She ran through a list, which he answered leaning back in the chair, his feet stretched out and his enormous hands steepled over his stomach. He was impressively articulate. At one point he said, 'I have answered this already.' To several other questions he said, 'Refer this to my attorney, Lon Chasewell.'

They pressed on, until she'd reached the end.

'So, Eloise,' he said, 'the sun has come out. Shall we go for a walk?'

They headed out into the grounds, Loafer following discreetly behind.

Eloise looked around, at the green estate, as well tended as a golf course, the lawns stretching away in gentle dips and mounds, the line of trees on the horizon, each straight trunk tipped with a plume of foliage, like a quill pen.

She said, 'Did you mean it when you said you could be murdered?'

'Sure. I'm supposed to have stolen hundreds of millions from Hollywood. The United States is after my ass.'

'But murder?'

'They carry out extra-judicial killings all the time. Using drones, assassins. I could be like the guy who was murdered in London with the tip of a poison umbrella. Or the guy they fed the cup of green tea and polonium in the sushi house.'

'The Russians did those.'

'Yes, but same principle.'

Eloise was trying to think it out. How would Arthur have approached this? What would he have told Hartmann — and not told him?

She launched in, with a reckless sense of unreality, 'You're a master hacker.'

'Sure. When I was young, in my country, the government paid me to break into its systems, looking for flaws.'

'Can I tell you about something?'

He paused. 'This is for Roysmith?'

'No, for me.'

'What do you have in mind?'

But not long after Eloise had started to explain, he held up his hand. 'On second thoughts, we will go to a place where it's good to talk. And let us give Chad our phones. He will put them in the chiller, in the golf cart.'

'Really?'

'Of course. Chad will look after your phone very carefully. And I must ask you, Eloise, to speak in a tiny little voice. I know I am tall, but you must do your best. You must whisper in my ear!'

While they were talking the rainbow appeared again, and behind it another shower, drawing a curtain of chainmail across the horizon. Over the Hartmann mansion, the sky was clear blue. It was hot down in the still air by the barn. They were wading among the chickens. Eloise admired the birds' shiny brown and black feathers. Their eyes were like holes. As she and Hartmann spread the feed the chickens rushed and then were still, they pecked and paused, their eyes were tiny circles of blackness.

She felt awkward to be whispering, but every time she raised her voice he frowned, held up his big hand.

He said, 'So you say there was a post-mortem. And someone made an unauthorised inquiry. From outside.'

'That's what I was told.'

'You think someone wanted to know the results of the post-mortem?'

'I don't know. I just wonder who inquired, and if there's anything unusual.'

'You think someone might have wanted to alter the results?'

Eloise stared at him. 'Alter them. I hadn't thought of that.'

Hartmann poured chicken feed from one palm to the other. 'I have to tell you, I am in a constrained position right now. I am being spied on. You could be being monitored, because you have interviewed me. I must ask, Eloise, why are you telling me these things?'

She paused.

Arthur, help me out. What's the best way to put this?

'I just thought, Mr Hartmann . . .'

A magnanimous wave of the huge hand. 'Please. Kurt.'

'I just thought of telling you about it, Kurt, because it concerns Ed Miles. The person Arthur called just before he died was staying at Rotokauri with David Hallwright. And David Hallwright's other house guest at the time was Ed Miles. The police looked into the phone calls, but didn't go any further with their inquiry after they got the post-mortem results, which said Arthur was drugged with sleeping pills when he went over the wall.'

Hartmann said slowly, 'Mr Ed Miles, Minister of Justice.'

Minister of Chustice.

'Yes. Back when he was police minister. And David Hallwright was prime minister.'

'Ed Miles. My nemesis.' He smiled, showing his wicked little teeth. The smile made him look so different.

Eloise took a breath. 'So I thought maybe you'd be interested, and, I don't know, have some advice. Anything.'

Hartmann stooped, and held out a palm full of chicken feed. He said, 'Mr Ed Miles, Minister of Justice, is a serious problem for me. He has done a great deal to facilitate my extradition. I have a feeling he talks directly to the White House. On a regular basis!'

Eloise laughed along nervously, watching the chickens. The way their heads shot out as their legs, swathed in feathers like big skirts, jerkily carried them over the dusty ground.

Sudden dizziness. When had she last eaten anything, apart from Hartmann's lollies? Last night? She said in a glazed tone, 'Ed Miles is going after Jack Dance's job. He wants to be prime minister. The PM is low in the polls. Ed Miles is backed by Hallwright. Hallwright's come back from France, and has been meeting with Miles. Like, plotting.'

Hartmann considered this. 'Jack Dance is in need of currency,' he said.

'Yes.'

Hartmann smiled. 'And so am I.'

'The thing is,' Eloise said, 'when Arthur died, I didn't ask any questions.'

'Well. We must question. It is our duty, as citizens. I, of all people, know this, Eloise.'

She nodded. How would you describe his tone? It was hard to pin down. Compulsively tongue-in-cheek, yet also searching, sharp. She was reasonably certain he was taking her seriously. Wasn't he?

The dust whirled in the shining air, catching in the back of her throat. Her cheeks were hot; she'd got sunburnt walking over the estate to the barn. Sweat stood out on Hartmann's face.

He waved out to summon Loafer, and Eloise was abruptly convulsed with such a paroxysm of sneezing she staggered about in the hay, raising more dust. Then Hartmann sneezed, a staccato series of small eruptions, surprisingly delicate in such a big man. He sneezed like a cat.

'*Gesundheit,*' he kept saying, ushering her across the grass towards the golf cart. Loafer opened the chiller and gave them back their phones.

She sat under the canopy, Hartmann's huge thigh pressed against hers as they trundled over the bright grass towards the house, the sneezes running between them in a relay.

They walked through dim rooms filled with black furniture. In many of them the curtains were drawn. 'There are eyes everywhere,' Hartmann whispered, laying a theatrical finger to his lips.

In a vast kitchen, tropical fish swam in an aquarium above the stove. There was a black bench, a black table. A silent woman in a smock silently left the room as they entered.

'I need,' Hartmann said, 'a snack. Would you like a snack, Eloise?'

He called out. 'Raquel! Precious! Are you there?'

Raquel or Precious emerged, winding her hair into a bun and fastening it on top of her head.

'Snackaroodles,' was Hartmann's command.

The woman turned smartly to the sink, opened the faucet with her elbow like a doctor, and soaped and washed her hands. She drew open the double doors of a giant fridge.

Hartmann squirted hand sanitiser on his palms and rubbed them vigorously. He offered the bottle to Eloise, who used it, lest he be offended.

'Over here,' he said, and led Eloise to a black table by the window, from which they could see the estate stretching away in a rolling series of grassy knolls.

'I joke all the time, Eloise,' he said, 'but I am serious about being watched. I must warn you, it's best not to discuss business in the house. Tell me about Roysmith. He is a charming man.'

'Scott's great. He's the most principled journalist I've ever met. And he's nice to work for. I love his wife, too. She's a photographer. She's cool.'

'I watch his show, *Roysmith*. He cares about social issues, about the poor. He uses that word all the time, what is it?'

'Splendid. Only I think he's cut down on that a bit.'

'He wears nice suits. Tell me, where does he get those suits?'

'Someone called Ronald.'

'Where do you live, Eloise?'

'On the Starlight Peninsula.'

'Where they demolished the old Starlight Hotel? Did you know STARLIGHT is a computer programme used by spies? It's a force multiplier.'

'Oh . . . What's that?'

'It turns data into actionable intelligence.'

The smocked woman arrived with club sandwiches and small bottles of Coke.

'I do not drink alcohol,' Hartmann said.

'Oh God, no. Me neither.'

They clinked bottles.

The woman watched from the kitchen door, silently removing the plates when they'd finished. Hartmann said he was due for a conference with his lawyer. He saw her to the door.

Out in the courtyard, under the rinsed blue sky, Eloise said in a low voice, 'If you're so watched, how do you contact people?'

'I have the best encryption, naturally.'

'Okay.'

He smiled. 'Don't worry, it's very straightforward. I can easily contact people without anyone knowing.'

'Oh.'

'Of course. This is my business. At the moment, I'm working on a system for encrypted Skype. One that is totally secure and works through the internet.'

'Wow. Great.'

'Anyone I want to talk to privately, I can send a message and we can meet if we need to.'

Eloise said, 'It's ridiculous, I've had the feeling lately that I'm being followed.'

Hartmann put his hands together. He pursed his lips, giving her a priestly, knowing look. 'It would not surprise me.'

'But why? I'm not doing anything wrong. I'm not up to anything.'

'Aren't you?' Hartmann said.

Silence.

'You are now,' he said.

'But I haven't . . .'

Hartmann looked thoughtful. 'In my experience, it is hard to say when something starts. You've started something coming to see me. But when you look back, it may be that you started it some time before.'

She sighed. 'I really don't know *what* that means.'

'Sometimes you take action, or start asking questions, before you realise what you are doing. And sometimes you find other people are asking too — the same questions.'

'I still don't know . . . ?'

'Put it this way. I believe there is such a thing as Collective Consciousness. Information runs through the world and, in certain circumstances, our minds can tap into it. The internet is a man-made construction of a phenomenon that is already there. So if there is an unanswered question, you may find others are moving towards it, too. That is why it is so hard to say when something has actually *begun*.'

'I've been wondering about ESP.'

'ESP? Call it Collective Consciousness. The information is out there. Sometimes more than one person will read it, or start moving towards it, at the same time.'

'It doesn't really explain why I might be being followed. To be honest, it's just as likely I've been imagining it. I've been living alone.'

'My guess would be you are not imagining it. Events are merely coming together. Put it another way: our actions are more instinctive than we think. You believe you have free will, right?'

'Yes.'

'But really, many of the things you do are automatic, instinctive. And sometimes as a group, as a society, we move in a certain direction instinctively. We are all animals.'

She said, 'The idea's been coming into my head lately: a layer of the world has been hidden from me.'

'And now you are alone, you are starting to make it out, to glimpse what has been hidden. You are not distracted. Your vision has cleared.'

They looked at each other. He raised both palms. *Voilà*.

Eloise frowned, smiled. She looked at him, searchingly. 'Do you really believe all this?'

'Sure. I love this kind of shit. I totally believe in it. By the way, do you play DroidWars? Or Tank Fighter? Not to blow my own horn, but I am world champion in both.'

'I don't really play computer games.'

'What philistinism. I am shocked. Next time you come, I will show you my gaming room, Eloise. I will teach you all you need to know.'

TWENTY-THREE

When Eloise dropped the Sparkler at Iris Roysmith's birthday party she felt a certain familial pride. The Sparkler was not only beautiful, with her smooth brown skin and her dimples, she had, what would you call it, poise? Little Iris, who was in the Sparkler's class at the poshest state primary in the city, was a magnet for the children in her year, because her father was Roysmith. They all wanted to be friends with Iris, and their mums and dads wanted to be friends with Scott and Thee. It was the power of television. Eloise felt that the Sparkler had something over all the other Western Bay girls, except for Iris herself, who was also impressive: a thin, intensely intelligent child. She was Scott and Thee's youngest, a late arrival after their much older daughters.

'Rachel Margery!' Scott boomed, throwing open the door. 'And her Aunty Eloise!'

Behind him, the slew and slum of a children's party; amid the trashed furniture the floor was strewn with balloons, blowing crazily this way and that in the breeze from the deck. From an upstairs window came a series of piercing screams.

Eloise held the box containing the giant Bionicle, allowing her eyes to adjust to the sight of Scott suitless. He was looking, by his standards, super casual, in jeans and a baggy T-shirt with a chocolate stain on the shoulder.

The Sparkler held her present for Iris against her shoulder like a spear. It was, she had explained in the car, a swingball set. She and Iris were interested in sports. They were both sprinters, and tennis players, and swimmers. The Sparkler was a left-hander, like her father Giles, which gave her, in Eloise's opinion, a different and interesting body language, something to do with having learned to move in a right-handed world. She hunched over the page when she wrote, and her handwriting sloped backwards. She was well co-ordinated, could smash a ball batting left or right, and moved with a kind of angular, boyish grace.

'How's it going?' Eloise said.

Scott had a hand to his forehead. 'Bedlam. And we've got *hours* to go.'

Eloise came in long enough to hand over the present to Iris, and to talk to Thee, who was gamely supervising a violent session of bullrush on the back lawn.

'I should have bought some damned earplugs,' Thee said. 'Oh, did Scott tell you? We found a lovely man for you. You'll like him. He's Irish.'

'Really?'

'Scott, the Irishman.'

From the deck Scott said, 'He used to work for the BBC.'

'That sounds good.'

'We'll go on a double date, if you like, 'Thee said. 'He's really nice. He's only got one leg.'

'One leg.'

'Yeah. We didn't ask why, or how. I mean you can't just come out with it. But he's very good-looking. Christ, what's with the screaming? Quiet, kids!'

Scott said, plaintive, 'E, can you blow up some of these balloons? Before I pass out?'

She blew up a few balloons, greeted Scott's glamorous older daughters, sardonic Sophie and sharp-eyed Sarah, admired Sarah's new hair (blonde dreadlocks) and arranged to pick up her niece in a few hours. Then she got out of there.

In the car, Silvio was waiting, his nose pressed to the glass.

Eloise watched Simon Lampton leave the house in his running gear. Silvio had just followed a scent from the crater, over the lip of the hill and down the western side of the mountain. He appeared far below her, running, his nose to the ground, alongside a boundary fence. She hurried after him, calling, shaking the leash. Not looking where she was going, she stuck her foot in a hole and went over sideways into the warm, dry grass.

Klaudia, everything is going wrong today. In the bathroom this morning I dropped the soap dish and it smashed on the floor. In the laundry, the bag of Silvio's despised dog biscuits slipped from my grasp, and the pungent pellets (no wonder he hates them) shot in all directions. Carina rang to ask if I would take the Sparkler to her party; talking to her while sweeping up dog biscuits I smashed my head on the open cupboard door.

Where was the dog? They needed to get down the hill, so as not to miss Lampton. But Silvio's head appeared above her, blocking out the sky. He loomed, panting, threatening to drool on her face.

She hurried him down the hillside, through the pedestrian path that led between the gardens. The fences sagged in places under the weight of milkweed and bougainvillea, the gardens were lush and silent under the sun, vegetable patches laid out in the black soil, divided by bamboo markers. The cicadas sawed and the bougainvillea petals made a red carpet along the path.

Slow down, Klaudia said. Be mindful. Breathe.

Savour beautiful things.

Eloise and Silvio took a short-cut across a lawn, and crossed a concrete driveway. Now they were on the road, where they could intercept Simon when he came back from the run.

Silvio lay down in the shade of a stone wall. Eloise waited, her mind on Klaudia and the outrage she'd committed. The betrayal. Oh yes. Klaudia had, at the end of their last session, smoothly announced that she couldn't see Eloise next time because she was going to attend a 'yoga retreat'.

Just like that. Bare-faced. Cool as a cucumber.

Eloise thought about it now, with bitterness. Klaudia was going to laze around with massages and yoga and a 'juice detox diet' for days, *days,* while Eloise could go off and die for all she cared. It had taken great self-control not to storm from the room, hotly denouncing Klaudia's monstrousness. She'd had to pretend she was having a panic attack about something else.

Not that she was getting dependent. God forbid.

The cicadas made their wall of sound, the clack and shimmer of the summer air. Silvio burrowed himself down in the cool grass, in the shade of the dry stone wall. Near Simon Lampton's gate, a cat leapt onto the fence and watched.

She heard the slow thump of his feet on the pavement. Towing Silvio, she stepped out from the shadow of the wall.

His voice was guarded, not warm. 'Eloise. I was wondering when I'd . . .'

'I've got my car,' she said. 'Can we talk?'

He bent over, his hands on his knees, breathing hard. He wiped his face on the bottom of his T-shirt, glanced up at the house.

'Okay.'

She led him to the car.

'You want me to get in?' He was going to refuse.

'Yes. Please, Simon.' She got Silvio to jump in the back seat.

He hesitated, shrugged. When he folded himself into the passenger seat, his knees pressed against the glovebox. He felt around under the seat for the lever and the seat shot backwards.

Eloise started the engine.

'Are we going somewhere?'

'It won't take long,' she said. 'Please?'

He pulled his sweaty T-shirt away from his chest. 'Where?'

'I've got something to tell you. And I'll show you something.'

They drove in silence. She could feel the heat coming off him.

'Don't you have air-con?' he said.

'It doesn't work.'

He wound down the window, wiping sweat off his face with his forearm. He sat very still as they drove along Mountain Road, and, as they were approaching Mt Eden, he asked again, sharply, 'Where are we going?'

The little car bounced over the cattle stop and began chugging up the hill road. Simon didn't say anything.

'I want to show you Arthur's flat,' Eloise said.

'No.' He looked at his watch.

'Why not?'

'I haven't got time. Karen, my wife, will miss me.'

'It's a private place, good for talking. It won't take long.'

She parked in the shade. 'Why don't we talk here?' he said. She insisted, and he got out finally, reluctant. They left Silvio in the car with the windows wound down, and she led him to the path below the crater, across the hillside and over the walking track, to the back of Arthur's flat.

'Here,' she said.

He glanced around. 'What are we looking at?'

They sat down in the grass above the concrete deck with its wooden trellis, the flowering wisteria vine, the silver water bowl set there for a dog or cat, a single deckchair, on which hung a coloured swimming towel and a bathing suit. The back door was closed; there was no sign of anyone at home.

She said, 'This was Arthur's flat.'

'Oh. Did he own it?' Simon's voice was toneless.

'No, rented it.'

'It's a lovely spot,' he said.

She caught the polite, artificial note in his voice. He didn't see what she was seeing: the beautiful, lost past. Their bolt-hole on the edge of the mountain. Summer evenings ranging on the hillside above the city, watching the sun go down over the Waitakere Ranges. Winter mornings with the huge rain roaring on the corrugated-iron roof, the melancholy singing of a thrush on the wet fence, the walking track turned into a brown water race, streaming down the hill.

Simon sat in the grass, his arms folded across his chest. There was such a stillness about him. His arms and legs were wiry and muscular; you could tell he was super fit for his age.

Now was the moment to explain, but she'd forgotten the lines she'd rehearsed, the approach she'd decided on. How had she meant to put it? Just give him an outline, don't tell him too much. Keep your cards close to your chest. Even though that means facing everything alone . . .

'You know I told you I didn't ask enough questions. I accepted what they told me about Arthur's death, and that was it.'

'Yes.' He put a hand to his neck and rubbed it, as if at a sudden pain.

'So, I've asked some. Questions.'

He looked at his watch again, and she understood: he was busy, things to do. There was only so much of her antics he would put up with.

'Asked who?' he said, wiping his forehead. She caught the sharp smell of his sweat.

'I spoke to Detective Da Silva again. You don't remember her.'

He shrugged. 'Maybe I do. Vaguely.'

But he had turned, his eyes fixed on her. She hesitated.

'So,' he said. 'What did you and the detective talk about?'

'About Arthur.'

'And?'

'That's it.'

She waited. Silence.

His expression had changed. He was patient, but she was pushing it. He looked hard at her and said, 'Eloise, I've tried to explain to you that I think you're getting carried away. I've told you: there's nothing to see here. But if you're going to keep approaching me and dragging me places, and talking to the police, and somehow involving me, I think you need to tell me exactly what you're doing.'

'Sorry. It's just, I'm trying to think it out by myself and . . .'

He thought for a moment. 'Look Eloise, I told you, politics in this country is boring, right? No conspiracies, just committees. Maybe . . . maybe I wasn't being entirely open with you, and that wasn't fair. I'll tell you one thing, if you keep it to yourself. All right? Ed Miles gives me the creeps. If anyone's up to anything, it's him. Now even just saying that aloud sounds fanciful to me. Because I'm a doctor. I treat patients — women. My life is very what you'd call down to earth. No glamour, no conspiracies, no politics. I'm just a doctor.'

'Okay.'

'I probably shouldn't say this, but I have a huge, successful practice, and you know why that is? Because women trust me. They come to me with their incredibly sensitive issues, and I help them. They trust me more than their husbands. They say to me, If you run into my husband in the ward, don't tell him what we talked about. As if I would. I'm there to help them. And to keep their secrets.' He touched her arm lightly. 'Do you know what I mean?'

'Yes.'

'You've been feeling very alone lately,' he said.

She lay back in the grass. The clouds were edged with bright seams. 'Yes.'

'I thought so.'

Eloise sat up. 'Okay. This is just between us, right?'

'Yes. Definitely.'

'The detective said someone made an inquiry about Arthur, from the outside. Maybe someone high up. She thought it might have been about his post-mortem.'

Simon was expressionless. 'So?'

'She got the sense she was being told not to investigate any further. And she thought maybe this was because they'd been getting a bit too close to the people at Rotokauri.'

Eloise paused, frowned. Had Da Silva actually said that? Yes. Well, near enough. She went on, 'So, I got an idea. Roysmith and I have just done a piece on the internet mogul Kurt Hartmann, right? Whom the Americans are trying to extradite. We interviewed him. I got the idea to ask Hartmann about Ed Miles.'

Silence.

Finally, Simon spoke. His tone was incredulous. 'But *I* was at Rotokauri, too.'

'Exactly. You said Ed Miles gives you the creeps. If there was something funny about Arthur's death, wouldn't you like to know?'

He let out a short laugh. 'Not specially.'

Eloise winced. He didn't have to sound so brutal.

Simon squeezed his hands together; he turned to her and said, 'Okay. Okay.'

Silence.

He started again, 'The people you're talking about. They're my friends.'

'I didn't get the impression Ed Miles is your friend.'

'The Hallwrights are more than friends; they're family.'

'I know. I wanted to tell you what I'd done because I thought you'd like to know.'

Again he looked incredulous. 'Thanks. You could have checked with me first.'

'Simon, you told me you'd think about it, and that you might even look into it. I thought you wanted to find out as much as I did.'

'Christ. You go off and unleash that giant ogre . . .'

'I haven't unleashed him. He's not an ogre actually, he's very nice. I just asked him if he knew anything about Ed Miles.'

Eloise looked at the red iron roof of Arthur's flat. She said in a slow, intent voice, 'A layer of the world has been hidden from me.'

'You didn't tell the policewoman about talking to Hartmann?'

'No. I won't. It's a secret.' She turned to him. 'I'm serious about this, Simon. I let Arthur down. I'm trying to make up for that. Even if there's nothing to find out, I'll know I've asked.'

Simon looked away, distracted. Birds rose from the trees along the walking track, flapping wings.

He said, 'Hartmann won't do anything.'

Eloise said, 'He might.'

'Why would he?'

'Ed Miles is Minister of Justice. Ed Miles wants Hartmann extradited. And Ed Miles was at Rotokauri.'

'Christ,' Simon said. 'Oh no.'

Eventually he held his hands out steady and said, 'Okay, you've done it now, so let's think it through.'

She waited, looking at his big hands.

'First of all, there's not going to be anything to find.'

'Probably not,' Eloise said. She watched the birds flying in formation over the suburb.

He said slowly, 'But if there *was* something, it would only relate to Ed Miles.'

'Why?'

'Process of elimination. It's nothing to do with me. All I did was field a few questions, first from Arthur, then from a couple of bored young cops. That was it. I didn't "look into" anything. David Hallwright was the prime minister, so looking into things wasn't his job. It was beneath his pay grade. The person who looked into things was Miles. He was the fixer, the person who calmed things down.'

'Calmed things down,' Eloise repeated. Like Klaudia — *she* had calmed things down, after Eloise had flown into a panic about the yoga retreat. Be mindful, Eloise. Breathe. Klaudia had taken deep breaths herself, to demonstrate. And Eloise had pretended she was upset about something else.

Simon moved closer and took hold of her arm. 'Eloise, the more I think about this, the more worried I get.'

'We're not doing anything wrong.'

'But think. Think what you've done. I must be out of my mind even talking to you. You've effectively set Kurt Hartmann on the Minister of Justice. It's about as serious as you can get. Even if there's nothing to find, and there won't be, you've set them against each other.'

She blinked nervously. 'They're set against each other already. If Ed Miles has done nothing wrong, then there's no harm in mentioning it to Hartmann . . .'

'He's the Minister of Justice. Whether he's done something wrong or not, what if he finds out what you've done?'

'Well, you and I won't tell him. And neither will Hartmann.'

'How do you know Hartmann won't?'

'He promised.'

'Oh. And he's Mr Reliable?'

'I believe him. All we did was have a conversation. He said my visiting him was a nice distraction. He needs to take his mind off things while he fights his extradition case. We had a long talk at his house, he said he's going to teach me some computer games.'

'At the Hartmann mansion? You went there?'

'Sure, I've been there twice.'

'Well, you do tend to bowl up to people's houses.' A new thought struck him. 'He's surely being watched. You will have been seen going there. Without Roysmith.'

'I had some extra questions for him, from Scott,' Eloise said with dignity. 'I was there on official business. Then we put our phones in the portable chiller on his golf cart, and talked down at the hen house.'

'The *hen house*.'

'He keeps chickens. They're his Zen.'

Simon let out a mirthless laugh. 'And how will you talk to him again?'

'He contacts people by encrypted email.'

'How James Bond.'

Eloise said, 'He did say a delicate approach was required.'

Simon said, 'A delicate approach. I don't know whether I'm talking to someone outrageously cunning or the village idiot.'

'Well, I know you don't follow politics, Simon. But Ed Miles is supposed to be after Jack Dance's job.'

'You mean information that makes life difficult for Miles is worth something. To Jack Dance. Christ, this just gets worse.'

'I don't know. Could it be? I told you, I just want to be able to say I asked.'

Simon sat silent, as if struggling to take it in.

Finally he said, 'Listen, I don't think you understand. What you've been doing is potentially dangerous. It could hurt my friends, or even me — not that I've done anything wrong.'

She turned to him with feeling. 'I don't want to hurt you.'

Is it possible, Klaudia, that I could be just slightly in love with Simon Lampton?

He said, 'I want you to promise you won't tell anyone about this. Not family, friends, workmates, no one. You and I can deal with this together.'

'Okay.'

'You should know that Ed Miles is a formidable and clever guy. And he is extremely ambitious. If anyone gets in his way, he does not play nice. His policy is: pay back double. So you — we — have to be careful.'

Simon looked at her searchingly. 'You're a good person, Eloise. You're sensitive about people's privacy, in a way that maybe Arthur wasn't — not because he was bad, but because he was driven. By his art. I know you're not trying to make mischief, to cause harm. You want to make up for something. You're trying to honour Arthur's memory.'

'*Yes.* That's exactly what I'm doing. Honouring Arthur. You understand it all. You *understand.*'

'Of course I do. Here, come here.'

He put his arm around her and they sat together in the long grass. His voice was low and soothing. He said, 'It's all right, Eloise. We'll work this out together. I know people, after all. Everything's going to be fine.'

TWENTY-FOUR

The Sparkler and Eloise walked Silvio across the dog park and returned in time for the news. Mariel Hartfield and Jack Anthony appeared in matching outfits, his tie the same electric blue as the stripe in her jacket.

'I used to think those two hated each other,' Eloise said.

The bulletin rolled smoothly towards the first commercial break: crime, crime, politics, crime, unusual weather events, Pacific affairs, an article (marketing disguised as news) about record demand for a new Apple product.

When Eloise went to the kitchen for a drink, the Sparkler switched to the cartoon channel. Eloise couldn't be bothered arguing. They watched as Soon, the obnoxious dwarf, behaved appallingly (he set fire to a building and began a blackmail plot) while his counterpart, conscientious Starfish, wrung his hands. The action involved the Bachelor, who rode around on a flying bed accompanied by his hissing girlfriends, the Cassowaries, and a visit from the Ort Cloud, the large purple mass with eyes and a mouth full of wicked teeth, who reminded Eloise of Kurt Hartmann.

Eloise watched, pressing the cold wine glass against her sunburnt cheeks. After a while she said, 'Is the giant purple cloud good or bad?'

The Sparkler didn't take her eyes off the screen. 'Good. His wife's bad. When the Ort Cloud and his wife fight, there's chaos in the universe.'

'How did Roza Hallwright come up with it all?'

The Sparkler had her fingers wound in Silvio's coat. 'Who?'

'The woman who made it up. Maybe the characters are based on real people.' Was David Hallwright in there? What about Simon Lampton? Perhaps he was Starfish, the good-hearted one, who tried to undo the wrongs committed by wicked Soon.

The Sparkler said, 'Yeah. It's based on a real dwarf and a real starfish.'

Eloise laughed. 'Sarky!'

Silvio jumped up with an explosion of barks, sending Eloise reeling back.

'I wish he wouldn't *do* that.'

The Sparkler had her hand up to her hair.

'Oh, God, sorry.' Eloise grabbed a tea towel on the way to the door, where Silvio was already up on his hind legs and scrabbling. She let Carina in.

Carina fought her way past the ecstatic dog.

Eloise said over her shoulder, wishing Silvio wasn't quite so pleased, 'The Sparkler's fine. Good party. She reeks of booze — only because I tipped a glass of wine over her head.'

'Okay . . .'

Eloise dabbed at the Sparkler's hair. 'Sorry. The dog's so loud.' She turned. 'You're staying for dinner, aren't you? Mum's on her way; she rang me. I'm cooking.'

Carina sniffed her daughter's wet hair. 'What're you cooking?'

'Either curry or pizza, or fish and chips.'

'Okay. Look at your couch. The footprints. You should kick him off.'

'I don't care. I love him. Silv can do no wrong.'

Eloise brought out more wine from the stash under the sink and poured another couple of drinks. Then Silvio went berserk all over again.

Demelza held out her car keys. 'Carina, dear. If you could just . . .'

Her dog, Gerald, waddled out on the deck and stood looking across to the dog park. He was like a little, fat, uneasy old man. Hands on his hips. Resigned. No escape.

While Carina went out to park the car, Demelza settled herself between muddy patches on the sofa and addressed the Sparkler.

'Daddy still overseas, dear? Goodness he's away a lot.' She looked up as Carina came in with the keys. 'Reminds me of Terrence. He always claimed it was work. But I knew.'

'You were a realist,' the Sparkler said.

'I was. You remember, dear. I believe in telling the truth. Men, you see, you'll never get them to be faithful.'

'Speak for yourself,' Carina said.

'And after women have children it's even harder. Ooh, the wear and tear childbirth causes. They marry someone young and lovely, and they end up with . . . Well, put it this way, Sparkles darling, some women start out with flesh like a raw chicken and end up like one that's been cooked! Some,' she lowered her voice, 'who have a lot of children, their insides start to fall. Not that I'm saying your mother . . . But when I see this mania for jogging (I know you like to go jogging, Carina, and I'm not meaning anything by it, mind) I think to myself, they're going to end up like Queen Victoria. I've just read a wonderful biography. After eight children, Sparkles dear, Queen Victoria herself had a terrible case of . . .'

'How's Dad?' Eloise said.

'Oh, dreadful. He's been under the doctor now for six months. The local GP's been wonderful, very attentive when I've rung in the middle of the night. I've needed a lot of prescriptions, what with the strain, and Terrence's snoring, which does keep me awake. It's like a death rattle.'

Demelza pushed back her hair with her fingers, in little sharp stabs. 'We've had Luna to stay, which doesn't improve Terrence's mood. My poor sister, she's mad, of course. She insists everyone sees the world as she does. She's deeply neurotic, an unweeded garden. Of course, she was a terrible mother. Always trying to get rid of her children, couldn't handle motherhood. She couldn't face things. A bolter. Shied away from the truth . . .'

She looked around. 'Goodness, the house is looking a bit worse for wear. There's mud everywhere. What are the Rodds going to say?'

'It's not their house.'

'It's their money, chuck.'

'Well, they've got a lot to spare,' Eloise said, turning to Carina. 'I heard a new theory on Baby O'Keefe. Bradley Kirk's the daddy.'

'That's a good one,' Carina said. 'Cross-party affairs must be rare. Because politics is fundamental.'

Demelza said, 'There's Eloise, mind, marrying a Rodd. Terrence and I brought you up in a good left-wing household and you went off with a right moneybags.'

Eloise said, 'Look where it got me.'

Carina said, 'I couldn't marry anyone who votes National.'

'But you liked Sean,' Eloise said. 'And I'm not that rigid.'

'Sean was all right, until he turned out to be a complete shit.' Carina stood up and went to the window.

Demelza said, 'And what about your silly Roysmith, what's his political persuasion?'

'He can't really say publicly. He has to appear balanced. He can't come on all opinionated, like Pilger.'

Demelza pursed her lips. 'But I must say, a lot of television people are quite open about their politics. They're all mad fans of Jack Dance. That pompous one with the spiky hair, and the funny one in the sandshoes.'

'But Scott's a *serious* journalist.'

'He's serious about his hairstyle. And his outfits.'

'What about his work on child poverty? He's a great journalist. He cares. He has high standards.'

'Ooh, hark at you, chuck. No need to get hot under the collar. I believe in telling the truth, that's all.' Demelza held out her empty glass. 'Eloise, if you could just . . . What are we having for dinner? Pizza again? Not with garlic, I trust. None of that foreign muck. I won't have anchovies or olives, and none of those capers. We could have a nice Hawaiian, if you wish. But hold the pineapple.'

'What about salami?'

'I don't eat salami!'

'Scallops?'

'Get away with you! Don't be silly!'

Demelza fanned herself with the pizza menu. 'You want to get that dog seen to. There's a right pong. Mud, is it? I don't see how you can even wash him, he's so woolly. Thank you, dear, I will have another glass. Now Sparkles, darling, how's school?'

Carina said, 'She loves school.'

'Takes after her father, does she. The genes will out. Even though he's so seldom present in the flesh. Now, Eloise, what's that shirt you're wearing? What a bright colour. It's so elegant. Look at that, Carina. Something to give you ideas. Eloise knows how to show off the best bits of her figure. Goodness knows we all need that skill, Carina. Especially those of us with Terrence's genes. Let's face it, all the women on his side are so heavy-boned. Bums too near the daisies, I always say. Sparkles, did you tell me your daddy's designing a bridge in Thailand? Ooh, such delicate, wand-like figures those Thai women have . . .'

Carina and the Sparkler left first, Carina having reached the end of her tolerance early on. This meant Eloise had to take Demelza's keys and manoeuvre her car out of the tight park outside the house.

Demelza stood waiting, holding Gerald.

Eloise was wishing she'd managed to keep Silvio. The Sparkler had prevailed, which was only fair. You couldn't commandeer someone else's pet. But she hated the thought of a night without him.

She held out the keys. The hot wind blew dust across the road; insects whirled around the streetlights. Out in the estuary there was a disturbance in the water, a faint splashing.

Demelza made a face. 'Must be a bit creepy living here by yourself.'

'I love the peninsula. I've got a nice neighbour. You met him, Nick Oppenheimer. And I'm going out with Scott and Thee this week, they've been incredibly kind. There's a man they want me to meet.'

'Nick. I remember. Handsome chap. Not quite as good-looking as Arthur was.'

'Here's your keys.' Eloise thrust them at her mother.

Arthur.

She tried to hold it back, but something broke. A great sob welled up, and another. Her body shook with them. Tears spilled and poured down her cheeks; she shuddered with crying.

She struggled, tried to control the sobbing, looked up.

Her mother was watching her, her eyes narrowed. Her smooth brown face had sharpened into an expression of intense interest. She had Gerald under one arm, and the other hand resting on her car. She didn't move, only looked, and then drummed her fingers, very slowly, on the car roof. Turning away, she opened the car door, and dumped Gerald in the passenger seat.

She walked slowly around to the driver's door.

'Goodbye, Eloise,' she said. 'God bless.'

What is there left, when everyone leaves? Only the hours of night, and no Silvio, and the black sky up there, the universe made of dark matter, dust and ash. The day is a bright mesh over the blackness; when the night pulls it away there's nothing between the raw self and the information beyond.

Over the shadowy dog park, the moon was a button made of bone.

He opened the door. 'You again.' But he was smiling, leaning against the wall in his old jeans, his denim shirt open.

'I had to give the dog back.'

'Ah. So you're all alone.'

'Want to come for a walk?'

They crossed the wooden bridge and wandered along the path through the cabbage trees and flax. Eloise said, 'I don't want to leave here.'

'Will you have to soon?'

'I haven't been to a lawyer yet. It's on my list.'

'Is there a mortgage?'

'No.'

'Really?'

'My husband's a Rodd. The Rodds are rich.'

'You *do* need to see a lawyer.'

'I know. I'll find an apartment, keep working.'

'Where do you want to be in five years? What do you want?'

'I have no idea.' *Not to be lonely.* She looked back at the house. 'If a house is a metaphor for the mind . . . I'm losing mine.'

'Mine's rather empty at the moment,' Nick said.

They did a turn around the park and stopped at the edge of her lawn.

'Coming in?' she asked.

'Do you want me to?'

'Yes.'

She took great pleasure in making two cups of tea. Because she didn't need to keep the night at bay by getting drunk. They went upstairs and he kicked off his boots and lay on her bed.

He said, 'When I was in South Africa, I knew a couple. They'd been ordinary white middle-class students when they were young — good kids — but apartheid turned them into terrorists. What they did was, they made a bomb. And they set it off. They were trying to help get rid of apartheid. They didn't kill anyone, but they caused a lot of damage. Decades later, when the Truth and Reconciliation Commission was set up, it was their chance to tell their story without punishment. Full amnesty. They had to decide whether to take the amnesty and tell the truth, or just leave it buried.'

'What did they do?'

'They told their story. But then their families wouldn't speak to them any more. They were outcasts.'

'That's sad.'

'They wanted to tell; it was their right. The truth is always there. To hell with those who don't like it. Sometimes you've just got to tell it like it is.'

TWENTY-FIVE

'So,' Eloise said, looking at Klaudia narrowly, 'how was the retreat?'

Klaudia's smile was shameless. 'Very refreshing, thank you.'

Eloise sat silent.

'How have you been, Eloise?'

'Oh *fine. Great.*'

'Is something on your mind? You seem a little . . .'

'Terrific. Box of birds, me.'

No sign of the rat out there. Perhaps it was on a little retreat of its own.

Klaudia had a fresh suntan. Her skin was glowing, her eyes were bright. When they'd entered her office, she'd done a little stretching routine before sitting down.

Eloise maintained a neutral expression.

'Do you have some things to tell me? How is the relationship with your neighbour?'

'It's fine.' Eloise roused herself. Sulking was such hard work. 'It would be great if I could trust him.'

'You don't?'

'I don't trust anyone. Well, that's not true, I trust my colleague Scott and his wife Thee, and my sister Carina. And Silvio. Not a huge line-up.'

'And me of course,' Klaudia said, archly.

Eloise waited, with a chilly smile, before saying, 'I hope so.'

'You know, Eloise, our sense of trust can develop very early. When we are young children.'

'Right. Blame your parents.'

'Unfortunately. Your parents might think it's unfair, but they are usually to blame for quite a lot! Our turn to be blamed comes when we are parents ourselves.'

Eloise said, 'While you were away on your *yoga retreat* . . .'

'Yes?'

'My mother was at my house. I burst into tears in front of her. I couldn't control myself. It was completely unexpected. Really big sobs. And it was the strangest thing, she just looked at me. Intently. She didn't move, except to drum her fingers very slowly on the roof of the car.'

'No hug? No kind words?'

'Her expression — it was like a cat looking at a mouse.'

'No empathy,' Klaudia said grimly. She made a note in her file.

As usual, Eloise tried to rein herself in, and gave up. 'Years ago, when Arthur had just died, I was numb, in shock. I had a moment when I came near to understanding properly that he was dead. I heard my mother coming up the stairs. I must have offended her, because she put her head around the door and said, Eloise, I just want to say, please do not be mean to me. Then she left.'

Klaudia nodded.

Eloise rushed on, 'In her mind, it was all about her. She had no conception of what I was dealing with.'

'I see.'

'It was devastating. Not only no hugs and no kind words, but actually no understanding at all. Just a void. It's like she lives in a hall of mirrors. Everywhere she looks, there's only herself.'

She paused. Klaudia was making a noise in her nose. Inhaling, in, out.

'Just breathe, Eloise. Deep breaths.'

'My father would say I'm imagining things.'

'Well, Eloise, all you have done is to say it finally: the emperor has no clothes.'

'So I'm not mad.'

'I would say not. You are calling a spade a spade. As I said before, telling our true story has to be existentially important.'

Klaudia glanced down at her notes. 'Have you heard from your ex-husband lately?'

'No. But I'm sure I will soon. I'm going to have to move out of the house. Which makes me sad.'

'Perhaps it will be good for you to live in a less challenging environment. You could find an apartment with a friend. Somewhere cosy.'

'I love the peninsula. I don't want to leave.'

Klaudia's eyes seemed to redden, to turn moist. She drew in a deep breath. 'But tell me. What do you dream of, Eloise? What would make you whole?'

Dream of? Whole? Eloise recoiled slightly. *Steady on, Klaudia. Less of the schmaltz. Hold the Americanisms.* She considered how to answer, watching for the rat. His pile of leaves had been swept away.

Finally she said, 'If the house is a metaphor for the mind, then what I would like is to fill it.'

'Fill the house? The mind?'

'Both. With people.'

'If I understand you, Eloise, this will involve trust.'

Don't say 'reaching out'.

'It will involve you in reaching out to people.'

Quite the cliché-monger today, Klaudia.

Eloise said with an attempt at dignity, 'It is possible that I have difficulty with trust. It takes me on average about seven years to make friends, and even then I can hardly stand it. If things get friendly too fast, I feel as if I'm facing a blinding searchlight. I have to retreat. The only way I've become so close to Scott is by working with him every day. And he's a lovely man.'

Klaudia was inhaling again. 'Breathe, Eloise.'

Had she raised her voice?

'Seven years to make friends, you say?'

'That was a joke. Hyperbole. I also love and trust Scott's wife. She's cool. And I loved Sean. I miss him. I miss him and he's gone off with that drip, bimbo, airhead . . .'

'Breathe Eloise!'

Klaudia waited.

Eloise found she was actually not breathing at all. She gripped the arms of the chair.

'Okay. I'm breathing.'

'I think you are a little anxious today.'

'I am a bit tense. There are things . . . I can't really say. I decided I wanted to ask some questions about Arthur's death. Because I failed him.'

'You did not fail him.'

'There are so many things I could tell you . . .'

'Please do tell me. We are completely confidential here.'

'I can't.'

'It helps to share, Eloise.'

'I've been back to Arthur's flat a couple of times. I took someone there. Not my neighbour, another man. We drove in my car, he'd been running, it was hot because the air-conditioning doesn't work in my car. He was sweating, I could smell him, sweat and aftershave.'

'Yes?'

'I don't know. I keep thinking about it.'

'You were attracted to this man?' Klaudia gave her sly smile. In the studiously light tone she used for teasing out information, 'This hot guy . . .'

Eloise frowned. 'He's quite old.'

'Old guys can be attractive.'

'I can't explain what I think about him.'

'Go back to the memory.'

'I can't, really. Klaudia, do you believe in Collective Consciousness?'

'I am not sure. Probably not.'

'You know we were talking about ESP. The girl in the bus stop is crying. One explanation for ESP is Collective Consciousness.'

Klaudia paused, considered. 'I believe in things that do not require a belief in the supernatural. The girl in the bus stop is explicable without mysticism. You received data into your subconscious, which fed it to your conscious mind without your remembering how you'd received it . . . Is something wrong, Eloise? Do you have a pain in your head?'

'The cups.'

'I am sorry?'

'Simon said "missing items". Our blue cups were missing.'

Klaudia's expression was polite, open. She waited.

'Our coffee cups were missing from Arthur's place. A special pair of blue mugs that I bought for the flat. I never saw them again. Arthur couldn't have broken both while I was away.'

'Okay . . .'

'They were definitely not there.'

Silence.

'Maybe someone had a coffee with Arthur that morning. And then took the cups to hide the fact.'

Klaudia scribbled notes on her pad. She considered. 'Isn't it just as likely that the police took them? Perhaps to test.'

'They did take some things away. But they showed them to me. I saw their exhibits. There were no cups. I remember they asked me if anything was missing from the flat and I said no.'

Another failure.

'They may not have shown you everything they took.'

Eloise stared out at the garden. 'Arthur's family cleared the flat, but I went in there before them with the police and took my own stuff. I would have taken the cups if they'd been there, as a memento. They were special. I took a few kitchen things that belonged to me. I've had the sense someone was in the flat with Arthur just before he died, and the cups are missing. Can it be a coincidence?'

Klaudia dropped her voice very low. 'I wonder if it would be better to look to the future, instead of beating yourself up over this.'

'But you're a great believer in digging up the past.'

'You must not blame yourself.'

'My past as a crime scene,' Eloise said in a glazed voice.

'Do you think you are perhaps trying to construct an explanation of what happened as a way to avoid fear?'

'Fear of what?'

'The unpredictable nature of life. That someone we love could be here one minute and gone the next, and only because of a random accident. Sometimes when we find life brutal and frightening, we try to construct explanations that make it easier for us to deal with emotionally.'

'So I'm making it all up.'

'I am just trying to think it through with you. Perhaps this mystery visitor is a symbol, perhaps he represents Chance or Death.'

'So Chance or Death went off with a couple of blue coffee mugs.'

Klaudia smiled, shrugged. 'Okay, I don't know. I'm thinking aloud. What I am concerned about is the amount of energy it is taking you to control all these negative thoughts. If we could talk about breathing . . .' She placed her fingertips lightly on her desk and began a spiel. 'When we express certain thoughts, if we could begin with a deep, in-drawn breath, and then speak while breathing out, but only for as long as that breath lasts . . .'

Eloise listened. You had to love Klaudia's voice. So lilting and softly accented, so kind. She loved Klaudia, and yet what was the point of that? What was Klaudia doing? Sitting there with her pretty blonde hair and her kindness and her crafty smile, making you love her, and yet you couldn't do anything with your love — your hopeless transference. You couldn't send it back. Maybe Klaudia was supposed to be teaching Eloise to love *per se* — to expand her repertoire, love other people beyond her small circle of Carina, Scott and Thee, the Sparkler. (And possibly Nick?) Was *that* what she was doing? So far, though, Eloise had only widened the circle by loving Klaudia, which was comically pointless. It was all very confusing.

Klaudia now said, 'I will email you some information about t'ai chi, Eloise.'

She roused herself. 'T'ai chi. Right. You're going to have me down the park. Waving my arms around in slo mo. With the old slopes.'

Klaudia looked at her, levelly. 'Slopes?'

'Sorry,' Eloise said. 'Bad choice of words. Wrong of me. But I just can't see myself doing t'ai chi. I mean, on the peninsula . . .'

Klaudia said softly, sorrowfully even, 'Eloise! You still express yourself with a degree of idealised aggression.'

'Aggression? Me? I don't want to hurt anyone.'

'But these dismissive jokes you make. This tough stance you assume. Do you know the words from Taoism: "The soft water breaks the stone"? There is a flip side to this harsh way of expressing yourself. It is that you direct the harshness towards yourself.'

'I know, I remember. Don't beat yourself up. Treat yourself well, all that.' Eloise sat back, and Klaudia resumed her spiel. They both looked out at the garden. The rat, Eloise now felt, would be lying on its back in the grass, chewing a stalk and dreamily watching the clouds.

She fixed her eyes on the photo of the soulful brown dog on Klaudia's desk, and her mind went back to the hillside behind Arthur's flat. The concrete deck, the silver water bowl, the wisteria vine growing over the open back door. Arthur crossing the deck, kicking the water bowl, making the water slop over the side, a beam of refracted light, painfully bright, playing on the weatherboard wall. Arthur carrying two blue cups, bringing coffee to a person who sits at the table on one of the frayed, faded deckchairs, a person who has left a space, a black outline cut in the harsh light of that stunned and reeling morning, when the mesh of expected life was ripped away, leaving all senses raw, open, receiving.

Eloise said in a slow, dazed voice, 'The person in Arthur's flat that morning. All this time I've thought maybe it was a woman. That Arthur was having an affair. But it was a man.'

'How do you know?'

'The smell. Aftershave. Arthur never used it.'

I must tell Simon.

TWENTY-SIX

'Can you smell the fennel? Did you know fennel masks scent for dogs? When I was a kid in Cape Town we knew if you hid in the fennel, police dogs couldn't find you.'

'Smells can be a reminder,' Eloise said. 'You can get nostalgia from a smell, or it can make you remember a bad time, like when you were sick.'

Nick bent a branch out of her way. 'Maybe, but memory's unreliable. The mind plays tricks. Where there's a gap in the data, the brain invents stuff to fill it in, and labels it as memory.'

They were walking through scrub at the far edge of the dog park, Nick leading the way and slashing at the bush with a stick. They were both hot and tired, their voices slow.

'If you and your sister, say, each wrote a memoir, it would be full of different impressions of the same events. And different takes on the same *people*, because people behave towards individuals in different ways.'

They came out of the scrub and waded through the long dry grass towards the creek.

'I'm an only child,' Nick went on. 'My mother left me in South Africa with my father and came back here. I always felt she'd abandoned me. So I was actually surprised when she left me the house. I was going to sell it straight away, but I'm starting to get attached to it.'

'Do you miss Cape Town?'

'Only sometimes. Once, back home, I was driving in a bad part of town, and I came to a barricade made of burning tyres. There was a group of youths dancing round it. I knew if I got out of the car, I'd be in deep trouble. So I drove through it.'

'How exciting.'

'It wasn't exciting. It was depressing. Too much violence. I'd like to have kids one day, and not feel like I have to live in a fortress.'

'Kids?'

'Sure. You?'

'I don't know. Do you know anything about encryption?' Eloise said.

'Not really. Except it means spooks can't read your emails.'

Eloise said, 'I love your accent.' She frowned. What a ridiculous thing to say.

'Thanks. I wanted to tell you, I saw the wolf. It was in the back of an SUV in the supermarket car park. I heard it, too — howling, just like you said.'

'Finally! So, was it a husky?'

'Well, maybe part. But I think it's at least part-wolf. It's huge.'

'I told you.'

'I believed you.'

'No you didn't.'

'I did.'

'Shall we go back via the pub?'

'Definitely.'

But when they reached the top of the peninsula, where a new fashionable bar had replaced the terrible old Starlight Hotel, Nick got a phone call. She waited, shading her face against the evening sun, while he wandered along the roadside, kicking at tufts of grass.

He came back, rubbing his head, making his hair stand on end. His eyes were bloodshot from the hot sun. 'Been summoned,' he said. 'Search and rescue.'

'Who's lost?'

'Two women went for a walk in the Waitakeres. They haven't come back.'

'Can't you have a drink first?'

'Certainly not. It's a serious business.'

'It's very inconsiderate of them. These women.'

He said, 'Will you walk back with me?'

'No, I'll go via the supermarket.'

'Shall I ring you if it gets called off?'

'Yeah. If they're found dead, give me a call.'

He kissed her cheek. Eloise waved and watched him go. Then she headed for the bar. Just one for the road, because he'll be away all night for sure, and Silvio's gone home, and there's a wind making a whine in the power lines, blowing dust along the peninsula road, and last night I dreamed I was watching violence in a crowd, people being attacked with knives; I was watching from a distance but before long the attackers were coming for me, and I woke so poisoned with adrenaline my whole body ached and burned.

She had a couple of wines, then walked back through the dust, under the high-pitched keening of the wires.

Back home, in the stillness of the stone house, it was a relief to get out of the wind, to close the windows and watch leaves and dust whirling across the lawn. She talked to Scott on the phone, but then he had to go. Carina was writing a feature and needed to be left in peace. If only she could ring Klaudia, summon her for an urgent house call. If only she had old Silvio draped across her legs. With no appetite for the ready-made curry in the fridge, she fixed a drink and lay on the sofa, reading.

Meanwhile Tania had woken up; she was looking with amazement and horror at her husband. He was talking, addressing the armchair, laughing and gesticulating; his eyes were gleaming and there was something strange in his laugh.

'Andrei, whom are you talking to?' she asked, clutching the hand he stretched out to the monk. 'Andrei! Whom?'

'Oh! Whom?' said Kovrin in confusion. 'Why to him ... He is sitting here,' he said, pointing to the black monk.

'There is no one here ... no one! Andrei, you are ill.'

Eloise's cell phone rang. It was her mother, and she let it ring. She lay on her back, looking at the ceiling. What would Arthur have done? He wouldn't have lain here, reading, drinking. The first thing he would have done was put everything down on paper. *I think things out by writing them down, Eloise. Getting them straight in my head. Sometimes I don't even have a thought until I'm writing it.*

Get it down: I talked to Kurt Hartmann about Arthur. I told him about Rotokauri and Ed Miles. I told Simon Lampton what I'd done. Simon understood that I am trying to honour Arthur's memory, to make up for the shabby, perfunctory way he was treated by everyone, including me. Simon also understood that Arthur could be insensitive, that he barged in. He shouldn't have asked about Mrs Hallwright's adopted child, but he only did it because he was driven. He believed in an ideal: the ruthlessness of the artist. He would have called it a romantic ideal. Art before everything. Art the greatest imperative. He loved the Woody Allen movie *Bullets Over Broadway*, remember, where the wannabe artist is soft and irresolute, and the true artist is a gangster so ruthless he shoots the bad actress who's ruining his play. What would Klaudia think? She would probably say Arthur was aggressive.

But Klaudia is not an artist.

Eloise looked at her glass and found it empty. She refilled, drank, turned the page.

A tall black column like a whirlwind or a waterspout, appeared on the further side of the bay. It moved with fearful rapidity across the bay, towards the hotel, growing smaller and darker as it came, and Kovrin only just had time to get out of the way to let it pass . . . The monk with bare grey head, black eyebrows, barefoot, his arms crossed over his breast, floated by him and stood in the middle of the room.

When Arthur was dying, I was on my way to the flat. At what point did he hit the concrete, and his soul go flying out into oblivion? At the moment I was getting in the taxi at the airport, or when I was sitting in the back seat, staring mindlessly out at the beautiful morning? When Arthur looked up at the sky and took his last breath, did he know he was going to die? I can't shake the belief: someone visited him on the morning he died. I believe, with little or no evidence, that it was a man. I think someone took our blue cups. Maybe it was the police. But if it wasn't the police, then who? The cups could only have been taken in order to hide something.

It's time to pull myself together, to assemble a record of my own.

———

She drove through the streets on the eastern side of Mt Matariki. Outside Simon's house she sat in the car and twisted the rear-view mirror towards herself. Confronting the close-up: sunburnt face, smudged eyes, hair plastered down on one side and sticking up on the other. She made some brisk adjustments, and got out.

At the door, no hesitation. She rang the bell and waited, eyeing the matted fronds of a nikau palm in the garden below. There were footsteps, heels clicking on the wooden floor. A woman opened the door and regarded her silently. Tanned skin, fine lines under the eyes, full symmetrical mouth, cosmetically whitened teeth. Behind her the wide hall, the glossy wooden floor, the sound of a television.

'Is Simon Lampton here?'

No answer. A manicured hand resting on the door frame. Blue eyes, looking her up and down.

'I'm Eloise from around the corner. I just wanted to talk to him about banging into his car the other day.'

'His car?'

'I dinged his car, at the corner. It was my fault. We were both in a hurry so he said just call around some time and we'd talk about it.'

Silence.

'Didn't he tell you?'

'He didn't mention it. He's at the hospital at the moment. I'll let him know you came. Where did you say you live?'

'Just on the corner. I backed out of our drive and . . . It was only a tap. He was incredibly nice about it, said it was nothing. I just wanted to check. Anyway, I'll come back later.'

She drove, keeping to the speed limit.

At home, she lay down on the sofa and carried on reading.

But the wind. Listen to it out there, screaming. She drifted off, then woke tingling with pins and needles, wondering where she was. She slept and woke again. Hours had passed. A fixed idea had entered her mind.

In the yard, dust flew into her eyes. The estuary was full and frothing with grey chop that glimmered in the lights from the last house on the peninsula. The tide was running, the wind churning the surface into waves.

She unlocked the boot of the Honda and felt around under the carpet.

At the intersection she jammed on the brakes, bringing the Honda to a shuddering stop. She had been driving too fast; it was lucky the road was dry. In front of her, beyond a slalom of traffic cones and cordons, workmen in day-glo jackets were supervising the progress of a giant truck, on which rested an entire wooden house. She watched as it inched by like a ship travelling along a canal, all rigged up with lights, the men scurrying around it in their hard hats, continually rearranging their rolling cordon.

A policeman waved her on.

It was night; he was at a hospital; he must be doing obstetric work. So she had driven to the City Hospital, the obstetric centre, where she remembered Carina had had the Sparkler. She left the Honda in the car park and went to the lobby. A security guard directed her. In the bright white light the corridors stretched away, branching off in a series of further hallways and rows of closed doors. She crossed through hushed, dim halls, entered areas that were suddenly busy. She reached a station manned by personnel, and was stopped; asking for Dr Lampton, she was told it wasn't possible to see him.

Another security guard directed her to a waiting area. She waited, then went forward, past the desk and reached another set of corridors, another desk. Again she was stopped, and directed to a different waiting area. This time a woman in a baggy pink cotton outfit pushing a trolley said, 'Can I help you?'

'Yes,' Eloise said. 'I'd like to speak to Dr Simon Lampton. He said he'd have time for a word.'

'Oh? He's just about finished up. What's your name?'

'Eloise Hay.'

The woman pushed her trolley up the corridor and Eloise poured herself a cup of water from the cooler. Breathe, Klaudia would have said. The icy water settled in her stomach; Simon appeared and the sight of him cut off her breath. He looked tired, unshaven, and furious.

'What are you doing here?' He hustled her into the empty waiting area.

'Your wife told me you were here.'

'My *wife*.'

'I went over there earlier this evening. I told her I was a neighbour, that I'd banged into your car and we'd agreed to talk about it.'

'But what do you want? You can't come here.'

'Simon, Arthur's file . . .'

'What? Christ, don't start getting upset. I'm at work. Have you got your car? Go and wait in the car park. I'm about to go home for a while. I'll come out.'

'Will you?'

'Yes. Just give me about half, three-quarters of an hour. Don't make a fuss, just go.'

She went back to the car and waited, listening to the radio.

After an hour he came out of the foyer wearing a jacket with the collar turned up. He walked through the lines of cars, looking for the Honda, saw her, opened the door and got in.

He sniffed. 'Have you been drinking?' he said sharply.

'Yes.'

'Great. So you don't care about killing people.'

'I've only had a few.'

'I'm a doctor. I've seen the consequences of "a few". People die, Eloise.'

'Like Arthur.'

He turned to her. His eyes were dark with exhaustion or anger.

She rested her hands on the steering wheel. 'Simon, Arthur's file is gone. The one I showed you. His notes. My photos. I hid it in the boot of the car and it's gone.'

He hesitated, rubbing his hands nervously across his jaw. 'Are you sure? Maybe you forgot where you put it.'

'No. I hid it in the car and it's gone. I think a man's been following me. He could have seen me put it in there.'

'What man?'

'A tall thin man with black hair. He has a dragonfly tattooed on his hand.'

Silence. Simon seemed to be trying to decide on something. He ruffled his hair, fidgeted, checked his phone a couple of times.

'A dragonfly. And who do you think this man is?' His tone was steady, but he was on the edge of something.

'I don't know. A guy visited my neighbour one evening and said he was a policeman. It could have been him.'

'Why would a policeman follow you?'

'I don't know, Simon. I'm so tired and confused. I can't sleep. I get drunk because I hate being alone. I don't know who to trust, and I've lost Arthur's file. The only important thing I had of Arthur's, and I couldn't keep it safe. I wanted to make up for failing Arthur, and I've only made things worse. His notes. The photos. All gone.'

Simon was peering out through the windscreen, watching a security guard cross the lit forecourt outside the lobby.

Eloise said, 'What if my neighbour, Nick, took it? Remember you met him, the guy with the red T-shirt. I like him very much, but I don't know whether to trust him. He says he's a black belt in karate, he says he does search and rescue; once he got sent out to find half a woman, since only half of her had turned up, and they had to pull the other bits of her out of a drain. Klaudia says I have to reach out to people and trust them but I don't even know who *she* is . . .'

Simon twitched his shoulders. 'Christ. Half a woman?'

Eloise drew in a breath, and tried to speak on the exhalation. Breathe Eloise!

'Arthur's file is gone. Someone has taken it. It means something.'

'Means what? That you got drunk and dropped it down the back of the couch.' His tone was harsh.

'No. Someone's taken it. It means it matters, Simon. It *matters.*'

'Nothing matters except I'm going to be seen out here with you and people are going to talk.'

'Someone wanted that file.'

'I've had enough. I need to go.'

'Simon. I've realised something.'

He had his hand on the door handle. He looked at her.

'Someone took our coffee cups.'

Silence. He glanced over at the security guard.

'There was a pair of blue coffee cups at the flat. I bought them, they were special. His and hers. They were gone after Arthur died and I never saw them again. Someone must have taken them. I could be mistaken, but since the file's gone too . . .'

His face was screwed up with weariness, irritation. He licked his dry lips. 'Coffee cups? But what does that mean?'

'It means someone visited Arthur that morning, and then took the cups. I feel sure of it. And there's something else.'

He waited.

'It was a man.'

He let out a strangled little laugh. 'Sherlock Holmes. How do you know that?'

'I know. Somehow. It's not mystical. Nothing supernatural. It's to do with the subconscious. Information came to me, and I've only processed it recently.'

His face was hard, his eyes held a glint of mockery. 'Did you have a séance?'

'I think it was a smell.'

'Oh. Are you a dog?'

'Yes. I'm a dog. We're all dogs.'

Another silence, after which he delicately rubbed his forehead and repeated, 'We're all dogs.'

She was angry, stung by his tone, but she was too tired to rouse herself more than to say, 'That morning, I arrived at the flat very soon after Arthur died. It was sheer bad luck I didn't turn up earlier.'

'I see.'

'I've never told anyone this: I changed my booking. I caught an earlier flight from Sydney without telling Arthur. I'd been nagging him about having too many projects. We'd argued about him using personal stuff in his writing. I felt he was up to something, that he'd started hiding things from me. I thought he might be seeing someone else. I was suspicious, and when I landed in Auckland I didn't text or ring him, I just got in the cab. I sensed a stranger had been in the flat. But I didn't tell the police because I didn't know then that I'd sensed it.'

'But you could "smell" it was a man? Or, you couldn't then, but you know now.'

'Yes, there was a smell. My theory is: aftershave.'

Simon looked at her.

'Arthur never wore it. Perfume gave him asthma.'

She leaned forward and put her head in her hands. 'A person visited Arthur the morning he died. The person was a man. He took our special blue cups.' She looked sideways. 'A layer of the world was hidden from me — *those facts* were hidden from me. Now, someone's taken Arthur's file.'

Simon sat in silence, not moving. A sudden gust of wind smacked the side of the car; paper rubbish blew up over the asphalt and whirled around in the air. In the neon light of the lobby, the security guard slowly paced from wall to wall.

Finally he looked at the back of his hands and said, 'Have you related any of this speculation to your policewoman friend?'

'No. I wanted to tell you first. I'm so tired and I don't know who to trust. Will you help me, Simon?'

'But how can I help you?'

'Can you drive me back to the peninsula? I can't get back there alone. You're right, it's terrible to drink and drive. I'll end up killing someone. You're a doctor. You know what's right.'

He looked at his watch. 'I need to get home.'

'Your wife will be asleep. She won't know the difference. You must stay the night at the hospital all the time. You could drive my car.'

He sat without speaking, deep in thought. After a while he rolled his shoulders, rubbed his neck and turned to her. His expression had changed; it was earnest, weary, troubled. He scratched the stubble on his chin and said,

'Eloise, I'm going to be frank with you. Up until now I've been inclined to think you're a bit nuts.' He crinkled his eyes, put a hand on her arm. 'I mean that in a caring way, as a friend, okay? Can I say we're friends? Good. I've thought you were strung-out, full of grief, needing help for your mental state, all that. And that you were probably not seeing things clearly. But what you've been telling me tonight, and the last time we talked, is really making me wonder. I'm starting to think maybe you're right to be worried. That you're right to be worried about *trusting* people. I think you and I need to work this out before we go telling anybody about it. Including the police. I mean, think about it. We're talking about matters that involve, although very indirectly, an ex-prime minister and a justice minister who used to be Minister of Police. These are powerful people, with powerful interests and a lot of reach. Let's not forget Ed Miles used to *run* the police. And now he's justice, he's got even more power. And worse, you've managed to mention Arthur's calling Rotokauri to Kurt Hartmann, which just makes me shudder, frankly. That's the craziest thing you've done — it's the fucking *definition*, excuse my language, of playing with fire. Hartmann is a complete wild card. No one knows who he really is, or what he's up to. And I'm sorry, but to me he's not an internet freedom-fighter or any of that bullshit, he's a pirate and a criminal, and he's going to end up in a US supermax. I'm glad you've come to me, that you trust me. I'm honoured by your trust, even though you're making me very worried. I want us to be friends, and I want to help. Okay?'

Eloise assented, with a watery sigh. Oh Arthur, the exquisite relief of not being alone.

At Simon's instruction, she started the car and drove out of the hospital parking lot. In the street, under the flame trees, they got out. She stumbled on the grass verge and he guided her around the side of the car into the passenger seat. She felt how tall he was, how strong and competent his big hands.

High in the branches, the tui were puffing out their feathers, starting up their repetitive early morning dirge. Simon folded himself into the tiny car, and cranked back the seat.

He looked at her, his face waxy in the grey dawn light. There were shadows under his eyes; his expression was fixed, intent.

'Tuis,' he said. 'What beautiful birds. I love their song, don't you?'

'Sure,' she said. Her eyes were closed. They listened to the tuis' morning song, five short piercing notes followed by three long liquid ones.

'Buckle up, Eloise.'

He started the engine, and began driving the small car carefully towards the harbour. In the east the wind had ploughed a track across the clouds, like the swipe of an animal's claw, and the city skyline was a honeycomb, shot through with liquid light. In the west, over the Starlight Peninsula, the night was still hanging on, inky black.

TWENTY-SEVEN

'What's all this?' Simon was looking at the material strewn over Eloise's kitchen table.

'I'm researching mass hysteria. Roysmith's doing a piece on it.'

He held up a page. 'Outbreaks of mystery illness are more common than we think.'

Eloise shuffled the pages into a rough pile. 'I've been reading about the Phantom Gasser of Illinois. People believed a man was spraying a poisonous mist into the bedrooms of teenage girls. In Washington in the 1950s, people who were worried about nuclear testing developed mass hysteria about cosmic rays. When groups of people are stressed out, they can catch psychosomatic illness from one another.'

'Why choose that subject?'

Eloise, who, along with everyone else at Q, had received management's slightly threatening plea for 'discretion' on the static shock issue, said, 'Human interest, sort of thing.'

Simon went to the ranch slider. 'Look at the sunrise.'

Beyond the dog park, the distant buildings were covered with a shawl of fire.

Eloise sighed. 'No point going to bed now.'

Simon said, 'Elke, our adopted daughter, never slept. When I was head of obstetrics at Auckland, I'd come home in the night and she'd be up. We spent a lot of night time together.'

'How many children do you have?'

'Two sons, two daughters.'

'Lot of kids.'

'One of my sons grew up elsewhere. William. He has a different family.'

'Oh?'

'Typical story. Nothing unusual.'

'When Arthur rang you . . .'

'He wanted to know about our daughter. That crossed a line. Journalists, writers of whatever kind, need to leave the children out of it.'

'He believed in the ruthlessness of the artist.'

'He wasn't ruthless,' Simon said.

Silence. They looked out at the sky, the clouds bleeding red light.

Eloise pointed, 'Those shafts of light, Maori call them the ropes of Maui.'

Simon put his hand on the glass. 'Politicians — now *they* can be ruthless.'

'Tell me about Rotokauri.'

'The place? It's more than a big house; it's a compound. The main house is called the Wedding Cake, on account of being big and white and three storeyed. There are smaller houses grouped around it. That summer, Karen and I were there with the Hallwrights, Miles and his wife, and the Cahanes. A big staff. The help, plus security. Roza Hallwright spent a lot of time telling her kid *Soon and Starfish* stories, which drove me up the wall. Who knew she was creating herself an empire. They've made more money out of the *Soon* franchise than David's made in business.'

'They had a housekeeper, a Chinese woman.'

'Yes, they did have a rather formidable Chinese housekeeper, although she left at some point. And a beautiful Niuean nanny. Roza disliked her.'

'Why?'

'She was lovely, kind, religious, and Roza's son loved her. Roza was jealous.'

'So, a ruthless group?'

'Well Miles is, obviously. Hallwright was so popular, he could afford to do a lot of smiling, and let Miles and Cahane be the assassins.'

'So there you were on holiday, and Arthur rang you. On your cell phone? How did he get your number?'

'No idea. Any number of ways he could have got it, through my office maybe. I was still going into work during the holiday; I had to be on call for patients.'

'Arthur had the housekeeper's cell phone number. It was in his notes.'

Simon gave her a forbearing look, as though he'd just swallowed something unpleasant. 'Did he. How enterprising.'

'He also wrote in his notes that Roza Hallwright used to be an alcoholic and drug user.'

A flash of irritation in his eyes. 'How did he know that?'

'So it's true? There was a reference to an old friend of Roza's, and a cell phone number.'

'I told you. He crossed a line.'

'It's true he always went too far. But that was one of the reasons I loved him. He was daring and fun; he was into everything. Kind of unstoppable. If you'd met him, talked to him properly, you'd know he was a good person. He was humane, interested in people.'

Simon said, 'Unstoppable. Really?'

He stood in front of the plate-glass window, looking out towards the city. The wind had died, and the sky was striped with long, delicate feathers of cloud. Over the dog park, a single star hung next to the thin curve of the moon, a ball of blackness edged with silver. The flax bushes and cabbage trees were motionless in the strange aquarium light.

He said, 'You're alone here.'

'So?'

He came towards her. 'Does it bother you?'

'Yes, it bothers me. Especially now someone's taken Arthur's file.'

He sat down on the sofa, winced, drew something out from under himself and held it up.

'Sorry. One of Silvio's bones. Just chuck it on the floor.'

His voice was slow, intent. 'There's something, what's the word, compelling, about talking. Remembering Rotokauri. I can see it must be a relief for people to go to a shrink.'

'I recommend it,' Eloise said. 'My shrink's great. I'll give you her card if you like.'

Would you like a new patient, Klaudia? He's a doctor. I may be slightly in love with him.

'No, thanks.' He rubbed his stubbly chin. A long pause. 'I've never told anyone about what it was like, those times when we were living right up against the Hallwrights. The pressure, the tightrope we had to walk. There was tension between Roza and my wife about our daughter. Hallwright's court was a minefield; Miles and Cahane were fighting for favour the whole time; Hallwright was playing them off against each other. Miles is such a mindreader he's practically clairvoyant. He finds people's weak spot and homes in. Cahane's an arrogant, smooth bastard, with a very scary wife. Roza's complex and a handful, and David, well, he's a phenomenon.'

'Are you still Hallwright's best friend?'

'I'd like to think so.'

'Do you visit them in France?'

'Sure. All the time.'

'St Tropez or whatever?'

Simon's smile was genuine, full of pleasure. 'Actually, they have a fuck-off big mansion on the Corniche, just outside Monte Carlo.'

She smiled back. 'Do they now. Fancy.'

'Yeah. Makes Rotokauri look a bit rustic.'

'I'm sure.'

'At Rotokauri back then, I was totally out of my depth, but I had this position, it kept me above the fray. It's still the most surprising thing that's ever happened to me: David chose me. He just decided — I was not only his friend, I was his "best friend". There I was every morning, having breakfast with the prime minister. No one else was allowed to join us, not even Miles. I felt . . . it's hard to describe. I have to admit, I was thrilled.'

'So he appointed you. You didn't have to earn it.'

Simon's smile vanished. 'I did actually. I very much felt I earned it.'

'Were you the greasiest courtier, the biggest fan?'

'No. The opposite. I was the one who never grovelled. I treated him as an equal. Only Roza and I managed that. Everyone else was star-struck, insincere, tip-toeing around him. I was straight with him. If he tried any tricks, I ignored him until he came round.'

'Tricks?'

'He had power moves. He used to freeze people out, isolate them, things like that. Play on their nerves. Divide and rule. I never responded. I had a father who used similar tactics, used to play power games with me and my brother. I was ready for that kind of bullshit.'

'So you were the tough guy.'

'I had to be. I needed to look after my family, my kids. I had to keep my practice going. My patients were depending on me. It was up to me to keep it together.'

'Sounds like a stressful holiday.'

'It had its moments,' Simon said.

Beyond the glass the sky was mottled, red and black.

Eloise said, 'You managed. And now life is less fraught.'

'It has been. I find *you* rather stressful.'

'Who is Mereana Kostas?'

'I have no idea.'

'Did Arthur talk about her on the phone?'

'No.'

'The detective said someone told her Mereana Kostas left the country years ago. But *she* thinks Mereana's dead. She said it's hard to disappear unless you have resources, and ordinary people who vanish are usually dead.'

'No doubt.'

'Who do you think took Arthur's file?'

'Well, Eloise, we don't know who you've stirred up with your enquiries. You've talked to the police . . .'

'The woman cop's not interested. She told me, she's overworked and it's a dead file.'

'And yet she may have a passing interest in what you turn up. Also, if she's made any noise herself as a result of your visit, she could have alerted other people.'

'Noise?'

Simon chewed his nails. 'And there's Jack Dance, threatened by Miles.'

'I thought you didn't follow politics.'

'Everyone knows Miles and Dance are out to get each other. The question is are you safe because you've spoken to the police?'

'Why would I not be safe?'

'If you weren't, you are now. That detective may not be interested at the moment, but she's not stupid. She's going to wake up smartly if you come to any harm.'

'I thought you didn't remember her.'

'She's come into focus, since you reminded me. Young. Crazy stack of blonde hair. Funny eyes.'

'And who would harm me?'

'I don't know. I suppose I'm thinking of Hartmann. The uber-criminal.'

'Hartmann wouldn't hurt a fly.'

'Oh sure, he's been teaching you to feed chickens and play computer games. Actually, he's a fugitive wanted by the United States. You seem extraordinarily naïve about him, if you don't mind my saying.'

'He's fine. He's a big softie. With his golf carts. His chickens.'

'Think he roasts his chickens for dinner?'

'No! They're his Zen.'

'His Zen. Christ. We all need some Zen.' Simon sighed and lay back with his feet up on the arm rest, as if he'd forgotten himself for a moment.

Look, Klaudia. His stubble, his curly hair, his big, steady hands.

'What a sky,' Simon said. 'Red sky in the morning. I used to see in the dawn all the time with Elke. My little insomniac. She'd ask me strange questions. She said, Since you're a doctor and you cut people open, would it be easy for you to kill someone? I told her, I *fix* people. When they're hurt, I make them better. It was as if she were trying to work out what makes us human.'

'I couldn't be a doctor. I'm too squeamish.'

'But when you know you're doing good, fixing people, there's no need for squeamishness. There's great satisfaction.'

'You can obviously stand the sight of blood.'

He said, 'Yes, I've seen a lot of blood. I can stand it.'

'The only dead person I've seen is Arthur.'

'I'm sorry.'

'I can see him now. He had a triangle of broken skull sticking up out of his head. His lips were sort of pursed. His neck was bent right over. There was stuff coming out his ears. And he had deep purple shadows under his eyes.'

'He would have fractured his skull, broken his neck.'

'It's terrible to think of, isn't it. Dying on the concrete, alone.'

'Yes, it's terrible.' Simon said. 'But he wouldn't have suffered, and no doctor could have helped him.'

'How do you know?'

'Because of that triangle of skull you describe, the angle of his neck and the fluid from his ears. An ambulance wouldn't have saved him.'

'Really? Are you sure?'

'Yes, I'm sure. You have this idea you should ask questions. I think you feel a kind of guilt. But you shouldn't torture yourself.'

'I didn't do enough.'

'You couldn't change anything. We all do our best. We do what we have to do.'

A tui started up in the flame tree by the stucco house. They listened.

Simon was lying on his back, his forearm over his face. After a long moment he said, 'Want to know what I think?'

'Sure.'

She waited.

He said, 'You were angry with Arthur. He had this idea of being a "ruthless artist". It meant he used things, private details, in his writing. You said he wrote caricatures of your mother. He used details from *your* life, too. Maybe he made light of stuff that was important, personal. And even though you understood the concept of the artist using material without fear or favour, you still felt invaded and hurt by it. You argued with him, and he started being a bit evasive. He stopped telling you what he was up to. You worried he might be cheating on you, right?'

Eloise listened. His voice, and behind it the chorus of the tui in the flame tree.

'You felt insecure, uncertain about him. So you booked an earlier flight back from Sydney, and when you'd landed at Auckland, you didn't ring or text to say you were coming home early. You wanted to catch him out. But here's what troubles you most: if you'd rung or texted him, he might not have died.'

Eloise's throat closed over.

'If you'd rung or texted him, you could have changed the course of events. But you didn't, because you were angry, and you were checking up.'

She wanted to speak, but she went on listening.

He carried on, 'You have to accept, what happened was not your fault. You did what you did partly because of *his* actions. You didn't ring him from the airport because you didn't trust him. You felt he'd somehow crossed a line, and you were trying to deal with that. You were acting in good faith. Events took a bad turn, outside your control.'

Simon lifted his arm from his eyes. His words had taken on a kind of rhythm. 'Imagine if something different had happened. Say you'd arrived earlier at the flat, you were angry, the pair of you argued. You told him he'd invaded your privacy by writing about you, that he'd damaged trust by keeping things from you. Say your dispute took place on the road outside and you decided to storm off, and there was some kind of tussle and he tripped and fell against the fence; it gave way, and he went over the wall. It wouldn't be your fault. It wasn't *his* fault either, it was a combination of circumstances. He played a part in it as much as you. It could have been *you* who fell down the wall, and in that case it wouldn't have been his fault either. We're all at the mercy of fate. The gods decide what's going to happen.'

'The gods . . .'

'Call it the gods or fate or chance. Look at the sky out there. Look at the universe. Does it care? No.'

Eloise looked at the red and black sky over the dog park. A phrase came to her. 'It's riddled with light,' she said, sitting up. She went to the shelves and found a book.

'This was Arthur's. Yeats.' She consulted the index, turned the pages. 'It's a poem called "The Cold Heaven".'

'I don't know any poetry,' Simon said.

'Neither do I, really.' She sat down beside him.

Suddenly I saw the cold and rook-delighting heaven
That seemed as though ice burned and was but the more ice,
And thereupon imagination and heart were driven
So wild that every casual thought of that and this
Vanished, and left but memories, that should be out of season
With the hot blood of youth, of love crossed long ago;
And I took the blame out of all sense and reason,
Until I cried and trembled and rocked to and fro,
Riddled with light. Ah! when the ghost begins to quicken,
Confusion of the death-bed over, is it sent
Out naked on the roads, as the books say, and stricken
By the injustice of the skies for punishment.

'I took the blame . . .' Simon repeated.

'Out of all sense and reason.'

They said nothing for a while. The sky was changing from red to orange, the first faint tints of light green, almost blue, appearing.

'So Arthur read poetry.'

'Some. I never used to read anything, myself. I just watched TV, went to movies. He was scandalised by that. I do read now, thanks to him.'

She let the book drop and said in a tranced voice, 'You understand. I loved Arthur. I was angry he used our private lives as material. I was hurt by his ruthless side, his secretiveness. But the way you talk, you make it sound as if nothing's anyone's fault. As if no one should be blamed for anything.'

Simon rested his arm over his eyes again. 'People have fewer choices than they think. Mostly they're just reacting to what's happening.'

'But a criminal, a murderer, say, has choices. Decides to kill.'

'Does he? Can one human being really change his circumstances? Where he was born, who his parents are, what they do to him, how he grows up, what random events life throws at him? How he reacts in any given moment? I don't know.'

'You're saying we're all animals.'

He lifted his arm, turned to her. 'You told me yourself, Eloise. We're all dogs.'

'Look.' She pointed. They could see a man walking along the edge of the creek, crossing the wooden bridge, following the path through the flax bushes. 'It's Nick. My neighbour.'

Simon stood up. 'I'd better go. You should get some sleep.'

'It's too late. I have to go to work.' She followed him to the front door. 'Will you come back here?'

He looked down at her, expressionless. 'Sure.'

'I won't be able to live here much longer. My husband wants to sell the house. I have to move.'

'Goodbye, Eloise.'

'Wait, I've just remembered. You've got no car.'

'I'll walk up to the main road and get a cab.'

'Call one from here.'

'No, I'd like to walk for a while. Clear my head.'

She watched him walk away up the peninsula road. There was a tapping sound; she locked the front door and went back through the house.

Nick was on the deck, his face close to the glass. She opened the ranch slider.

'I saw the light on in the kitchen. You're up early,' he said.

'Did you find them?'

'Yes.'

'In one piece?'

'Both alive, fortunately. Relieved to be found. They were twenty metres off the track. In the bush, sense of direction's the first thing to go.'

His South African accent was soft, pleasing. He sounded exhausted. She said, 'Congratulations. Would you like to come in?'

She started making coffee, but by the time it was ready he had fallen sideways and was asleep on the sofa. She covered him with a rug.

It was nearly time to get ready for work. She sat down, drinking her coffee. Her temples were pulsing with weariness. Tiny sparks flashed at the edges of her eyes.

Nick, sleeping beside her, smelled of sweat and aftershave.

She went through the open door onto the deck and looked out over the dog park. The owners were clustered on the grass, the dogs speeding out from them, circling, running back. She watched a man throwing a ball, the dog tearing in pursuit, its body rippling as it raced over the grass. Nearby, on the edge of the creek, an old man led the way for an ancient, puffing corgi. The mangrove leaves shone in the morning light, the flax bushes quietly rattled, and all along the peninsula the early sun picked out delicate detail: the thin shadows of the cabbage trees, the tui high in the flame tree.

In the corner of Eloise's eye there was a squiggle of light that mirrored the rippling effect of the running dog. It was like looking at her own thought, an electrical spark arcing along the neural pathway. At first it was only obliquely visible; if she turned towards it, it moved away. The ripple of brightness formed itself into a question.

The question was coming at her, out of a sky riddled with light. It was burning as it came nearer, hurting her eyes.

TWENTY-EIGHT

'Okay. Tell me about the Mad Gasser.'

Scott had his feet up on the desk, a coffee in his hand.

Eloise consulted her iPad. 'The Mad Gasser of Mattoon, also known as the Anesthetic Prowler, Fritz the Phantom Anesthetist, and the Mad Gasser of Roanoke. Widely reported to have made holes in people's windows and shot poison gas into their houses, causing nausea, faintness and vomiting. Investigations concluded that many of the complaints arose as a result of reports that generated mass hysteria . . .'

She paused, frowned. 'Scott?'

'Mmm?'

'You felt the shocks. They weren't mass hysteria.'

'You and I aren't hysterical types.'

'You mean other people are?'

'Take Selena: the woman was hysterical the whole time.'

'You refuse to take this seriously!'

'Can you blame me? By the way, did I show you Thee's photos? She emailed me a whole bunch. Have a look.'

He took his feet off the desk and brought up pictures on his big computer screen, mostly photos of Iris's birthday party: Scott looking harassed, children running amok in the trashed house, a shot of the Sparkler and Iris jumping through a sprinkler on the lawn.

'That niece of yours, Rachel Margery, she's a bit of an old soul.'

Eloise looked at the crowded pictures, the domesticity, the careless, beautiful, romping children. She felt something, what would you call it? An ache, a pang.

She rested her chin on her fist and said irritably, 'What does that even mean, an old soul?'

'Dunno.'

'You mean, she's kind of a powerful child.'

'Yeah. She's intelligent. And confident. Very real and present.'

He clicked through the pictures. 'Here's the opera, *Marriage of Figaro*, look, the Hallwrights with that fundraising dragon, what's her name, Lady Trish Ellison. Hamish Dark looking like Nosferatu.'

'Nice one of you and Mariel.'

'Mmm. I'm not sure about the suit. Do you like that one?'

They looked at pictures of Scott. His expressions, the dial, as always, slightly turned up: rapt attention, joyfulness, frowning seriousness. There was Hamish Dark listening to the Sinister Doormat while studiously 'keeping a straight face'. The Hallwrights in conversation with a red-faced woman, Roza Hallwright looking beyond her, across the room.

Scott's phone rang, he answered.

Eloise went on clicking through the photos. There was one of herself, flushed, raising a wine glass and looking on as Scott talked, a group of women eyeing him. Another of the Hallwrights among a circle of the invited guests: an actor, a DJ, a TV executive, Jack Anthony. One of the film director, Sir Peter Jackson. A shot of a plate-glass window with city lights shining in the darkness behind it. Leaning against the glass, Mariel Hartfield and Simon Lampton, both talking on their phones, so close their elbows were nearly touching.

'Hartmann's here,' Scott said.

'Why?'

'He wants to talk about the interview. I should have told him we're busy with the Phantom Gasser. Can you go down to reception for him, E. I've got a headache. Hartmann gives me a headache. He gives me mass hysteria. I can't understand what he's talking about half the time.'

'You need Fritz the Phantom Anesthetist. No, you need some Panadol. Go and take some drugs. I'll see what he wants.'

'Thanks, E, you're a pal.'

She went down to reception. Hartmann was leaning against the desk, conferring with Chad Loafer. Eloise paused, struck by the sight of Hine, the receptionist, looking minuscule next to Hartmann's giant frame.

'Eloise Hay,' Hartmann said, turning with a smile that struck her as genuine, even sweet. Tossing his scarf over one shoulder, hitching up his pants, he told Loafer impressively, 'Chad. Wait here.'

'You look pleased about something,' Eloise said.

He came close, squinted down at her. 'I have something for you.'

'Okay. I'll take you up to Scott.'

The lift doors closed on Chad Loafer, on Hine. They were alone in the metal box. Hartmann said quietly, without looking at her, 'You have an office? Let's go there before I speak to Scott.'

They went to her room — more a nook than an office — and closed the door. Hartmann's bulk filled the small space. She could hear the rasp of his effortful breathing. He took some sheets of paper out of his bag and held them up.

'I have located historical exchanges, mostly email and Facebook messaging. I will not tell you how I got them, except to say an expert friend accessed them from a website that had suffered a denial of service attack, leaving it vulnerable for a short time. I'm going to show them to you because you led me to them.'

She reached out, but he held the sheets back.

'You have a personal interest in what's recorded here. But I want to make something clear between us. I found the material — actually my friend did — so I am going to retain the right to use it in the way I see fit.'

'What do you mean?'

'I want to decide how to use the material. I want your agreement on this.'

She felt like Scott: unable to understand what he was talking about.

He seemed to be waiting for a reply. When she didn't say anything he went on, 'Eloise, I think you want to see what I've found. But I will only show it to you if you agree that I control it, and you keep this conversation between us. No telling anyone about it, or about the material. If you don't agree, I won't show it to you.'

'Okay . . .' She thought about it. 'How can I agree if I don't know what you're talking about?'

'It's your choice. Agree now, or I go away and we don't speak any more.'

She folded her arms. 'What if I agree now, then look at the stuff and change my mind — decide I do want to tell someone about it?'

'You won't want to do that.'

'Why not?'

'It wouldn't be in your interests.'

'Is that a threat? You mean you'll set your tiny bodyguard on me?'

He smiled, showing his wicked little teeth. 'No threats. Just a gentleperson's agreement.' He held out his hand. 'I am only going to show it to you, not give it to you. I'm not going to leave you today with any proof. So if you wanted to talk about this material, you'd have to work pretty hard to convince people it really exists. Without proof, you face a lot of trouble. Also a defamation suit. I'm sorry but that's the only way I can proceed. You want to see what I've got, don't you?'

'So, let me get this straight. I've apparently helped you to find something, but you're going to keep it all for yourself.'

'Precisely, Eloise. Sorry. But *you* would not have been able to find it.'

He was holding out his hand. She shook it.

'These are exchanges between Roza Hallwright and Mr Ed Miles, at the time they were on holiday at the Hallwright residence, Rotokauri. They are exchanges made before people knew this kind of messaging is not secure — that it can never be secure. They thought they were speaking in absolute privacy.

'Let's sit down, and I will show you. See, here is the date, the time, and here are the names of the pair talking. Roza and Ed.'

Who is he? He rang one of the numbers in the main house. He spun some line and got the idiot girl to bring me the phone. He mentioned Jung Ha. He said something about 'your housekeeper'. She's always spied on us. I think she gave him the house numbers. It's got to be her. He asked about Elke, about my past, my AA/NA and he talked about my friend Tamara Goldwater. Whose name he could have got from Jung Ha. I'm going to fire JH today. He's asking about very personal stuff. He knows stuff.

Don't worry. I will look into it.

I Googled him. Have a look. Am going to see if I can get rid of Jung Ha straight away. Or if I have to give her notice. Do I? I will ask D.

Okay.

Ed, have you seen the paper. Weeks. He's dead. What is going on?

Ed????

Don't worry. No need to freak out. You've done nothing wrong obv. I will find out what's happened — sounds like accident.

Ed, have you found out what he was doing? How he knew stuff? Did he talk to JH?

I told you, don't worry. I have checked. You're right, it is the kind of thing media like to blow into story: journalist harasses PM's wife about her eventful past. Is found dead(!) I will calm things down.

Eventful . . . I need to talk to you. Are you at the house today?

Hello Ed? Are you still in Auck?

Roza, cheer up. Talked to Quilliam this a.m. — at dawn actually — usual awful Waitangi torture. I told him prejudicial outweighs probative value vis a vis your pest caller. I gave him the message from me and by impl from D: there is nothing to see here. Move on. He got the idea. He is going to look into it, also check the path report. I told him: Call off the dogs. Quieten things down.

D's right, you're the best. Good karma . . .

All fine. No need to feel you owe me. Only I can't do much about your Tamara friend shooting mouth off about your private stuff, AA etc. That's yours to deal with.

Okay.

My advice, Roza — do what I do: Pay back double.

Hartmann said, 'The police commissioner, you probably remember, was the late Rodney Quilliam. He and Miles were at the dawn service at Waitangi that year. I have found an exchange between Quilliam and a third party that suggests serious interference by Miles.'

'So Miles told him to stop looking into Arthur's death.'

'Miles saw it could turn into a tabloid thing, Arthur ringing Hallwright's wife, then dying. Police investigating, maybe finding out what questions Arthur was asking her. It could have fuelled conspiracy theories, right. So he told Quilliam to act. Miles went outside his ministerial powers. He wasn't allowed to interfere in police operational matters.'

'I had no idea Arthur talked to Roza Hallwright.'

'I guess he got her worried. Asking about her past, talking to some woman she knew. Maybe he found out some bad stuff. These politicians are so alert to the possibility of bad publicity, they will dampen anything down if they can. Even if they haven't actually done anything wrong. It's about perception. Miles would have made less of a problem for himself if he had been less proactive. But he had the boss's wife nagging him to do something. See his line, *No need to feel you owe me.* Meaning, You owe me. Big time.'

'Oh, Arthur.' Eloise closed her eyes. Why did he have to go so far? To think of him, spinning a line, somehow luring Roza Hallwright to a phone in the compound, asking her about personal stuff, about her past. Perhaps he really was ruthless.

She said, 'He used to get obsessed with ideas, with projects. No wonder he was being secretive. He would have known I'd object to him ringing her. The prime minister's wife, for God's sake. I would have said, You can't do that.'

Her phone pinged. Scott sending a text: *where are you?*

She said, 'This shows Miles didn't know anything about Arthur's death, and neither did Roza Hallwright. They were only worried how it would look.'

Hartmann moved to the window and looked out, his hands on his hips. He said, 'You can see why I smiled when my friend gave me this material. It answers your question, Eloise. It tells you: these people did not hurt your friend. He probably just had an accident. And it answers my question: does Ed Miles have an Achilles heel?'

Eloise thought about this. 'I had a file belonging to Arthur. It wasn't much, just photos mostly, but there were notes he'd written about the people staying at Rotokauri. I hid it, not very well, in the boot of my car, and someone's taken it.'

'Are you sure?'

'Yes. It's been stolen.'

'Also, you said you were being followed.'

'I thought I was, although it seemed so fanciful. Unbelievable. But now someone's taken Arthur's file, maybe I wasn't imagining it.'

'I don't see why you would be imagining it. It is like I said, people are not as independent as they think. Just like the herd at the waterhole, suddenly pricking up the ears and moving: they start responding to outside forces, moving in the same direction at the same time. When you started to ask questions, other people started asking, too. Who knows what signals come from the universe.'

'Signals?'

'People want the same thing you've been looking for: the same information.'

'I don't know about all that. The universe . . .'

'Jack Dance, for one, will have started asking questions about the guy who's trying to take his job: Ed Miles. And about his super-rich backers, Mr and Mrs Soon Empire.'

Hartmann folded the sheets of paper and put them in his bag.

Eloise said, 'Why don't you give me a copy?'

'Finders keepers,' he said.

'Right.'

He put his big hand on her arm. 'Do you understand, Eloise, if you tell anyone about this, all you'll do is attract unwelcome attention. You will make people angry with you. And you will have no proof to back your claim. Zero gain for you.'

'So *give* me the proof.'

'No.'

'Why not?'

'That would not be in *my* interests.' Hartmann stood up and held out his hand. 'I want to thank you. The information has currency.'

'What are you going to do with it?'

He said, 'I am going to spend it very quietly, Eloise.'

'On what?'

'Well, let's see. I have had so much negativity from Mr Ed Miles, that I really don't want to hear another word from him.' He smiled and fussily arranged his scarf. 'And so, Eloise, I am going to talk to our esteemed Prime Minister. I am going to reach out to Jack Dance!'

He turned to go. 'I want you to know, Eloise, I care about you. I care about your safety. I am protecting you by not giving you a copy of the messages. Ed Miles is a powerful man, and so is Hallwright. I, don't forget, have nothing to lose. I'm a wanted guy. Mr Obama wants me. Mr Biden wants me. They say I'm the biggest copyright thief in the world. They call me "Bond villain". I'm like something out of a movie except, guess what, I'm real! I could be bumped off, why not? It would be cheaper for them.'

Eloise smiled. 'The poison umbrella. The radioactive cup of tea.'

'Exactly. So let *me* be the one to play with fire. And you be content you have your answer. Okay?'

'It seems wrong. I have to think about it.'

Hartmann said, 'You have more time than I do. I have a suggestion. You say Arthur's file is stolen. So make a file of your own. Write down everything you know, everything you suspect. Make a list of times, names, dates, and keep it. Who knows, one day it might all come out. It is useful to put things in order. Give it a name: that's what I would do.'

'A name?'

'Operations and files need a name, Eloise. For focus, purpose. It's what spooks do, with their ridiculous FIVE EYES and SPEARGUN and PRISM. Something that sums it up: the Hallwrights, Ed Miles, Arthur, your hope that one day all will be explained.'

'Arthur used to say the same thing: write it down.'

'Okay, there you go. Now, let's go and say hi to Scott.'

She followed him out, not listening to his talk about the weather, his health, his battles with the court over his finances.

Shall I follow his advice, Klaudia? Call it the Rotokauri File. The Last Days of Arthur Weeks. I will put it down on paper, make my own file. Soon.

TWENTY-NINE

'So, Eloise, it's been a few weeks. I am sorry I had to attend a relative's funeral in Germany. It was very cold back in my home town, I can tell you!'

Eloise let this latest betrayal pass without comment.

She waited for a moment, then said, 'I've decided to write a record, my own file on Arthur. To replace the one I lost. And to make up for the fact I didn't ask enough questions.'

Klaudia swallowed, placed her fingertips on the page in front of her and said, 'It can be useful to note down your thoughts.'

'The morning Arthur died I wasn't there. I was absent. By the time I arrived at the flat he was gone; there was only the memory of him. He'd disappeared through a door in the air, he was just an outline, the black shape of a man . . .'

Klaudia listened. The light, pouring in through the window behind her, caught her blonde hair, illuminating the fine strands. The air was full of specks of shiny dust. When Klaudia listened intently, she had a way of wrinkling her sharp nose and turning her mouth up at the corners that made her look sly, silken, complicit.

Eloise briefly considered this: Klaudia is at her most charming when she is listening. Just as Simon Lampton is at his most fetching when he drops his smile, turns serious.

She went on, 'I thought someone had been in the flat, but perhaps it was just the outline of Arthur I sensed. The presence of his absence.'

'Perhaps. That is a little obscure.'

'Obscure? I suppose. It's possible seeing you has made me much less sane.'

Klaudia looked at her steadily. She was wearing glasses today. She put her index finger on the frame and lightly pushed.

'My mother would say, Stay away from shrinks. With their corniness and their mumbo jumbo. They'll turn you mad.'

Klaudia smiled. 'Oh dear.'

'She's a kind of emotional prude. Beyond stiff upper lip.'

'Too much stiffer lip equals dead,' Klaudia said coolly.

Eloise let out a slightly wild laugh. She covered her mouth. 'Sorry.'

Klaudia's mouth turned up in her Joker smile. She seemed larger, more solid today, with a slight edge of irritation in her smile. The glasses made her blue eyes severe. Eloise looked at Klaudia's big, pale hand, the square fingers, a tight bronze bracelet pinching the skin on her wrist. She was wearing her paua shell necklace. Also a rather flattering shirt. She probably had a date.

Eloise sighed. *How about you cancel your date, Klaud, and come over to my place. I'll forgive you for putting a trivial 'funeral' ahead of me. I'll cook you something. Ready-made curry, sushi, pizza, whatever you like. I'll show you the peninsula, before I have to leave it. I'm so sad I won't be living there any more.*

'I'm going to have to move. Leaving the house will feel like losing my mind,' she said.

'How are you getting on with your neighbour?' Klaudia's voice sounded thick, sleepy.

Eloise, who'd been hoping for more of a reaction, looked for the rat (no sign) and said, 'He's South African.'

'Yes?'

'When he visits, I have a feeling of . . .'

'Yes?'

Don't do it, Klaudia. Don't look at your watch.

Klaudia glanced at her watch.

With a sense of sorrow (*Klaudia, you break my heart!*), Eloise said, 'When he comes over, I have a terrific feeling of being safe.'

Klaudia smiled. 'That is good, Eloise!'

Safe. How nauseatingly corny Demelza Hay would find *that*.

At home on the peninsula, Eloise phoned Carina and voiced the opinion that Silvio was yearning for a visit. 'Pining for it. The park. The wide open spaces.'

Her sister wearily promised to discuss the matter with the Sparkler.

'Bring *her*, too,' Eloise said.

She phoned Scott's and spoke to Thee. Who said, 'So, this neighbour. Do we like him?'

Eloise said, 'Want to meet him?'

'Definitely. Bring him over.'

Eloise said slowly, 'Maybe you and Scott could come over here. And the girls.' It was the new idea: filling the house with people. Not that she'd be living here much longer. She was waiting for the call from Jaeger's: Scott's secretary, Voodoo, would call to schedule a meeting with whichever Tulkinghorn or Jackal Sean had engaged to act for him. They would summon her to the Jaeger's boardroom, sit her down in front of a photo of the new girlfriend and tell her: fifty-fifty. Or, just as likely: go away. Not fifty-fifty, one hundred-zero. Why was she so paralysed, so unable to rouse herself to consult a lawyer of her own?

Thee was saying something enthusiastic. They'd love to come over, and bring Iris. Perhaps Rachel Margery would be free, too?

Eloise looked around the sitting room. The place had turned into a bit of a dump lately, it had to be said. Amigo had been languid, once-over-lightly. Dreamily wafting his feather duster. Waving his Hoover around like a light sabre. Last week he'd gone so far as to call in sick.

Eloise wondered whether she actually owned a vacuum cleaner, and, if so, whether it worked. Had it gone up in the fire?

She lay down with Chekhov. For thoroughness (which Arthur believed in) she was reading the notes at the back of the book. The composer Shostakovich was enthralled by 'The Black Monk', she read, which he believed was connected to his fifteenth symphony. He told his biographer, 'I am certain Chekhov constructed "The Black Monk" in sonata form.'

Eloise read the sentence twice. She sipped her tumbler of wine. What did the story mean? When Kovrin believes in the existence of the black monk he's happy, but mad. When he realises the black monk is an apparition, he's miserable.

Now, she conjured up Klaudia. *Glass of wine, Klaud? How about a slice of this disgusting pizza? Make yourself comfortable. Loosen that paua shell necklace. What a pretty shirt you're wearing! Now, tell me. Do we need our madness in order to be happy? If you cure someone of their illusions, do you risk that you will render them bereft, or even insane?*

Write down your thoughts, Eloise. And don't forget to breathe!

She sat up and opened her laptop.

When I arrived at the flat, Arthur was already dead. Remember the sky that morning, the hard, bright light on the side of the

mountain, the cicadas making their shimmering wall of sound.
He walked out through a gap in the air, leaving a black outline
in the fabric. There was only a space, the absence of his presence.
Is that what I sensed in the flat — the photographic negative of
Arthur?

But what was the question that came at her out of the air, hurting her eyes?
A bright squiggle of light, as if she were looking at her own thought . . .

'When Mum's angry with me, she calls me Rachel.'

The Sparkler and Silvio were sitting on the couch, side by side,
watching TV.

Eloise took her head out of the hall cupboard and said, 'Remember
the fire?'

'Yeah.'

'Did we . . . do you think it involved a vacuum cleaner?'

The Sparkler wrinkled her nose, thought about it. 'No!'

'But maybe it was in the initial layers? The sort of pile underneath?'

'There'd be bits of it left,' the Sparkler said.

Eloise looked at her niece. Her muddy sneakers and knobbly knees.
Her vivid, intelligent little face.

'I suppose you're right. Maybe Amigo's gone off with it. Or Sean.
No, that's not likely. We'll have to go and buy a new one.'

Eloise paused and looked vacantly at the Sparkler's cartoon. Soon,
the fiendish dwarf, and his virtuous brother Starfish were consulting the
oracle known as the Red Herring. An object hovered in the lurid mauve
sky above them: it was the Bachelor, swooping down on his flying bed,
accompanied by his hissing girlfriends, the Cassowaries.

The Cassowaries were birdlike, as the name suggested, also
bedizened, colourful and insanely jealous.

'It's kind of psychedelic,' Eloise said, of the cartoon. 'Trippy. Maybe

Mrs Hallwright was stoned when she wrote it.'

'Wot?' the Sparkler said in a glazed voice. She had her small hand twined in Silvio's wool. Her eyes had turned dreamy.

'Cassowaries — the actual birds — are really dangerous. Have you ever seen one?'

The Sparkler shook her head.

'They're Australian. I saw some in a wildlife park, behind a high fence. They have really bright feathers. They're huge and they chase you, run after you, try to peck you to death.'

The Sparkler went on watching. The Red Herring, having consulted various scrolls, was delivering a pearl of wisdom: Too many cooks spoil the broth.

Eloise said, 'Okay. Dinner. Nasty pellets for Silv. What about you and me?'

'Too many cocks spoil the breath,' the Sparkler said.

'What? Who told you that? That's disgusting!'

The Sparkler laughed behind her small, grubby hand. 'Let's have fish and chips.'

'What about your food groups. Your vitamins.'

The cartoon finished on a cliffhanger: Soon and Starfish were taken prisoner by a villainous and camp old woodsman called Uncle Wayne.

Eloise ordered her niece to switch to the news. Beyond the windows, the estuary was brimming with a high tide, the bay as smooth and glassy as a pond. In the golden evening light, the dog owners were making their way towards the park.

Jack Anthony and Mariel Hartfield appeared in matching shades of blue, gold and red: her jacket, his shirt, his tie. Her heavily lashed eyes were smoky and calm. Behind them was a large photo of the Justice Minister, Ed Miles.

Mariel's throaty voice: 'Justice Minister Ed Miles stunned his colleagues in the National Party today with the shock announcement that he is resigning from politics. Prime Minister Jack Dance earlier appeared blindsided by the news that his long-serving cabinet minister, one of the most experienced members of the government front bench, is to leave Parliament, reportedly to pursue opportunities in the private sector. Miles, who was widely touted as a leadership prospect, and the subject of much speculation recently about his leadership ambitions, especially in light of the Prime Minister's low approval ratings, announced his decision at a press conference this afternoon.

'Sources are describing Prime Minister Jack Dance as "surprised and flabbergasted" by Mr Miles's sudden decision.'

Silvio erupted in an explosion of barks. He shot off the sofa, scrabbled on the wooden floor, threw himself towards the ranch slider.

Nick was standing on the deck. Eloise let him in.

Political reporter Sarah Lane, was speaking outside Parliament: 'Indeed, there has been intense speculation today, Mariel, as to why a long-serving, hitherto highly ambitious minister, strongly favoured as a leadership contender, with politics, you could say, running in his veins, has chosen this moment to resign for a career in the private sector. Mariel, earlier we sought comment from one of Mr Miles's oldest political allies and backers, former prime minister Sir David Hallwright, who had this to say.'

Eloise got a beer for Nick. They watched David Hallwright, interviewed in front of an ivy-covered wall.

'His hair's got darker. What's he wearing? Is that a cravat?'

'He's had his teeth whitened.'

'Look at his tan.'

Hallwright said, 'This is a loss to politics, sure. However, Ed Miles has given several decades of service to this country. And I think if you go out there, you'll find that the vast overwhelming bulk of New Zealanders will recognise that a talented individual like Ed Miles now has a fantastic contribution to make to the country's growth in the private sector. For me, personally, my focus is on the party, and the superb job that Prime Minister Jack Dance is doing. I am going to continue to put my weight behind Mr Dance, and to play my part, actually, to help New Zealanders understand the benefits the Dance government is bringing to the economy, and to the country as a whole. Jack Dance has made some tough calls, and frankly he deserves credit for them. There's a whole raft of exciting things my wife and I plan to continue to be involved in, to help Jack Dance achieve a second term.'

Sarah Lane again: 'So there you have it, Mariel. A week is indeed a long time in politics. After the recent speculation that Ed Miles and Sir David Hallwright might have been seeking to unseat Prime Minister Dance, who has been struggling with his approval ratings, we have a different picture today. A resignation from Ed Miles, and a ringing endorsement for Mr Dance from powerful National Party figure David Hallwright. Mariel?'

The Sparkler moved closer to Nick on the sofa.

'C'n I have a sip?' she said. He passed her the beer bottle. She raised it, clinking her teeth on the glass.

'Hey,' Eloise said, distracted, her eyes on the television.

Nick stretched out his long legs. He said, 'That Mariel Hartfield. She's kind of sleepily gorgeous. The glossy hair and white teeth. The velvet voice.'

'The eyes,' the Sparkler said in a cartoon-ghostly voice, curling her hand into a telescope.

Nick nudged her. 'Give me my beer, kid. How much have you drunk? And her eyes. They're amazing. With her beautiful brown skin. She's Maori, but with green eyes. Kind of unusual.'

Eloise said, 'She grew up in Australia. But her accent is New Zealand. She doesn't have Australian vowels.'

'No. It's pure Kiwi.'

Mariel Hartfield's eyes. Her voice.

Nick was speaking, 'Wait, here's something about Minister O'Keefe. Maybe Miles is resigning so he can be a house husband. Do Baby O'Keefe's nappies. Push the stroller around the park.'

They watched. No, Minister O'Keefe was revealing nothing more than a comment about social housing: the government would like to sell all of it to private providers.

The Sparkler was tying up her laces. She looked up and said, 'Mum got told at work. Eloise is right. The baby's father is the leader of the Labour Party.'

'Bradley Kirk. The old dog,' Nick said. 'Eloise, shall we take this kid out to dinner?'

Eloise was thinking: Thee's photos of the opera. Mariel Hartfield and Simon Lampton leaning against the plate-glass window, their elbows nearly touching. Simon's words, 'One of my sons grew up in a different family.' He said a name. William?

Note for the Rotokauri file: Leaf through copies of the *Woman's Day* and the *New Idea*. Those shots of Mariel and Hamish Dark shopping, arriving at airports, leaving cafés. Look at pictures of Mariel Hartfield's tall, curly-haired son. His name is William.

Is this what you were looking for, Arthur? Some fact that was hidden in the world you wanted to write about? You couldn't decide whether you were a fiction writer or a journalist. Why pry the way you did, why not just make the story up?

Remember, Arthur, I used to think I was observant. What is Mariel Hartfield like? She is popular, a celebrity. Her husband, Hamish Dark, is a friend of the National Party. She is Maori, she has green eyes. She has a narrow waist, strong hands, is slim and tall, with a pulpy scar on her index finger. Every evening, Mariel Hartfield tells the nation how it's spent its day. She lives her life in the public eye; she lives in plain sight.

'The girl in the bus stop is crying,' Eloise said.

––––––––––

In the morning, leaving Nick and the Sparkler to escort Silvio to the dog park, she drove across town and parked the Honda, barely bothering to line it up against the kerb. The Lamptons' door was opened by a woman holding a mop and a bucket filled with cleaning fluids, who said, 'Mr? Wait, I will get.'

Voices. He walked into the hallway. When he saw her, he came straight out onto the porch.

'Let's go up there,' she said, and pointed at Mt Matariki. He took one look at her face and didn't say a word.

Now they sat on the park bench at the edge of the green crater. Below them the suburbs stretched away, crossed by racing cloud shadows.

'I've been writing things down,' Eloise said.

She turned to him. 'Arthur had the idea, Art before everything. No fear or favour. He used people's personal details. He caricatured my mother. She appeared in a lot of his stuff, very thinly disguised. When we had arguments, he'd make them into comic sketches, or describe them in his columns. Nothing was sacred, everything was material. It made me angry. Hurt sometimes.'

Simon nodded slightly.

'But he didn't do it out of malice. He didn't do it in order to offend. It wasn't revenge or cruelty. He just did what all artists do. If you didn't know him or us, you wouldn't have recognised what material he was using.'

'Okay.'

'He went too far with the Hallwrights. Asking them about private details. It was . . . aggressive. He was obsessed with the idea of finding out, because he didn't have access to their world. I guess he was prepared to be a bit too ruthless.'

'To stalk them,' Simon said. He cleared his throat. His voice was light, without conviction. He was sitting very still.

'Not stalk them, just be enterprising. A cheeky journalist.'

Simon was looking at the backs of his hands.

She said, 'Arthur wrote a note: your name and the name of a woman who's missing. Simon Lampton/Mereana Kostas.'

Silence.

'You used the words "missing items".'

He looked at her.

'When you said that, you reminded me the blue cups were missing from the flat. I wouldn't have thought of it.'

He shrugged.

'You wear some kind of aftershave. I could smell it after you'd been running, when we were in the car.'

He looked straight ahead. 'Right . . . ?'

'You said I shouldn't feel guilty that I didn't call or text Arthur from the airport. You said, Imagine if I'd come back earlier, if Arthur and I had argued on the edge of the road and he'd tripped and fallen down the wall. You said he would be as much to blame for the fall as I was, because his behaviour had contributed.'

She looked out over the suburb, the grids of roads and houses. She went on, 'You were talking about yourself. It was you. You were in the flat. You took the cups. You left some trace, some outline of yourself. It was you.'

He twisted to face her. 'No. You're wrong, Eloise.'

'You said to me, Imagine if you and Arthur argued and he fell against a fence, and it gave way.'

'So?'

Her voice rose. 'I never told you he fell against a fence and it gave way. I *never* told you that detail. And it's what happened. How could you know unless you were there? You were there. Why were you there? Was he asking you about your adopted daughter, about Mrs Hallwright? Or the missing woman?'

He was looking at his hands, squeezing them, turning them this way and that. He scratched his chin hard, thinking.

Silence.

Finally he took a breath, rolled his shoulders, rubbed his neck, turned to her.

'Eloise,' he said, 'I have to tell you something. It's going to sound strange.'

She waited. She wasn't breathing.

'I care about you very much,' he said.

'What?'

'You. You and all your chaos. I'm old and married, and I really care about you. I think about you. You look stunned. Don't worry, I'm not mad. It doesn't mean anything other than that. You're young and lovely; it's no wonder I can't get you out of my head. As for what you just said . . . Don't get up, don't fly off the handle. Wait. Just hear me out. Please.'

She stared.

'Eloise. In your usual headlong way, you've constructed something out of the air. You've mounted a case against me, and it's half fact, and half your beautiful, clever, imaginative mind making all kinds of leaps. I know you're lonely. You spend too much time alone and you dream up connections, because that's what lonely people do. You feel bad about Arthur, you feel sad and guilty, you have this idea you didn't ask questions when he died, and so you're trying to fit it all together in a way that isn't random. Because we fear the random. We want things to make sense, to have a logic, a justice. The idea that people can die by pure, freak accident is terrible. You've fastened on the idea you should have rung or texted Arthur when you landed at the airport, you didn't because you didn't trust him, and as a result he died. And the story you're making up is so important to you, so much a part of your . . . recovery, that I'm almost reluctant to put you right. But I have to, because in the end you won't be served by getting fixated on something that isn't true.

We have to get at the truth. We agreed, remember, to work this out together. We've been thrown together by weird circumstance, and I'm actually not sorry about that, not sorry to have been spending time with you — although the cleaner's sure to tell my wife I've been talking to a pretty young woman who came to the house while she was out. She'll be thinking we're having an affair, and we're going to have to work out what to say. We don't want her knowing what we're talking about, because she's incredibly indiscreet.

'Now don't say anything, just let me finish. Eloise. Darling. Just listen. Just breathe. I mentioned the fact that Arthur fell against a flimsy fence for the simple reason that the police told me he had. It's just a detail I remember from their questions. I said something like, How the hell does a guy fall off a wall in broad daylight anyway? And they said, He stumbled against a fence and the whole thing gave way. Freak accident. Simple as that. Maybe I mentioned missing items. I don't remember. I put on aftershave, sure. But so do most other men I know. Arthur wrote some woman's name next to mine in a note, okay, but I have no idea why he did that, except I assume he was intending to contact both of us at some stage. He rang me. He was probably going to ring her next, whoever she was, or is. I have no idea.

'Eloise, don't look at me like that. Please just let me tell you, I've become fond of you, and I want us to be friends. I don't mind what you said. I don't mind you accusing me. You've had a hard time of it lately. I understand your feelings of guilt. I understand them. Let's work on them together. Your husband left you, you've had a lot to deal with emotionally.

'It's okay, Eloise. Everything's going to be fine. I just wonder, I really do. My lovely, chaotic friend. *How could you have got this so wrong?*'

The bump, the grind, of the rings of light. The interval between the words could be expressed as a forward slash.

Bright light made her screw her eyes shut. They had walked down from the mountain. Now, Simon stood next to her by the pool. The heat struck up off the concrete patio and she could feel his eyes on her, the intensity of his watchfulness, his calculation. But she felt as weightless and insubstantial as the wavering rings dancing on the blue walls of the pool.

She turned and looked at the big, square villa, its weatherboard walls and orange tiled roof.

'It's a beautiful house,' she said, and then added carelessly, 'The house is a metaphor for the mind.'

'I know it is,' he said, which surprised her.

'Do you?'

'Or it represents security. One of my patients had a marital crisis. She told me about it: when it was all going badly, she dreamed about broken-down, ruined houses, also houses she was locked out of. When she got back with her husband and all was well, she dreamed about beautiful mansions.'

'I'm trying to get my mind back in order,' Eloise said. 'That's why I've been seeing a therapist.'

'It's a good idea. To process your feelings of guilt.'

Eloise looked at him. 'Shall we sit down for a minute.'

'Sure.' He pulled up a deckchair and they sat looking down the length of the lawn to the base of Mt Matariki.

She faced him. 'I know who Mariel Hartfield is,' she said. 'She is Mereana Kostas. Her son is your son, William.'

Simon sat very still, his hands in his lap.

'Detective Da Silva described her: tall, slim, Maori, unusual green eyes. Scar on index finger. In the past, she had a criminal conviction. She was jailed. She left the country, changed her identity. She must have had help to do that. No, don't get up. Don't fly off the handle. Hear me out, Simon. Just breathe. You said it, we're working it out together, remember. I assume Arthur found out there was a connection between the two of you, he came looking for you. He was pushy, ruthless. He invaded your private life, and he didn't care if it hurt you. You've told me the rest. You told me when you came to my house.'

Simon turned to look at her. His eyes had no light, no depth in them. His face was expressionless. He said, 'How have you come up with this fantasy?'

'The information was out there. It came to me.'

'You mean there's gossip?'

'No. Definitely not. No one knows.'

His voice was harsh. 'It's completely untrue. A fairy story. One that could cause damage to innocent people. Good luck with putting it about. You'll get slapped with a defamation suit, just for starters.'

'I'm not going to put it about. I just want one thing.'

He waited. His eyes were opaque, his face was set. But she could sense something rising in him.

She said, 'You're right, I've been wracked with guilt about Arthur. I failed him. My husband's left me. I've been unhappy, lonely, lost. I want security; I want to put my mind in order. I'm seeing the shrink, but there's something else that would properly put my mind at ease.'

She gestured towards the house behind them.

'You said it to me, Simon, you know people.'

He squeezed his hands into fists and said in a quiet, dogged voice, 'What do you want?'

'I want a house,' Eloise said. 'I want my own home.'

THIRTY

Dear Klaudia,

I regret the necessity of the therapeutic blank screen: the fact that you know everything about me, and I know almost nothing about you. I have only a few details, an outline, with which to construct a picture. You own a soulful brown dog called Linus. Your mouth turns up like the Joker's when you are amused. You have blonde hair, a sharp nose, and a sly, crafty smile. When you are irritable, your eyes turn darker blue behind your glasses, and your face sets in a square frown. Before you speak, you pause, swallow, and rest your blunt fingertips on the desk. You are at your most charming when listening. Your familiar, and therapeutic assistant, is a large, brown rat.

I have to tell you, Klaudia, my ex-husband came to the peninsula. My neighbour, Nick, and I were walking back from the dog park when Sean turned up with an entourage: his secretary Voodoo, and a Jaeger's lawyer. For a moment, we stood on the path between the flax bushes, watching them milling around on the deck. They spent a bit of time peering at the fire damage along the fence. (The grass is growing back in patches, but the bushes are black.) Voodoo got her high heel stuck between the boards of the deck. Assisting her, Sean looked plump and uneasy, and even quite short — shorter than Nick, I noted.

The Jaeger's solicitor told me a lot of things. He was extraordinarily verbose. Sean paced about, looking agonised. I watched him covertly. I miss him, but he's determined, it seems, to stick with his actress girlfriend.

Eventually, they told me there is one point on which I can put my mind at rest. I won't have to leave the peninsula. After discussions with advisors and his Jaeger's partners, in a spirit of magnanimity, Sean, with the blessing of Lady Cheryl and Sir Jarrod Rodd, has offered to let me have the house. There will be no forced sale. I will be given sole ownership. I have been advised to consult my own lawyer on other matters, and further negotiations are pending, but I sit here now in my own house, knowing I won't have to pack my bags.

As I write, the tide is racing in the creek, the seagulls are crying over the house, and the sun is going down. There is a change in the air; it's the beginning of that special kind of iron light, signalling autumn is on the way. The sky is bright, hard, blue; the air is very clear. Along the peninsula road, the windows are lit up with red fire. In the living rooms, Mariel Hartfield, all smoky eyes and sleepy, enigmatic smile, is telling the nation how it spent its day.

A layer of the world was hidden from me. I wanted to ask questions, and with your help I found the courage to do so. I received answers, and I have also let some questions, as Sean would put it, 'lie on the record'.

The Rotokauri file, which documents the last days of Arthur Weeks, remains an open one. I've done as Kurt Hartmann jokingly advised me, and given it a spook-style working title: SOON.

I asked Kurt Hartmann, 'Do you think I'm being followed?'

His answer was unequivocal: Yes.

There was a man with black hair and a dragonfly tattooed on his hand. I haven't seen him lately. Was he a phantom in a migraine dream? I was so ill and lonely — perhaps, now Nick is always near, and I'm drinking less and I feel safe, I've stopped seeing ghosts. I don't really believe this. Did the dragonfly man vanish once he'd stolen Arthur's file? Or once I'd stopped talking to Hartmann? What about the figure I saw in the abandoned stucco house? These questions are why I'm keeping the file open. It won't be closed. Because I am still watching. And across town, Simon Lampton is watching, too.

That morning, when we saw in the dawn together, under a sky 'riddled with light', Simon Lampton and I came close — as close as two people whose interests are implacably opposed could come. Do you understand what I mean, Klaudia? We came close, and I made a choice, based on what I had. You probably won't approve, but I made the kind of choice Arthur wanted to make. He loved the Woody Allen film, *Bullets Over Broadway*; he wanted to be ruthless, like the gangster in the film. He thought that would mean he was a real artist. But he wasn't so tough. Arthur was a good person. I loved him for his goodness. I don't think he knew just how ruthless the world can be.

You told me the past is a dead star, its light still reaching me. You told me to try to live in the Now. And you also said, Klaudia, that a house is a metaphor for the mind. I came close to losing mine. What I want to do now is fill my house with people.

For lunch this weekend, I've invited Nick, and Scott Roysmith and Thee Davis, and their three daughters, Sophie, Sarah and the indomitable Iris. Scott and I will, no doubt, discuss our upcoming story on mass hysteria. He will argue in favour of balance, but in this case, I suspect management will be hoping for something thoroughly one-sided.

My sister Carina and the Sparkler are coming, along with Silvio, and Carina's husband Giles, on a rare break from his bridge-building project in Thailand. Nick has offered to help me with the food. I suggested my usual, takeaway pizzas, but he had the quaint idea that he and I should cook.

I would like to invite you to come, Klaudia. I feel as if you've spent a lot of time here on the peninsula, in the haunted house of my mind. Assuming it would be professionally inappropriate for you to accept a lunch date, I will send you these thoughts instead. And I will dedicate this record —

To the memory of Arthur Weeks. And to you.

Eloise Hay
Starlight Peninsula
4 April 2014